HAVE BABY, NEED BILLIONAIRE

BY
MAUREEN CHILD

Maureen Child is a California native who loves to travel. Every chance they get, she and her husband are taking off on another research trip. The author of more than sixty books, Maureen loves a happy ending and still swears that she has the best job in the world. She lives in southern California with her husband, two children and a golden retriever with delusions of grandeur. Visit Maureen's website at www.maureenchild.com.

For Carter
He's never met the lonely Bunny
But he loves the little Critters

One

Simon Bradley didn't like surprises.

In his experience, any time a man let himself be taken unawares, disaster happened.

Order. Rules. He was a man of discipline. Which is why it only took one look at the woman standing in his office to know that *she* wasn't his kind of female.

Pretty though, he told himself, his gaze sweeping her up and down in a brisk, detailed look. She stood about five foot four and looked even shorter because she was so delicately made. She was tiny, really, with short blond hair that clung to her head in chunky layers that framed her face. Big silver hoops dangled from her ears and her wide blue eyes were fixed on him thoughtfully. Her mouth was curved in what appeared to be a permanent half smile and a single dimple winked at him from her right cheek. She wore black jeans, black boots and a bright red sweater that molded itself to her slight but curvy body.

He ignored the flash of purely male interest as he met her gaze and stood up behind his desk. "Ms. Barrons, is it? My assistant tells me you insisted on seeing me about something 'urgent'?"

"Yes, hi. And please, call me Tula," she said, her words tumbling from her delectable-looking mouth in a rush. She walked toward him, right hand extended.

His fingers folded over hers and he felt a sudden, intense surge of heat. Before he could really question it, she shook his hand briskly, then stepped back. Looking past him at the wide window behind him, she said, "Wow, that's quite a view. You can see all of San Francisco from here."

He didn't turn around to share the view. He watched her instead. His fingers were still buzzing and he rubbed them together to dissipate the sensation. No, she wasn't his type at all, but damned if he wasn't enjoying looking at her. "Not all, but a good part of it."

"Why don't you have your desk facing the window?"

"If I did that, I'd have my back to the door, wouldn't I?"

"Right." She nodded then shrugged. "Still, I think it'd be worth it."

Pretty, but disorganized, he thought. He glanced at his wristwatch. "Ms. Barrons—"

"Tula."

"Ms. Barrons," he said deliberately, "if you've come to talk about the view, I don't really have time for this. I've got a board meeting in fifteen minutes and—"

"Right. You're a busy man. I get that. And no, I didn't

come to talk about the view, I got a little distracted, that's all."

Distractions, he thought wryly, *are probably how this woman lives her life.* She was already letting her gaze slide around his office rather than getting to the point of her visit. He watched her as she took in the streamlined office furniture, the framed awards from the city and the professionally done photos of the other Bradley department stores across the country.

Pride rose up inside him as he, too, took a moment to admire those photos. Simon had worked hard for the last ten years to rebuild a family dynasty that his father had brought to the brink of ruin. In one short decade, Simon had not only regained ground lost, thanks to his father's sloppy business sense, he'd taken the Bradley family chain of upscale shopping centers further than anyone else ever had.

And he hadn't accomplished all of that by being distracted. Not even by a pretty woman.

"If you don't mind," he said, coming around his desk to escort her personally to the door, "I am rather busy today...."

She flashed him a full smile and Simon felt his heart take an odd, hard lurch in his chest. Her eyes lit up and that dimple in her cheek deepened and she was suddenly the most beautiful thing he'd ever seen. Shaken, Simon brushed that thought aside and told himself to get a grip.

"Sorry, sorry," Tula said, waving both hands in the air as if to erase her own tendency to get sidetracked. "I really am here to talk to you about something very important."

"All right then, what is it that's so urgent you vowed to

spend a week in my waiting area if you weren't allowed
to speak to me immediately?"

She opened her mouth, shut it again, then suggested,
"Maybe you should sit down."

"Ms. Barrons…"

"Fine," she said with a shake of her head. "Your call.
But don't say I didn't warn you."

Pointedly, he glanced at his watch.

"I get it," she told him. "Busy man. You want it and
you want it now. Okay then, here it is. Congratulations,
Simon Bradley. You're a father."

He stiffened and any sense of courtesy went out the
window along with his sense of bemused tolerance.
"Your five minutes are up, Ms. Barrons." He took her
elbow in a firm grip and steered her toward the door.

Her much shorter legs were moving fast, trying to
either keep up or slow him down, he wasn't sure which.
Either way, it didn't make a difference to him. Beautiful
or not, whatever game she was playing, it wasn't going
to work. Simon was no one's father and he damn well
knew it.

"Hey!" She finally dug the heels of her boots into
the lush carpet and slowed his progress a bit. "Wait a
second! Geez, overreact much?"

"I'm not a father," he ground out tightly. "And trust
me when I say that if I had ever slept with you, I would
remember."

"I didn't say I was the baby's mother."

He didn't listen. Just kept moving toward the door at
a relentless pace.

"I would have worked up to that little declaration
slower, you know," she was babbling. "You're the one
who wanted it direct and fast."

"I see. This was for my benefit."

"No, it's for your son's benefit, you boob."

He staggered a little in spite of knowing that she had to be lying. A son? Impossible.

She took advantage of the momentary pause in his forced march toward the door to break free of his grip and step back just out of reach. He was unsettled enough to let her go. He didn't know what she was trying to pull, but at the moment, her eyes looked soft but determined as she met his gaze.

"I realize this is coming as a complete shock to you. Heck, it would be for anybody."

Simon shook his head and narrowed his eyes on her. Enough of this. He didn't have a son and he wasn't going to fall for whatever moneygrubbing scheme she'd come up with in her delusional fantasies. Best to lay that on the line right from the start.

"I've never even seen you before, Ms. Barrons, so obviously, we don't have a child together. Next time you want to convince someone to pay for a child that doesn't exist, you might want to try it on someone you've actually slept with."

She blinked up at him in confusion, then a moment later she laughed. "No, no. I told you, I'm not the baby's mother. I'm the baby's aunt. But you're definitely his father. Nathan has your eyes and even that stubborn chin of yours. Which does not bode well, I suppose. But stubbornness can often be a good quality, don't you think?"

Nathan.

The imaginary baby had a name.

But that didn't make any of this situation real.

"This is insane," he told her. "You're obviously

after something, so why not just spill it and get it over with."

She was muttering to herself as she walked back to his desk and Simon was forced to follow her. "I had a speech all prepared, you know. You rushed me and everything's confused now."

"I think you're the only thing confused here," Simon told her, moving to pick up his phone and call security. They could escort her out and he'd be done with this and back to work.

"I'm not confused," she said. She read his expression and added, "I'm not crazy, either. Look, give me five minutes, okay?"

He hung up. Wasn't sure why. Maybe it was the gleam in her blue eyes. Maybe it was that tantalizing dimple that continued to show itself and disappear again. But if there was the slightest chance that what she was saying was true, then he owed it to himself to find out.

"All right," he said, checking his watch. "Five minutes."

"Okay." She took a deep breath and said, "Here we go. Do you remember dating a woman named Sherry Taylor about a year and a half ago?"

A thin thread of apprehension slithered through Simon as he searched his memory. "Yes," he said warily.

"Well…I'm Sherry's cousin, Tula Barrons. Actually, Tallulah, named after my grandmother, but that's such a hideous name that I go by Tula…."

He was hardly listening to her now. Instead his mind was focused on those nebulous memories of a woman in his past. Was it possible?

She took another steadying breath and said, "I know

this is hard to take in, but while you two were together, Sherry got pregnant. She gave birth to your son six months ago, in Long Beach."

"She *what?*"

"I know, I know. She should have told you," the woman said, lifting both hands as if to say it wasn't her fault. "I actually tried to convince her to tell you, but she said she didn't want to intrude on your life or anything, so…"

Intrude on his life.

That was an understatement. God, he could barely remember what the woman looked like. Simon rubbed at the spot between his eyes as if somehow that might clear up the foggy memories. But all he came up with was a vague image of a woman who had been in and out of his life in about two weeks' time.

And while he'd gone on his way without a backward glance, she'd been *pregnant?* With *his* child? And didn't even bother to *tell* him?

"What? Why? How?"

"All very good questions," she said, smiling at him again, this time in a sympathetic fashion. "I'm really sorry this is such a shock, but—"

Simon wasn't interested in her sympathy. He wanted answers. If he really did have a son, then he needed to know everything.

"Why now?" he demanded. "Why did your cousin wait until now to tell me, and why isn't she here herself?"

Her eyes filmed over and he had the horrifying thought that she was going to cry. Damn it. He hated when women cried. Made a man feel completely helpless. Not something he enjoyed at all. But a moment later, the woman had gotten control of her emotions and managed to stem the tide of those tears. Her eyes still glittered with them, but she refused to let them fall and Simon found, unexpectedly, that he admired her for it.

"Sherry died a couple of weeks ago," she said softly.

Another quick jolt of surprise in a morning that felt full of them. "I'm sorry," he said, knowing it sounded lame and clichéd, but what else was there to say?

"Thanks," she said. "It was a car accident. She died instantly."

"Look, Ms. Barrons…"

She sighed. "If I *beg,* will you please call me Tula?"

"Fine. Tula," he amended, thinking it really was the least he could do, considering. For the first time in a very long time, Simon had been caught completely off guard.

He wasn't sure how to react. His instinct, of course, was to find this baby and if it was his son, to claim him. But all he had was this stranger's word, along with memories that were too obscure to trust. Why in the hell would a woman get pregnant and not tell the baby's father? Why wouldn't she have come to him if that child really was his?

He scrubbed one hand across his jaw. "Look, I'm sorry to say, I don't really remember much about your cousin. We weren't together long. I don't see why you're so sure this baby is mine."

"Because Sherry named you on the baby's birth certificate."

"She gave the baby my name and didn't bother to tell me?" He didn't even know what to say to that.

"I know," she said, her tone soothing.

He didn't want to be soothed. Or understood. "She could have put anyone's name down," he pointed out.

"Sherry didn't lie."

Simon laughed at the ridiculousness of that statement. "Is that right?"

Tula winced. "All right, fine. She lied to you, but she wouldn't have lied to her son. She wouldn't have lied about Nathan's name."

"Why should I believe that the boy is mine?"

"You did have sex with her?"

Scowling, Simon admitted, "Well, yes, I did, but—"

"And you do know how babies are made, right?"

"That's very amusing."

"I'm not trying to be funny," she told him. "Just honest. Look, you can do a paternity test, but I can tell you that Sherry would never have named you as Nathan's father in her will if she wasn't sure."

"Her will?" The silent clang of a warning bell went off in his mind.

"Didn't I already tell you that part?"

"No."

She shook her head and dropped into one of the chairs angled in front of his desk. "Sorry. It's been a busy couple of weeks for me, what with Sherry's accident and arranging the funeral and closing up her house and moving the baby up here to my house in Crystal Bay."

Sensing that this was going to go on far longer than the original five minutes he'd allowed her, Simon walked around the edge of his desk and took a seat. At the very least, he was now in the position of power. He watched the pretty blonde and asked, "What about the will?"

Tula reached into the oversize black leather bag she had slung over her shoulder. She pulled out a large manila envelope and dropped it onto his desk. "That's a copy of Sherry's will. If you look, you'll see that I've been named temporary guardian of Nathan. Until I'm sure that you're ready to be the baby's father."

Her voice, her words, were no more than a buzz of sound in his head. He read through the will quickly, scanning until he found the provisions for the child Sherry had named as his. *Custody of minor, Nathan Taylor, goes to the child's father, Simon Bradley.*

He sat back in his chair and kept rereading those words until he was fairly certain they'd been burned into his brain. Was this true? Was he a father?

Lifting his gaze to hers, Simon found Tula Barrons studying him through those wide, brilliant blue eyes. She was waiting for him to say something.

Damned if he knew what it should be.

He'd been careful, always, in his relationships with women. He'd had no desire to be a father. And yet he had a vague memory of being with Sherry Taylor. The woman herself was hardly more than a smudge in his memories—but he did remember the night the condom had broken. A man didn't forget things like that. But she'd never said anything about a baby, so he'd forgotten about the incident.

It was possible.

He might really have a son.

Tula watched as Simon Bradley came to terms with a whole new reality.

She gave him points. Sure, he'd been a little edgy, temperamental…all right, *rude,* at first. But she supposed that was to be expected. After all, it wasn't every day you found out you were a father, for heaven's sake.

Her gaze moved over him while he was reading the

will and Tula had to admit that he wasn't at all what she'd been expecting. She and her cousin Sherry hadn't been close, by any means, but Tula would have bet that she would at least know Sherry's taste in men.

And tall, dark, gorgeous and crabby wasn't it. Normally, Sherry had gone for the quiet, sweet, geeky type. Simon was about as far from that description as a man could get. He practically radiated power, strength. Ever since she had walked into the room, Tula had felt a sizzle of attraction for him that she was still battling. She so didn't need yet one more complication at the moment.

"What exactly is it you want from me?"

His voice shattered her thoughts and she met his gaze. "I should think that would be obvious."

He dropped the sheaf of papers to his desktop. "Well, you would be wrong."

"Okay, how about this? Why don't you come out to my place in Crystal Bay? Meet your son. Then we can talk and figure out our next move together."

He scrubbed one hand across the back of his neck. She'd dumped a lot of information on him all at once, Tula told herself. Of course he was going to need a little time to acclimate.

"Fine," he said at last. "What's your address?"

She told him, then watched as he stood up behind his desk in a clear signal of dismissal. Well, that was all right with her. She had things to do anyway and what more was there to say at the moment? Tula stood up, too, and held her right hand out toward him.

A moment's pause, then his hand engulfed hers. Again, just as it had happened earlier, the instant their palms met a bolt of heat shot up her arm and ricocheted around her chest like a manic Ping-Pong ball. He must have felt the same thing because he dropped her hand and shoved his own into his pocket.

She took a breath, blew it out and forced a smile that felt wobbly. "I'll see you tonight then."

As she left, Tula felt his gaze on her and the heat engendered by his stare stayed with her on the long ride home.

Two

"How'd it go?"

Tula smiled at the sound of her best friend's voice. Anna Cameron Hale was the one human being on the face of the planet that Tula could count on being on her side. So, naturally, the moment she'd returned from San Francisco and facing down Simon Bradley, she dialed Anna's number.

"About as you'd expect."

"Ouch," Anna said. "So he had no idea about the baby?"

"Nope." Tula turned to look at Nathan, sitting in his bouncy seat. The babysitter, Mrs. Klein, had said that the baby was "good as gold" the whole time she was gone. Now, as he bounced and pushed off with his toes, the springs squeaked into motion, jolting him up and down in the small kitchen.

Tula's heart gave a little Nathan-caused twinge that she was starting to get used to. How was it possible to love someone so much in the span of a couple of short weeks?

"In his defense, it must have been a shock for him to be faced with this out of the blue," Anna said.

"True. I mean I knew about Nathan and it was still a stunner when Sherry died and suddenly I'm responsible for him." Although, she thought, it hadn't taken more than five minutes for her to adjust. "But when I told Simon, he looked like he'd been hit with a two-by-four."

"God, honey, I'm sorry it didn't go well. So what do you do now?"

"He's coming here tonight to meet Nathan and then we're going to talk." Tula thought briefly about the little buzz of sensation she'd received when he shook her hand and then pushed that thought right out of her mind. There was already plenty going on at the moment. She *so* didn't need anything else to think about.

But her mind couldn't quite keep from remembering him as he stood over her, all fierce and furious.

"He's going to your house?" Anna asked.

Tula shook her head and paid attention. "Yeah, why?"

"Nothing. But maybe I could come over and help you get ready."

She knew exactly what Anna was thinking and Tula couldn't help laughing. "You are not coming over to clean my house. He's not visiting royalty or something."

Anna laughed, too. "Fine. Just warn him when he walks in to watch where he steps."

Tula stepped away from the kitchen counter and shot

a look into her tiny living room. Toys littered the floor, her laptop was sitting open on the coffee table and her latest manuscript was beside it. She was doing revisions for her editor and when she was working, other things— like picking up clutter—tended to go by the wayside.

Shrugging, she silently admitted that though her house was clean, it did tend to get a little messy. Especially now that she had Nathan living with her. She hadn't had any idea just how much *stuff* came along with a baby.

"Why did I call you again?" Tula asked.

"Because I'm your best friend and you know you need me."

"Right, that was it." Tula smiled and reached out one hand to smooth the wispy hairs on the top of Nathan's head as he scooted past, babbling happily. "It was weird, Anna. Simon was crabby and rude and dismissive and yet…"

"Yet *what?*" Anna prompted.

There was a buzz of interest, Tula thought but didn't say. She hadn't expected it, hadn't wanted it, but hadn't been able to ignore it, either. The suit-and-tie kind of guy was *so* not what she was interested in. And for heaven's sake, the last thing she needed was to be attracted to Nathan's father. This situation was hard enough. Yet she couldn't deny the flash of heat that had flooded her system the moment her hand had met his.

Didn't mean she had to do anything about it though, she assured herself firmly.

"Hello?" Anna said. "Finish what you were saying! What comes after the 'yet'?"

"Nothing," Tula said with sudden determination. One thing she didn't need was to indulge in an attraction for a man she had nothing in common with but a baby they were both responsible for. "Absolutely nothing."

"And you expect me to just accept that?"

"As my friend, I'm asking you to, yeah."

Anna sighed dramatically. "Fine. I will. For *now*."

"Thanks." She'd accept the reprieve, even though she knew that Anna wouldn't let it go forever.

"So what're you going to do tonight?"

"Simon comes here and we talk about Nathan. Set something up so that he can get to know the baby and I can watch them together. I can handle Simon," she said a moment later and wasn't sure whether she was trying to convince Anna or herself. "I grew up around men like him, remember?"

"Tula, not every man who wears a suit is like your dad."

"Not all," she allowed, "but most."

She was in the position to know. Her entire family had practically been born wearing business suits. They lived stuffy, insular lives built around making and keeping money. Tula was half convinced that they didn't even know a world existed beyond their own narrow portion of it.

For example, she knew what Simon Bradley would think of her tiny, cluttered, bayside home because she knew exactly what her father would have thought of it—if he'd ever deigned to visit. He would have thought it too old, too small. He would have hated the bright blue walls and yellow trim in the living room. He'd have loathed the mural of the circus that decorated her bathroom wall. Mostly though, he would have seen her living there as a disgrace.

She had the distinct impression that Simon wouldn't be any different.

"Look, the reality is it doesn't matter what Nathan's father thinks of me or my house. Our only connection is the baby." As she spoke, she told her hormones to listen up. "So I'm not going to put on a show and change my life in any way to try to convince a man I don't even know that I am who I'm not."

A long second passed, then Anna laughed gently. "What does it say about me that I completely understood that?"

"That we've been friends too long?"

"Probably," Anna agreed. "Which is how I know you're making rosemary chicken tonight."

Tula smiled. Anna did know her too well. Rosemary chicken was her go-to meal when she was having company. And unless Simon was a vegetarian, everything would go great. Oh, God—what if he *was* a vegetarian? No, she thought. Men like him did lunch at steak houses with clients. "You've got me there. And once we have dinner, I'll talk to Simon about setting up a schedule for him to get to know Nathan."

"You?" Anna laughed. "A schedule?"

"I can be organized," she argued, though her words didn't carry a lot of confidence. "I just choose to not be."

"Uh-huh. How's the baby?"

Everything in Tula softened. "He's wonderful." Her gaze followed the tiny boy as he continued on his path around the kitchen, laughing and making noises as he explored his world. "Honestly, he's such a good baby. And he's so smart. This morning I asked him where his nose was and he pointed right to it."

Well, he had been waving his stuffed bunny in the air and hit himself in the face with it, but close enough.

"Harvard-bound already."

"I'll sign him up on the waiting list tomorrow," Tula agreed with a laugh. "Look, I gotta go. Get the chicken in the oven, give Nathan a bath and…ooh, maybe myself, too."

"Okay, but call me tomorrow. Let me know how it goes."

"I will." She hung up, leaned against the kitchen counter and let her gaze slide over the bright yellow kitchen. It was small but cheerful, with white cabinets, a bright blue counter and copper-bottomed pans hanging from a rack over the stove.

She loved her house. She loved her life.

And she loved that baby.

Simon Bradley was going to have to work very hard to convince her that he was worthy of being Nathan's father.

The scent of rosemary filled the little house by the bay a few hours later.

Tula danced around the kitchen to the classic rock tunes pouring from the radio on the counter and every few steps, she stopped to steal a kiss from the baby in the high chair. Nathan giggled at her, a deep, full-belly laugh that tickled at the edges of Tula's heart.

"Funny guy," she whispered, planting a kiss on top of his head and inhaling the sweet, clean scent of him. "Laughing at my dance moves isn't usually the way to my heart, you know."

He gave her another grin and kicked his fat legs in excitement.

Tula sighed and smoothed her hand across the baby's wisps of dark hair. Two weeks he'd been a part of her life and already she couldn't imagine her world without him in it. The moment she'd picked him up for the first time, Nathan had carved away a piece of her heart and she knew she'd never get it back.

Now she was supposed to hand him over to a man who would no doubt raise Nathan in the strict, rarified world in which she'd been raised. How could she stand it? How could she sentence this sweet baby to a regimented lifestyle just like the one she'd escaped?

And how could she avoid it?

She couldn't.

Which meant she had only one option. If she couldn't stop Simon from eventually having custody of Nathan— then she'd just have to find a way to loosen Simon up. She'd loosen Simon up, break him out of the world of "suits" so that he wouldn't do to Nathan what her father had tried to do to her.

Looking down into the baby's smiling eyes, she made a promise. "I'll make sure he knows how to have fun, Nathan. Don't you worry. I won't let him make you wear a toddler business suit to preschool."

The baby slapped one hand down onto a pile of dry breakfast cereal on the food tray, sending tiny O's skittering across the kitchen.

"Glad you agree," she said as she bent down, scraped them up into her hand and tossed them into the sink. Then she washed her hands and came back to the baby. "Your daddy's coming here soon, Nathan. He'll probably be crabby and stuffy, so don't let that bother you. It won't last for long. We're going to change him, little man. For his own good. Not to mention *yours.*"

He grinned at her.

"Attaboy," she said and bent for another quick kiss just as the doorbell sounded. Her stomach gave a quick spin that had her taking a deep breath to try to steady it. "He's here. You're all strapped in, so you're safe. Just be good for a second and I'll go let him in."

She didn't like leaving Nathan alone in the high chair, even though he was belted in tightly. So Tula hurried across the toy-cluttered floor of her small living room and wondered how it had gotten so messy again. She'd straightened it up earlier. Then she remembered she and the baby playing after she put the chicken in the oven and—too late to worry about it now. She threw open the door and nearly gulped.

Simon was standing there, somehow taller than she remembered. He wasn't wearing a suit, either, which gave her a jolt of surprise. She got another jolt when she realized just how good he looked when he pried himself out of the sleek lines of his business "uniform." Casual in a charcoal-gray sweater, black jeans and cross trainers, he actually looked even more gorgeous, which was just disconcerting. He looked so…different. The only thing familiar about him was the scowl.

When she caught herself just staring at him like a big dummy, she said quickly, "Hi. Come on in. Baby's in the kitchen and I don't want to leave him alone, so close the door, will you, it's cold out there."

Simon opened his mouth to speak, but the damn woman was already gone. She'd left him standing on the porch and raced off before he could so much as say hello. Of course, he'd had the chance to speak, he simply hadn't. He'd been caught up in looking at her. Just as he had earlier that day in his office.

Those big blue eyes of hers were…mesmerizing somehow. Every time he looked into them, he forgot what he was thinking and lost himself for a moment or two. Not something he wanted to admit, even to himself, but there it was. Frowning, he reminded himself that he'd come to her house to set down some rules. To make sure Tula Barrons understood exactly how this bizarre situation was going to progress. Instead, he was standing on the front porch, thinking about just how good a woman could look in a pair of faded blue jeans.

Swallowing the stab of irritation at himself, he followed after her. Tula wasn't his main concern here, after all. He was here because of the child. His son? He was having a hard time believing it was possible, but he couldn't walk away from this until he knew for sure. Because if the baby was his, there was no way he would allow his child to be raised by someone else.

He'd been thinking about little else but this woman and the child she said belonged to him since she'd left his office that morning. With his concentration so unfocused, he'd finally given up on getting any work done and had gone to see his lawyer.

After that illuminating little visit, he'd spent the last couple of hours thinking back to the brief time he'd spent with Sherry Taylor. He still didn't remember much about her, but he had to admit that there was at least the possibility that her child was his.

Which was why he was here. He stepped inside and his foot came down on something that protested with a loud *squeak*. He glanced down at the rubber reindeer and shook his head as he closed the door. His gaze swept the interior of the small house and he shook his head. If more than two people were in the damn living room, they wouldn't be able to breathe at the same time. The house was old and small and…bright, he thought, giving the nearly electric blue walls an astonished glance.

The blue walls boasted dark yellow molding that ran around the circumference of the room at the ceiling. There was a short sofa and one chair drawn up in front of a hearth where a tiny blaze sputtered and spat from behind a wrought-iron screen. Toys were strewn across the floor as if a hurricane had swept through and there was a narrow staircase on the far wall leading to what he assumed was an even tinier second story.

The whole place was a dollhouse. He almost felt like Gulliver. Still frowning, he heard Tula in the kitchen, talking in a singsong voice people invariably tended to use around babies. He told himself to go on in there, but he didn't move. It was as if his feet were nailed to the wood floor. It wasn't that he was afraid of the baby or anything, but Simon knew damn well that the moment he saw the child, his world as he knew it would cease to exist.

If this baby were his son, nothing would ever be the same again.

A child's bubble of laughter erupted in the other room and Simon took a breath and held it. Something inside him tightened and he told himself to move on. To get this first meeting over so that plans could be made, strategies devised.

But he didn't move. Instead, he noticed the framed drawings and paintings on the walls, most of which were of a lop-eared bunny in different poses. Why the woman would choose to display such childish paintings was beyond him, but Tula Barrons, he was discovering, was different from any other woman he'd ever known.

The child laughed again.

Simon nodded to himself and followed the sound and the amazing scents in the air to the kitchen.

It didn't take him long.

Three long strides had him leaving the living room and entering a bright yellow room that was about the size of his walk-in closet at home. Again, he felt as out of place as a beer at a wine tasting. This whole house seemed to have been built for tiny people and a man his size was bound to feel as if he had to hunch his shoulders to keep from rapping his head on the ceiling.

He noted that the kitchen was clean but as cluttered as the living room. Canisters lined up on the counter beside a small microwave and an even smaller TV. Cupboard doors were made of glass, displaying ancient china stacked neatly. A basket with clean baby clothes waiting to be folded was standing on the table for two and the smells pouring from the oven had his mouth watering and his stomach rumbling in response.

Then his gaze dropped on Tula Barrons as she straightened up, holding the baby she'd just taken from a high chair in her arms. She settled the chubby baby on her right hip, gave Simon a brilliant smile and said, "Here he is. Your son."

Simon's gaze locked on the boy who was staring at him out of a pair of eyes too much like his own to deny. His lawyer had advised him to do nothing until a paternity test had been arranged. But Harry had always been too cautious, which was why he made such a great lawyer. Simon tended to go with his gut on big decisions and that instinct had never let him down yet.

So he'd come here mainly to see the baby for himself before arranging for the paternity test his lawyer wanted.

Because Simon had half convinced himself that there was no way this baby was his.

But one look at the boy changed all that. He was stubborn, Simon admitted silently, but he wasn't blind. The baby looked enough like him that no paternity test should be required—though he'd get one anyway. He'd been a businessman too long to do anything but follow the rules and do things in a logical, reasonable manner.

"Nathan," Tula said, glancing from the baby on her hip to Simon, "this is your daddy. Simon, meet your son."

She started toward him and Simon quickly held up one hand to keep her where she was. Tula stopped dead, gave him a quizzical look and tipped her head to one side to watch him. "What's wrong?"

What wasn't? His heart was racing, his stomach was churning. How the hell had this happened? he wondered. How had he made a child and been unaware of the boy's existence? Why had the baby's mother kept him a secret? Damn it, he had had the right to know. To be there for his son's birth. To see him draw his first breath. To watch him as he woke up to the world.

And it had all been stolen from him.

"Just…give me a minute, all right?" Simon stared at the tiny boy, trying to ignore the less-than-pleased expression on Tula Barrons's face. Didn't matter what she thought of him, did it? The important thing here was that Simon's entire world had just taken a sharp right turn.

A father.

He was a father.

Pride and something not unlike sheer panic roared

through him at a matching pace. His gaze locked on the boy, he noticed the dark brown hair, the brown eyes—exact same shade as Simon's own—and, finally, he noticed the baby's lower lip beginning to pout.

"You're making him cry." Tula jiggled the baby while patting him on the back gently.

"I'm not doing anything."

"You look angry and babies are very sensitive to moods around them," she said and soothed the boy by swaying in place and whispering softly. Keeping her voice quiet and singsongy, she snapped, "Honestly, is that scowl a permanent fixture on your face?"

"I'm not—"

"Would it physically kill you to smile at him?"

Frustrated and just a little pissed because he had to admit that she was at least partially right, Simon assumed what he hoped was a reassuring smile.

She rolled her eyes and laughed. "That's the best you've got?"

He kept his voice low, but didn't bother to hide his irritation. "You might want to back off now."

"I don't see why I should," she countered, her voice pleasant despite her words. "Sherry left *me* as guardian for Nathan and I don't like how you're treating him."

"I haven't done anything."

"Exactly," she said with a sharp nod. "You won't even let him get near you. Honestly, haven't you ever seen a child before?"

"Of course I have, I'm just—"

"Shocked? Confused? Worried?" she asked, then continued on before he could speak. "Well, imagine how Nathan must feel. His mother's gone. His home is gone.

He's in a strange place with strangers taking care of him and now there's a big mean bully glaring at him."

He stiffened. "Now just a damn min—"

"Don't swear in front of the baby."

Simon inhaled sharply and shot her a glare he usually reserved for employees he wanted to terrify into improving their work skills, fully expecting her to have the sense to back off. Naturally, she paid no attention to him.

"If you can't be nice and at least *pretend* to smile, you'll just have to go away," she said. Then she spoke to the baby. "Don't you worry, sweetie, Tula won't let the mean man get you."

"I'm not a mean—oh, for God's sake." Simon had had enough of this. He wasn't going to be chastised by anybody, least of all the short, curvy woman giving him a disgusted look.

He stalked across the small kitchen, plucked the baby from her grasp and held Nathan up to eye level. The baby's pout disappeared as if it had never been and the two of them simply stared at each other.

The baby was a solid, warm weight in his hands. Little legs pumped, arms waved and a thin line of drool dripped from his mouth when he gave his father a toothless grin. His chest tight, Simon felt the baby's heartbeat racing beneath his hands and there was a… connection that he'd never felt before. It was basic. Complete. Staggering.

In that instant—that heart-stopping, mind-numbing second—Simon was lost.

He knew it even as he stood there, beneath Tula Barrons's less than approving stare, that this was his son and he would do whatever he had to to keep him.

If this woman stood in his way, he'd roll right over her without a moment's pause. Something in his gaze must have given away his thoughts because the small blonde lifted her chin, met his eyes in a bold stare and told him silently that she wouldn't give an inch.

Fine.

She'd learn soon enough that when Simon Bradley entered a contest—he never lost.

Three

"You're holding him like he's a hand grenade about to explode," the woman said, ending their silent battle.

Despite that swift, sure connection he felt to the child in his arms, Simon wasn't certain at all that the baby wouldn't explode. Or cry. Or expel some gross fluid. "I'm being careful."

"Okay," she said and pulled out a chair to sit down.

He glanced at her, then looked back to the baby. Carefully, Simon eased down onto the other chair pulled up to the postage-stamp-sized table. It looked so narrow and fragile, he almost expected it to shatter under his weight, but it held. He felt clumsy and oversize. As if he were the only grown-up at a little girl's tea party. He had to wonder if the woman had arranged for him to feel out of place. If she was subtly trying to sabotage this first meeting.

Gently, he balanced the baby on his knee and kept one hand on the small boy's back to hold him in place. Only then did he look up at the woman sitting opposite him.

Her big eyes were fixed on him and a half smile tugged at the corner of her mouth, causing that one dimple to flash at him. She'd gone from looking at him as if he were the devil himself to an expression of amused benevolence that he didn't like any better.

"Enjoying yourself?" he asked tightly.

"Actually," she admitted, "I am."

"So happy to entertain you."

"Oh, you're really not happy," she said, her smile quickening briefly again. "But that's okay. You had me worried, I can tell you."

"Worried about what?"

"Well, how you were going to be with Nathan," she told him, leaning against the ladder back of the chair. She crossed her arms over her chest, unconsciously lifting her nicely rounded breasts. "When you first saw him, you looked…"

"Yes?" Simon glanced down when Nathan slapped both chubby fists onto the tabletop.

"…terrified," she finished.

Well, that was humiliating. And untrue, he assured himself. "I wasn't scared."

"Sure you were." She shrugged and apparently was dialing back her mistrust. "And who could blame you? You should have seen me the first time I picked him up. I was so worried about dropping him I had him in a stranglehold."

Nothing in Simon's life had terrified him like that first moment holding a son he didn't know he had. But he wasn't about to admit to that. Not to Tula Barrons at any rate.

He shifted around uncomfortably on the narrow chair. How did an adult sit on one of these things?

"Plus," she added, "you don't look like you want to bite through a brick or something anymore."

Simon sighed. "Are you always so brutally honest?"

"Usually," she said. "Saves a lot of time later, don't you think? Besides, if you lie, then you have to remember what lie you told to who and that just sounds exhausting."

Intriguing woman, he thought while his body was noticing other things about her. Like the way her dark green sweater clung to her breasts. Or how tight her faded jeans were. And the fact that she was barefoot, her toenails were a deep, sexy red and she was wearing a silver toe ring that was somehow incredibly sexy.

She was *nothing* like the kind of woman Simon was used to. The kind Simon preferred, he told himself sternly. Yet, there was something magnetic about her. *Something*—

"Are you just going to stare at me all night or were you going to speak?"

—Irritating.

"Yes, I'm going to speak," he said, annoyed to have been caught watching her so intently. "As a matter of fact, I have a lot to say."

"Good, me too!" She stood up, took the baby from him before he could even begin to protest—not that he would have—and set the small boy back in his high chair. Once she had the safety straps fastened, she shot Simon a quick smile.

"I thought we could talk while we have dinner. I made chicken and I'm a good cook."

"Another truth?"

"Try it for yourself and see."

"All right. Thank you."

"See, we're getting along great already." She moved around the kitchen with an economy of motions. Not surprising, Simon thought, since there wasn't much floor space to maneuver around.

"Tell me about yourself, Simon," she said and reached over to place some sliced bananas on the baby's food tray. Instantly, Nathan chortled, grabbed one of the pieces of fruit and squished it in his fist.

"He's not eating that," Simon pointed out while she walked over to take the roast chicken out of the oven.

"He likes playing with it."

Simon took a whiff of the tantalizing, scented steam wafting from the oven and had to force himself to say, "He shouldn't play with his food though."

She swiveled her head to look at him. "He's a baby."

"Yes, but—"

"Well, all of my cloth napkins are in the laundry and they don't make tuxedos in size six-to-nine months."

He frowned at her. She'd deliberately misinterpreted what he was saying.

"Relax, Simon. He's fine. I promise you he won't smoosh his bananas when he's in college."

She was right, of course, which he didn't really enjoy admitting. But he wasn't used to people arguing with him, either. He was more accustomed to people rushing to please him. To anticipate his every need. He was not used to being corrected and he didn't much like it.

As that thought raced through his head, he winced. God, he sounded like an arrogant prig even in his own mind.

"So, you were saying…"

"Hmm?" he asked. "What?"

"You were telling me about yourself," she prodded as she got down plates, wineglasses and then delved into a drawer for silverware. She had the table set before he gathered his thoughts again.

"What is it you want to know?"

"Well, for instance, how did you meet Nathan's mother? I mean, Sherry was my cousin and I've got to say, you're not her usual type."

"Really?" He turned on the spindly seat and looked at her. "Just what type am I then?"

"Geez, touchy," she said, her smile flashing briefly. "I only meant that you don't look like an accountant or a computer genius."

"Thanks, I think."

"Oh, I'm sure there are attractive accountants and computer wizards, but Sherry never found any." She carried a platter to the counter and began to slice the roast chicken, laying thick wedges of still-steaming meat on the flowered china. "So how did you meet?"

Simon bristled and distracted himself by pulling bits of banana out of the baby's hair. "Does it matter?"

"No," she said. "I was just curious."

"I'd rather not talk about it." He'd made a mistake that hadn't been repeated and it wasn't something he felt like sharing. Especially with *this* woman. No doubt she'd laugh or give him that sad, sympathy-filled smile again and he wasn't in the mood.

"Okay," she said, drawing that one word out into three

or four syllables. "Then how long were the two of you together?"

Irritation was still fresh enough to make his tone sharper than he'd planned. "Are you writing a book?"

She blinked at him in surprise. "No, but Sherry was my cousin, Nathan's my nephew and you're my...well, there's a relationship in there somewhere. I'm just trying to pin it down."

And he was overreacting. It had been a long time since Simon had felt off balance. But since the moment Tula had stepped into his office, nothing in his world had steadied. He watched her as she moved to the stove, scooped mashed potatoes into a bowl and then filled a smaller dish with dark green broccoli. She carried everything to the table and asked him to pour the wine.

He did, pleased at the label on the chardonnay. When they each had full glasses, he tipped his toward her. "I'm not trying to make things harder, but this has been a hell—" he caught himself and glanced at the baby "—heck of a surprise. And I don't much like surprises."

"I'm getting that," she said, reaching out to grab the jar of baby food she'd opened and left on the table. As she spooned what looked like horrific mush into Nathan's open mouth, she asked again, "So how long were you and Sherry together?"

He took a sip of wine. "Not giving up on this, are you?"

"Nope."

He had to admire her persistence, if nothing else.

"Two weeks," he admitted. "She was a nice woman but she—we—didn't work out."

Sighing, Tula nodded. "Sounds like Sherry. She never did stay with any one guy for long." Her voice softened in memory. "She was scared. Scared of making a mistake, picking the wrong man, but scared of being alone, too. She was scared—well, of pretty much everything."

That he remembered very well, too, Simon thought. Images of the woman he'd known in the past were hazy, but recollections of what he'd felt at the time were fairly clear. He remembered feeling trapped by the woman's clinginess, by her need for more than he could offer. By the damp anxiety always shining in her eyes.

Now, he felt…not guilt, precisely, but maybe regret. He'd cut her out of his life neatly, never looking back while she had gone on to carry his child and give birth. It occurred to him that he'd done the same thing with any number of women in his past. Once their time together was at an end, he presented them with a small piece of jewelry as a token and then he moved on. This was the first time that his routine had come back to bite him in the ass.

"I didn't know her well," he said when the silence became too heavy. "And I had no idea she was pregnant."

"I know that," Tula told him with a shake of her head. "Not telling you was Sherry's choice and for what it's worth, I think she was wrong."

"On that, we can agree." He took another sip of the dry white wine.

"Please," she said, motioning to the food on the table, "eat. I will, too, in between feeding the baby these carrots."

"Is that what that is?" The baby seemed to like the stuff, but as far as Simon was concerned, the practically neon orange baby food looked hideous. Didn't smell much better.

She laughed a little at the face he was making. "Yeah, I know. Looks gross, doesn't it? Once I get into the swing of having him around, though, I'm going to go for more organic stuff. Make my own baby food. Get a nice blender and then he won't have to eat this stuff anymore."

"You'll make your own?"

"Why not? I like to cook and then I can fix him fresh vegetables and meat—pretty much whatever I'm having, only mushy." She shrugged as if the extra effort she was talking about meant nothing. "Besides, have you ever read a list of ingredients on baby food jars?"

"Not recently," he said wryly.

"Well, I have. There's too much sodium for one thing. And some of the words I can't even pronounce. That can't be good for tiny babies."

All right, Simon thought, he admired that as well. She had already adapted to the baby being in her life. Something that he was going to have to work at. But he would do it. He'd never failed yet when he went after something he wanted.

He took a bite of chicken and nearly sighed aloud. So she was not only sexy and good with kids, she could cook, too.

"Good?"

Simon looked at her. "Amazing."

"Thanks!" She beamed at him, gave Nathan a few more pieces of banana and then helped herself to her own dinner. After a moment or two of companionable quiet, she asked, "So, what are we going to do about our new 'situation'?"

"I took the will to my lawyer," Simon said.

"Of course you did."

He nodded. "You're temporarily in charge…"

"Which you don't like," she added.

Simon ignored her interruption, preferring to get everything out in the open under his own terms. "Until *you* decide when and if I'm ready to take over care of Nathan."

"That's the bottom line, yes." She angled her head to look at him. "I told you this earlier today."

"The question," he continued, again ignoring her input, "is how do we reach a compromise? I need time with my son. You need the time to *observe* me with him. I live in San Francisco and have to be there for my job. You live here and—where do you work?"

"Here," she said, taking another bite and chasing it with a sip of wine. "I write books. For children."

He glanced at the rabbit-shaped salt and pepper shakers and thought about all of the framed bunnies in her living room. "Something to do with rabbits, I'm guessing."

Tula tensed, suddenly defensive. She'd heard that dismissive tone of his before. As if writing children's books was so easy anybody could do it. As if she was somehow making a living out of a cute little hobby. "As a matter of fact, yes. I write the Lonely Bunny books."

"Lonely Bunny?"

"It's a very successful series for young children." Well, she amended silently, not *very* successful. But she was gaining an audience, growing slowly but surely. And she was proud of what she did. She made children happy. How many other people could say that about their work?

"I'm sure."

"Would you like to see my fan letters? They're scrawled in crayon, so maybe they won't mean much to you. But to me they say that I'm reaching kids. That they enjoy my stories and that I make them happy," She fell back in her chair and snapped her arms across her chest in a clear signal of defense mode. "As far as I'm concerned, that makes my books a success."

One of his eyebrows lifted. "I didn't say they weren't."

No, she thought, but he had been thinking it. Hadn't she heard that tone for years from her own father? Jacob Hawthorne had cut his only daughter off without a dime five years ago, when she finally stood up to him and told him she wasn't going to get an MBA. That she was going to be a writer.

And Simon Bradley was just like her father. He wore suits and lived in a buttoned-down world where whimsy and imagination had no place. Where creativity was scorned and the nonconformist was fired.

She'd escaped that world five years ago and she had no desire to go back. And the thought of having to hand poor little Nathan off to a man who would try to regulate his life just as her father had done to her gave her cold chills. She looked at the happy, smiling baby and wondered how long it would take the suits of the world to suck his little spirit dry. The thought of that was simply appalling.

"Look, we have to work together," Simon said and she realized that he didn't sound any happier about it than she was.

"We do."

"You work at home, right?"

"Yes…"

"Fine, then. You and Nathan can move into my house in San Francisco."

"Excuse me?" Tula actually felt her jaw drop.

"It's the only way," he said simply, decisively. "I have to be in the city for my work. You can work anywhere."

"I'm so happy you think so."

He gave her a patronizing smile that made her grit her teeth to keep from saying something she would probably regret.

"Nathan and I need time together. You have to witness us together. The only reasonable solution is for you and him to move to the city."

"I can't just pick up and leave—"

"Six months," he said. He drained the last of his wine and set the empty goblet onto the table. "It won't take that long, but let's say, for argument's sake, that you move into my house for the next six months. Get Nathan settled. See that I'm going to be fine taking care of my own son, if he is my son, and then you can move back here…" He glanced around the tiny kitchen with a slow shake of his head as if he couldn't understand why anyone would willingly live there. "And we can all get on with our lives."

Damn it, Tula hadn't even considered moving. She loved her house. Loved the life she'd made for herself. Plus, she tended to avoid San Francisco like the plague.

Her father lived in the city.

Ran his empire from the very heart of it.

Heck, for all she knew, Simon Bradley and her father

were the best of friends. Now there was a horrifying thought.

"Well?"

She looked at him. Looked at Nathan. There really wasn't a choice. Tula had promised her cousin that she would be Nathan's guardian and there was no turning back from that obligation now even if she wanted to.

"Look," he said, leaning across the table to meet her eyes as though he knew that she was trying and failing to find a way out of this. "We don't have to get along. We don't even have to like each other. We just have to manage to live together for a few months."

"Wow," she murmured with a half laugh, "doesn't that sound like a good time."

"It's not about a good time, Ms. Barrons…"

"If we're going to be living together, the least you could do is call me Tula."

"Then you agree, *Tula?*"

"Do I get a choice?"

"Not really."

He was right, she told herself. There really wasn't a choice. She had to do what was best for Nathan. That meant moving to the city and finding a way to break Simon out of his rigid world. She blew out a breath and then extended her right hand across the table. "All right then. It's a deal."

"A deal," he agreed.

He took her hand in his and it was as if she'd suddenly clutched a live electrical wire. Tula almost expected to see sparks jumping up from their joined hands. She knew he felt it, too, because he released her instantly and frowned to himself.

She rubbed her fingertips together, still feeling that sizzle on her skin and told herself the next few months were going to be very interesting.

Four

Two days later, Simon swung the bat, connected with the baseball and felt the zing of contact charge up his arms. The ball sailed out into the netting strung across the back of the batting cage and he smiled in satisfaction.

"A triple at least," he announced.

"Right. You flied out to center," Mick Davis called back from the next batting cage.

Simon snorted. He knew a good hit when he saw it. He got the bat high up on his shoulder and waited for the next robotic pitch from the machine.

While he was here, Simon didn't have to think about work or business deals. The batting cages near his home were an outlet for him. He could take out his frustrations by slamming bats into baseballs and that outlet was coming in handy at the moment. While he was concentrating on fastballs, curveballs and sliders, he couldn't think about big blue eyes. A luscious mouth.

Not to mention the child who was—might be—his son.

He swung and missed, the ball crashing into the caged metal door behind him.

"I'm up two now," Mick called out with a laugh.

"Not finished yet," Simon shouted, enjoying the rush of competition. Mick had been his best friend since college. Now he was also Simon's right-hand man at the Bradley company. There was no one he trusted more.

Mick slammed a ball into the far netting and Simon grinned, then punched out one of his own. It felt good to be physical. To blank out his mind and simply enjoy the chance to hit a few balls with his friend. Here, no one cared that he was the CEO of a billion-dollar company. Here, he could just relax. Something he didn't do often. By the time their hour was up, both men were grinning and arguing over which of them had won.

"Give it up." Simon laughed. "You were outclassed."

"In your dreams." Mick handed Simon a bottle of water and after taking a long drink, he asked, "So, you want to tell me why you were swinging with such a vengeance today?"

Simon sat down on the closest bench and watched a handful of kids running to the cages. They were about nine, he guessed, with messy hair, ripped jeans and eager smiles. Something stirred inside him. One day, Nathan would be their age. He had a son. He was a father. In a few years, he'd be bringing his boy to these cages.

Shaking his head, he muttered, "You're not going to believe it."

"Try me." Mick toasted him with his own water and urged him to talk.

So Simon did. While late-afternoon sunshine slipped through the clouds and a cold sea wind whistled past, Simon talked. He told Mick about the visit from Tula. About Nathan. About all of it.

"You have a *son?*"

"Yeah," Simon said with a fast grin. "Probably. I'm getting a paternity test done."

"I'm sure you are," Mick said.

He frowned a little. "It makes sense, but yeah, looking at him, it's hard to ignore. I'm still trying to wrap my head around it myself. Hell, I don't even know what to do first."

"Bring him home?"

"Well, yeah," he said. "That's the plan. I've got crews over at the house right now, fixing up a room for him."

"And this Tula? What's she like?"

Simon pulled at his ice-cold water again, relishing the liquid as it slid down his throat to ease the sudden tightness there. How to explain Tula, he thought. Hell, where would he begin? "She's...different."

Mick laughed. "What the hell does that mean?"

"Good question," Simon muttered. His fingers played with the shrink-wrapped label on the water bottle. "She's fiercely protective of Nathan. And she's as irritating as she is gorgeous—"

"Interesting."

Simon shot him a look. "Don't even go there. I'm not interested."

"You just said she's gorgeous."

"Doesn't mean a thing," he insisted, shooting a look

at the boys as they lined up to take turns at the cages. "She's not my type."

"Good. Your type is boring."

"What?"

Mick leaned both forearms on the picnic table. "Simon, you date the *same* woman, over and over."

"What the hell are you talking about?"

"No matter how their faces change, the inner woman never does. They're all cool, quiet, refined."

Now Simon laughed. "And there's something wrong with that?"

"A little variety wouldn't kill you."

Variety. He didn't need variety. His life was fine just the way it was. If a quick image of Tula Barrons's big blue eyes and flashing dimple rose up in his mind, it was nobody's business but his own.

He'd seen close-up and personal just what happened when a man spent his time looking for *variety* instead of *sensible*. Simon's father had made everyone in the house miserable with his continuing quest for amusement. Simon wasn't interested in repeating any failing patterns.

"All I'm saying is—"

"Don't want to hear it," Simon told him before his friend could get going. "Besides, what the hell do you know about women? You're *married*."

Mick snorted. "Last time I looked, my beautiful wife *is* a woman."

"Katie's different."

"Different from the snooty ice queens you usually date, you mean."

"How did we get onto the subject of my love life?"

"Beats the hell outta me," Mick said with a laugh.

"I just wanted to know what was bugging you and now I do. There's a new woman in your life *and* you're a father."

"Probably," Simon amended.

Mick reached out and slapped Simon's shoulder. "Congratulations, man."

Simon smiled, took another sip of water and let his new reality settle in. He was, most likely, a father. He had a son.

As for Tula Barrons being in his life, that was temporary. Strangely enough, that thought didn't have quite the appeal it should have.

"I don't know what to do about him," Tula said, taking a sip of her latte.

"What *can* you do?" Anna Hale asked from her position on the floor of the bank.

Tula looked down at the baby in his stroller and smiled as Nathan slapped his toy bunny against the tray. "Hey, do you think it's okay for the baby to be in here while you're painting? I mean, the fumes…"

"It's fine. This is just detail work," Anna said, soothing her, then she smiled. "Look at you. You're so mom-like."

"I know." Tula grinned at her. "And I really like it. Didn't think I would, you know? I mean, I always thought I'd like to have kids some day, but I never really had any idea of what it would really be like. It's exhausting. And wonderful. And…" She stopped and frowned thoughtfully. "I have to move to the city."

"It's not forever," Anna told her, pausing in laying down a soft layer of pale yellow that blended with the bottom coat of light blue to make a sun-washed sky.

"Yeah, I know," Tula said on a sigh. She walked to Anna, sat down on the floor and sat cross-legged. "But you know how I hate the idea of going back to San Francisco."

"I do," Anna said, wiping a stray lock of hair off her cheek, leaving a trace of yellow paint in her wake. "But you won't necessarily see your father. It's a big city."

Tula gave her a halfhearted grin. "Not big enough. Jacob Hawthorne throws a huge shadow."

"But you're not in that shadow anymore, remember?" Anna reached out, grabbed her hand, then winced at the yellow paint she transferred to Tula's skin. "Oops, sorry. Tula, you walked away from him. From that life. You don't owe him anything and he doesn't have the power to make you miserable anymore. You're a famous author now!"

Tula laughed, delighted at the image. She was famous in the preschool crowd. Or at least, her Lonely Bunny was a star. She was simply the writer who told his stories and drew his pictures. But, oh, how she loved going to children's bookstores to do signings. To read her books to kids clustered around her with wide eyes and innocent smiles.

Anna was right. Tula had escaped her father's narrow world and his plans for *her* life. She'd made her own way. She had a home she loved and a career she adored. Glancing at the baby boy happily gabbling to himself in his stroller, she told herself silently that she was madly in love with a drooling, nearly bald, one-foot-tall dreamboat.

What she would do when she had to say goodbye to that baby she just didn't know. But for the moment, that time was weeks, maybe months, away.

If ever she'd seen a man who wasn't prepared to be a father, it was Simon Bradley.

Instantly, an image of him popped into her brain and she almost sighed. He really was far too handsome for her peace of mind. But gorgeous or not, he was as stuffy and stern as her own father and she'd had enough of that kind of man. Besides, this wasn't about sexual attraction or the buzzing awareness, this was about Nathan and what was best for him.

So Tula would put aside her own worries and whatever tingly feelings she had for the baby's father and focus instead on taking care of the tiny boy.

She could do this. And just to make herself feel better, she mentally put her adventure into the tone of one of her books. *Lonely Bunny Goes to the City.* She smiled to herself at the thought and realized it wasn't a bad idea for her next book.

"You're absolutely right," Tula said firmly, needing to hear the confident tone in her own voice. "My father can't dictate to me anymore. And besides, it's not as if he's interested in what I'm doing or where I am."

The truth stung a bit, as it always did. Because no matter what, she wished her father were different. But wishing would never make it so.

"I'm not going to worry about running into my father," she said. "I mean, what are the actual odds of that happening anyway?"

"Good for you!" Anna said with an approving grin. Then she added, "Now, would you mind handing me the brush shaped like a fan? I need to get the lacy look on the waves."

"Right." Tula stood, looked through Anna's supplies and found the wide, white sable fan-shaped brush. She handed it over, then watched as her best friend expertly laid down white paint atop the cerulean blue ocean, creating froth on water that looked real enough Tula half expected to hear the sound of the waves.

Anna Cameron Hale was the best faux finish artist in the business. She could lay down a mural on a wall and when she was finished, it was practically alive. Just as, when this painting on the bank wall was complete, it would look like a view of the ocean on a sunny day, as seen through a columned window.

"You're completely amazing, you know that, right?" Tula said.

"Thanks." Anna didn't look back, just continued her painting. "You know, once you're settled into Simon's place, I could come up and do a mural in the baby's room."

"Oooh, great idea."

"And," Anna said coyly, turning her head to look at Tula, "it would be good practice for the nursery Sam and I are setting up."

A second ticked past. Then two. "You're—"

"I am."

"How long?"

"About three months."

"Oh my God, that's huge!" Tula dropped to her knees and swept Anna into a tight hug, then released her. "You're gonna have a baby! How'd Sam take it?"

"Like he's the first man to introduce sperm to egg!" Anna laughed again and the shine in her eyes defined just how happy she really was. "He's really excited. He called Garret in Switzerland to tell him he's going to be an uncle."

"Weird, considering you actually dated Garret for like five minutes."

"Ew." Anna grimaced and shook her head. "I don't like to think about that part," she said, laughing again. "Besides, three dates with Garret or a lifetime with his brother...no contest."

Tula had never seen her friend so happy. So content. As if everything in her world were exactly the way it was supposed to be. For one really awful moment, Tula actually felt envious of that happiness. Of the certainty in Anna's life. Of the love Sam surrounded her with. Then she deliberately put aside her own niggling twist of jealousy and focused on the important thing here. Supporting Anna as she'd always been there for Tula.

"I'm really happy for you, Anna."

"Thanks, sweetie. I know you are." She glanced at the baby boy who was watching them both through interested eyes. "And believe me, I'm glad you're getting so much hands-on experience, Aunt Tula. I don't have a clue how to take care of a baby."

"It's really simple," Tula said, following her friend's gaze to smile at the baby that had so quickly become the center of her world. "All you have to do is love them."

Her heart simply turned over in her chest. Two weeks she'd been a surrogate mom and she could hardly remember a time without Nathan. What on earth had she done with herself before having that little boy to snuggle and care for? How had she gotten through her day without the scent of baby shampoo and the soft warmth of a tiny body to hold?

And how would she ever live without it?

* * *

Simon knew how to get things done.

With Mick's assistant taking care of most of the details, within a week, Simon's house had been readied for Tula and Nathan's arrival.

He had rooms prepared, food delivered and had already lined up several interviews with a popular nanny employment agency. Tula and the baby had been in town only three days and already he had arranged for a paternity test and had pulled a few important strings so that he'd have the results a lot sooner than he normally would have.

Not that he needed legal confirmation. He had known from his first glance at the child that Nathan was his. Had felt it the moment he'd held him. Now he had to deal with the very real fact of parenthood. Though he was definitely going to go slowly in that regard until he had proof.

He'd never planned on being a father. Hell, he didn't know the first thing about parenting. And his own parent had hardly been a sterling role model.

Simon knew he could do it, though. He always found a way.

He opened his front door and accidentally kicked a toy truck. The bright yellow Dumpster was sent zooming across the parquet floor to crash into the opposite wall. He shook his head, walked to the truck and, after picking it up, headed into the living room.

Normally, he got home at five-thirty, had a quiet drink while reading the paper. The silence of the big house was a blessing after a long day filled with clients, board meetings and ringing telephones. His house had been a sanctuary, he thought wryly. But not anymore.

He glanced around the once orderly living room and blew out an exasperated breath. How could one baby have so much...stuff?

"They've only been here three days," he muttered, amazed at what the two of them had done to the dignified old Victorian.

There were diapers, bottles, toys, fresh laundry that had been folded and stacked on the coffee table. There was a walker of some sort in one corner and a discarded bunny with one droopy ear sitting in Simon's favorite chair. He stepped over a baby blanket spread across a hand-stitched throw rug and set his briefcase down beside the chair.

Picking up the bunny, he ran his fingers over the soft, slightly soggy fur. Nathan was teething, Tula had informed him only that morning. Apparently, the bunny was taking the brunt of the punishment. Shaking his head, he laughed a little, amazed anew at just how quickly a man's routine could be completely shattered.

"Simon? Is that you?"

He turned toward the sound of her voice and looked at the hall as if he could see through the walls to the kitchen at the back of the house. Something inside him tightened in expectation at the sound of Tula's voice. His body instantly went on alert, a feeling he was getting used to. In the three days she and the baby had been here, Simon had been in a near-constant state of aching need.

She was really getting to him, and the worst of it was, she wasn't even trying.

Tula was only here as Nathan's guardian. To stay until

she felt Simon was ready to be his son's father. There was nothing more between them and there couldn't be.

So why then, he asked himself, did he spend so damn much time thinking about her? She wasn't the kind of woman who usually caught his eye. But there was something about her. Something alive. Electric.

She smiled and that dimple teased him. She sang to the baby and her voice caressed him. She was here, in his house when he came home from work, and he didn't even miss the normal quiet.

He was in serious trouble.

"Simon?"

Now her voice almost sounded worried because he hadn't answered her. "Yes, it's me."

"That's good. We're in the kitchen!"

He held on to the lop-eared bunny and walked down the long hallway. The rooms were big, the wood gleaming from polish and care and the walls were painted in a warm palate of blues and greens. He knew every creak of the floor, every sigh of the wind against the windows. He'd grown up in this house and had taken it over when his father died a few years ago.

Of course, Simon had put his own stamp on the place. He'd ripped up carpeting that had hidden the tongue-and-groove flooring. He'd had wallpaper removed and had restored crown moldings and the natural wood in the built-in china cabinets and bookcases.

He'd made it his own, determined to wipe out old memories and build new ones.

Now he was sharing it with the son he still could hardly believe was his.

Stepping into the kitchen, he was surrounded by the scented steam lifting off a pot of chili on the stove. At the table, Tula sat cross-legged on a chair while spooning something green and mushy into Nathan's mouth.

"What is that?" he asked.

"Hi! What? Oh, green beans. We went shopping today, didn't we, Nathan?" She gave the boy another spoonful. "We bought a blender and some fresh vegetables and then we came home and cooked them up for dinner, didn't we?"

Simon could have sworn the infant was listening to everything Tula had to say. Maybe it was her way of practically singing her words to him. Or maybe it was the warmth of her tone and the smile on her face that caught the baby's attention.

Much as it had done for the boy's father.

"It's so cold outside, I made chili for us," she said, tossing him a quick grin over her shoulder.

The impact of that smile shook him right down to the bone.

Mick had been right, he thought. Tula was nothing like the cool, controlled beauties he was used to dating.

And he had to wonder if she was as warm in bed as she was out of it.

"Smells good," he managed to say.

"Tastes even better," she promised. "Why don't you come over here and finish feeding Nathan? I'll get dinner for us."

"Okay." He approached her and the baby cautiously and wanted to kick himself for it. Simon Bradley had a reputation for storming into a situation and taking charge. He could feed a baby for God's sake. How difficult could it be?

He took Tula's chair, picked up the bowl of green

bean mush and filled a spoon. Behind him, he could sense Tula's gaze on him, watching. Well, he'd prove not only to himself, but to her, that he was perfectly capable of feeding a baby.

Spooning the green slop into Nathan's mouth, he was completely unprepared when the baby spat it back at him. "What?"

Tula's delighted laughter spilled out around him as Simon wiped green beans from his face. Then she leaned in, kissed him on the cheek and said, "Welcome to fatherhood."

An instant later, her smile died as he looked at her through dark eyes blazing with heat. Her mouth went dry and a sizzle of something dark and dangerous went off inside her.

They stared at each other for what felt like forever until finally Simon said, "That wasn't much of a kiss. We'll have to do better next time."

Next time?

Five

Tula remembered sitting in her own kitchen thinking that this was not a good idea. Now she was convinced.

Yet here she was, living in a Victorian mansion in the city with a man she wasn't sure she liked—but she really did want.

Last night at dinner, Simon had looked so darn cute with green beans on his face that she hadn't been able to stop herself from giving in to the impulse to kiss him. Sure, it was just a quick peck on his cheek. But when he'd turned those dark brown eyes on her and she'd read the barely banked passion there, it had shaken her.

Not like she was some shy, retiring virgin or anything. She wasn't. She'd had a boyfriend in college and another one just a year or so ago. But Simon was nothing like them. In retrospect, they had been boys and Simon was all man.

"Oh God, stop it," she told herself. It wouldn't do any good of course. She'd been indulging in not so idle daydreams centered on Simon Bradley for days now. When she was sleeping, her brain picked up on the subconscious thread and really went to town.

But a woman couldn't be blamed for what she dreamed of when she slept, right?

"It's ridiculous," she said, tugging at her desk to move it into position beneath one of the many mullioned windows. A stray beam of rare January sunlight speared through the clouds and lay across her desktop. She didn't take the time to admire it though, instead, she went back to getting the rest of her temporary office the way she wanted it.

She didn't need much, really. Just her laptop, a drawing table where she could work on the illustrations for her books and a comfy chair where she could sit and think.

"Hmm. If you don't need much stuff, Tula, why is there so much junk in here?" A question for the ages, she thought. She didn't *try* to collect things. It just sort of…happened. And being here in the Victorian where everything had a tidy spot to belong to made her feel like a pack rat.

There were boxes and books and empty shelves waiting to be filled. There were loose manuscript pages and pens and paints and, oh, way too many things to try to organize.

"Settling in?"

She jumped about a foot and spun around, holding one hand to her chest as if trying to keep her heart where it belonged. He stood in the open doorway, a half smile on his handsome face as if he knew darn well that he'd scared about ten years off her life.

Giving Simon a pained glare, she snapped, "Wear a bell or something, okay? I about had a heart attack."

"I do live here," Simon reminded her.

"Yeah, I know," As if she could forget. She'd lain awake in her bed half the night, imagining Simon in his bed just down the hall from her. She never should have kissed him. Never should have breached the tense, polite wall they'd erected between them at their first meeting.

Only that morning, they'd had breakfast together. The three of them sitting cozily in a kitchen three times the size of her own. She had watched Simon feeding a squirming baby oatmeal while dodging the occasional splat of rejected offerings and darned if he hadn't looked...cute doing it.

She groaned inwardly and warned herself again to get a grip. This wasn't about playing house with Simon.

He strolled into her office with a look of stunned amazement on his face. "How do you work in this confusion?"

She'd just been thinking basically the same thing, but she wasn't about to give him the satisfaction of knowing it. "An organized mind is a boring mind."

One dark eyebrow lifted and she noticed he did that a lot when they were talking. Sardonic? Or just irritated?

"You paint, too?" he asked, nodding at the drawing table set up beneath one of the tall windows.

"Draw, really. Just sketches," she said. "I do the illustrations for my books."

"Impressive," he said, moving closer for a better look.

Tula steeled herself against what he might say once he'd had a chance to really study her drawings. Her father had never given her a compliment, she thought. But in the end that hadn't mattered, since she drew her pictures for the children who loved her books. Tula knew she had talent, but she had never fooled herself into believing that she was a great artist.

He thumbed through the sketch papers on the table and she knew what he was seeing. The sketches of Lonely Bunny and the animals who shared his world.

His gaze moving to hers, he said softly, "You're very good. You get a lot of emotion into these drawings."

"Thank you." Surprised but pleased, she smiled at him and felt warmth spill through her when he returned that smile.

"Nathan has a stuffed rabbit. But he needs a new one. The one he has looks a little worse for wear."

She shook her head sadly, because clearly he didn't know how much a worn, beloved toy could mean to a child. "You never read *The Velveteen Rabbit?*" she asked. "Being loved is what makes a toy real. And when you're real, you're a little haggard looking."

"I guess you're right." He laughed quietly and nodded as he looked back at her sketches. "How did you come up with this? The Lonely Bunny, I mean."

Veering away from the personal and back into safe conversation, she thought, oddly disappointed that the brief moment of closeness was already over.

Still, she grinned as she said, "People always ask writers where they get their ideas. I usually say I find my ideas on the bottom shelf of the housewares department in the local market."

One corner of his mouth quirked up. "Clever. But not really an answer, either."

"No," she admitted, wrapping her arms around her middle. "It's not."

He turned around to face her and his warm brown eyes went soft and curious. "Will you tell me?"

She met his gaze and felt the conversation drifting back into the intimate again. But she saw something in his eyes that told her he was actually interested. And until that moment, no one but Anna had ever really cared.

Walking toward him, she picked up one of the sketches off the drawing table and studied her own handiwork. The Lonely Bunny looked back at her with his wide, limpid eyes and sadly hopeful expression. Tula smiled down at the bunny who had come along at just the right time in her life.

"I used to draw him when I was a little girl," she said more to herself than to him. She ran one finger across the pale gray color of his fur and the crooked bend of his ear. "When Mom and I moved to Crystal Bay, there were some wild rabbits living in the park behind our house."

Beside her, she felt him step closer. Felt him watching her. But she was lost in her own memories now and staring back into her past.

"One of the rabbits was different. He had one droopy ear, and he was always by himself," she said, smiling to herself at the image of a young Tula trying to tempt a wild rabbit closer by holding out a carrot. "It looked to me like he didn't have any friends. The other rabbits stayed away from him and I sort of felt that we were two of a kind. I was new in town and didn't have any friends, so I made it my mission to make that bunny like me. But no matter how I tried, I couldn't get him to play with me.

"And believe me, I tried. Every day for a month. Then one day I went to the park and the other rabbits were there, but Lonely Bunny wasn't." She stroked her fingertip across her sketch of that long-ago bunny. "I looked all over for him, but couldn't find him."

She stopped and looked up into eyes filled with understanding and compassion and she felt her own eyes burn with the sting of unexpected tears. The only person she had ever told about that bunny was Anna. She'd always felt just a little silly for caring so much. For missing that rabbit so badly when she couldn't find him.

"I never saw him again. I kept looking, though. For a week, I scoured that park," she mused. "Under every bush, behind every rock. I looked everywhere. Finally, a week later, I was so worried about him, I told my mother and asked her to help me look for him."

"Did she?" His voice was quiet, as if he was trying to keep from shattering whatever spell was spinning out around them.

"No," she said with a sigh. "She told me he had probably been hit by a car."

"*What?*" Simon sounded horrified. "She said *what?*"

Tula choked out a laugh. "Thanks for the outrage on my behalf, but it was a long time ago. Besides, I didn't believe her. I told myself that he had found a lady bunny and had moved away with her."

She set the drawings down onto the table and turned

to him, tucking her hands into her jeans pockets. "When I decided to write children's books, I brought Lonely Bunny back. He's been good for me."

Nodding, Simon reached out and tapped his finger against one of her earrings, setting it into swing. "I think you were good for him, too. I bet he's still telling his grandbunnies stories about the little girl who loved him."

Her breath caught around a knot of tenderness in the middle of her throat. "You surprise me sometimes, Simon."

"It's only fair," he said. "You surprise me all the damn time."

Seconds ticked past, each of them looking at the other as if for the first time. Simon was the first to speak and when he did, it was clear that the moment they had shared was over. At least for now.

"Do you have everything you need?"

"Yes." She took a breath and an emotional step back. "I just need to move my chair into place and—"

"Where do you want it?"

She looked up at him. He was just home from work, so he was wearing a dark blue suit and the only sign of relaxation was the loosening of the knot in his red silk tie.

"You don't have to—"

He shrugged out of his suit jacket. His tailored, long-sleeved white shirt clung to a truly impressively broad chest. She swallowed hard as she watched him grab hold of the chair and she wondered why simply taking off his suit jacket in front of her seemed such an intimate act.

Maybe, she thought, it was because the suit was who he was. And laying it aside, even momentarily, felt like an important step.

As soon as that thought entered her mind, Tula pushed it away.

Nothing intimate going on here at all, she reminded herself. Just a guy, helping her move a chair. And she'd do well to keep that in mind. Anything else would just be asking for trouble.

"Over there," she said, pointing to the far corner.

"You want to move that box out of the way?"

She did, pushing the heavy box of books with her foot until Simon had a clear path. He muscled the oversize chair across the room, then angled it in a way so that she'd be facing both windows when she sat in it.

"How's that?"

"Perfect, thanks."

He looked around the room again. "Where's the baby?"

"In his room. He took a late nap today."

"Right." He wandered around the room now, peeking into boxes, glancing at the haphazard stacks of papers on her desk. "You know, I've got some colored file folders in my office you could use."

She bristled. "I have my own system."

Simon looked at her and lifted that eyebrow again. "Chaos is a system?"

"It's only chaos if you can't find your way around. I can."

"If you say so." He moved closer. "Is there anything else I can do?"

"Um, no thanks," Tula whispered, feeling the heat of him reach for her. This was her fault, she told herself as tension in the room began to grow. If she hadn't given him that impulsive kiss, they'd still be at odds. If she hadn't opened herself up, causing him to be so darn sweet, they wouldn't be experiencing this closeness now.

So she spoke up fast, before whatever was happening between them could go any further. "Why don't you go check on Nathan while I finish up in here? I've still got a lot of unpacking to do."

She stepped past him and dug into a carton of books, deliberately keeping her back to him. Her heart was pounding and her stomach was spinning with a wild blend of nerves and anticipation. Pulling out a few of the books, she set them on the top shelf and let her fingertips linger on the bindings.

But Simon didn't leave. Instead, he went down on one knee beside her, cupped her chin and turned her face toward him.

"I don't know what's going on between us any more than you do. But you can't avoid me forever, Tula. We're living together, after all."

"We're living in the same house, that's all," she corrected breathlessly. "Not together."

"Semantics," he mused, a half smile tugging at one corner of his mouth.

Oh, she knew what he was thinking because she was thinking the same thing. Well, actually, there was very little *thinking* going on. This was more feeling. Wanting. Needing.

She shook her head. "Simon, you know it would be a bad idea."

"What?" he asked innocently. "A kiss?"

"You're not talking about just a kiss."

"Rather not talk at all," he admitted, his gaze dropping to her mouth.

Tula licked her lips and took a breath that caught in her lungs when she saw his eyes flash. "Simon…"

"You started this," he said, leaning in.

"I know," she answered and tipped her head to one side as she moved to meet him.

"I'll finish it."

"Stop talking," she told him just before his mouth closed over hers.

Heat exploded between them.

Tula had never known anything like it before. His mouth took hers hungrily, his tongue parting her lips, sweeping inside to claim all of her. He pulled her tightly against him until they were both kneeling on the soft, plush carpet. His hands slid up and down her back, dipping to cup the curve of her behind and pull her more tightly against him.

Tula felt the rock-hard proof of just how much Simon wanted her and that need echoed inside her. Her mind blanked out and she gave herself up to the river of sensations he was causing. She tangled her tongue with his, leaning into him, wrapping her arms around his neck and holding on as if she were afraid of sliding off the edge of the world.

He tore his mouth from hers, buried his face in the curve of her neck and whispered, "I've been thinking about doing this, about *you,* ever since you first walked into my office."

"Me, too," she murmured, tipping her head to give him better access. Her body was electrified. Every cell was buzzing, and at the core of her she burned and ached for him.

He dropped his hands to the hem of her sweater and slid his palms beneath the heavy knit material to slide across her skin. She felt the burn of his fingers, the sizzle and pop in her bloodstream as he stoked flames already burning too brightly.

Oh, it had been way too long since anyone had touched her, Tula thought, letting her head fall back on a soft sigh. And she'd *never* been touched like this before.

"Let me," he murmured, drawing her sweater up and off, baring breasts hidden beneath a bra of sheer, pink lace.

Cool air caressed her skin in a counterpoint to the heat Simon was creating. One corner of her mind was shrieking at her to stop this while she still could. But the rest of her was telling that small, insistent voice to shut up and go away.

"Lovely," he said, skimming the backs of his fingers across her nipples.

She shivered when his thumbs moved over the tips of her hardened nipples, the brush of the lace intensifying his touch to an almost excruciating level of excitement. Tula trembled as he unhooked the front clasp of her bra and sucked in a quick breath when he pushed the lacy panel aside and cupped her breasts in his hands.

He bent his head to take first one nipple and then the other into his mouth and Tula swayed in place. Threading her fingers through his thick hair, she held him to her and concentrated solely on the feel of his lips and tongue against her skin.

She wanted him naked, her hands on his body. She wanted to lie back and pull him atop her. She wanted to feel their bodies sliding together, to look up into his eyes as he took her to—

An insistent howl shattered the spell between them.

Simon pulled back from her and whipped his head around to stare at the doorway. "What was that?"

"The baby." Still trembling, Tula grabbed the edges of her bra and hooked it together. Then she reached for her sweater and had it back on in a couple of seconds. "I've got the baby monitor in here so I could hear him while I worked."

She waved one hand at what looked like a space-age communication device and Simon nodded. "Right. The monitor."

Scrambling to her feet, Tula backed away from him quickly.

"Don't do that," Simon said, standing up and reaching for her. "I can see in your eyes that you're already pretending that didn't happen."

"No, I'm not," she assured him, though her voice was as shaky as the rest of her. Pushing one hand through the short, choppy layers of her hair, she blew out a breath and admitted, "But I should."

"Why?" He winced when the baby's cries continued, but didn't let go of her.

Tula shook her head and pulled free of his grasp. "Because this is just one more complication, Simon. One neither one of us should want."

"Yeah," he said, gaze meeting hers. "But we do."

"You can't always have what you want," she countered, taking a step back, closer to the open doorway. "Now I really have to go to the baby."

"Okay. But Tula," he said, stopping her as she started to leave. "You should know that I *always* get what I want."

When Tula carried Nathan into her office half an hour later, she found a stack of colored file folders lying on top of her desk. There was a brief note. "Chaos can be controlled. S."

"As if I didn't know who put them there," she told the baby. "He had to put his initial on the note?"

She set the baby down on a blanket surrounded by toys, then took a seat at her desk. Her fingertips tapped against the file folders until she finally shrugged and opened one.

"I suppose it couldn't hurt to try a little filing, right?"

Nathan didn't have an opinion. He was far too fascinated by the foam truck with bright red headlights he had gripped in his tiny fists.

Tula smiled at him, then set to work straightening up her desk. It went faster than she would have thought and though she hated to admit it, there was something satisfying about filing papers neatly and tucking them away in a cabinet. By the time she was finished, her desktop was cleared off for the first time in...ever.

Her phone rang just as she was getting up to take the baby downstairs for his dinner. "Hello?"

"Tula, hi, this is Tracy."

Her editor's voice was, as always, friendly and businesslike. "Hi, what's up?"

"I just need you to give me the front matter for the next book. Production needs it by tomorrow."

"Right." For one awful moment, Tula couldn't remember where she'd put the letter to her readers that always went in the front of her new books. She liked adding that extra personal touch to the children who read her stories.

The scattered feeling was a familiar one. Despite what she had bragged to Simon about knowing where everything was, she usually experienced a moment of sheer panic when her editor called needing something. Because she knew that she would have to stall her while she located whatever was needed.

"It's okay, Tula," Tracy said as if knowing exactly what she was thinking. "I don't need it this minute and I know it'll take you some time to find it. If you just email the letter to me first thing in the morning, I'll hand it in."

"No, it's okay," Tula said suddenly as she realized that she had just spent hours filing things away neatly. "I actually know right where it is."

"You're kidding."

Laughing, she reached out, opened the once-empty file cabinet and pulled out the blue folder. *Blue for Bunny Letters,* she thought with an inner smile. She even had a system now. Sure, she wasn't certain how long it would last, but the fun of surprising her editor had been worth the extra work.

"Poor Tracy," Tula said with sympathy. "You've been putting up with my disorganization for too long, haven't you?"

"You're organized," Tracy defended her. "Just in your own way."

She appreciated the support, but Tula knew very well that Tracy would have preferred just a touch more organizational effort on her writer's part. "Well, I'm trying something new. I am holding in my hand an actual file folder!"

"Amazing," Tracy said with a chuckle. "An organized writer. I didn't know that was possible. Can you fax the letter to me?"

"I can. You'll have it in a few minutes."

"Well, I don't know what inspired the new outlook, but thanks!"

Once she hung up, Tula faxed in the letter, then filed it again and slipped the folder back into the cabinet with a rush of pride. Wouldn't Simon love to know that he'd been right? As for her, she'd managed to straighten up a mess without losing her identity.

Grinning down at the baby, she asked, "What do you think, Nathan? Can a person have chaos *and* control?"

She was still wondering about that when she carried the baby downstairs to the kitchen.

A few hours later, Tula said sharply, "You have to make sure he doesn't slip."

"Well," Simon assured her, "I actually knew that much on my own."

He was bent over the tub, one hand on Nathan's narrow back while he used his free hand to move a soapy washcloth over the baby's skin. "How is it you're supposed to hold him and wash him at the same time?"

Tula grinned and Simon felt a hard punch to his chest. When she really smiled it was enough to make him want to toss her onto the nearest flat surface and bury himself inside her heat.

The kiss they'd shared only a couple of hours before was still burning through him.

He still had the taste of her in his mouth. Had the feel of her soft, sleek skin on his fingers.

Now, as she leaned over beside him to slide a wet washcloth over Nathan's head, he inhaled and drew her light, floral scent into his lungs. He must have let a groan slip from his throat because she stopped, leaned back and looked up at him.

"Are you okay?"

"Not really," he said tightly, focusing now on the baby who was slapping the water with both hands and chortling over the splashes he made.

"Simon—"

"Forget it, Tula. Let's just concentrate on surviving bath time, okay?"

She sat back on her heels and looked up at him. "Now who's pretending it didn't happen?"

He laughed—a short, sharp sound. "Trust me when I say that's not what I'm doing."

"Then why—"

Giving her a hard look, he said, "Unless you're willing to finish what we started, drop it, Tula."

She snapped her mouth closed and nodded. "Right. Then I'll just go get Nathan's jammies ready while you finish. Are you good on your own?"

Good question.

He always had been.

Before.

Now he wasn't so sure.

"We'll be fine. Just go."

She scooted out of the bathroom a moment later and Nathan drew his first easy breath since bath time had started. He looked down into the baby's eyes and said, "Remember this, Nathan. Women are nothing but trouble."

The tiny boy laughed and slapped the water hard enough to send a small wave into his father's face.

"Traitor," Simon whispered.

Six

A few nights later, Simon had had enough of slipping through his own house like a damn ghost. Ever since the kiss he had shared with Tula, he'd kept his distance, staying away not only from her, but from the baby as well. He wondered where in the hell the paternity test results were and asked himself how he was supposed to keep his mind on anything else when memories of a too brief kiss kept intruding.

Hell, it wasn't just the kiss. It was Tula herself and that was an irritation he hadn't expected. She was in his mind all the time. Moving through his thoughts like a shadow, never really leaving, always haunting.

She walked into the room and he felt a hard slam of desire pulse through him. His body was hard and his hands itched to touch her. But she seemed blissfully unaware of what she was doing to him, so damned if he'd let her know.

"Maybe we should talk about how this is going to work," he said when Tula walked into the living room.

Lamplight shone on her blond hair and glittered in her eyes so that it almost looked as if stars were in their depths, winking at him. She was nothing like the women he was usually drawn to. And she was everything he wanted. God, knowing that she was there, in his house, right down the hall from his own bedroom, was making for some long, sleepless nights.

Oblivious of his thoughts, she smiled at him, crossed the room and dropped into a wingback chair on his right. Curling her feet up beneath her, she said, "Yes, the baby went right to sleep as soon as I laid him down. Thanks for asking."

He frowned to himself and silently admitted that, no, he hadn't been thinking about the baby. Hardly his fault when she was so near. He dared any man to be able to keep his mind off Tula Barrons for long. "I assumed he was sleeping since he's not with you and I can't hear him crying."

She studied him for a thoughtful moment. "Don't you think you should start being a part of the whole putting-Nathan-to-bed routine?"

"When I get the results of the paternity test, I will."

Until then, he was going to hang back. Taking part in bath time a few nights ago had taught him that he was too damn vulnerable where that baby was concerned. He had actually thought of himself as the boy's father.

What if he found out Nathan wasn't his?

No, better to protect himself until he knew for sure.

"Simon, Nathan is your son and pretending he isn't won't change that."

"That's what we need to talk about," he said, standing

to walk to the wet bar across the room. "Do you want a drink?"

"White wine if you've got it."

"I do." He took care of the drinks then sat down again opposite her. Outside, night was crouched at the glass. A fire burned in the hearth and the snap and hiss of the flames was the only sound for a few minutes. Naturally, Tula couldn't keep quiet for long.

"Okay, what did you want to talk about?"

"This," he said, sweeping one hand out as if to encompass the house and everything in it.

"Well, that narrows it down," Tula mused, taking a sip of wine. "Look, I get that you're a little freaked by the whole 'instant parenthood' thing, but we can't change that, right?"

"I didn't say—"

"And I've closed up my house and moved here to help you settle in—"

"Yes, but—"

"You'll get to know the baby. I'll help as much as I can, but a lot of this is going to come down on you. He's your son."

"We don't know that for sure yet and I think—"

She ran right over him again and Simon was beginning to think that he'd never get the chance to have any input in this conversation. Normally, when he spoke, people listened. No one interrupted him. No one talked over him. Except Tula. And as annoying as it was to admit, even to himself, he liked that about her. She wasn't hesitant. Not afraid to stand up for herself or Nathan. And not the least bit concerned about telling him exactly what she thought.

Still, he was forced to grind his teeth and fight for patience as she continued.

She waved her glass of wine and sloshed a bit onto her denim-covered leg. She hardly noticed.

"So basically," she said, "I'm thinking a man like you would feel better with a clear-cut schedule."

That got his attention. "A man like *me?*"

She smiled, damn it and his temperature climbed a bit in response.

"Come on, Simon," she teased. "We both know that you've got a set routine in your life and the baby and I have disrupted it."

This conversation was not going the way he'd planned. He was supposed to be the one taking charge. Telling Tula how things would go from here. Instead, the tiny woman had taken the reins from his hands without him even noticing. Simon took a sip of the aged scotch and let the liquor burn its way down his throat. It sat like a ball of fire in the pit of his stomach and he welcomed the heat. He looked at Tula, watching him with good humor sparkling in her eyes and not a trace of the sexual pull he'd been battling for days.

Irritating as hell that she could so blithely ignore what had been driving him slowly insane. Fresh annoyance spiked at having her so calmly staring him down, pretending to know him and his life and not even once allowing that there was something between them.

Plus, in a few well-chosen words, Tula had managed to both insult and intrigue him.

"I don't have a routine," he grumbled, resenting the hell out of the fact that she had made him sound like a doddering old man concentrating solely on his comfortable rut in life.

She laughed and the sound filled the big room with a warmth it had never known.

"Simon, I've only been in this house a handful of days and I already know your routine as well as you do. Up at six, breakfast at seven," she began, ticking items off on her fingers. "Morning news at seven-thirty, leave for the office at eight. Home by five-thirty..."

He scowled at her, furious that she was reducing his life to a handful of statistics. And even more furious that she was right. How in the hell had that happened? Yes, he preferred order in his life, but there was a distinct difference between a well-laid-out schedule and a monotonous habit.

"A drink and the evening news at six," she went on, still smiling as if she was really enjoying herself, "dinner at six-thirty, work in your study until eight..."

Dear God, he thought in disgust, had he really become so trapped in his own well-worn patterns he hadn't even noticed? If he was this transparent to a woman who had known him little more than a week, what must he look like to those who knew him well? Was he truly that *predictable?* Was he nothing more than an echo of his own habits?

That thought was damned disconcerting.

"Don't stop now," he urged before taking another sip of scotch. "You're on a roll."

"Well, there my tale ends," she admitted. "By eight I'm putting the baby to bed and I have no idea what you do with the rest of your night." She leaned one elbow on the arm of the chair and grinned at him. "Care to enlighten me?"

Oh, he'd like to enlighten her. He'd like to tell her she was wrong about him entirely. Unfortunately, she wasn't. He'd like to take her upstairs and shake up *both* of their routines. But he wasn't going to. Not yet.

"I don't think so," he said tightly, still coming to grips with his own slide into predictability. "Besides, I didn't want to talk about me. We were going to talk about the baby."

"For us to talk about the baby," she countered with a satisfied nod, "you would have to actually spend time with him. Which you manage to avoid with amazing regularity."

"I'm not avoiding him."

"It's a big house, Simon, but it's not that big."

He stood up, suddenly needing to move. Pace. Something. Sitting in a chair while she watched him with barely concealed disappointment was annoying.

Simon knew he shouldn't care what she thought of him, but damned if he wanted her thinking he was some sort of coward, hiding from his responsibilities. *Or* an old man stuck in a routine of his own devising. He walked to the wide bay window with a view of the park directly across the street. Moonlight played on the swing sets and slides, illuminating the playground with a soft light that looked almost otherworldly.

"I haven't gotten the paternity test results back yet," he said, never taking his gaze from the window and the night beyond the glass.

"You know he's yours, Simon. You can feel it."

He looked down at her as she walked up beside him. "What I feel isn't important."

"That's where you're wrong, Simon," she said sadly, looking up at him. "In the end, what you feel is the *only* important thing."

He didn't agree. Feelings got in the way of logical

thought. And logic was the only way to live your life. He had learned that lesson early and well. Hadn't he watched his own father, Jarod Bradley, nearly wipe out the family dynasty by being so chaotic, so disordered and flighty that he neglected everything that was important?

Well, Simon had made a pledge to himself long ago that he was going to be nothing like his father. He ran his world on common sense. On competency. He didn't trust "feelings" to get him through his life. He trusted his mind. His sense of responsibility and order.

Which was how he'd slipped into that rut he was cursing only moments ago. His father hadn't had a routine for anything. He'd greeted each day not knowing what was going to happen next. Simon preferred knowing exactly what his world was doing—and arranging it to suit himself when possible.

Besides, despite what Tula thought, he wasn't so much actively avoiding Nathan as he had been avoiding *her*. Ever since that kiss. Ever since he'd held her breasts cupped in his hands he hadn't been able to think of anything else but getting his hands on her again. And until he figured out exactly what that would mean, he was going to keep right on avoiding her.

Damn it, things used to be simple. He saw an attractive woman, he talked her into his bed. Now, Tula was all wrapped up in a tight knot with the child who was probably his son and Simon was walking a fine line. If he seduced her and then dropped her, couldn't she make it more difficult for him to get custody of Nathan? And what if he had sex with her and didn't *want* to let her go? What then?

There was no room in his life for a woman as flighty

and unorganized as she was. She thrived in chaos. He needed order.

They were a match made in hell.

"Are you even listening to me?"

"Yes," he muttered, though he was actually trying to *not* listen to her.

Which was no more successful than trying not to think about her.

Tula wasn't comfortable in the city.

Ridiculous, of course, since she'd spent so much of her childhood there. Her parents separated when she was only five and her mother, Katherine, had moved them to Crystal Bay. Close enough that Tula could see her father and far enough away that her mother wouldn't have to.

Crystal Bay would always be home to Tula. Right from the first, she'd felt as though she belonged there. Life was simpler, there were no piano lessons and tutors. Instead, there was the local public school where she'd first met Anna Cameron. That friendship had really helped shape who she was. The connection with Anna and her oh-so-normal family had helped her gain the self-confidence to eventually face down her father and refuse to fall in line with his plans for her life.

Now being in San Francisco only reminded her of those long, lonely weekends with her father. Not that Jacob Hawthorne was evil, he simply hadn't been interested in a daughter when he'd wanted a son. And the fact that his daughter didn't care at all about business was another big black mark against her.

Funny, Tula thought, she had long ago gotten past the regrets she had for how her relationship with her father had died away. Apparently though, there was still a tiny spark inside her that wished things had been different.

"It's okay though," she said aloud to the baby who wasn't listening and couldn't have cared less. "I'm doing fine, aren't I, Nathan? And you like me, right?"

If he could speak, she was sure Nathan would have agreed with her and that was good enough for now.

She sighed and pushed the stroller along the sidewalk. Nathan was bundled up as if they were exploring the Arctic Circle, but the wind was cold off the bay and the dark clouds hanging over the city threatened rain.

She and the baby had been in that house for days and it was harder and harder to be there without thoughts of Simon filling her mind. She knew it was pointless, of course. She and Simon had nothing in common except that flash of heat that had practically melded them together during that amazing kiss.

But she couldn't help where her mind went. And lately, her mind kept slipping into wildly inappropriate thoughts of Simon. Which was exactly why she had bundled Nathan up for a walk. She needed to clear her head. Needed to get back to work on the book that was due by the end of the month. It was hard enough eking out the time for illustrations and storyboards while the baby was napping. Forcing herself to work on the Lonely Bunny's antics while daydreaming about Simon made it nearly impossible.

Whenever Tula was having a hard work day, she would take a walk, just to feel the bite of the fresh air, see people, listen to the world outside her own mind. Ideas didn't pop into an idle mind. They had to be fostered, engendered. And that usually meant getting out into the world.

Actually, one of her most popular books had been born at the grocery store in Crystal Bay. She remembered watching a pallet of vegetables being delivered and immediately, she'd felt that magic "click" in her brain that told her an idea was forming. Soon, she'd had the story line for *Lonely Bunny Visits the Market.*

"So see, Nathan, we're actually working!" She chuckled a little and picked up the pace.

There were so many people scurrying along the sidewalks, Tula felt lost. But then she'd been feeling a little lost since settling into Simon Bradley's house. She hadn't written a word in three days and even her illustrations were being ignored. She couldn't keep this up much longer. She had deadlines to meet and editors to appease.

And Simon was taking up so many of her thoughts, she was afraid she wouldn't be able to think of anything else.

The only bright side was that she knew Simon was feeling just as frustrated as she was. That he wanted her as much as she did him. And she couldn't help relishing that sweet rush of completely feminine power that had filled her when he'd practically thrown her out of the bathroom during Nathan's bath time a few days ago. He hadn't trusted himself around her.

Which was just delicious, she thought. Of course it would be crazy to surrender to whatever it was that was simmering between them. She had Nathan to think about, after all. She couldn't just give in to what she was feeling and not think about the consequences.

Don't I sound responsible? she thought with surprise.

Well, she was. Now. Now that she had Nathan in her

life, she had to judge every decision she made along the measurement of what was good for him. And sleeping with his father couldn't be a good idea. Especially knowing that it was up to *her* to decide when Simon was ready for custody.

She stopped short.

Was that why he had kissed her?

Was he trying to seduce her into giving him Nathan?

"Now, that's a horrible thought," she said aloud.

"I beg your pardon?"

"Hmm?" Tula looked at the older woman who had stopped on the sidewalk to look at her. "Oh, sorry. I was actually talking to myself."

"I see." The woman's eyes went wide and she hurried past.

Tula laughed a little, then stepped to the front of the stroller to check on Nathan. "Well, sweetie, I think that nice lady thought I was crazy."

He kicked his legs, waved his arms and grinned at her. All the approval she needed, Tula thought, and stepped around to push him along the sidewalk again.

There were stores, of course. Small boutiques, coffee bars and even a cozy Italian restaurant with tables grouped together on the sidewalk.

But what caught her eye was the bookstore.

"Let's go see, Nathan."

She stepped inside and paused long enough to enjoy the atmosphere. An entire store devoted to books and the people who loved them. Was there anything better? Crossing to the children's section, Tula smiled at the parents indulging their kids by sitting on the brightly colored rugs to pick out books.

When she saw a little girl reading *Lonely Bunny Makes a Friend* Tula's heart swelled with pride.

She wandered over to the shelf where her books were lined up and, taking a pen from her purse, began signing the copies there.

A few minutes later, a voice stopped her mid-scrawl.

"Excuse me."

Tula looked at a woman in her mid-forties with a name tag that read Barbara and smiled. "Hi."

The woman looked her up and down, taking in her faded jeans, blue suede boots and windblown hair before asking, "What are you doing?"

Tula dug into her purse and pulled a roll of gold-and-black autographed copy stickers that she always carried with her. "I'm the author and I thought since I was here I would just sign your stock, if that's all right."

She had never had trouble before. Usually bookstores liked having signed copies of the books on the shelves to help with sales.

"You're Tula Barrons?" Barbara asked with a wide grin. "That's wonderful! My daughter loves your books and I can tell you they sell very well for us here in the store."

"I'm always glad to hear that," Tula said and hurried her signature as Nathan started to fuss.

"You live locally?" Barbara asked.

"Temporarily," Tula told her and felt a slight wince inside at the admission. She didn't know how long she would be staying in the city, but she was already dreading having to leave both Nathan and Simon.

"Would you be interested in doing a signing here at the store?" the woman asked. "We could set it up for you to do a reading at the same time. I think the kids would love it."

"Uh," Tula hedged, not sure if she should agree or not. Normally, she would have, of course. But now that she had Nathan to worry about…

"Please consider it," Barbara urged, looking around the children's area at the brightly colored floor rugs, the tiny tables and chairs. "I know most authors hate doing signings, but I can promise you a success! Your books are very popular here and I know the children would get a big kick out of meeting the woman who writes the Lonely Bunny stories."

Tula followed her gaze and looked at the dozen or so kids sprinkled around the area, each of them lost in the wonders of a book. Yes, her life was a little up in the air at the moment, but a couple hours of her time wasn't that much of a sacrifice, was it?

"I'd love to," she finally said.

"That's *great*," Barbara replied. "If you'll just give me a number where I can reach you, we'll set something up. How does three weeks sound?"

"It's fine," Tula told her. While Barbara went to get a pad and pen to take down her information, Tula told herself that in three weeks, she might be back living in Crystal Bay. Alone. That would mean a drive into the city for the signing, but if she was gone from Simon's life, she would at least be able to stop in and see Nathan while she was here.

Her heart ached at the thought. That baby had become so much a part of her life and world already, she couldn't even imagine being nothing more than a casual visitor to him. She put the signed book back on the shelf, walked to the front of the stroller and went down to her knees.

Running her fingers across the baby's soft cheek, she looked into brown eyes so much like his father's it was eerie and said, "What will I do without you, Nathan? If I lose you now, you won't even remember me, will you?"

He laughed and kicked his legs, turning his head this way and that, taking in all the primary colors and the bright lights.

Her already aching heart began to tear into pieces as she realized that Nathan would never know how much she loved him. Or how much it hurt to think of not being a part of his life.

She'd agreed to be the baby's guardian for her cousin Sherry's sake. But Tula had had no idea then that doing the right thing was going to one day destroy her.

Simon got home early the following day and no one was there to appreciate it.

Damned if he'd be so boring that Tula could set her watch—if she had the organizational skills to wear one—by him. He was still fuming over her monologue the night before, ticking off his daily routine and making him sound as exciting as a moldy rock.

In response, Simon had been shaking up his routine all day long. He had gone through the flagship of the Bradley department stores, stopping to chat with clerks. He'd personally talked to the managers of the departments, instead of sending Mick to do it. He had even helped out in the stockroom, walking a new employee through the inventory process.

His employees had been surprised at his personal

interest in what was happening with the store. But he had also noted that everyone he talked with that day was pleased that he'd taken the extra time to listen to them. To really pay attention to what was happening.

Simon couldn't imagine why he hadn't done it years ago. He was so accustomed to running his empire from the sanctity of his office, he'd nearly forgotten about the thousands of employees who depended on him.

Of course, Mick had ribbed him about his sudden aversion to routine.

"This new outlook on life wouldn't have anything to do with a certain children's book author, would it?"

Simon glared at him. "Butt out."

"Ha! It does." Mick followed him out the door and down the hall to the elevator. "What did she say that got to you?"

He was just aggravated enough by what Tula had had to say the night before that he told Mick everything. He finished by saying, "She ticked off my day hour by hour, on her fingers, damn it."

Mick laughed as the elevator doors swept closed and Simon stabbed the button for the ground floor of the department store. "Wish I'd seen your face."

"Thanks for the support."

"Well come on, Simon," Mick said, still chuckling. "You've got to admit you've dug yourself a pretty deep rut over the years."

"There's nothing wrong with a tight schedule."

Mick leaned against the wall. "As long as you allow yourself some room to breathe."

"You're on her side?"

Grinning, Mick said, "Absolutely."

Grumbling under his breath at the memory, Simon

stalked up the stairs, haunted by the now unnatural silence. For years, he'd come home to the quiet and had relished it. Now after only a few days of having Tula and the baby in residence...the silence was claustrophobic. Made him feel as if the walls were closing in on him.

"Ridiculous. Just enjoy the quiet while you've got it," he muttered. At the head of the stairs, he headed down the hall toward his room, but paused in front of the nursery. The baby wasn't there, but the echo of him remained in the smell of powder and some indefinable scent that was pure baby.

He stepped inside and let his gaze slide across the stacked shelves filled with neatly arranged diapers, toys and stuffed animals. He smiled to himself and inspected the closet as well. Inside hung shirts and jackets, clustered by color. Tiny shoes were lined up like toy soldiers on the floor below.

In the dresser, he knew he would find pajamas, shorts, pants, socks and extra bedding. A colorful quilt lay across the end of the crib and a small set of bookshelves boasted alphabetically arranged children's books.

Tula might thrive in chaos herself, he mused, but here in the baby's room, peace reigned. Everything was tidy. Everything was calm and safe and...perfect. He'd had a crew in to paint the room a neutral beige with cream-colored trim, but Tula had pronounced it too boring to spark the baby's inner creativity. It hadn't taken her long to have pictures of unicorns and rainbows on the walls, or to hang a mobile of primary-colored stars and planets over the crib.

Shaking his head, Simon sat down in the cushioned rocker and idly reached to pull one of the books off the shelves. *Lonely Bunny Finds a Garden*.

"Lonely Bunny," he read aloud with a sigh. Now that he'd heard her story, he could imagine Tula as a lonely little girl with wide blue eyes, trying to make friends with a solitary rabbit. He frowned, thinking about how her mother had so callously treated her daughter's fears.

He was feeling for Tula. Too much.

Opening the book, Simon read the copyright page and stopped. Her name was listed as Tula Barrons Hawthorne.

He frowned as his memory clicked into high gear, shuffling back to when he was dating Nathan's mother, Sherry. He remembered now. She had been living here in the city then and she'd told him that her uncle was in the same business as Simon.

"Jacob Hawthorne." Simon inhaled slowly, deeply, and felt old anger churn in the pit of his stomach.

Jacob Hawthorne had been a thorn in his side for years. The man's chain of discount department stores was forever vying for space that Simon wanted for his own company. Just three years ago, Jacob had cheated Simon out of a piece of prime property in the city that Simon had planned to use for expansion of his flagship store.

That maneuver had cost Simon months in terms of finding another suitable property for expansion.

Not to mention the fact that Jacob had bought up several of the Bradley department stores when Simon's father was busily running the company into the ground. The old man had taken advantage of a bad situation and made it worse. Hell, he'd nearly succeeded in getting his hands on the Bradley *home*.

By the time Simon had taken over the family business, it was in such bad shape he'd spent years rebuilding.

Jacob Hawthorne was ruthless. The old pirate ran his company like a feudal lord and didn't care who he had to steamroll to get his own way.

At the time Simon had briefly dated Sherry, he'd enjoyed the thought of romancing a member of Hawthorne's family, knowing the old coot would have been furious if he'd known. But Sherry's own clingy instability had ended the relationship quickly. Now, though, he had a son with the woman—which made his child a relative of Jacob Hawthorne.

There was a bitter pill to choke down. And he figured it would be even harder for the old pirate to swallow it. But there was more, too. If Sherry and Tula were cousins, then Tula was also a relative of Jacob Hawthorne. Interesting. But before his thoughts could go any further, his cell phone rang.

"Bradley."

"Simon, it's Dave over at the lab."

He tensed. This was the call he'd been waiting for for days. The results of the paternity test were in. He would finally know for sure, one way or the other.

"And?" he asked, not wanting to waste a moment on small talk when something momentous was about to happen.

"Congratulations," his old friend said, a smile in his tone. "You're a father."

Everything in Simon went still.

There was a sense of rightness settling over him even as an unexpected set of nerves shook through him. He was a father. Nathan was really his.

"You're sure?" he asked, moving his gaze around the

room, seeing it now with fresh eyes. His *son* lived here. "No mistakes?"

"Trust me on this. I ran the test twice myself. Just to be sure. The baby's yours."

"Thanks, Dave," he said, tossing the book onto the nearby tabletop and standing up. "I appreciate it."

"No problem."

When his friend hung up, Simon just stared down at his phone. *No problem?*

Oh, he could think of a few.

Such as what to do about the woman who was making him insane. The very woman who stood between him and custody of *his* son.

Seven

Tula knew something was different, she just couldn't put her finger on what it was exactly. Ever since she and Nathan had returned from their walk, Simon had been...watching her. Not that he hadn't looked at her before, but there was something more in his gaze now. Something hungry, yet wary.

There was a strained sense of anticipation hanging over the beautiful house that only added to the anxiety she had been feeling for days. She was on edge. As though there were tightened wires inside her getting ready to snap.

Just being around Simon was difficult now. As it had been ever since that kiss. He made her want too much. Need too much. And now, with those dark eyes locked on her and heat practically rolling off of him in waves, she could hardly draw a breath.

She made it through dinner and through Nathan's bath time and was about to read the baby his nightly story. Oh, she knew the baby didn't understand the words or what the stories meant, but she enjoyed the quiet time with him and felt that Nathan liked hearing the soft soothing tones of her voice as he fell asleep. Before she could begin, Simon walked into the nursery.

Tula smiled in spite of the coiled, unspoken strain between them. For the first time, he was inviting himself to Nathan's nightly ritual. "Hi."

"I thought I'd join you tonight." Simon looked at her for a long moment, then shifted his gaze to the tiny boy in the crib. Slowly, he walked across the floor and Tula sensed that she was witnessing something profound. Simon's features were taut, his eyes unreadable. There was a careful solicitude in his attitude she'd never seen before.

Leaning over the crib, Simon looked down at the boy in the pale blue footed jammies as if really seeing him for the first time.

"Simon?" she asked quietly, as if hesitant to break whatever spell was spinning out into the room. "What is it? You've been weird all night. Is something wrong?"

He shifted a quick look at her before turning his gaze back on Nathan. The baby stared up at him, then rubbed his eyes and sighed sleepily.

"Wrong?" Simon echoed in a thick hush of sound. "No. Nothing's wrong. Everything's right. I got the paternity test results this afternoon."

She sucked in a breath of air. Of course, from the beginning, she had known that Simon was Nathan's father. Sherry wouldn't have lied about something like that. But Tula could understand that Simon, a demon for rules and order and logic, would have to wait to be convinced.

"And?" she prompted.

"He's my son." Three words, spoken with a sort of dazed wonder that sent a flutter of something warm racing along her spine.

He reached into the crib and cupped one side of Nathan's face in the palm of his hand. The baby smiled up at him and Simon's eyes went soft, molten with emotions too deep to speak. Tula watched it all and felt her own heart melt as a man recognized his son for the very first time.

Seconds ticked past and still it was as if the world had taken a breath and held it. As if the planet had stopped spinning and the population of the earth had been reduced to just the three of them.

This small moment was somehow so intense, so important, that the longer it went on the more Tula felt like an outsider. An intruder on a private scene. That thought hurt far more than she would have thought it could.

For weeks now, she alone had been the baby's entire universe. When she was forced to share Nathan with Simon, she was still the central figure because Nathan's father was, if nothing else, a stubborn man. Determined to hold himself emotionally apart even while making room in his life for the boy. Now she saw that Simon had accepted the truth. He knew Nathan was his and he would be determined to have his son for himself.

As it should be, Tula reminded herself, despite the pain ratcheting up in the center of her chest. This was what Sherry had wanted—that Nathan would know his father. That Simon and his son would make a family.

A family, she told herself sadly, of *two*.

With that thought echoing over and over through her mind, Tula stepped back from the crib, intending to leave the two of them alone. But Simon reached out and grabbed her arm, pulling her to a stop.

"Don't go."

She looked up at him. The room was dark but for the night-light that projected constellations of stars onto the ceiling. In the dim glow of those stars, she watched his eyes and shook her head. "Simon, you should have a minute alone with Nathan. It's okay."

"Stay, Tula." His voice was low, hardly more than a dark rumble of sound.

"Simon…"

He pulled her closer until he could wrap one arm around her shoulders. Then he turned her toward the crib and they both looked down at the boy who had fallen asleep. There would be no story tonight. Nathan's tiny features were perfect, the picture of innocence. His small hands were flung up over his head, his fingers curling and relaxing as if in his dreams he was playing catch with the angels.

"He's beautiful," Simon whispered.

Tula's throat tightened even further. It was a miracle, she thought, that she could even breathe past the hard knot of emotion clogging her throat. "Yes, he is."

"I knew he was mine, right from the first," he admitted. "But I had to be sure."

"I know."

He turned his head to look down at her. Emotions charged his eyes with sparks that dazzled her. "I want my son, Tula."

"Of course you do." Her heart cracked a little further.

He would have Nathan and she would have…Lonely Bunny.

"I want you, too," he admitted.

"What?" Jolted out of her private misery, she could only stare up into brown eyes that shimmered with banked heat. This she hadn't seen coming. She hadn't expected. Something inside her woke up and shivered. Was he saying…

"Now," he said, drawing her from the room into the hall, leaving the sleeping infant laying beneath his night-light of floating stars.

"Simon—"

"I want you now, Tula," he repeated, drawing her close, framing her face with his hands.

Ah, she thought. He wanted Nathan forever. He wanted her *now*. That was the difference. She chided herself silently for even considering that he might have meant something different. A twist of regret grabbed at her but she relentlessly pushed it aside.

She'd been in his home for nearly a week. She knew Simon Bradley was a cool, calm man who didn't make decisions lightly. He liked to think he responded to his gut instincts, but the truth was, he looked at a situation from every angle before making a decision.

He wasn't the kind of man who would take some sexual heat and a shared love for a child and build it into some crazy happily-ever-after scenario. That was all in her mind.

And her heart.

She should have known better. *How silly,* she told herself, staring up into his eyes. How foolish she'd been to allow herself to care for him. To idly spin daydreams that had never had a chance to come true.

The three of them weren't a family. They were a temporary unit. Until Simon and Nathan had found their way together. Then good old "Aunt Tula" would go home and maybe come to the city once in a while for a visit.

As Nathan got older, he would no doubt resent time spent with her as simply time lost with his friends. He would be awkward with her, she thought, her heart breaking at the realization. Kind to a distant relative when his father forced him to be polite.

The little boy she loved so much wouldn't remember her love or the comfort he had derived from it. How she had sung to him at night and played peekaboo in the mornings. He wouldn't know that she would have done anything for him. Wouldn't recall that they had once been as close as mother and son.

He would have no memories of these days and nights, but they would haunt *her* forever.

She would be alone again. But this time, it would be so much worse. Because this time, she would know exactly what she was missing.

"Tula," Simon whispered, drawing her back from thoughts that were threatening to drown her in misery. He tipped her face up until their gazes were locked, his searching, hers glittering with a sheen of tears she refused to shed for the death of a dream that should never have been born.

So very foolish, she thought now, looking up at Simon Bradley. Until this very moment, Tula hadn't had any idea that she was more than halfway in love with a man she would never have.

"What is it?" he demanded. "Are you crying?"

"No," she said quickly because she couldn't let him

know that she had just said goodbye to a fantasy of her own making. "Of course not."

He accepted her word for that as his thumbs traced over her cheekbones.

"Come to my room with me, Tula," he said softly, his voice an erotic invitation she knew she couldn't resist. More, she knew she didn't want to resist it. She'd let the fantasy go but she would be a fool to turn her back on the reality, however brief it might be.

Reaching up, she covered his hands with her own and gave him the answer they both needed. "Yes, Simon. I'll come with you. I want you, too. Very much."

"Thank God." He bent and kissed her, hard and fast.

"Just let me turn the monitor on first," she said, walking back into the nursery, shooting a quick look at the baby as he sighed and smiled through his dreams. She flipped the switch on the monitor, knowing the receivers in hers and Simon's rooms would pick up every breath the baby made during the night.

She stared down at Nathan for a long moment, then turned her gaze on the doorway. There Simon stood, dark eyes burning with a fire that thrummed inside her just as hotly. Her body ached, her core went damp with need. She moved toward him and as she stepped into the hallway, he pulled her in close, then swung her up into his arms.

"I can walk, you know," she said wryly, the last of her sorrow draining away against a tide of rising passion. In spite of her protest, she secretly delighted in being carried against his hard, strong body.

"But why walk when you can ride?" One of his eyebrows lifted into the arch that she knew so well and she had to admit that being snuggled against Simon's broad chest was much preferable to a long walk down a silent hall.

The house sighed like a tired old woman settling down for a good night's rest. The creaks and groans of the wood were familiar to her now and Tula felt as though she were wrapped in warmth.

Warmth that suddenly enveloped her in heat as Simon dipped his head to claim another brief, fierce kiss. When he broke the kiss, his dark eyes were flashing with something that sent a quick chill racing along Tula's spine. Passion and just a hint of something more dangerous shone down at her and Tula's stomach erupted with a swarm of what felt like bees.

Head spinning, heart pounding, she linked her arms around his neck as he strode into his bedroom and headed for the wide, quilt-covered bed. She had never been in his room before and she glanced around at the huge space. Wildly masculine, the room was done in brown and dark blue. Deep brown leather chairs were drawn up in front of a blazing tiled fireplace. Twin bay windows overlooked the street, the park beyond and the distant ocean. The bed was big enough, she thought wryly, to sleep four comfortably and moonlight poured through the windows to lay in a silver path along the mattress. As if someone, somewhere, had drawn them a road map to where they both wanted to go.

"Gotta have you. Now," he muttered thickly, dropping her to the bed and following after.

"Yes, Simon," she answered, reaching for the buttons on his shirt, tearing at them when they refused to give.

Simon was half-crazed with wanting her. Everything

he had planned to say to her tonight dried up in the face of the overwhelming need clutching at him. Pulling at the hem of her bloodred sweater, he dragged it up and over her head to display the silky pink camisole she wore beneath. His gaze locked on her pebbled nipples. No bra. That was good. Less time wasted.

Simon hadn't been able to keep his mind on anything but Tula for hours. The question of his son's parentage had been answered and any other damn questions could just wait their turn. This was what he needed. What he had to have. Her.

Just her.

He pulled the camisole up, exposing her breasts to his hungry gaze and his mouth watered for a taste of her. He shrugged out of his shirt as she pushed the material down his arms, but beyond that, he couldn't be bothered.

Clothes would come off when they needed to. For now...he bent his head to her breasts and took first one nipple, then the other into his mouth. She gasped and arched off the bed, pushing herself into him, silently begging for more.

He gave her what she wanted.

Lips, tongue, teeth ran across the pink, sensitized tips of her breasts. Her taste filled him, her sighs inflamed him. Her fingers threaded through his hair, holding him to her breast as she squirmed under him, desperate for more. For everything.

He knew that feeling and shared it. His body ached. He was so hard for her he felt as though he might combust if he didn't get inside her. Tearing his mouth from her breasts, he worked his way down her incredibly lush body.

"So small, so perfect," he whispered, his breath hot against her skin.

"I'm not small," she countered, then gasped when his tongue traced a line around her belly button. "You're just abnormally tall."

He grinned and glanced up at her.

She shrugged. "Fine. I'm short."

"And curvy," he added, flicking the snap of her jeans and drawing down the zipper in one smooth move. His fingertips slid across her skin and she whimpered.

Simon smiled again and tugged at the jeans keeping him from her. They slid off her legs and fell to the floor. He paused then to admire the scrap of pink lace that made up the thong she wore. "If I'd known those jeans were hiding something like this, we'd have made it here long before now."

She ran her tongue across her bottom lip and everything in Simon fisted.

"Now that you know," she teased, "what are you planning on doing about it?"

In answer, he tugged the lace down her legs and off, shifted position and pulled her to the edge of the bed.

"Thought I'd start with this," he said and ran his tongue across the most sensitive spot on her body.

She jolted and instinctively squirmed beneath his strong hands holding her in place. But Simon wasn't letting her go anywhere. Instead, he pulled her closer to him, draped her legs across his shoulders and took her core with his mouth.

Tula groaned helplessly against the onslaught of emotions, sensations rampaging through her system. She looked down the length of her own body to watch him as he kissed her more intimately than anyone ever had before.

It was erotic. Sensuality personified, to see him licking her, tasting her and at the same time to feel what he was making her feel. Spirals of need and want clung together inside her and twisted into a frantic knot that seemed to pulse along with the beat of her heart.

And as her heartbeat quickened so did the tension coiling inside her. Tighter, faster, she felt herself nearing a precipice that swept higher with every passing moment. She raced toward it, surrendering to the incredible sensations coursing through her. She held nothing back—sighing, groaning, whispering his name as he pushed her further along the twisting road to completion.

Her breath was strangled in her lungs. She reached for the explosion she knew was coming and when the end came, her hands clenched the quilt beneath her and Tula held on as if for her life. The world rocked and her mind simply shut down under the onslaught of too many tiny shuddering ripples of pleasure.

Even before the last rolling sigh of satisfaction had settled inside her, Simon was there, moving her on the mattress, levering himself over her.

Staring down into her eyes, he entered her and Tula gasped at yet one more sensation. One more amazing invasion of her heart and mind and body. She held on to his shoulders and looked into dark brown eyes that were shadowed with secrets and shining with the same overpowering passion that held her in its grip. Again and again, his body claimed hers in the most intimate way possible. Again and again, she gave herself up to him, holding nothing back. Again and again, he pushed her higher and faster than she'd ever gone before.

The mind-numbing, soul-shattering climax, when it rushed through her, was enough to steal what little breath she had left. Moments later, she felt his release pound through him and heard him groaning her name. Then he collapsed atop her, his breath wheezing from his lungs, his heartbeat hammering in his chest.

Tula wrapped her arms around him and held him close, not wanting him to move yet. Not wanting to let go of the closeness that was somehow even more intimate than what they had just shared.

What could have been minutes or hours passed in a sensual haze of completion. Finally, he lifted his head, met her gaze and gave her a smile that at once made him look sexy and playful. That one smile slipped inside her and gave her the last nudge she needed to take the slippery slide into something she feared was probably, heaven help her, *love*.

"What is it?" he asked, voice quiet. "You look worried."

She was. Worried for her own sanity. Her own well-being. Falling in love with Simon would be a huge mistake, Tula thought grimly, so she just wouldn't do it. She would refuse to take that last step. It wouldn't be easy, she knew, but protecting herself was too important. Instinctively she realized she needed protection, too. Because loving and *losing* Simon would be enough to devastate her.

"Worried?" she echoed lamely, scrambling for something to say.

"I used protection," he assured her. "You weren't really paying attention, but I did."

"Oh. Thanks," she said, though a part of her wondered if it might not have been better if he hadn't. Then she would have had a chance at having a baby of her own. A child that would help fill the hole that losing Nathan was going to dig in her heart.

"Tula—" He pushed himself up on his elbows, took a breath and said, "We should talk about what just happened."

"Do we have to?" she asked, hating for this time to end with what couldn't possibly be good news. Whenever a man told a woman they had to talk, it was rarely to say, "Boy, that was great, I'm really happy."

He rolled to one side, and the chill in the room settled over her skin the moment he left her. He stacked pillows against the headboard and leaned back, his gaze on her. "Yeah. We do. Look, this was…inevitable, I think."

"Like death and taxes you mean?" she muttered, already hating how this conversation was going.

"You know what I'm talking about."

"Yeah, I do. And you're right," she sighed in agreement and sat up beside him on the bed.

He was sprawled naked, completely at ease. But Tula was suddenly feeling a little fragile. A little exposed. So she grabbed the edge of the quilt and tossed it over her, covering herself from breasts to knees. "Simon, you don't have to feel guilty or make a speech. I wanted this, too. You didn't seduce me into anything."

"I know."

"Well," she said with a small, self-conscious laugh. "Thanks for noticing."

"Not the point, Tula," he said. "The point is, we're still involved over Nathan and I want to make sure we understand each other."

She turned her head to look at him. "What are you talking about?"

Frowning, he pushed one hand through his hair. "Just that, you hold the strings when it comes to Nathan's custody."

She nodded, unable to look away from his eyes, once so warm and now looking as cold as the damp winter night outside. Somehow, he had taken a step away from her without actually leaving her side. Amazing that he could pull that off naked, but he managed.

"I don't want this," he continued, voice hard and flat, "what just happened here between us, to affect that."

Stunned, Tula could only stare at him, dumbfounded. This was not what she had been expecting. She'd thought that he was about to deliver the old, that-was-a-mistake-that-won't-be-repeated speech. Instead, he was intimating… *"What?"*

His mouth flattened into a grim line and that one eyebrow lifted. Surprisingly, she found it far less charming this time.

"Are you serious?" she demanded, indignant fury driving her words. "You really think I'm the kind of person who would use *this* against you somehow?"

"I didn't say that."

"Oh, yes you did," she told him, tossing the quilt aside and scooting off the bed. She grabbed her jeans and pulled them on over bare skin when she couldn't spot her lace thong. "I can't believe this. After what we just did, you could think that I, how could you think that? Amazing. And I'm so stupid. I should have seen this coming."

"Just wait a damn minute—"

She glanced at him over her shoulder. "That is about the most insulting thing anyone's ever said to me."

"I wasn't trying to insult you."

"So it's just a bonus then."

He climbed off the bed and went to grab his own jeans. Tugging them on, he said in a patient, calm tone that made her want to throw something, "Tula, you're overreacting. We're two adults, we should be able to talk about this without getting emotional."

"Emotional? Oh, could I show you emotional. Right now I want to throw something at that swelled head of yours."

"Not helpful," he pointed out, then looked around as if judging what she might grab and hurl at him.

"There's one of the differences between us, Simon," she snapped, whipping her head around to glare at him as she grabbed up her sweater. "Throwing things sounds very helpful to me right now. See, I'm not *afraid* to get emotional."

"What the hell are you talking about?" Now it was his turn to look insulted. "Who said I was afraid? This isn't even about fear."

"Really? Looks that way to me. My God, Simon." She cocked her head and narrowed her eyes on him. Shaking her head, she said, "You relaxed for like what? Twenty minutes? Was I on your schedule? Did you pencil me in—*Sex with Tula*—then back to business?"

"Don't be ridiculous," he muttered.

"Oh, now I'm ridiculous," she echoed, tossing both hands high then letting them fall. "You're the one making this into something it never was. This little speech you're making isn't about Nathan at all. It's about you backing away from allowing yourself to feel something genuine."

"Please." He scoffed at her and that one eyebrow winged up. "This isn't about feelings, Tula. We both had an itch and we scratched it. That's all."

She hissed in a breath and her eyes narrowed even farther until the slits were so tiny it was practically a miracle she could see him at all. "An *itch?* That's what you call what just happened?"

"What do you call it?" he asked.

Good question. She wasn't about to call it anything nice *now*. She wouldn't give him the satisfaction. So instead, she ignored the subject entirely. "Honestly, Simon, the very minute you felt close to me at all, you pulled back and hid behind that stiff, businessman persona you wear as if it were just another three-piece suit."

"Excuse me?"

"Oh," she said, warming to her theme and riding on bruised feelings and insult, "I'm just getting started. You're worried that now that I've been in the fabulous Simon Bradley's bed I might try to use that in deciding Nathan's future? Well, trust me when I say that sex with you won't sway my decision about you taking custody…"

He folded his arms over his chest. "Was there an insult in there?"

"Quite possibly, but I wasn't finished."

"Finish then. I knew there was more coming."

"You haven't proved to me yet that you're anywhere near ready to take care of a baby. Heck, until you were absolutely sure he was your son, you hardly went near him."

"And that's bad?"

"It is when you're too busy protecting yourself to give a child a chance."

"That's not what I was doing."

They stared at each other, gazes simmering with passions that had nothing to do with sex.

"This was clearly a mistake," Tula said a moment later, when she thought she could speak without shrieking. "But thankfully it's one that doesn't have to be repeated."

"Right. Probably best." Simon shoved one hand through his hair and said, "I still want you."

Tula looked at him for a long moment before admitting, "Yeah. Me, too. Good night, Simon."

She left the room and he didn't stop her. But she couldn't help turning back for one last look as she walked out. He looked powerful. Sexy.

Very alone.

And even after everything that had just happened, something inside her urged Tula to go back to him. Wrap her arms around him and hold on.

She had to remind herself that he had *chosen* solitude.

Eight

"I handled it badly, I know that."

"Yeah," Mick agreed cheerfully the following day. "That about covers it. Were you *trying* to piss her off?"

"No," Simon said, shaking his head as he thought about the night before. Hell, he couldn't remember much besides the urgent need he had felt to get her under him. Although the fight afterward was etched clearly enough in his mind. He still wasn't sure how it had happened. He hadn't meant to alert her to the fact that he was aware of the power she held in the situation. Hadn't meant to throw down a gauntlet just so that she could hit him over the head with it.

All he had really wanted to do was let her know that he wasn't going to be led around by his groin. That he was more than his passions. That sex with her, no matter how astounding, wasn't going to change him.

Simon made the rules.

Always.

But somehow, when he was around Tula, rational thought went out the window. Today, here in his office, away from the woman who was making him crazed, he was able to think more clearly. Now what he needed to know was what exactly Mick had found out about Tula Barrons Hawthorne.

"Never fight with a woman after sex," Mick was telling him. "They're feeling all warm and cozy and whatever. Men want to sleep. So hell, even *talking* after sex can be dangerous—if you ever want sex again."

Oh, he did, Simon thought. He wanted her the moment she left his room. He had wanted her all night and had awakened that morning aching for her. *Want* wasn't the issue.

"Just skip the advice and tell me what information you turned up."

Mick frowned at him and Simon thought that this was the downside of having your best friend work for you. He was less likely to take orders well and more likely to deliver his opinion whether Simon wanted it or not. "What did you find out? I know she's related to Jacob Hawthorne, but how? Niece?"

"A lot closer than that, as it turns out. She's his daughter."

"His what?" Simon went on alert. "His *daughter?*"

His mind raced as he listened to Mick give him more details.

"Hawthorne and his ex split when Tula was a kid. Mom moved with her to Crystal Bay. Tula visited her father often, but several years ago, she appears to have cut all ties with people here completely—including her father. My source didn't know much about it, just that Tula's a sore spot with the old man."

He had already known about her moving to that little town with her mother, Simon thought. But why would she cut all ties with everyone here, including her father? And why had he never heard about a daughter before? Was the old bastard protecting his child? Simon wouldn't have thought Jacob Hawthorne capable of familial loyalty.

"And," Mick added, "seems that when she started publishing children's books, she began using her middle name, Barrons. It's a family name, after her maternal grandmother. That grandmother left a will that provided a trust for Tula so that she—"

He straightened up in his desk chair and leaned both forearms on the neatly stacked files on his desk. "How big a trust?"

Mick thumbed through the papers he held. "To you, fairly small. To most of the world, very nice. It at least allowed her to buy her house and support herself while writing."

"Her books don't earn much?"

Mick shook his head. "She has a small, but growing readership for her Lonely Bunny series. The money will probably improve, but between her writing and the trust, she gets along and lives well within her limited means."

"Interesting." Her father was rich and she lived in a tiny house nearly an hour away from the city. What was the story behind that? he wondered.

"She hasn't seen her father in a few years that I can

find," Mick continued. "But then, the old man almost never leaves the city, either."

Hell, Simon thought, Jacob hardly left the Hawthorne building. He had a penthouse suite at the top of the structure that was his company's headquarters. He ruled his world from the top of his tower and rarely interacted with the "little people."

But as he thought that, Simon had to wince. Until the other day when he had deliberately gone through the store chatting with his employees, people could have said the same thing about him. There were some very uncomfortable similarities between Simon and his enemy.

"Is there anything else?" he asked, mainly to get his mind off that realization.

"No," Mick said, laying the sheaf of papers on his lap. "I can probably get more if you want me to dig deeper."

He thought about that for a moment. If he turned Mick loose and told him to dig, he'd have every piece of information available on Tula Barrons within a couple of days. But did he need more? He now knew who she was. He knew that she was the daughter of his enemy.

That was plenty.

While Mick talked, offering advice that he wasn't listening to, Simon tried to consider the situation objectively. He was attracted to Tula, obviously. The passions she stirred in him were like nothing he'd ever known. But now he knew who she was and damned if he could bring himself to trust a Hawthorne. So where did that leave him?

"What're you planning?"

He glanced at Mick. "I don't know what you're talking about."

"Right. I've seen that look before," his friend said, settling into the chair in front of Simon's desk. "Usually just before you're plotting some major takeover of an unsuspecting CEO."

Simon laughed and missed his point deliberately. "No CEO is ever unsuspecting."

"Damn it, Simon, what're you up to?"

"The less you know, the better off you are," he said, knowing that his friend would try to argue him out of the plan quickly forming in his mind.

"You mean the less you have to listen to my objections."

"That, too."

Mick slapped one hand down hard on the arm of his chair. "You're crazy, you know that? So what if she's a Hawthorne? Her father's a miserable old goat. She's got nothing to do with him."

"Doesn't matter."

"Damn it, Simon," Mick continued. "She split with him years ago. Doesn't even use her real name for God's sake."

"She's still his daughter," Simon insisted. "Don't you get it? The daughter of the man who tried to destroy my family is now in *charge* of when I get custody of my own son. How the hell am I supposed to take that, Mick? What if she just decides to never approve my custody of Nathan?"

"You really think she'd do that?"

"She's a Hawthorne." As far as he was concerned, that explained everything. God, he was an idiot. He had actually begun to trust Tula. He'd *felt* for her. More than he had anyone else in his life. Now he finds out this? For all he knew, Jacob had manufactured Nathan's mother's will. Maybe he and his daughter were in this together. Conspiring to dangle his son in front of him only to snatch him back.

He sprang to his feet as if the thought of sitting still another moment was going to kill him. Turning his back on his friend, he stared out the wide window at the view of San Francisco that Tula had admired so the first day he met her.

But instead of the high-rises and the glittering bay beyond the city, he saw *her*.

Her eyes. Her smile. That damn dimple in her cheek. He heard her sigh, felt the ripples of satisfaction rolling through her body as they took each other.

It had been one night since he had been with her and he wanted her again so badly, it was gnawing at him. Had she planned that, too? Had she deliberately set out to seduce him just so she could crush him later and sit with her father to enjoy the show?

His guts tightened and a cold, hard edge wrapped itself around his heart. The nebulous plan still forming in his mind was looking better and better by the moment.

"If you screw this up, you could be risking your son," Mick reminded him unnecessarily.

"No," Simon said, glancing back over his shoulder at his friend. "Don't you get it? A *Hawthorne* is in charge of whether or not I'm fit to care for my son. How could I possibly make that any worse?"

"Let me count the ways," Mick muttered darkly.

"You'll see," Simon told him, warming to his plan even as it took final shape in his mind. "I'm going to seduce Tula—" *again,* he added silently "—until she can't think straight. By the time I'm finished, she'll support me getting custody of Nathan. And when I'm sure of that, I'll go to her father and tell him that I've been sleeping with his daughter. If that doesn't give the old man a stroke, nothing will."

"What'll it do to her?" Mick asked quietly.

For one brief second, Simon considered that. Considered how it would be when she found out that she'd been used by him. But he let that thought go as soon as he remembered that she was a Hawthorne and that her family was more than accustomed to using and being used.

"Doesn't matter," he ground out.

"Whatever you say." Mick stood up and shook his head. "I'm heading home now, but before I go, one more piece of advice."

"I'm not going to like it, am I?"

Mick shrugged. "Whoever likes unsolicited advice?"

"Good point. Okay, let's have it."

"Don't do it."

"Do what?"

"Whatever it is you're planning, Simon." Mick locked his gaze with his friend's and said in all seriousness, "Just let this go."

Simon shook his head. "Hawthorne cheated me."

"His daughter didn't."

"She lied to me. About who she was. Maybe about why she's in my damn house."

"You don't know that. You could just ask her."

Sending a warning glare at his friend, Simon said, "You don't understand."

"You're right," Mick told him, turning for the door.

"I don't. For the last week or so, you've been almost… happy. I'd hate to see you screw that up for yourself, Simon."

He didn't say anything as Mick left. Hell, what was there to say? There was an opportunity here. A chance to get back at Jacob Hawthorne while at the same time indulging himself in a woman he wanted more than he was comfortable admitting.

An image of Tula filled his mind and his body went hard and heavy almost instantly. Remembering how responsive she was in bed had him wanting her so desperately, he'd have done anything to have her that minute. Even that damned fight they'd had hadn't cooled him off any. Instead, it had stoked the fires already inside him. He'd never enjoyed a fight more.

Didn't mean anything though, he told himself. Yes, he'd admitted to liking her. But that was before he knew who she really was. Now he didn't know if he could believe the person she'd shown herself to be. Maybe it was all an act. Maybe everything she had done since arriving at his house had all been part of an elaborate show.

If it was, he would have the last laugh. If it wasn't… he shook his head. He wouldn't consider that. Tula *Hawthorne* was a grown woman. She could make her own decisions. And if she decided to join him in his bed—and she would, *again*—that would be her choice.

She'd be fine.

He'd have his revenge.

And his son.

* * *

"He was a complete jerk," Tula said into her cell phone, then caught the baby watching her warily. She didn't care what some people thought about children and their awareness to the world around them. She knew that Nathan was sensitive to tone and her moods, so she instantly forced a smile, despite the sheen of ice that felt as though it was coating her insides.

"Honey," Anna's sympathetic voice came over the phone. "You're the one who always reminded me that most men are jerks at one point or another."

"Yes, but at *that* point?" Tula said in a hiss, still smiling for Nathan's sake. "Seriously, Anna the glow hadn't even begun to fade and he turned on me like a rabid dog."

"Well, I hope you gave it right back to him."

"I did," she said, remembering their fight last night. It had completely colored everything that went before it and that was saying something.

Sex with Simon had been even more amazing than she had imagined it could be. But to have it all ruined because Simon had donned his metaphorical suit right after was just infuriating.

"Nothing I said got through to him though, so it hardly matters that I fought back," she mused, plucking a windblown brown leaf from the blanket and tossing it into the air. "He was so cold. So..."

"Believe me I know," Anna assured her. "Remember how awful Sam was in the beginning?"

"That's different."

"Really, how?"

Tula laughed halfheartedly. "Because this is about *me*."

"Ah, well sure. Now I see."

Another laugh shot from Tula's throat helplessly. "Fine, fine. You suffered, all women suffer. But *my* suffering is happening now."

"Okay, there you've got me."

"Thanks. So. Advice?"

"Plenty, but advice isn't what you need, Tula. You already know how to handle this."

"Really, how's that?"

"Get Simon ready for Nathan and then come home. Where you belong."

Where she belonged.

For so many years, the tiny house in Crystal Bay had been just that. Tula's haven. The one spot in the world where she felt as if she'd carved out a place for herself. But now, thinking about going back to her old life of work and friends sounded somehow...empty.

Her gaze turned on the baby laying on a blanket spread over the grass of Simon's backyard. She didn't know if she *could* go back home. Her small house would now be crowded with memories of a baby that had brightened it so briefly. She would hear Nathan's cries in the night, find his toys tucked under the couch. She would wonder, always, how he was, what he was doing.

Just as she would wonder about Simon.

The bastard.

How dare he make her care for him and then become just...a *man?* How could he have experienced what they had shared and then turn his back on it all so mechanically? How could he simply flip a mental switch and shut off his emotions as easily as turning off a lightbulb?

Or maybe she was reading too much into him.

Giving him too much credit. Maybe he didn't *have* any emotions. Maybe that suit that so defined him had stunted any natural human feelings. Hadn't she warned herself the very first day she had met him that he was too much like her father? Too caught up in the world of corporate finances for her to be interested in him?

She should have listened to herself.

Then she remembered the look on his face as he had stared down at Nathan, knowing the baby was his son. His features had been easy enough to read. The man was capable of love. He simply wasn't interested in it.

At least, not with her.

"Yoo-hoo?"

"Huh? What?" Tula shook her head and said, "Sorry, sorry. Wasn't listening."

"Yeah, I got that," Anna said wryly. "You're not ready to come home yet, are you?"

"I can't. The baby and—"

"No." Anna's voice was soft and filled with understanding sympathy. "I mean, you're not ready to walk away from Simon yet, are you?"

Tula's shoulders slumped in resignation, though her friend couldn't see it. "No, guess I'm not. That makes me some kind of grand idiot, doesn't it?" Then, without waiting for her friend's response, she answered her own question. "Of course it does. Why would I think I could have feelings for a man so much like my father? Why didn't I stop myself?"

"Because sometimes you just can't, honey." Anna laughed. "Look at me! I took that mural job Sam offered me because I needed the money. I even told him to his face that I couldn't stand him! Now look where I am...

married and pregnant. Sometimes, the heart just wants what it wants and you can't do anything to change it."

"Well, that's not fair at all."

"And so little is," Anna commiserated. "Now, back to my original question with this phone call…do you still want me to come to the city this weekend? Do the mural on Nathan's wall?"

Tula thought about that. Knew Simon would probably hate it—he of the beige-with-cream-trim designing skills. Then Tula looked at the baby, waving his little arms at the naked tree branches high overhead. And she knew that if she couldn't be with him, then at least she could leave behind a physical reminder of her presence. One that both Nathan and Simon would see every day.

"Yeah, I do," Tula told her friend. "Nathan's room needs some brightening up."

"Great! I've already got some fabulous ideas."

"I trust you," Tula said, then added, "I've only got one request."

"What's that?"

"Paint in the Lonely Bunny somewhere, will you?" She reached out and smoothed her fingertips along Nathan's cheek. "That way it will almost be like I'm still here, watching over him. Even after I'm gone."

"Oh, sweetie…"

She heard the sympathy in her friend's voice and steeled herself against it. Tula didn't want pity. In fact, she wasn't sure what exactly she *did* want. Beyond Simon, of course, and that was never going to happen.

It would have been easier to seduce Tula if they hadn't already been to bed only to have the fight that had left both of them furious.

But Simon was nothing if not determined.

He dismissed Mick's warnings that seemed to repeat over and over again in his mind. After all, Mick was married. He and Katie had been together since college. They fit together so well, it was hard to believe they hadn't started out life joined at the hip. So how could his best friend understand the tension, the stubborn refusal to back down once a position was taken? How could he know anything about the sexual heat that flared during an argument?

How could he ever understand the enmity Simon felt for the Hawthorne family?

Simon knew exactly what he was doing—as he always did. And the fact that Mick disagreed wasn't going to stop him.

This plan of his was going to kill two birds with one impressive stone, he told himself. Not only would he be able to indulge himself with Tula—something he hadn't been able to stop thinking of—but he'd also have the revenge on her father that he had been dreaming of for three years. It would absolutely fry that old man when he found out that his daughter had been in Simon's bed.

But first things first. Before his plan could get into motion, Simon had to start making arrangements for when he had custody of Nathan. He wouldn't have Tula to care for the baby while he was at work, so he would need someone responsible for the job.

He didn't let himself think about the fact that when that day came, Tula would be out of their lives.

Nine

An hour later, he was home early again and didn't even stop to admit that since Tula had come into his life, he'd found less and less reason for hanging around the company. Instead, he seemed to be drawn to this old house and the woman inside it.

Simon found Tula in the backyard, watching Nathan squirm on a blanket beneath the winter sun. She turned to look at him and he could actually *see* her freeze up. A part of him regretted being the cause of that. He was too accustomed to her easy smile and ready laugh. Seeing her so wary, so cold, gave him a pause that none of Mick's not so subtle warnings had managed to do.

But he reminded himself that she was a Hawthorne and had never bothered to mention it. How much did he owe her anyway? Besides, he had a plan now and once Simon picked a direction, he didn't deviate. That would indicate that he doubted himself and he never did that.

Stuffing his hands into the pockets of his slacks, he walked down the flagstone steps that led to the landscaped yard. Each step was slow, deliberately careless, letting her know that though she might be angry, he was just fine.

Liar.

His brain shouted out that single word and he recognized the truth in it. But damned if he'd let her know.

"Isn't it a little cold out here for him?" Simon asked, nodding at the boy who was wearing a shoulder-to-toes zip-up blanket sleeper.

"Fresh air's good for him," she said stiffly. She countered, "You're home early."

He grinned, pleased that she'd noticed. "I am. I wanted to talk to you."

"Oh, can't wait," she said, sarcasm coloring her tone. "Our last conversation went so well."

Good, he told himself. She was still bothered. He liked knowing that what they'd shared had hit her as hard as it had him. And more, he wanted to share it all again. A lot.

He took a seat beside her on the blanket and hid a smile when she scooted away a bit. As if she didn't trust herself too near him. He knew just how she felt.

At the moment, all he really wanted to do was grab her and hold her and—

"What can you possibly have left to say that you didn't say last night?"

"Plenty," he admitted, drawing one knee up and resting his forearm on it.

"Let me guess," she said, her blue eyes snapping with banked fury. "You've found a way to blame me for global warming? Or am I a spy of some kind, sent to ferret out all of your secrets and feed them to your enemies?"

He just stared at her. Was that last statement for show or was she actually trying to tell him why she was really there? "Is that a confession?"

"Oh, for heaven's sake, Simon," she snapped in a whispered hiss. "You know darn well it's not. I'm just trying to guess how you'll insult me next."

He wondered, but let it go for now. "As a matter of fact, I don't want to talk about you at all," he said. "Now that we're committed to getting me ready to take over custody of Nathan, we have to find a competent nanny."

"A *nanny?*" she asked in the same tone she might have used to ask, *You want to hire an axe murderer?*

He nodded, pleased with her reaction. Even if he was confused about her motivation for being there, with him, he knew for a fact that she loved Nathan.

"I'll still have to work, so when you leave, I'll need someone here with the baby. I think a live-in nanny would be the best way to go, don't you?"

"I don't know," she said, glancing down at the babbling baby. "I hadn't really thought about someone else caring for him on a day-to-day basis."

Actually, Simon didn't much care for the idea of a stranger in his house taking care of his son while he wasn't there. But he couldn't see any way around it, either. No matter how his plan ended up working out, Tula wouldn't be here for him and Nathan to count on.

He really didn't like the thought of that, but refused to explore the reasons why.

"He can't go to work with me," Simon said abruptly, watching her reaction.

"No, I suppose not."

"Is there a problem?"

Her gaze flicked to his, fired for an instant, then cooled off again until those beautiful blue eyes of hers shone like the surface of a frozen lake. "No. No problem."

"Good," he said. "So I'll call the employment agency and have them send people over. Are you interested in interviewing them or would you prefer I do it?"

She looked torn and he was forced to admit silently that he felt the same way. Funny, this conversation about hiring a nanny didn't have anything to do with his plan. It had only seemed like a reasonable way for him to open communications with Tula again. Besides, theoretically, a caretaker for Nathan had sounded acceptable enough.

In practice though...looking down at his son— innocent, helpless, at the mercy of whoever his father hired to look after him...it felt wrong, somehow. Instantly, half-forgotten news reports flashed through his mind, stories about nannies and babysitters and preschools, all of whom were supposedly devoted caregivers. And how the children in their charge had paid the price for their negligence or apathy.

Frowning, Simon told himself this situation would be different. He would have the nanny he hired screened completely. He wouldn't trust just anyone with his son's safety.

But the scowl on his face deepened as he realized

that the only person he really trusted with Nathan's well-being was the woman beside him. The very woman who he already knew to be a liar. She hadn't told him the truth about who she was, so why should he trust her?

But he did. Instinctively, he knew he could trust Tula with his son. But she was also the woman who would be leaving someday soon.

The woman he was planning on using for his own taste of revenge.

Tula thanked the woman for coming and once she'd seen her out, closed the door and leaned back against it. A sigh of defeat slid from her throat.

That was the third prospective nanny she had interviewed in the last two days and she hadn't liked any of them.

"What was wrong with that one?"

Startled, she looked up at Simon, leaning against the newel post of the banister. His eyes were amused and his mouth was curved at one end as if he were trying to hide a smile that hadn't quite made it to his features.

"What're you doing here?" He had the most disconcerting habit of sneaking up on a person. And this new habit of his, splintering the routine he had clung to when she first came to the city, was even more disquieting. He was up to something, she figured. She just didn't know what. Which just put her that much more on guard.

He tossed his suit jacket over the newel post and loosened his red silk tie. "I live here, as I've pointed out before."

"Yes, but it's the middle of the afternoon. On a workday. Are you sick?"

He chuckled. "No, I'm not sick. I just left the office early. No big deal. Now, what was wrong with the woman you just sent packing?"

Still wary, she asked, "Didn't you see the bun she was wearing?"

"Bun?"

She saw the confusion on his face and explained. "Her hair. It was pulled into a taut little knot at the back of her head."

"So? An unattractive hairstyle makes for a bad nanny?"

It sounded silly when he said it, but Tula was going with her instincts. Nathan was too important to take any chances with his safety and happiness. She would find the *right* nanny for him or she just wouldn't leave.

Unless, she thought, that's exactly what she was subconsciously hoping for. That she could stay. That she could be the one raising Nathan, loving him. A worry for another day, she supposed.

"The woman's hair was scraped so tightly, her eyelids were tilted back. Anyone that rigid shouldn't be in charge of a child."

"Ah," he said as though he understood, but she knew he didn't. He was patronizing her.

"So the one yesterday afternoon, with her hair long and loose and curling…?"

She scowled at him. "Too careless. If she doesn't care what her hair looks like, she won't care enough about Nathan."

"And the first one?"

"She had mean eyes," Tula said with no apologies. She just knew that woman was the kind who made children sit in dark closets or go to bed without dinner. She would never leave Nathan with a cold-eyed woman.

Simon's eyebrow lifted again. She was getting to the point where she could judge his moods by the tilt of that eyebrow alone. Right now, she told herself with an inner grumble, he was entertained. By *her*.

Perhaps he had a point. Tula knew what she was doing wasn't fair to the women who had come looking for a job. Except for the mean-eyed one, they seemed nice enough. Certainly qualified. The agency Simon was dealing with was the top one in the city, known for representing the absolute best in nannies.

But how could she be expected to turn over a little boy she loved to a stranger?

He was still watching her with just the barest hint of amusement on his face. An expression she found way too attractive for her own well-being.

"All right," she conceded grudgingly, "maybe I'm being a little too careful in the selection process."

"Maybe?"

She ignored that. Because even if she was being overprotective, it wouldn't hurt that baby any. It would only help ensure that the best possible person would be in charge of him. And if anything, as the baby's father, Simon should appreciate that.

"This is important, Simon. No one knows better than I do just how much the people in a child's life can impact their character. The way they look at the world. The way they think of themselves."

She caught herself when she realized that she was headed in a verbal direction she had had no intention of going.

"Speaking from experience," he mused and she knew

he was remembering the story she'd told him about the bunny she had once tried to befriend. And about her mother's less than maternal attitude toward her.

"Is that so surprising?" she countered. "Doesn't everyone have some sort of issue with their parents? Even the best of them make mistakes, right?"

"True," he acknowledged, but his gaze never left hers. She felt as if he were trying to see inside her mind. To read her thoughts and display all of her secrets.

As if to prove her right, he spoke again.

"Who had that impact on you, Tula?" he asked, voice quiet. "Was it just your mom?"

"This isn't about me," she told him, refusing to be drawn into the very discussion she had unwittingly initiated.

"Isn't it?" he asked, pushing away from the banister to walk toward her.

"No," she insisted with a shake of her head. She felt the intensity of his gaze and flinched from it. Tula didn't need sympathy and wasn't interested in sharing her childhood miseries with a man who had already made it clear just how he felt about her. "This is about Nathan and what's best for him."

He kept coming and was close enough now that she had to hold her breath to keep from inhaling the scent of him. A blend of his aftershave and soap, it was a scent that called to her, made her remember lying beneath him, staring up into his eyes as they flashed with passion. Eyes that were, at the moment, studying her.

"You said it yourself," he told her, "we're all affected by who raised us. And whoever raised you will affect who you choose to care for Nathan."

Instantly, her back went up. He'd somehow touched on the one thing that had given her a lot of misgivings over the years. She had thought about how she was raised and about her parents and had wondered if she should even have a child of her own. But the truth was, Tula's heart yearned for family. Hungered for the kind of love and warmth she used to dream about. And she had always known she would be a good parent because she knew just what a child wanted. Craved.

So she was completely prepared and ready to argue this point with Simon.

"No, Simon. You're wrong about that. The initial input a child is given is important, I agree. And when we're kids and growing up, it pushes us in one direction or another. But at some point, responsible adults make choices. *We* decide who we are. Who we want to be."

He frowned as he thought about what she said. "Do we? I wonder. Seems to me that we are always who we started out to be."

Uncomfortable with being so close to him and unable to touch, she walked into the living room. She wished Nathan were awake right now because then she could claim that she didn't have time to talk. That she had to take care of the baby. But it was nap time and that baby really enjoyed his naps. Ordinarily, she loved that about him because she could get a lot of her own work done. Today, when she could have used Nathan's presence, she had to admit there would be no help coming from that quarter.

She kept walking farther into the huge room and didn't stop until she was standing in front of the bay window. Naturally, Simon followed her, his footsteps sure and slow, sounding out easily against the wood floor.

"So," he said, "you're saying your parents had nothing to do with who you are today?"

Tula laughed to herself but kept the sound quiet, so he wouldn't know just how funny that statement really was. Of course her parents had shaped her. Her mom was a lovely woman who was simply never meant to be a mother. Katherine was more at home with champagne brunches than PTA meetings. Impatient with clumsiness or loud noises, Katherine preferred a more formal atmosphere—one without the clamor of children.

Being responsible for a child had cut into Katherine's lifestyle, though it had significantly increased her alimony when she and Jacob divorced.

But when her stint at motherhood was complete, Katherine left. She moved out of Crystal Bay the morning of her daughter's eighteenth birthday.

Tula still remembered that last hug and brief conversation.

The airport was crowded, of course, with people coming and going. Excitement simmered in the air alongside sorrow as lovers kissed goodbye and family members waved and promised to write.

"You'll be fine, Tula," her mother said as she moved toward her gate. "You're all grown up now, I've done my job and you're entirely capable of taking care of yourself."

Tula wanted to ask her mother to stay. She wanted to tell Katherine that she so wasn't ready to be alone. That she was a little scared about college and the future. But it would have been pointless and she knew that, too. A part of her mother was already gone. Her mind and heart were fixed in Italy, just waiting for her body to catch up.

Katherine was renting a villa outside Florence for the summer, then she would be moving on—to where, Tula had no idea. The only thing she was absolutely sure of was that her mother wouldn't be back.

"Now, I can't miss boarding, so give me a kiss."

Tula did, and fought the urge to hug her mom and hold on. Sure, her mother had never been very maternal, but she had been there. Every day. In the house that would now be empty. That would echo with her own thoughts rattling around in the suffocating silence.

Her father was in the city and Tula wouldn't be seeing him anytime soon, so she was truly on her own for the first time ever. And though she could admit to a certain amount of anticipation, the inherent scariness of the situation was enough to swamp everything else.

Thank God, Tula thought, she still had Anna Cameron and her family. They would be there for her when she needed them. They always had been. That knowledge made saying goodbye to her mother a bit easier, though no less sad.

She'd often dreamed that she and her mother could be closer. She had wished she had the sense of family that Anna had. Though Anna's mom had died when she was a girl, her father and stepmother had supported and loved her. But wishes changed nothing, she told herself firmly, then pasted a bright smile on her face.

"Enjoy Italy, Mom. I'll be fine."

"I know you will, Tula. You're a good girl."

Then she was gone, not even bothering to glance back to see if her daughter was still watching.

Which Tula was.

She stood alone and watched until the plane pulled away from the gate. Until it taxied to the runway. Until it took off and became nothing more than a sun-splashed dot in the sky.

Finally, Tula went home to an empty house and promised herself that one day she would build a family. She would have what she had always longed for.

Simon was watching her, waiting for her to answer his question. She scrubbed her hands up and down her arms and said, "Of course they influenced me. But not in the way you might think. I didn't want to be who they were. I didn't want what they wanted. I made a conscious decision to be myself. *Me.* Not just a twig on the family tree."

A flash of surprise lit his eyes and she wondered why.

"How's that working out for you?"

"Until today," she admitted, "pretty good."

He walked closer and Tula backed up. She was feeling a little vulnerable at the moment and the last thing she needed was to be too near Simon. She kept moving until the backs of her knees hit the ledge of the cushioned window seat. Abruptly, she sat down and her surprise must have shown on her face.

He chuckled and asked, "Am I making you nervous, Tula?"

"Of course not," she replied, while her mind was screaming, *Yes!* Everything about him was suddenly making her nervous and she wasn't sure how to handle it. Since she'd met him, he'd irritated her, intrigued her. But this anxiousness was a new sensation.

Tula knew everyone thought of her as flaky. The crazy artist. But she wasn't really. She had always known what she wanted. She lived the way she liked and made no apologies for it. She always knew who was in her life and what they meant to her.

At least, she had until Simon. But he was a whole different ball game. He went from insulting her to seducing her. He made her furious one moment and hot and achy the next. For a man who had so loved his routine, he was becoming entirely too unpredictable.

She couldn't seem to pin him down. Or guess what he was going to do or say. She had thought him just another staid businessman, but he was more than that. She simply wasn't sure what that meant for her. Which made her a little nervous, though she'd never admit to it. So to keep herself steady, she started talking again.

"You've heard my story, so tell me, how did wearing a three-piece suit by the age of two affect you?"

He gave her a half smile and sat down beside her on the window seat. Turning his head, he stared through the glass at the winter afternoon behind them.

A storm was piling up on the horizon, Tula saw as she followed his gaze. Thunderclouds huddled together in a dark gray mass that promised rain by evening. Already, the wind was picking up, sending the naked branches of the trees in the park into a frenzied dance. Mothers gathered up their children as the sky darkened further and soon the park was as empty as Tula felt.

When Simon finally spoke, his voice was so soft, she nearly missed it. "You think you've got me figured out, do you?"

She studied him, trying to read his eyes. But it was as if he'd drawn a shutter over them, locking himself away from her.

"I thought so," she admitted and her confusion must

have been evident in her tone. "When I first met you, you reminded me of…someone I used to know," she said, picturing her father, fierce gaze locked on some hapless employee. "But the more I got to know you, the more I realized that I didn't know you at all. Well, that made no sense," she ended with a laugh.

"Yeah, it did," Simon said, shifting to look at her again, closing off the outside world with the intensity of his gaze. Making her feel as if she were the only thing in the world that mattered at the moment.

"Simon…"

"Nobody is what they look like on the surface," he murmured, features carefully blank and unreadable as he studied her. "I'm just really realizing that."

Ten

He was looking at her as if he had never seen her before. As if he were trying to see into her heart and mind again, searching out her secrets. Her desires.

"I don't know what you mean," Tula said.

"Maybe I don't, either." He took a breath, blew it out and after a long, thoughtful moment, changed the subject abruptly. "You know, I grew up here, in this house. My great-grandfather built it originally."

"It's a lovely house," she said, briefly allowing her gaze to sweep the confines of the room. "It feels *warm*."

"Yeah, it does." His gaze was still locked on her. "Now, more than ever."

Why was he telling her this? Why was he being… nice? Weren't they at odds? Didn't their argument still hang in the air between them? Only a few minutes ago, he had looked at her with cool detachment and now everything felt different. She just didn't understand *why*.

"Several years ago, my father almost lost the house," he said, forcing an offhand attitude that didn't mesh with the sudden stiffness of his shoulders or the tightness in his jaw. "Bad investments, trusting the wrong people. My dad didn't have a head for business."

"I can sympathize," she muttered, remembering how many times her own father had made her feel small and ignorant because she hadn't cared to learn the intricacies of keeping ledgers and accounts receivable.

He kept talking, as if she hadn't spoken at all. "He was too unorganized. Couldn't keep anything straight." Shaking his head, he once more stared out at the gathering storm and focused on the windowpane as the first drops of rain plopped against it. But Tula knew he wasn't looking at the outside world so much as he was staring into his own past. Just as she had moments ago.

"My dad entered a deal once with a man who was so unscrupulous he damn near succeeded in taking this house out from under us. This man cheated and lied and did whatever he had to in his effort to bury my father and the Bradley family in general." Simon shook his head again. "My father never saw it coming, either. It was sheer luck that kept this house in the family. Luck that saved what was left of our business."

She heard the old anger in his voice and wondered who it was that had almost cost his family so much. Whoever it was, Simon was still furious with the man and she wished she could say something that would ease that feeling. Tula knew all too well that hanging on to anger didn't hurt the one it was focused on. It only made *you* miserable.

"I'm glad it worked out that way," she said simply. "I can't imagine how hard it must have been for your father. And you."

He looked at her as if judging what she'd said, trying to decide if she had meant it. Finally though, he accepted her words with a nod. "In a way, I guess it wasn't my dad's fault. He went into the family business because his father wanted it that way. My dad hated his life, knew he wasn't any good at it and that must have been hard, living with a sense of failure every day."

"I know what that's like."

He tipped his head to one side and narrowed his eyes. "Do you?"

She smiled, actually enjoying this quiet time with him. The talking, the sharing of old pains and secrets. She had never really talked about her father with anyone but Anna. But somehow, it seemed right now, to let Simon know that he wasn't alone in his feelings about the past.

"My father had plans for me, too," she said sadly. "And they didn't have anything to do with what I wanted."

He nodded again thoughtfully. "For me, I watched what happened with my dad and I learned."

"What?" she prompted, her voice soft and low. "You learned what?"

His eyes narrowed as he watched her and Tula felt the heat of his stare slide into her bones.

"I learned to pay attention. To make rules and follow them. To never let anyone get the best of me. There's no room in my life for chaos, Tula," he said.

There was no subtext there and she knew it. He was saying flat out that there was no room in his life for *her*. She had figured that out for herself, of course. But somehow hearing him say it out loud left a hollow feeling in the pit of her stomach.

"I saw exactly what happens when a man loses focus," Simon added. "My dad couldn't concentrate on work he hated, so he didn't pay attention. I never lose focus. I guess I did the same thing you did. Made my own choices in spite of the early training by my father."

And those choices would keep them apart. He couldn't have been any clearer. So why, she wondered, was he looking at her as if he wanted nothing more than to grab her and carry her up to his bed? Heat filled his eyes even as a chill colored his words. The man was a walking contradiction and Tula really wished she didn't find that so darned attractive.

She shook her head as if to rid herself of that thought and asked, "What about your mother? Didn't she have some impact on you, too?"

"No," he said abruptly. "She died in a car wreck when I was four. Don't remember her at all."

"'I'm sorry' doesn't sound like much," she told him, "but I am."

"Thanks." He looked at her again and this time there was emotion glittering in his eyes. She just wished she could decipher it. Simon Bradley touched her in ways she had never experienced before. Even knowing that nothing was going to come of what was simmering between them couldn't stop her from wishing things were different.

Wishing that just once in her life, someone would see her for who she was and want her.

"Tell me more about your father," Simon said suddenly. "What's he like?"

"Like you," she blurted without thinking.

"Excuse me?"

Tula thought it a little weird that he could look so insulted without even knowing who her father was. "What I mean is, he's a businessman, too. He practically lives in his office and can't see anything in his life if it's not on his profit-loss statements. He's a workaholic and he likes it that way."

He leaned back against a pillow tucked up to the wall. "And that's how you see me?"

"Well, yeah." Grateful to be off the subject of her own family, Tula said, "You're a lot like him. Go to work early, come home late—"

"I'm home early today. Have been for the last few days."

"True and I don't know what to make of that."

"I intrigue you?"

"You confuse me."

"Even better."

"No," she said, inching back on the window seat to keep plenty of room between them. "It's really not, Simon. I don't need more confusion in my life and you've already made it pretty clear what you think about me."

"That fight we had, you mean?"

"Yes."

"Didn't mean a thing," he told her and leaned forward.

"That's not how you felt *then*," she reminded him, trying not to notice that he was just within reach of her.

"As I remember it, you had plenty to say, too."

"Okay, yes. I did. You made me mad."

"Oh, trust me, you made that perfectly clear."

"Good then. We both remember that argument."

"That's not all we remember," he said, voice low, thick. He reached for her hand before she could pull back and rubbed his thumb across her palm.

Tula shivered. It wasn't her fault, she thought frantically. It's not like she *chose* to be this attracted to him. It was simple chemistry. A biological imperative. Simon touched her and she went up in flames.

But she could choose to step back from the fire.

"Simon…"

"Tula, we were good together."

"In bed, sure, but—"

"Let's just concentrate on the bed for right now, huh?"

Oh, that sounded really good, she silently admitted. That featherlight touch on her palm was already firing up every nerve ending in her body. She took a breath, held it, then released it on a sigh.

Oh, Tula, she thought wildly, *you're going to do it, aren't you?*

Even as that disappointed-in-herself sigh wound through her mind, Tula was leaning in toward Simon.

It was inevitable.

Her gaze locked with his as his mouth touched hers. A whispered groan slid from her throat at that first, gentle contact. And she realized just how much she'd missed him. Missed *this*. It didn't seem to matter that they were constantly butting heads. He was right. For now, all she had to concentrate on was what she felt

when she was with him. When she surrendered herself
to the magic of his touch, his kiss.

No doubt, there would be plenty of time for regrets
in the coming weeks and months. For right now there
was only *him*.

As if a floodgate had been opened somewhere inside
her, emotions churned, fast and furious throughout her
system. She leaned in closer, allowing him to deepen the
kiss. His arms closed around her, holding her tightly to
his chest and suddenly, the wide window seat seemed
too narrow. Too public.

He tumbled her to the floor, assuring that he landed
on the hardwood and she was cushioned against his
chest.

Her breath left her in a whoosh of sound. She lifted
her head, looked down into his eyes and grinned. "You
okay?"

He winced, then smiled back. "I'm fine. And I'm
about to be better."

"Promises, promises…"

A wide smile dazzled his eyes and made her heartbeat
jump into a gallop. His hands swept up and down her
spine and paused long enough to give her behind a quick
squeeze.

"I know a challenge when I hear one," he said and
lifted his head from the floor to kiss her again. Harder,
deeper, his tongue swept past her defenses and tangled
with hers in a sensual dance that stole her breath.

She cupped his face in her palms, loving the feel
of his whiskers against her skin. She shivered as his
arms tightened around her, holding her so closely she
could feel the pounding of his heartbeat shuddering
through her.

He rolled over, cradling her in his arms until she was on her back and his heavy weight pressed down on her. Tula sighed, loving the feel of him on top of her. She didn't mind the hardness of the floor beneath her, because he was too busy making sure she felt nothing but pleasure.

He tore his mouth from hers, buried his face in the curve of her neck and nibbled at her throat, sending tiny jolts of sensation across her skin. Tula fought for breath and ran her hands up and down his broad back. His heavy muscles tensed and flexed beneath her fingertips and she smiled at the knowledge of how much her touch affected him.

Staring up at the beamed ceiling overhead, Tula lost herself in the flash of heat swamping her. His hands moved over her body with finesse and determination. He left trails of fire in his wake. She felt as though she were burning up from the inside and all she could think of was the need for even more flames.

His mouth moved over her skin, her throat, her jaw and up again to her mouth where he kissed her until she couldn't breathe, couldn't think. Only sensation was left to her.

Then passion crashed down on them both in the same searing instant. Hands moved quickly, freeing buttons, undoing snaps and zippers and in seconds, they were naked, entwined tightly together on the living room floor.

Rain beat a counterpoint to the gasps and moans sounding out in the dimly lit room. From outside came the muffled heartbeat of the world. Cars whizzing past, wheels on wet streets sounding like steaks sizzling on a grill. Wind rattled the windowpanes and sighed beneath the eaves. From the nearby monitor came the quiet, steady breathing of the child upstairs in his bed.

And none of those sounds were enough to intrude on this moment. Around them, the world continued. But in that room, time stood still. There was only the two of them, Tula thought. Just she and Simon and for this one amazing instant she was going to forget about everything else. Stop trying to read the future, or hide from the past, long enough to enjoy the present.

Instead, she would lose herself in a pair of chocolate-brown eyes that saw too much and revealed too little.

"You're thinking," he accused, one corner of his mouth lifting into a half smile.

"Sorry," she said, smoothing her fingertips across his jaw. "Don't know how that happened."

"Let's just see what I can do about shutting down that busy brain of yours."

"Think you're up to the challenge?" she teased.

"Baby," he assured her, "I'm *very* up for it."

A surprised laugh shot from her throat and Tula sighed with happiness. Having a lover who could make her laugh at the most astonishing times, was really a gift. And maybe, she thought, there were even *more* layers to Simon Bradley than she had assumed. Maybe—

Then he began his quest to shut off her thoughts and he was more than successful. Tula groaned when his mouth came down on her breast. He licked and nibbled and she twisted beneath him, trying to take more of what he offered. Needing to feel all she could of him. Needing—just *needing*.

He suckled her and she gasped, arching into him, holding his head to her breast, as his mouth pulled at her breast. Her fingers speared through his thick, soft hair. She loved the feel of his mouth on her and thought frantically that she could happily spend the rest of her life like this.

He smiled against her skin. She felt the curve of his mouth against her breast and she knew he was aware of the effect he had on her. But she wasn't interested in hiding it from him anyway. Why shouldn't he know that he could splinter her body and shatter her soul with a kiss? A touch?

The wood floor beneath her bare back was cool, but the heat he built within her was more than a match for it. He lay between her thighs and she felt the tip of him prodding at her center. She wanted that invasion of body into body. Wanted to feel the slick slide of his heat into hers.

She lifted her hips in silent welcome, but he didn't respond to her invitation. Instead, he rolled over, taking her with him until she was splayed atop him, staring down into those eyes that fascinated her so.

"The floor's not real comfortable," he told her, reaching up to cup her breasts in the palms of his hands. "Thought we'd just change position for awhile."

"Change is good," she said, straddling him, keeping her gaze fixed on his. Her hands moved over his sculpted chest. At her touch, he hissed in a breath.

Simon looked up at her and felt his mind blur. He'd been planning this seduction for days and now that it was here, his plans meant nothing. The only thing that mattered was her. The feel of her. The taste of her. The soft sighs that drifted from her throat at his touch.

Shadowy light played on her choppy blond hair and winked off the silver hoops in her ears. Her big blue eyes were glazed with the same passion claiming him.

He kneaded her breasts with a firm, gentle touch and tweaked her hardened nipples between his thumbs and forefingers. He loved watching the play of emotion on her face as she hid nothing from him.

Her eager response to lovemaking only fed the fires inside him, pushing at him to take more, to give more. Her hips were rocking instinctively and his own body was hard and tight.

He set his hands at her hips and lifted her high enough off him that he could position himself to slide inside her. She closed her eyes, tipped her head back and, taking control of the situation, slowly, inch by inch, took him inside. She settled herself over him with a deliberately slow slide that was both tantalizing and exasperating. He tried to hurry her, to push himself into her harder, deeper, but the tiny, curvy woman was in control now, whether he liked it or not.

"You're just going to have to lay there and take it," she said, a sly, purely female smile on her lips.

His eyes crossed as she finally settled on top of him, with his body sheathed completely inside hers. She was tight and damp and so damn hot he couldn't think of anything but the sensations crashing down on him.

She moved, just a slight wiggle of her hips, but that small action shot through him with the force of a nine-point earthquake. He felt the world tremble. Or at least his corner of it. And he wanted more.

Didn't matter *why* he'd seduced her, he assured himself. All that mattered now was what they created together. The impossible heat. The incredible friction of two bodies moving as one toward a climax that would be, he knew, richer and more all-encompassing than anything else he'd ever known.

He didn't care who Tula was. Didn't want to remember that he was, in effect, setting her up to be used as a weapon against her own father. What he wanted to concentrate on now was how well they meshed. How their bodies joined so easily it was as if they were two pieces in the same puzzle.

She moved on him again, her hips rocking, taking him in and releasing him in a slow rhythm that built steadily into a pace that stole his breath and the last of his thoughts.

She arched her back, pushing her breasts higher. Her hands were on his chest, bracing herself as she rode him with a frenzied, honest passion that shook him to the core. Hands at her hips, he stared up into her eyes as she moved, and he was caught by the light glittering in those blue depths.

He felt swept up by both passion and emotion and just for that one, staggering moment, Simon forgot about everything else but Tula. She cried out his name as her release claimed her and a single heartbeat later, his body joined hers.

Blindly, Simon reached for her, pulling her down to his chest where he could cradle her close. Where, for a few brief seconds, he could forget that he had maneuvered her into this and instead pretend that what they had just shared was real.

Eleven

It had changed nothing.

And everything.

Two days later, Tula was still trying to understand the shift in her and Simon's relationship. If she could even call it that. Connected by a child, they were two people currently sharing a bed. Did that actually constitute a "relationship"?

Simon was kind and funny and warm and so attentive in bed, she'd hardly had any sleep at all the last two nights. Which, of course, she wasn't exactly complaining about. But was there anything else in his heart for her? Was it just desire? Was it expediency, since she was right there in his house and would be until she decided to hand over custody of Nathan?

She'd given herself to the man she loved with no assurances at all that he would care for her in return. Yes, she loved him. And it was too late now to change that.

How could she have let this happen? Hadn't she made a vow to herself not to take that last slippery step into love? But how could she possibly have avoided it? she asked herself. Simon was so much more than she had originally thought him to be. She had seen glimpses of his caring nature that he fought to bury so deeply. She had watched him with his son and been touched by the gentleness he showed Nathan. She had laughed with Simon, fought with him and made love with him in every possible way.

She couldn't avoid the simple truth any longer. She was in love with a man who was only in lust.

"This can't end well."

"That's the spirit," Anna cheered sarcastically.

Tula just looked at her friend and shook her head. "How you can expect me to be optimistic about this is beyond me. Anna, he doesn't love me."

"You don't know that."

A snort of laughter shot from her throat. "He hasn't said it. Hasn't shown any signs of admitting it. I think that's a good clue."

"All that means is that he's a man," Anna said, her gaze locked on the mural she was painting. "Sweetie, none of them ever want to admit to being in love. For some bizarre reason, the male brain deliberately will jump in the opposite direction the first time the word 'love' is used. They're just naturally skittish."

Tula laughed out loud. The baby on her hip enjoyed the sound and gurgled happily. She planted a quick kiss on his forehead before answering her friend.

"Simon? Skittish?" Shaking her head, she imagined the man in her mind and the idea of him being nervous about anything seemed even more ludicrous. "He's a force of nature, Anna. He sets down rules and expects everyone else to abide by them. And they *do*."

"You don't," she pointed out.

"No, but I'm different."

"He doesn't even expect you to do what he says, does he?"

"Not anymore," Tula assured her. "He knows better."

"Uh-huh." Anna maneuvered her paintbrush across the wall and still kept the conversation going. "So he's broken his own rule when it comes to you."

She thought about that for a second. "I suppose, but only because I made fun of his stupid schedule."

"How did he react?"

"He was all insulted," Tula told her with a laugh. Then she remembered. "But he started changing up his schedule. Coming home early, skipping meetings…"

"Hmm," Anna mused.

"That doesn't mean anything," Tula protested, but her mind was working.

"Only that Mr. I-have-a-schedule-set-in-stone is changing himself because of you."

"But—"

"Men don't do that if they don't care, Tula. Why would they?"

"No," Tula said, shaking her head, "you're wrong. Simon doesn't care about me. Beyond the obvious pluses about having me in his bed and here, taking care of Nathan."

"I don't know…"

"I do," Tula insisted, closing her mind to thoughts of Simon for a minute as she stared at the baby settled at her hip. She wasn't going to pretend everything was great. It wasn't. And it wasn't only the question of Simon's feelings that had her wrapped up so tightly.

Every day that passed she was that much closer to having to say goodbye to Nathan. She was going to lose the child that felt like her own. She was going to lose his father and the illusion of family she'd been living in for weeks. She was going to lose everything that mattered to her and that knowledge was tearing a hole in her heart.

"I'm going to have to leave soon, Anna. I'll have to walk away from Nathan *and* Simon. And the thought of it is just killing me."

Sitting back on her heels, Anna looked up at her. "Who are you and what have you done with Tula?"

"What's that supposed to mean?"

"It means that you are the world's biggest optimist," Anna told her, turning back to the mural she had been working on since the day before. "Even when you had no reason for it, you always maintained the upbeat attitude. Heck, Tula. Even your dad didn't rock your boat. If you wanted something, you went after it, no matter how many people tried to tell you it couldn't be done. So what's happening?"

Tula sat down, balancing Nathan in the circle of her crossed legs. "He did," she said, dropping a kiss onto the baby's head. "This little guy changed everything for me, Anna. I can't just go my own way anymore. Not when I have him to think about."

"Ah," her friend said, "so this isn't about Simon at all? You've been kidding yourself and me? You're just worried about Nathan, huh? Not pining away for the baby's father?"

Eyes narrowed, Tula warned, "No one likes a know-it-all."

"Oooh. Scored a point!" Smiling, Anna swept paint over the forest on the wall, wielding her paintbrush as expertly as a surgeon used his scalpel. "Come on, honey. This sudden case of the poor me's is about more than Nathan. More even than Simon. This is about you finally finding the place you want to be and thinking you have to leave it."

Tula cringed inside because Anna was exactly right.

"You found the home you've been looking for since you were a kid, sweetie." Anna looked at her, understanding and sympathy shining in her eyes. "You love Simon and Nathan both. But it's what they are to you together that's making this so hard. They're the family you always dreamed about. Your heart took them both in, made them yours and now you believe you have to let the dream die."

Nathan babbled and slapped playfully at Tula's hands on his legs. The scent of paint hung in the air despite the two opened windows. Anna's mural was almost complete. Once the woman got started on a painting, she was a whirlwind of activity. Tula looked at the realistic scene of a forest, with a flower-strewn meadow stretching out into the distance. And she smiled at Lonely Bunny, right up front, sitting under a tree and smiling out at the room.

From the house next door, the sound of wind chimes played like a distant symphony. As time passed in a lazy, unhurried way, Tula thought about what her friend had said and admitted silently that Anna was right. She did love Simon and Nathan both. She did love the family the three of them had become, however temporarily. She hated knowing that she was the one who didn't fit. The one who didn't belong. And knowing that she would have to walk away from what might have been was desolating.

"You're right," she finally said.

"The one time I wish I weren't," Anna told her.

"But what can I do? I can't stall Simon forever. He has a right to be his son's father. And I can't stay once I sign over custody."

"It's a problem," Anna agreed. "But there's always a solution. Somewhere."

Tula sighed. "You know, it was a lot easier on me when *you* were the one with man problems."

"I bet," Anna said on a laugh. "But it's your turn now, girl. The question is, what are you going to do about it?"

"What can I do?"

The last few days had been wonderful. And confusing. She had Nathan to care for and work of her own to accomplish during the day. But every night, she and Simon found each other. They shared taking care of Nathan, and once the baby was in bed it was their time.

The sex was incredible. It only got better each time they came together. But for Tula, it was bittersweet. She loved being with him—the problem was, she *loved* him. More than she had ever thought it possible to love someone. Every day here dragged her deeper and deeper into what was going to become a pit of despair one day soon.

Though even as she thought it, she realized that neither of them had so much as hinted about that situation lately.

It might still be the eight-hundred-pound gorilla in the middle of the room, but if no one was talking about it, did it matter?

Nathan babbled happily and Tula sighed.

"Honey, if you want him, why don't you go for it?"

"Oh, I am," she assured her friend.

Laughing, Anna said, "I'm not talking about sex, Tula. I'm talking about love. I know you love Simon. Heck, I can see it. Chances are he can, too."

"Oh, God," she said with a groan. "I hope not."

"Why?" Anna turned to look at her. "Why should you hide what you feel? Didn't you tell me to go for what I wanted?"

"Yes, but—"

"If he doesn't love you back, that's different." She rubbed her nose and transferred a streak of green paint. "Although, I'm willing to bet he does love you. I mean, how could he not? What's not to love? Besides, I saw you two together yesterday and again this morning. The way he looks at you…"

"What?" Hope rose up in Tula's chest.

"As if you're the only thing in the room," Anna said with a smile. "But Tula, you'll never know for sure what he feels if you don't try to get him to admit it."

"How am I supposed to do that?"

Anna grinned. "The best opportunity for getting a man to talk and lower his defenses at the same time? Right after sex. They're happy, they're relaxed and *very* open to suggestion."

Sometimes, she thought. Other times, they were too crabby entirely. Still it was worth a shot. Tula shook her head in admiration. "Does Sam know how truly devious you can be?"

"Sure he does," Anna replied, still grinning devilishly. "But by the time he figures out that I'm sneaking up on him, it's too late."

"I don't know…"

"Who was it who said all's fair in love and war?"

"I don't know that, either," Tula admitted. "But I'll bet it was a man."

"So," Anna said softly, "if it's okay for a man to be sneaky, why can't we try it? Look," she added, "while you're here, don't hold anything back. You can't tell him you love him, but you can show him. Make him want what you could have together. That's all I'm saying."

While her friend turned her attention back to the mural, and Nathan studied his toes with fierce concentration, Tula started thinking.

"You're going to do it, aren't you?"

"Do what?" Simon didn't take his gaze off the pitching machine. Getting hit by a ninety-mile-an-hour fastball didn't sound like a good time.

"Tula. You're going to mess it all up and toss it aside, aren't you?"

Simon hit the pitch high and left. Only then did he glance at Mick in the next cage over. "I don't know what you're talking about."

"Oh, forget it, Simon. I've known you too long to be fooled."

"Have you known me long enough to butt out?"

"Apparently not," Mick said good-naturedly. "Besides, you can always fire me if you don't like what I'm saying."

Simon snorted. "Sure. I fire you, then your wife comes over to kick my butt."

"There is that," Mick said, a pleased note in his voice. "So. About Tula."

"Let it go, Mick. I'm doing what I have to do."

"No," his friend insisted, "you're doing what your damn pride is telling you to do. There's a difference."

Simon hit a curveball dead center, line drive. "This isn't about my pride," he muttered darkly, irritated that his best friend wasn't on his side in this.

Mick was normally an excellent barometer for Simon. If the two of them agreed on something, it turned out to be a good idea. The times when Simon hadn't listened to Mick's advice were a different story. But this time, Mick was wrong. Simon knew it. He felt it.

Ever since her friend left last weekend, after painting a mural of a forest glade, complete with Lonely Bunny sitting beneath a tree, things had been...different.

Actually, the last few days with Tula had been great. Better than great. Amazing even. But it wasn't real. It had all been staged by him. They'd laughed and talked and gone for picnics and out to dinner. They took Nathan for walks and set him in a swing for the first time, making them both nervous. He had felt closer to her than he had to anyone else in his life, he thought darkly.

But none of Tula's responses to him were real because he had seduced her back into his bed for a deliberate reason. So if what he had done wasn't on the up-and-up, how could her reactions be genuine?

If he felt the occasional twinge of guilt over tricking her into being a weapon to use against her father...Simon dismissed the feeling. He didn't do guilt. Plus there was the fact that Tula was an adult, he assured himself, able to make her own choices. And she had *chosen* to be in his bed.

Yet, even as he told himself that, a voice in the back of his mind whispered the question, *Would she still have chosen to be with you if she knew what you were really doing? If she knew she was nothing more to you than a sword to wield against her father?*

Uncomfortable with what the answer to that might have been, he dismissed the mental question. Besides, he argued with himself, Tula wasn't *only* a weapon he'd waited years to find against Jacob Hawthorne. She was more, damn it. He actually…cared about her. Hadn't meant to, but he did.

Which was why he was standing at the batting cages arguing with himself while his best friend ragged on him. But the bottom line was, just because what he and Tula had together was mutually enjoyable, it didn't mean it was necessarily more than that, did it?

Besides, this wasn't even about Tula.

It was about her father.

After hearing what little she'd told him about her parents, she might even be grateful that he had found a way to take a slap at Jacob Hawthorne.

He snorted to himself and hit the next pitch, a slider, into right field. Sure. She'd *thank* him for using her. God, what universe was he living in anyway?

"This is all about your pride, Simon. You got cheated by a guy with no principles."

"Damn right I did," he snapped, turning his head to glare briefly at Mick. "And it wasn't just me, remember. Jacob maneuvered my father, too. That miserable old thief almost cost us our house, damn it."

He hated knowing that Jacob Hawthorne was out there, still chortling over getting the best of two generations of Bradleys. The need for revenge had been gnawing on him for years. Was he expected to now just put it aside because he had feelings for a woman? *Could* he put it aside?

"And your answer to that is to become as unprincipled as the old pirate himself?"

"What the hell are you talking about?"

Mick shook his head, clearly disgusted. "If you do this. If you use Tula to get at her old man, then you're as big a louse as he is."

Simon chewed on those words for a minute or two, then shook them off, determined to stay his course. He'd made a plan, damn it. Now he had to follow through. That was how he lived his life and he wasn't about to change now. Wasn't even sure he could change if he wanted to.

"It's not who you are, Simon," Mick told him. "I hope you remember that before it's too late."

A few days later, Tula was happy.

Anna had been right, she thought. Though she hadn't actually confessed her love for Simon, she had tried to show him over the last several days just how important he had become to her. She was sure she was getting through to him. She felt it. In his easy smile. His touch. The whispered words in the night and the gentle strength in his arms when he held her as she slept.

He hadn't mentioned again the subject of hiring a nanny. They hadn't talked about him taking full custody of Nathan. Instead, the three of them were in a sort of limbo. Locked into a paralyzing state where they didn't move forward and didn't go back. It was as if they were caught in the present, while Tula and Simon tried to decide what might be waiting for them in the still hazy future.

She didn't like waiting. She never had been a patient person, Tula admitted silently. But she was trying to fight her natural inclination—which would be grabbing Simon and shaking him until he admitted he loved her—so she could have the time to show Simon exactly how good they were together.

"Maybe this will work out, Nathan," she told the baby as she zipped up his tiny sweatshirt for their walk to the bookstore. "Maybe we will become a *real* family."

The baby laughed at the idea and clapped his hands together as if applauding her.

"That's my boy." She kissed him, then picked up the baby she thought of as her son and settled him into his stroller. "Now, Nathan, what do you say we go see the nice lady at the bookstore and talk about the signing this weekend?"

For days Simon had been living in two different worlds.

In one, he experienced a kind of happiness that he had never known before. In the other, there was a black cloud of misery hanging over his head, making him feel as though he was about to make the biggest mistake of his life.

He walked down the crowded sidewalk in the heart of downtown San Francisco and hardly noticed the bustle around him. His gaze fixed dead ahead, the expression on his face was ferocious enough to convince other pedestrians to give him a wide berth.

His mind raced with too many thoughts to process at once. Something he wasn't accustomed to at all. His

concentration skills were nearly legendary. But even
the inner workings of the Bradley department store
chain couldn't keep him fixated for long anymore. That
acknowledgment shook him to his bones. The Bradley
chain had always been his focus. The one mainstay of
his life. Rebuilding what the family had lost. Growing
the company until it was the biggest of its kind in the
country.

Those were tangible goals.

His entire life for the last ten years had been dedicated
to making those dreams a reality. But lately, they weren't
his only goals.

Tula.

Everything came back to her, he thought and waited
impatiently for the light to change and the Walk symbol
to flash green. Around him, a teenager danced along to
whatever music he had plugged into his ears. A young
mother swayed, keeping the baby in her arms happy.
Taxis honked, someone shouted and the world, in general, kept spinning.

For everyone but him.

Simon knew he didn't have to go through with
this. Didn't have to walk into the exclusive restaurant
precisely at twelve-thirty and "accidentally" meet the
man he'd waited years to take down. He knew he still
had a chance to turn away from his plan. From the
decision he had made before Tula became so damned
important to him.

Tula.

She was there again. Front and center in his thoughts.
Her short, soft hair. Her quick grin. That dimple that
continued to devastate him every time he saw it flash in
her cheek. She was there with her stories about lonely

children befriending rabbits. She was there, rocking Nathan in the middle of the night. She was in the kitchen, dancing to the radio as she cooked. He saw her in her tiny house in Crystal Bay. So small, yet so full of life. Of love.

Tula had waltzed into his life and turned everything he had ever known upside down.

The light changed and he walked with the crowd, a part of them, yet separate.

For days now, he and Tula and Nathan had been what he had never thought to have...a family. Laughing with the baby in the evening, holding Tula all through the night and then waking up with her curled up against him every morning. It was enough to drive a man out of his mind.

This wasn't how Simon had planned for his life to go.

Never before had he made room in his thoughts for babies and bunnies and smart-mouthed women who kissed him as if he contained the last breath on earth. Now he couldn't imagine his life without any of them.

And he didn't damn well know what to do about it.

The wind off the ocean was icy, chilling the blood in his veins until he felt as cold and grim as his thoughts. Outside the restaurant, Simon actually paused and considered the situation.

If Mick was right, then going inside to face down Jacob would ruin whatever he might have with Tula. On the other hand, if he *didn't* go inside and nothing came of whatever was happening between him and Tula, then he had wasted his one opportunity to get back at a man he'd spent too many years hating.

Scrubbing one hand across the back of his neck,

Simon stood in the sea of constantly moving pedestrians like a boulder in the middle of a rushing stream. For the first time in his life, he wasn't sure what his next move should be.

For the first time ever, he wondered if he shouldn't be putting someone else ahead of his own needs.

"Make up your damn mind," he muttered, shifting his gaze to take in the wide windows and the diners seated in leather booths affording a view of downtown.

That's when he saw Jacob Hawthorne.

Everything in Simon went still as ice. The old man was lording it over a group of businessmen at his table. Seated like a king before supplicants, the old thief was clearly holding court. And who knew what he was up to? Who knew which company Jacob was trying to destroy now?

Thoughts of Tula rose up in Simon's mind as if his subconscious was combating what he was seeing. Reminding him of what he could have. What he might lose.

Tula. The daughter of his enemy. Simon shouldn't have been able to trust her. But he did. He shouldn't have cared about her. But he did.

Still, it wasn't enough, he told himself, already reaching for the door handle and tugging it open.

He owed it to his father. Hell, he owed it to *himself* to give Jacob the set down the man had practically been begging to receive for years.

And nothing was going to stop him.

Twelve

There were posters of her latest book cover standing on easels at the front entrance of the bookstore. Management had even put her picture on the sign announcing the author reading and signing that weekend. Cringing a little, Tula tried not to look at her own image.

"Ms. Barrons!"

She turned to smile as Barbara, the employee responsible for all of this, hurried over. "Hi, nice to see you again."

Barbara shook the hand Tula offered and then waved at the sign. "Do you approve?"

"It's very nice," she said, idly noting that she really needed a new publicity picture taken. "Thank you."

"Oh, it's no bother, believe me," Barbara told her. "We've sold so many of your books already, you'll be signing for hours this weekend."

"Now that *is* good news," Tula replied, reaching down to lift Nathan from his stroller when he started to complain. "It's okay, sweetie, we won't be long, then we'll go to the park," she promised.

"You have a beautiful son," Barbara cooed, reaching in to take one of Nathan's tiny hands in hers.

Pleased, Tula didn't correct her. Instead, she felt her own heart swell with longing, pride and love. She looked at the tiny boy in her arms and smiled when he gave her a toothless grin. Kissing him tenderly, she looked at Barbara and said simply, "Thank you."

Simon walked to Jacob's table, dismissing the hostess who tried to intercept him. His gaze locked on the old man; he paid no attention to the other diners or even to the three older men at Jacob's table.

All he could see was the man he'd waited years to get even with. The man who had destroyed Simon's father and nearly cost him the business his family had built over generations.

He stopped beside the table and looked down at the man who was his enemy. Tula had gotten her blue eyes from her father, but the difference was there was no warmth in Jacob's eyes. No silent sense of humor winking out at him. She was nothing like her father at all, Simon thought, wondering how someone as warm as Tula could have sprung from a man with ice in his veins.

"Bradley," the older man said, glancing at him with a sniff of distaste. "What are you doing here?"

"Thought we could have a chat, Jacob," Simon said, not bothering to acknowledge the other men at the table.

"I'm busy. Another time." Jacob turned to the man on his right.

"Actually, now works best for me," Simon said, keeping his voice low enough that only those at the table were privy to what he had to say.

The older man sighed dramatically, turned to face him and said, "Fine. What is it?"

For the first time, Simon glanced at the other men. "Maybe we should do this in private."

"I don't see any need for that," Jacob argued. "This is a scheduled business meeting. You're the intruder here."

Right again. It was only thanks to Mick's reluctantly given information that Simon had known where to find the old goat. Now he didn't argue, he merely turned his flat, no-negotiation stare on the other men at the table. It didn't take them long to excuse themselves and stand up.

"Five minutes," Jacob told them.

"I don't need even that long," Simon assured him as the three men left, heading for the bar.

The steak house was old, moneyed and exclusive. The walls were paneled in dark oak, the carpet was bloodred and the booths and chairs were overstuffed black leather. Candles flickered on every table and wall sconces burned with low-wattage bulbs, making the place seem like a well-decorated cave.

Simon took a seat opposite the old man and met that hard stare with one of his own. This was the moment he had waited for and he wanted to savor it. Jacob had taken something from him. Had tried to destroy Simon's father and almost had. Now Simon had taken something from Jacob.

Payback, the old man was about to learn, really was a bitch.

"What's this about?" Hawthorne leaned back in the seat and draped one arm negligently along the back of the booth. "Come to complain about my getting the property you wanted again? Because if that's it, I'm not interested. Ancient history."

"I'm not here to talk about your dubious business practices, Jacob," Simon told him.

"What you call dubious, I call smart. Efficient." The old man snorted. "Then if that's not what's chewing on you, what is it, boy? I'm a busy man. No time to waste."

"Fine. I'll get right to it then," Simon said, even while that voice in the back of his mind urged him to shut up, stand up and leave before it was too late. But looking into Jacob's eyes, seeing the barely concealed sneer of superiority on his face, made it impossible for Simon to listen.

"Well?" Impatience stained Jacob's tone.

"Just wanted you to know that while you were out stealing that property from me, I stole something from you."

"And what's that?"

"Your daughter." Simon hated himself for doing it, but he watched and waited for the old man's reaction. When it came, it wasn't what he had expected.

Those icy blue eyes frosted over and emptied in the space of a single heartbeat. "I have no daughter."

"You do," Simon argued, leaning forward, lowering his voice. "Tula. She's at my house right now."

Jacob speared him with a hard look. "Tallulah Barrons is not my daughter. Not anymore. If that's what you came for, we're finished."

"You'd deny your own flesh and blood?" Shocked in spite of how badly he had always thought of Jacob Hawthorne, Simon could only stare at him.

Jacob looked away and signaled for the hostess. When she arrived, he said, "Please tell my guests I'm ready to continue our meeting. You'll find them in the bar."

"Yes, sir," she said and hurried off.

"You really don't give a damn about Tula, do you?" Simon hadn't moved. Couldn't force himself to look away from the old man's eyes.

"Why the hell should I?" Jacob countered. "She made her choice. Now what she does—or," he added snidely, "*who* she does it with—is nothing to me. We're done here, Bradley."

Stunned to his bones, Simon realized he actually felt dirty.

Just sitting at the same table with the man. Strange, but he had always pictured the moment of his revenge as tasting sweet. Being satisfying in a soul-deep way. He'd imagined that he would be vindicated. That he would walk away from Hawthorne, head held high, secure in the knowledge that he had bested the old thief. That he had *won*.

Finally.

Instead, years of anticipation fell flat. He felt as though he'd climbed down into the gutter to wrestle a rat for a bone. Mick had been right, of course. Simon had lowered himself to Jacob Hawthorne's level and now he was left with a bitter taste in his mouth and what felt like an oil spill on his soul.

Thoughts of Tula ran through his mind like a soft,

cool breeze on a miserable day. She was the openhearted person he had never been. She was all of the smiles and warmth and joy that he had never known. Everything about her was the opposite of everything he was. Everything her parents had been. Somehow, she was the very heart that he hadn't even realized was missing from his life.

And he'd betrayed her.

He had used her for leverage against a man who didn't even see what an amazing woman his daughter was. But if Jacob Hawthorne was blind, then so had Simon been. Now, though, he could see. Now that it was too late.

Standing up slowly, Simon looked down at the man. Shaking his head, he had the last word as he told Jacob, "You know, I've wasted a lot of years hating your guts. Turns out, you just weren't worth it."

Simon found Tula in the living room, curled up on the window seat reading. She looked up when he walked into the room and the smile she gave him, complete with dimple, tore at his insides. He had made up his mind to tell her the truth. All of it. But he knew the moment he did, everything would be ruined. Over. And he would have to live with the knowledge that he had hurt the one person in the world he shouldn't have.

"Simon? What's wrong?" She came up off the window seat and walked to him, concern in her eyes.

He held up one hand to hold her off, not trusting himself to go through with this confession if she came into his arms. Once he had the feel of her against him again, he might not be able to force himself to let her go. And that's what he had to do.

"I saw your father today," he blurted, knowing there was no easy way to say any of this.

Her jaw dropped and her blue eyes suddenly looked wary. "I didn't realize you knew him."

"Oh, yeah," Simon said tightly. "Remember when I told you about the man who nearly stole this house from my father? The man who stole a piece of property out from under my nose?"

"My father."

"Yeah." Simon walked past her and headed to the wet bar. There he poured himself a short scotch and tossed it down his throat like a gulp of medicine designed to take the inner chill away.

"See, when I found out who you were," he mused aloud, staring down at the crystal glass in his hand before shifting his gaze to hers, "I had the bright idea of somehow using you to get back at your father."

She actually winced. He saw the tiny reaction and, even from across the room, he felt her pain and hated himself for causing it. But he couldn't stop now. Had to tell her everything. Didn't someone say that confession was good for the soul? He didn't think so. It was more like ripping your soul out, piece by piece.

"I told him today that we were together." He waited for a reaction. The only sign she had heard him was the expression of resigned sorrow on her face.

"I could have told you," she finally said into the strained silence, "that he wouldn't care. My father disowned me when I chose to, as he put it, 'waste my brain writing books for sniveling brats.'"

"Tula…" He heard the old pain in her voice and saw her misery shining in her eyes. Everything in him pushed at him to go to her. To hold her. To…love her as she deserved to be loved. But he knew she wouldn't welcome his touch any longer and that brought a whole new world of pain crashing through him.

"He's an idiot," Simon muttered, then added, "and so was I. I didn't want to tell you any of this, but you had the right to know."

"Oh," she said sadly, "*now* I had the right to know."

He gritted his teeth and still managed to say, "I didn't mean to hurt you."

"No," she agreed, "probably not. It was just a by-product of you going after what you wanted. In a way, I'm not surprised. I knew when I first met you that you were like him. Like my father. Both of you only know about business and using people."

He took a step toward her, but stopped when she moved back, instinctively. How could he argue with that simple truth? Maybe, he told himself, he was even worse than her father. He had actually *seen* Tula for who she really was and had lied to her, used her, anyway.

Simon thought back to his meeting with Jacob Hawthorne. He had seen firsthand just what kind of man the old pirate was. And unless he made some changes in his own life, Simon knew he would end up just as cold and ruthless and empty as Jacob was.

Choosing his words carefully, he said, "I know you have no reason to believe me, but I'm not the man I was when you first came here. More, I don't want to be that man."

"Simon," she said softly, shaking her head.

"Let me finish." He took a breath, and said, "There are a lot of things I should say to you, but maybe I don't have the right anymore. So instead, I think the only way to prove to you that I'm not who you think I am, is to let you go."

"What?"

"Hell," he laughed shortly, shoving one hand through his hair with enough strength to yank it all out. "It's the only decent thing to do." He looked into her eyes. "We both know I'm ready to take care of Nathan. I'll hire the best nanny in the country to help me out. And you can go home. Get away from here. From me. It's the right thing to do."

Tula felt the world tip out from under her feet. She swayed under the blow of the unexpected slap. Bad enough to hear that the man she loved had only been pretending to care so that he could use her against the father that didn't give a damn about her anyway. Bad enough to know that her hopes and dreams had just been shattered at her feet.

Now, she was being sent away. From the baby. From Simon.

For her own good.

Pain was a living, breathing entity, and it roared from inside her as it settled in, making a permanent home in the black emptiness where her heart used to be. Hurt, humiliated and just plain tired of being used by the very people in her life she should have been able to count on, Tula sighed.

"Don't you see, Simon?" she whispered sadly. "Even in this, you're still acting like my father."

"No," he argued, but she cut him off because she just didn't want to hear anything else he had to say.

"Letting me go isn't about *me*. It's about *you*. About how you feel about what you did. About assuaging some sense of honor you believe you've lost."

"Tula, that's not—"

"What if I didn't want to go?" she asked, watching him. "What then?"

Naturally, he didn't have an answer for her. But then, it didn't matter, because Tula wasn't waiting for one. It was too late for them and she knew it. She had to go, whether leaving would rip her heart to pieces or not.

Softly, she said, "Nathan's asleep upstairs. If it's all the same to you, I'll leave now, before he wakes up. I don't think I can say goodbye to him."

"Tula, damn it, at least let me—"

"You've done enough, Simon," she told him, turning for the stairs. "Have your lawyer contact me. I'll sign whatever papers are necessary to turn over custody of Nathan to you. And Simon," she added, "promise me you'll love him enough for both of us."

Over the next few days, Simon and Nathan were miserable together.

Nothing was the same. Simon couldn't work—he didn't give a damn about mergers or acquisitions or the price of the company stock. He hated having Mick telling him *I told you so* every five minutes. The memory of Tula in his house was so strong that her absence made the whole place seem cavernous and as empty as a black hole.

He and his son were lost without the only woman either of them wanted.

Nathan cried continuously for the only mother he remembered. Simon comforted him, but it was a hollow effort since he knew exactly how the baby felt. And there was no comfort for either of them as long as Tula wasn't there.

Simon hadn't even hired a nanny. He didn't want some other woman holding Nathan. He wanted Tula back home. With them. Where she belonged. Every day without her was emptier than the one before. His dreams were filled with images of her and his arms ached to hold her.

He had fallen in love with the one woman who probably couldn't stand the sight of him. He had had a family, damn it, and he wanted it back. Yes, he had been a first-class idiot. A prize moron. But Tula had a heart big enough, he hoped, to forgive even him.

If she hadn't promised to do this signing, Tula didn't know if she would have had the nerve to return to the city. Used to be she avoided San Francisco because there were memories of her father here. Now it was so much more.

Nathan and Simon were only blocks from this bookstore. They were in that Victorian that she'd come to love and think of as her own. They were no doubt settling into life with a nanny and she wondered if either of them missed her as desperately as she missed them.

She sat cross-legged in the middle of the "reading rug" at the bookstore and looked at the shining, expectant faces surrounding her. Parents stood on the periphery, watching their children, enjoying their excitement. And Tula knew that she couldn't simply walk away from Simon and Nathan.

Yes, Simon had hurt her. Desperately. But he had told her everything, hadn't he? It couldn't have been easy for him to admit to what he had done. It said something that he'd eventually been honest with her.

Through her pain, through her misery, one truth

had rung clear over the last few days. Despite what had happened, she still loved Simon. And when the book signing was over, she was going to see him. She would just show up at the house and tell Simon Bradley that she loved him. Maybe he wouldn't care. And maybe, if she took a chance, they could start fresh and rebuild their family.

With that thought in mind, she smiled at the kids and asked, "Are you ready to hear about the Lonely Bunny and how he found a friend?"

"Yes!" A dozen childish voices shouting in unison made her laugh and she felt lighter in her soul than she had since walking out of Simon's life.

Opening the book, Tula began to read and for the next half hour gave her young audience her complete attention. When the story of the Lonely Bunny and a white kitten ended, children applauded and parents picked up copies of her books.

Tula smiled to herself as she signed her books and spent a minute or two with each of the children, giving them Lonely Bunny stickers to fix to their shirts. She was enjoying herself even while a corner of her mind worried over going to see Simon.

Through the noise and confusion, Tula felt someone watching her. Her skin prickled and her heartbeat quickened in reaction even before she looked up—directly into Simon's dark brown eyes. Instead of one of his sharply cut business suits, he was wearing jeans and a T-shirt with the Lonely Bunny logo. He held Nathan in his arms and she noticed that the baby wore a matching T-shirt.

Tula laughed and held her breath, afraid to read too much into this surprising visit. Maybe he had simply come to give her the chance to say goodbye to Nathan. Maybe the emotions she read in Simon's eyes were only regret and fondness. And maybe she would make herself nuts if she didn't find out.

She stood up slowly, never taking her gaze from his. Her heart doing somersaults in her chest, Tula tried to speak, but her mouth was dry. When Nathan reached out pudgy arms to her, she took him, grateful to feel his warm, solid weight as he snuggled in with a happy sigh.

Simon shrugged and said, "I, uh, saw the sign out front advertising that you would be here today."

"And you came," she whispered, running one hand up and down the baby's back.

"Of course I came," Simon said, gaze locked with hers, silently telling her everything she had ever wanted to hear. It was all there for her to read. He wasn't hiding anything anymore. So neither would she.

"I was going to come and see you after the signing."

He smiled and moved closer. "You were?"

"I had something to tell you," she said.

He must have seen what he needed to see written on her face because he spoke quickly. "Let me go first. I have so much I want to say to you, Tula."

She laughed a little and glanced around at the kids and their parents, all of them watching with interest. "Now?"

He looked at their audience, then shrugged them off as inconsequential. "Right here, right now."

To her amazement, he went down on one knee in front of her and looked up into her eyes. "Simon..."

"Me first," he said with a smile and shake of his head.

"Tula, I can't live without you. I tried and I just can't do it. You're the air I breathe. You're the heart of me. You're everything I need and can't do without."

Someone in the audience sighed but neither of them paid any attention.

"Oh, Simon—" Tears filled her eyes. She blinked them away because she didn't want to miss a moment of this.

He took her hand and slowly stood up to face her. "I love you. I should have told you that first. But I'll make up for that by saying it often. I love you. I love you."

Tula laughed a little, then harder when Nathan gurgled and laughed along with her. "I love you, too," she told Simon, her heart feeling as though it could pop out of her chest and fly around the room. "That's what I was coming to tell you. I love you, Simon."

"Marry me," he said quickly as if half-afraid she would change her mind. "Marry me. Be my wife and Nathan's mother. Be with me so neither of us ever has to be like your Lonely Bunny again."

"Yes, Simon," Tula said, moving into the circle of his arms. "Oh, yes."

As he stood in the bookstore, with his entire world held close to him, Simon listened to the cheers from the watching crowd. Staring down into Tula's blue eyes, he bent to kiss her and knew that like the Velveteen Rabbit she had told him about, it hurt to become real.

But it was worth it.

Epilogue

A year and a half later, Simon urged, "Push, Tula! Don't stop now, you're almost there!"

"You push for awhile, okay?" she asked, letting her head drop to the pillow. "I'm taking a break."

"Hey," the doctor called out from the foot of the bed, "nobody gets a coffee break yet!"

Simon laughed, planted a hard, fast kiss on Tula's forehead and said, "As soon as this is over, we're *both* taking a break. And, I swear, we'll never do this again."

"Oh, yes, we will," she told him with a sudden gasp. "I want at least six kids."

"You're killin' me," Simon said with a groan. He added, "Come on, honey, one more push."

Tula grinned up at him despite the pain he could see shining in her eyes. "Nag, nag, nag…" Then her features stiffened and she took a breath. "Here it comes again."

Simon had never been so terrified and so excited at once in his life. His gorgeous wife was the bravest, strongest, most miraculous human being in the world. He was humbled by her and so damn grateful to have her in his life.

"You're a warrior, Tula. You can do this. I'm right here, honey, just get it done." And *please* do it fast, he added in a silent prayer.

Mick had warned him that labor was hard on a husband. But Simon had had no idea what it would be like to stand beside the woman he loved and watch her suffer. But typically Tula, she had insisted on going through with this naturally.

Silently, Simon promised that if they ever did this again, God help him, he was going to demand that she take drugs. Or he would.

"Here we go," Doctor Liz Haney called out in encouragement. "Just a little more, Tula!"

She bore down, gritted her teeth and took Simon's hand in a crushing grip that he swore later had pulverized his bones. But then a thin, wailing cry split the air. Tula laughed, delighted, and Simon took his first relieved breath in what felt like months.

"It's a boy!" Doctor Liz reached out and laid the red-faced, squalling, beautiful child across Tula's chest.

"He's amazing," Simon said, "just like his mother."

"Hello, little Gavin," Tula said with a tired sigh as she stroked her newborn son's back. "We've been waiting for you. Your big brother is going to be so excited to meet you."

Simon's heart was so full it was a wonder he could

draw a breath. His world was perfect. Tula was safe and they had another beautiful son.

His exhausted wife looked up at him. "You should call Mick and Katie to check on Nathan—and to tell them our little Gavin is here."

"I will," Simon said, bending down to kiss her reverently. "Have I mentioned lately that I love you?"

"Only every day," she whispered back, her eyes tired but bright with happiness and satisfaction at a job well done.

"We'll just take the baby and clean him up," one of the nurses said, scooping Gavin into her arms.

Tula watched them go, then smiled at Simon when his cell phone chirped, alerting him to an incoming email. "I thought you were turning that off," she said.

"I meant to but I got distracted," he said, grinning as he read the email. "Hey, this isn't about me," he told her. "Your agent emailed to say your latest book just hit the *New York Times* list! Congratulations, honey."

Tula grinned. As exciting as that news was, it couldn't compare to what she felt every day of her life. Taking Simon's hand, she said, "I knew this book would do well. How could it miss with that title?"

He grinned and leaned over her for another kiss. *"Lonely Bunny Finds a Family,"* he whispered, then added, "I hope he's as happy as I am with mine."

* * * * *

THE BOSS'S
BABY AFFAIR

BY
TESSA RADLEY

Tessa Radley loves traveling, reading and watching the world around her. As a teen Tessa wanted to be an intrepid foreign correspondent. But after completing a bachelor of arts degree and marrying her sweetheart, she became fascinated by law and ended up studying further and practicing as an attorney in a city firm.

A six-month break spent traveling through Australia with her family reawoke the yen to write. And life as a writer suits her perfectly—traveling and reading count as research, and as for analyzing the world…well, she can think "what if?" all day long. When she's not reading, traveling or thinking about writing, she's spending time with her husband, her two sons or her zany and wonderful friends. You can contact Tessa through her website, www.tessaradley.com.

For Karen Solem
Fantastic agent and fabulous friend

One

Home meant…Jennie.

Nicholas Valentine stared at the glossy black front door and drew a deep breath. The imposing lion-head brass knocker had been one of the few touches he'd selected for the modern three-story Auckland house.

Ignoring the lion's ferocious expression, he keyed a security code into the access pad concealed in the doorframe. The heavy door swung inward.

Pocketing the keys to his Ferrari, Nick stepped forward. Carrara marble gleamed under spotlights that illuminated a triptych of tangled forms painted on three canvases facing the front entrance. He should've been pleased to be home. He should've been elated following a week of success after several months of living on the lip of a volcano.

Instead, he was too jet-lagged to care. He wanted a shower and a bed…but first he had to see Jennie.

It wasn't going to be a comfortable moment, but it had to

be done, regardless of the feelings her existence aroused in him.

Nick stopped at the foot of the white-marble stairs that ascended halfway up the two-story lobby. Resisting the urge to flee into the safety of the living room, where he could take refuge in the television remote, he placed a foot on the first stair.

He hadn't seen Jennie for almost a month.

Nick couldn't identify whether his overwhelming response was guilt—or relief. How was it possible that he could deal with a multimillion-dollar company, several hundred employees and a barrage of reporters without missing a beat, yet Jennie scared him witless? Not that he'd ever admit that to another living soul. Or even a dead one...

At the top of the stairs, a landing ran the length of the house. To the right lay two king suites, to the left four bedrooms with en suites, one of which had been converted into a nursery. In front of the four bedrooms the landing widened into a sitting area decorated in black, gray and white, and highlighted with colors that Jilly had referred to as pistachio and chartreuse yellow.

Nick paused. The usual clutter-free look of the designer-decorated space had given way to bright yellow and pink storage bins he didn't recognize. The glass coffee table had been pushed to one side, and foam squares patterned with numbers covered the area between two white love seats.

Someone—his sister?—clearly had high aspirations for Jennie's mathematical abilities. Nick was positive he hadn't been away long enough for Jennie to learn to count—after all, she was only six months old. A little farther along, some sort of contraption was rigged up on the white wool carpet.

What—?

The door to Jennie's nursery stood ajar. Nick pushed it open and entered.

One sweeping glance revealed that the room was empty.

Three strides took him past a tea party of teddy bears sitting on the floor, to the wall of windows overlooking the pool deck. There was no sign of the child or her motherly nanny—Nick couldn't remember the woman's name—by the pool, or on the expanse of manicured lawn rolling down to the edge of the cliffs overlooking the Pacific Ocean.

He glanced at his watch. Five o'clock. He knew from the schedule he'd memorized that it was Jennie's dinnertime. The baby should be home. Mrs. Busby, his housekeeper, would have an answer.

Downstairs, Mrs. Busby was not in the high-tech chrome-and-black kitchen. Where had all his staff gone? Impatient now, Nick rang the bell.

Long minutes later, Mrs. Busby appeared through the swing doors that led to the basement suites where the staff lived. At the sight of him, the housekeeper tugged at her dress collar. "I'm sorry, Mr. Valentine. I didn't know you were home yet."

Nick didn't bother to tell her that he'd gotten an earlier connection; instead, he got to the crux of what he wanted to know. "Where is Jennie?"

"Candace took her to the park—you can reach her on her cell phone." The housekeeper headed for the kitchen island with its bank of drawers. "I'll get the number—"

"Wait!" Nick's brows jerked together. The nanny's name wasn't Candace. He would've remembered that. "Who is Candace?"

Mrs. Busby hesitated, clearly flustered. "The new nanny. Didn't Mrs. Timmings let you know?"

New nanny? His sister hadn't said a word about any such thing. "What happened to…?" He searched his memory for the woman's name and came up blank.

"When Jennie got sick, Margaret resigned," Mrs. Busby explained hurriedly.

Nick tensed. "Jennie's sick?" He hadn't been notified. "What's wrong with her?"

Mrs. Busby looked increasingly uncomfortable. "She's much better now—Candace has been looking after her. Mrs. Timmings didn't want me worrying you about it." For a moment the housekeeper looked as if she wanted to say something more. Then she added, "She thought it best to wait for you to come back."

Nick's mouth compressed as he bit back his rising impatience. Mrs. Busby looked like she was about to faint with apprehension. But it wasn't her fault he hadn't been told. "I'll speak to my sister."

Relief softened Mrs. Busby's round features. "That would be best. What can I make you to eat, Mr. Valentine?"

Nick waved a dismissive hand as he headed for the double doors leading to the lobby. "I ate on the plane." At her crestfallen expression, he relented. "Maybe one of your special omelets, Mrs. Busby. But first get me the nanny's number. I'll be in the sitting room."

The nanny's cell phone must be off, Nick decided after reaching a crisp, recorded message for the second time. Impatiently, he scrolled through his phone's contacts list for his sister's number.

"Why didn't you let me know Jennie was ill? What happened?" Nick demanded as soon as Alison answered. He paused his pacing in front of the tall glass doors that folded back to reveal the pool deck, and stared unseeingly out over the expanse of water.

Silence hummed across the telephone line. "How about 'Good evening. How are you, Alison?'"

He ignored the sarcasm and started to pace again. "What's wrong with her?"

"An ear infection. I took her to the doctor, we watched it

very carefully—I didn't want to disturb you…" Her voice trailed away.

"She's my daughter." He said it with more conviction than he felt. "You should've given *me* the choice."

"Nicky, she's fine."

"So Mrs. Busby told me." He switched the phone to his other ear. "Do you know how it made me feel to hear from my housekeeper that Jennie had been ill and I didn't know anything about it?"

"I'm sorry, Nicky." His sister sounded subdued. "I should've let you know. Even Richard said so. But I thought you had your hands full—"

He cut her off. "Richard was right." Sometimes Nick pitied his long-suffering brother-in-law.

"I heard on the news that the unrest is over in Indonesia. I've been so worried—you might have let *me* know."

"Your Valentine's stock is safe. And I've managed to source the eco-friendly furniture and statuettes we need for the garden centers."

"That's not what I've been worried about. Though I should tell you we've had an offer on our stock."

"An offer?"

Nick was too tired to follow as his sister leapfrogged from one topic to the next. Yet that one phrase stuck out.

He knew how desperately Alison and Richard needed to liquidate their Valentine's stock to shore up the losses their chain of appliance stores had taken during the recent recession. Out of loyalty to Nick, they'd held off selling to give him an opportunity to buy their Valentine's stock—an impossibility until his usurious debt to his father-in-law, Desmond Perry, had been settled. And now the end was in sight. Tomorrow he would pay Perry every last cent that he owed—it would give Nick more satisfaction than anything in his life to throw the final check down on his former father-in-law's desk.

Of course, that would leave him with no liquid funds, but

if Alison and Richard could hang on for a few months more, he'd be able to acquire their Valentine's stock outright.

With people going out less and spending more time at home, his business was expanding aggressively. To Nick's satisfaction every sizable town in New Zealand's North Island now boasted a Valentine's Garden Center—just as he'd dreamed of when he first started out. People were flocking to his centers in ever-increasing droves, seeking the leisurely family lifestyle that the red heart of the Valentine's logo had come to promise.

Landscaping advice. Tranquil water features. Outdoor furnishings and art. Every plant under the sun. Customers could find it all at a Valentine's Garden Center. He had plans to carry the expansion into South Island and then farther afield into Australia. While the land the centers stood on and the business assets were worth millions, making Nick wealthy beyond his wildest dreams, the rapid expansion had left him short of cash. The repayments to his father-in-law had only made the situation tougher.

Nick knew the end was in sight. But Alison's mention of an offer for their stock had caused a frisson of unease.

"When was the offer made?" he asked.

"A few days ago." His sister sounded suspiciously vague.

"Alison..." he said warningly.

"Nicky, I was much more worried about Jennie's ear...and you." After recent riots in the capital, Alison hadn't been too keen on his trip to Indonesia. "Tell me *you* are okay."

Nick wasn't in the mood to talk about his roller-coaster month away from home. He was focused on Desmond Perry's calling in the final installment of the multimillion-dollar loan three months early. It had—much against his will—forced Nick to consider selling one of the more successful of the garden centers. He'd held off, and now he was relieved that he had.

In the long run, liquidating a center would cost them all. Him. Alison and Richard—and the other stockholders. Each center had been carefully selected for its position; in time every center was going to be a crown jewel. But future profits didn't help his sister; she needed help now.

"I'm okay. I've told you before, you fuss too much," he stalled.

"That's right. Shut me out, Nicky—as you always do. I suppose I should be grateful you at least speak to Richard... although that's only about business, I suppose. Not about your marriage, about what it's been like waiting for the sword of Damocles to drop."

Nick sighed. "Alison—"

"Don't worry, I know! Your marriage is none of my business. I should know by now that you never give an inch... never talk about what matters. One day you'll need to learn to let someone inside that hard shell you've grown."

He rubbed his hand over his eyes—God, he was tired—and resisted the urge to tell his sister that she was overreacting, that the hard shell she harped on was all in her imagination. Whatever he said, she'd only argue.

Instead, he crossed over to the white leather sofa and sank into its cushioned depths. Propping his feet onto one of the four mirrored cubes that together acted as a coffee table, he said, "Well, I want to talk now. Why didn't you let me know the nanny had walked out? That you'd seen fit to hire someone else?"

"Candace isn't really a nanny—she's a nurse."

At once fear flooded him. His hand clenched around the phone. "A *nurse?* Is there something you haven't told me?" Was Jennie a lot sicker than his sister had led him to believe? "Alison—"

"Jennie is fine! And Candace is a godsend—she's very capable. I met her at the hospital. We hit it off instantly and when she heard that Margaret had left—"

"Why *did* Margaret leave?"

"Her blood pressure had risen and when Jennie got ill she said it was too much for her."

Nick closed his eyes and suppressed the urge to swear.

He hadn't known the woman had high blood pressure or he might have had second thoughts when Jilly had hired her. Which was probably why she hadn't mentioned it on her resume. Margaret had seemed so perfect. An older, maternal-looking woman from a reputable agency with impeccable references. He'd been pleased with Jilly's choice. Now it appeared that she hadn't been quite so perfect.

"What do you know about this other woman?"

"She's a pediatric surgery nurse by training. She's been away from the hospital for a little while—traveling or something. But she has fabulous references and the hospital snapped her up to do overflow shifts in the emergency room as soon as she came back." His sister paused to draw a breath, but rushed on before Nick could get a word in edgewise. "Surely even you can see the benefit of Jennie having a nanny who can take care of her if she gets ill, as babies so often do? It certainly sets my mind at ease. I'm sure it's what Jilly would've wanted."

"Let's leave aside what Jilly would've wanted."

Nick wasn't about to let his sister change the focus of the conversation to his mixed-up emotions about his late wife... and Jennie.

"Once you meet Candace, you'll see that she's absolutely perfect." His sister changed direction, one of those frog-leaps Nick was finding more difficult than usual to follow. "I don't know what we'll do when she decides to go back to full-time nursing."

"Hire a real nanny?" suggested Nick, closing his eyes. "So that when I come home from being away for weeks on end Jennie is at least here to greet me?"

A scarlet Ferrari occupied the space that had been empty since Candace had arrived to take care of Jennie.

Candace's mouth set into a firm line as she eased the station wagon that had come with the job in between the sleek sports car and a silver Daimler. So Nick Valentine was home. About time. The electronically activated garage door lowered with a hum behind her. But her ire toward her neglectful employer didn't extend to his daughter. Opening the rear door, Candace crooned to the baby as she lifted her out of the car seat and she was rewarded with a happy smile.

Jennie was the sweetest baby in the world. In her job as a pediatric surgery nurse, Candace had seen many, but this one was special.

Her face softened and she tightened her arms. Jennie made a snuffling sound of contentment against her T-shirt and Candace's heart melted like honey in summer sunshine. Poor little motherless thing. The first time she'd held the baby she'd felt the inexplicable bond. This wasn't her child, she had to remind herself—Jennie belonged to someone else. Yet she couldn't help being smitten…and more than a little envious of the gift that Nick Valentine treated with such cavalier disregard.

Pushing the door leading into the house open, Candace tiptoed into the glossy marble-and-silver perfection of the foyer that made her feel like she'd stumbled into the pages of an architectural design magazine every time she entered the house. No plants softened the hard edges; no flowers spilling out of vases broke the palette of black, silver, icy lemon and white.

The baby in her arms was the only real thing there.

She glanced through to the black-and-chrome kitchen. It was empty. Across the lobby she could hear the blare of the television. Her pulse quickened and her stomach tied itself up in knots. She resisted the urge to flee upstairs. No point putting this meeting off. The sooner she met her boss the better.

Hoisting Jennie higher into her arms, she halted in the

doorway to the sitting room. A tremor of shock quaked through her.

Nick Valentine lay sprawled across a white leather sofa in front of a wide-screen television. His dark-as-midnight hair was rumpled as though he'd raked his fingers through the strands. His suit jacket had been abandoned over the back of the couch and the top two buttons of his striped business shirt had been undone to reveal a patch of bare, tanned skin. He was so much more than she'd bargained for—Candace hadn't expected his sheer physical presence.

Thankfully, the man was asleep.

Candace swallowed. Hurriedly, she forced her delinquent gaze away. A fluffy omelet lay untouched on a tray next to his highly shined shoes, which were propped up on the outsize glass cube serving as a coffee table. A half-empty tumbler of amber liquid sat beside him on the couch.

What had she expected?

A father who couldn't wait to see his baby? Nick Valentine was a businessman—first and always. Jilly Valentine had told her that. Her gaze flicked to the mirror table cube. The kind of man who drank Scotch rather than eating a carefully prepared meal, and fell asleep in front of a sports channel rather than seeking out his daughter after a month's absence.

The hope that perhaps she'd misjudged the man flickered out. Turning away, Candace hugged Jennie closer, suddenly desperate to get away from the baby's uncaring father.

Upstairs it was time to bathe the baby. Afterward, with Jennie changed and ready for bed, Candace headed for the fridge set under the counter in the corner of the nursery where the bottles she'd sterilized earlier waited. In fact, every modern convenience a baby could possibly need was at Candace's fingertips.

There were certainly uses for Nick Valentine's millions. But what did they help a baby whose father showed so little interest in her?

Candace grimaced on discovering that the formula was finished and she'd forgotten to bring another container up. Now she'd have to go fetch it from the well-stocked pantry in the kitchen downstairs.

Putting Jennie in the crib, she shut her ears to the wails of complaint as she made for the door. "I'll only be a moment, Jennie."

A profound sense of disorientation shook Nick.

The bright screen flickering out into the darkness confused him, and he blinked to escape the drowsiness that pressed down on him like smog.

Jennie.

Guilt knifed him. The hectic rush of the past few weeks was no excuse for his reluctance to see the baby. If he'd stayed away much longer, she wouldn't have recognized him.

Nick staggered to his feet. This time the stairs seemed to take forever to climb. And this time the nursery door was firmly closed—not open as he'd left it earlier. Relief flooded him. Jennie might already be sleeping, then he'd be off the hook.

He advanced into the nursery.

A snuffling noise told him the baby was still awake. Swallowing, he took another step. A pool of muted light surrounded the crib where Jennie lay. A quick glance around revealed that the party of teddy bears had been put away...and the rocker that Jilly had insisted on ordering for the nursery was empty. Jennie was alone.

Where the hell was that fancy nurse his sister had raved about?

Three strides took him to the side of the crib.

Once there, he hesitated, fighting his reluctance to pick up the baby. At last he managed to master the fears little Jennie would never know about.

"Hello, Jennie."

The baby fell silent. Her head turned, and wide-spaced eyes gazed up at him. Their color had lightened from the navy blue they'd been the last time he'd seen her. Jilly's eyes had been sapphire blue while his own were a much darker indigo shade. Neither hue was apparent in the cloudy gray depths of Jennie's eyes.

The unspoken dread deepened.

There was a moment of stillness when neither of them moved as they examined each other. Then Jennie gave a coo and stretched out a hand. Nick stilled. What did the past matter? This was a baby…innocent of it all.

He touched her hand with one finger.

Jennie's hand clutched his forefinger. They gazed at each other. Nick held his breath. The silence in the nursery was absolute, the moment powerful and intense.

He cleared his throat, told himself he was being fanciful. Yet something had changed—even as Jennie's fingers wrapped more tightly around his.

It was too much. And too soon. Nick gently shook the baby's fingers loose and turned blindly for the door, head down, desperate to escape, his hand groping for the door handle.

Before he'd found it, the door swung open.

Nick caught sight of a blur of movement and the next instant a hard object thudded against the side of his head.

"Ow! What the—?"

He glared down into the most angelic face he'd ever seen. Wide-spaced silver-gray eyes, an upturned nose, a sweetly curved pink mouth and cascading golden curls.

Nick was in no mood to be converted.

Yet the sudden pull of attraction unsettled him. Fingering the tender spot above his ear, he straightened to his full height, and snarled. "Do you always rush in without looking where you're going?"

* * *

Candace stared up in horror at the man blocking her way to the nursery.

Nick Valentine.

She must've said it out loud, because his glare intensified. "Who else were you expecting?"

"Uh…" She scanned the hard features. The strong, square jaw. The bladed nose, and an ancient scar that cut through one black eyebrow, giving him a dangerous air. Eyes so dark a blue as to appear black. He was much bigger than newspaper photos had suggested, at least six foot three.

Awake and up close, the handsome features were even more forbidding—not helped by that piratical scar and the almost-black eyes. Her heartbeat grew faster.

"I thought you were still downstairs, sleeping." Damn. Damn. Damn. "I'm so sorry."

"I'm going to have a lump like an egg," he accused, rubbing his head.

She stared at his fingers, cursing herself for being in such a hurry. "We should get some ice on it."

"Get some ice on it? That's all you're going to say about assaulting me?"

He was furious. Her pounding heart sank into the comfortable Ugg boots she'd taken to wearing inside to protect her feet from the acres of shiny marble. Her first meeting with her new boss couldn't have gone any worse.

Candace became conscious of how close he was standing. The warm, tangy scent of him swirled around her. "It was an accident," she protested halfheartedly. The force of the contact had jarred her elbow. It must hurt him like blazes. She started to apologize again.

"You need to watch where you're going," he said.

The unfairness of the accusation caused her to flush. "You ran into me," she defended herself.

His fingers probed along his hairline above his ear. "What the hell was the weapon?"

"A tin of formula."

The other hand released her arm, and his gaze followed hers to the floor. "A tin of baby formula?"

The disbelief in his voice compounded the realization that she'd hurt her boss, and her knees went weak. Was he going to think she was totally incompetent?

She sagged against him and mumbled, "I'm truly sorry."

Thankfully, this time he didn't say anything.

And this close to him it was even more difficult to think clearly. Nick's body was taut and unexpectedly muscled under the crumpled, striped business shirt, and much warmer than she'd expected. Much firmer, too. It wasn't the body of a man who sat behind a desk all day.

What was she doing thinking about Nick Valentine's taut and admittedly well-honed body? It struck her that she wasn't giving him a very good impression of her professionalism. Candace jerked upright as a quiver of fear feathered across her heart. If Nick Valentine doubted her ability to look after his daughter, he'd dismiss her without a second thought.

She searched for something to restore normality and asked a little breathlessly, "What did you come upstairs for?"

He didn't answer. Instead, he studied her. Candace shifted nervously. In the dimness of the doorway she couldn't clearly make out his expression. Of course, every emotion on her face would be visible to him under the overhead light. Could he see her apprehension? Was he really going to fire her for her clumsiness?

"You're Candace."

She flinched, and waited a heartbeat. Yet there was no dawning recognition in the narrowed gaze.

"Yes, I'm Candace," she conceded at last. "And you're Nick Valentine."

He inclined his head. "You have the advantage on me. I don't know your last name."

"Morrison." She gave it with reluctance, tensing as she waited warily for his reaction.

Nothing changed in the enigmatic navy-blue eyes. *Her name meant nothing to him.* Only by sheer willpower did she prevent herself from closing her eyes in relief. The longer he remained in ignorance, the better for her. Candace suppressed the notion that he deserved to know, then dismissed the momentary scruple and told herself he wouldn't care. If he'd been the kind of man to care, everything would've played out differently.

Even as she grappled with what to do next, Jennie let out a howl of protest in the room behind them.

Two

Candace could've kissed the baby for the timely distraction.

Nick spun around and hurried into the nursery, and she followed quickly in his wake.

He peered into the crib. "What's wrong with her?"

"She's tired and she wants her bottle." Candace scooped the baby into her arms and handed her to Nick.

He hesitated.

"Hold her while I get the bottle ready," she said hurriedly. "Otherwise, she's going to howl the place down."

On cue, Jennie's protests grew louder. Nick clumsily reached for the baby. Candace hovered, worried that he might drop her. He made some grunting noises, apparently intended to comfort the baby, but they only made Jennie scream more loudly.

"If you hold her a little more firmly, she'd settle."

Watching him, Candace was visited by the insane notion that Nick had never held the baby before. It wasn't possible. Yet he didn't appear familiar with the baby at all.

Her heart ached for Jennie. Poor motherless tyke. Nick was an ambitious businessman who spent more time chasing deals than with his child. Of course, having a full-time nanny made it all too easy for Nick to avoid his parenting responsibilities.

Candace wasn't ready to analyze the surge of emotions that flooded her. Instead, she grabbed his wrist. "Put one hand here..." she placed it behind Jennie's bottom "...and the other here."

"She's *my* daughter. I know how to hold her."

Who was he trying to fool? Yet the warmth of his skin beneath her fingertips drew her attention back to Nick, making Candace aware that her hand still gripped his wrist.

She released him as if she'd been scorched and stepped back, out of his force field, and ordered, "Walk with her."

He gave her a brooding look, then complied.

Jennie's bitter complaints forced Candace to hurriedly retrieve the tin of formula off the floor, open it and mix up a bottle. The howls turned to querulous grumbles that finally abated. Candace didn't pause to see what had caused the change; she kept focused on what she was doing. By the time the bottle was ready, she turned to find Nick holding a bunch of keys in front of the baby, flaunting the famous Ferrari tag with its rearing horse.

Jennie was enthralled. Her plump fingers clutched the keys as she tried to shove them into her mouth. Nick was looking confounded, struggling to keep the keys a safe distance from little madam's face. Every time Jennie opened her mouth, he flinched. What was he expecting—the baby to devour the keys or holler with frustration?

At the sight of Candace, relief darkened his indigo eyes to the shade of midnight. "Take her."

Normally she would've jumped at the invitation. She loved feeding the baby, and the last bottle of the day had become a special shared ritual for them both. The quiet of the nursery, the old-fashioned tick-tock of the antique grandfather clock in the corner, the warmth of the baby's body cuddled up against her. Moments to treasure forever.

Yet his terse command, the way he was ready to rid himself of the baby at the first opportunity, all caused the aching sympathy for the baby to deepen. He was Jennie's father, after all.

Even though he appeared to have forgotten all about her for the past month.

Candace had to try to get through to him, show him what he was missing. No one knew better than she how it felt to yearn for a child…

"Sit in the chair."

He gave her an oddly panic-stricken look. "The rocking chair?"

From his expression she might as well have said electric chair. Not as comfortable with his daughter as he'd like her to believe.

"Yes." She nodded to underscore her answer. Grim humor sparked through her as the millionaire businessman dropped into the purple-painted rocker that was plumped up with lime cushions. If his board of directors could see him now…

She suppressed her mirth and passed him the bottle. "Normally, you'd test the heat against the inside of your wrist but we won't bother this time. I've already done it and Jennie has reached the end of her patience."

The baby was flapping her hands furiously.

As Nick gave her the bottle, she latched desperately on to it, her hands clutched around his. The sight of her little plump fingers against Nick's large, tanned hands caused a strange sensation to flutter in Candace's chest.

His head was bent, his focus on Jennie absolute. In that moment Candace felt unaccountably excluded. For weeks the baby had been her responsibility—these secret moments had been hers alone to treasure.

Now he'd usurped them. She fought the riot of emotions that his presence here in the nursery aroused.

Then Nick raised his head.

The look on his face caused Candace's breath to catch. It held an intensity—pain mingled with something more elusive. For weeks she'd been furious at Nick Valentine's desertion of his daughter. She'd never expected to feel empathy for him—to see the darkness of hell in his eyes.

For the first time, she became aware of Nick Valentine as someone other than a busy, enterprising millionaire—someone other than Jennie's father. He was a man. A man tormented by the loss of his wife…a man who had been saddled with the lonely responsibility of raising their daughter.

A pang pierced her. It couldn't be easy.

The least she could do was grant him a few moments of privacy to deal with whatever demons plagued him. Candace edged to the door. "I'll go and fetch some ice for your head."

The baby had fallen asleep.

Nick studied the bundle in his arms. She radiated heat against his heart and the warmth of her body had spread through him, almost sending him to sleep, too. No doubt the long flight hadn't helped.

Shaking off the drowsiness that threatened to overtake him, Nick rose slowly to his feet. He carried the baby across to the crib and carefully settled her down before covering her with a fleecy blanket. To his relief, she didn't stir. Yawning, Nick turned out the light and let himself out the nursery.

The nanny—Candace, he amended—was coming toward him, her tread soundless on the thick pile of the pale carpet.

"Sorry I took so long. I couldn't find the ice trays." She held up a plastic bag filled with ice.

"It doesn't matter." Nick was so drugged with tiredness he'd forgotten that she'd gone to fetch ice. "Jennie's sleeping," he said to fill the sudden, awkward silence that stretched between them. "She went out like a light."

Candace smiled, and it transformed her face. The serious eyes sparkled with silver glints. "Yes, it's amazing how quickly that happens."

"I'm about to do the same." Resisting the urge to gawk like a teenager, Nick started to walk past her, but her hand came out and rested lightly on his shirtsleeve. "Let me ice your head."

A jolt of electricity buzzed under where her fingers rested. She was barely touching him. Gazing down at her, he found himself falling into wide, gray eyes as clear as a mountain lake. Nick shook his head roughly to rid himself of the illusion.

Jet lag was definitely setting in with a vengeance, he decided.

"I'll be fine," he said brusquely.

Her smile vanished and she blinked, shattering the unwelcome spell that bound him.

"Even ten minutes will make a difference to any possible bruise marks," she wheedled.

"Okay." To make amends for his terseness, Nick gave her a wry smile. "Then I won't have to explain how I came to have a bruise."

Her eyes clouded over. She was about to start apologizing again. Nick hadn't intended that. She'd relaxed a little since leaving him with Jennie. He didn't want to see her looking wretched—he wanted to see her smile. The generous, spontaneous smile that lit up her whole face...and made him feel like a ray of sunlight had stolen into the night.

"Don't worry—it will take more than a bump in the night to keep me down." Reluctantly he moved away from her toward the sitting area off the upstairs lobby and slumped down into the closest sofa, his head falling back against the pile of cushions as he closed his eyes. Man, he was tired.

The sudden cold of the ice pack against his skull made him flinch.

"Try not to move." Candace spoke from behind him. "I'll hold it here for a few minutes."

Despite the pressure of the freezing pack, a bit of peace seeped into him. It was the first time in weeks that he'd done nothing at all.

Candace leaned forward. "Not too cold?"

"At least it's keeping me from falling asleep."

She laughed, a joyous peal of sound. Nick forgot the coldness of the ice pack against his head and became aware of the wholesome scent of baby powder, soap and the hint of something more spicy and sexy that enveloped her.

The surge of desire that thrummed through his blood startled him. How long had it been since he'd allowed himself to feel that heady heat? And now it had happened with a woman he didn't know—his daughter's nanny, for God's sake.

He must be desperate.

Jeez, he *was* desperate.

How long had it been…?

"Relax. Your shoulders are all bunched up. Do you want me to rub them?" The angel's wickedly seductive voice interrupted his out-of-control thoughts.

"No." Nick closed his eyes against the tempting suggestion. He was already far too aware of the woman. If she touched him…

To Nick's intense discomfort, his body instantly reacted to the idea of her hands rubbing his skin. If Candace glimpsed his lap, she would see the humiliating effect her proximity had had on him from his tented trousers. *Damn.* He was trapped until this wayward impulse subsided.

Candace shifted, adjusting the ice pack, her breath soft against the top of his head.

Nick tensed, moving his hands surreptitiously to his trouser front, shielding any bulge from her view. "That's fine. It's late. Why don't you call it a night and go to bed?"

"I want to check on Jennie first before I retire." She straightened with a rustle of fabric, and he could no longer feel her breath ruffling his hair. Her voice had taken on a different note, too. Brisk and all business. Nick missed the concern, the caring note. Then he jerked himself back to reality.

He'd been aroused by his child's nurse. It was like a bad-taste comedy. Nick didn't grope the hired help...or seduce his secretaries.

He had to get away from her.

"I'll hold the ice pack on the lump. You can let go," he said gruffly, suddenly desperate for her to leave. But even that didn't block out the heightened awareness he'd developed of Candace...where she stood...as he strained his ears trying to figure out what she was doing.

The ice pack shifted. A curl brushed against his cheek.

"Oops!" Her voice was breathless.

The ice pack slipped from her hold and landed in his lap. Nick made a grab for it and, growling with frustration, closed his eyes and prayed for control.

The sudden silence that followed stretched his nerves to breaking point.

Nick opened his eyes.

She'd moved, and now stood in front of him, staring at him, and she flushed as he caught her gaze. "I should go check on Jennie."

"Yes, you should." It came out as a low, feral growl. Wide awake now, all his weariness evaporated, he cleared his throat and held the ice pack out. "Thanks for the ice."

She reached for it the same moment that he unfolded his length from the sofa. They bumped into each other and she laughed awkwardly. Nick didn't smile. He had never felt less like laughing in his life.

"Sorry—"

"I'm sorry—"

They both broke off, her laughter coming to an abrupt end as their eyes met. Nick didn't know how it happened, but he'd taken a step forward. She didn't retreat. He couldn't have stopped what happened next if he'd tried...

Her lips were soft. Softer than any he'd ever kissed.

Hunger clawed at his belly. He fought to keep the kiss gentle, not to unleash the ferocity that lurked within him. She tasted so sweet. He pressed soft kisses along the seam of her lips, leashing the feral urge to grab her by her shoulders, yank her to him and kiss her with all the hunger that churned inside him.

Instead he concentrated on their only point of contact: their lips.

But it wasn't enough. His hands came up and cupped her jaw.

She jerked, breaking the thrall that held them both.

"No!"

Candace pulled back sharply. Nick's hands dropped away from her face. They were shaking. And he wasn't the only one affected. Her breasts were rising and falling under the snug fit of her T-shirt, the ice pack clutched between her white-knuckled hands.

Nick forced his gaze away, back to her face.

Damn. He was out of his mind. "That should not have happened."

Her eyes had gone dark. "You're right."

"It won't happen again," Nick vowed, putting the length of the sitting room between them and retreating toward the top of the stairs...then edging to the safety of his suite that lay beyond. "I wouldn't lose any sleep over it—I certainly don't intend to."

* * *

Once he'd reached his own wing of the mansion, Nick made for the luxurious bathroom, where he stripped off the travel-soiled suit pants and unbuttoned the business shirt. He was wired now. All thoughts of sleep banished.

He spread his hands on the glass vanity slab. Lowering his head, he drew in a deep breath and slowly exhaled.

In the past half hour he'd experienced swings of emotion that had badly rattled him. The vulnerability when he'd held Jennie, the realization as he fed her the night bottle that this little scrap depended on him for everything in her life. And the need to get the hell out of that nursery before the safety of his world cracked wide open.

Only to find himself over the edge of the precipice. Shuddering, he relived the torrential surge of desire that Candace had aroused. Had he walked away while he could? No, he'd acted on it.

Kissed her.

Double damn.

Bracing his weight on his arms, Nick raised his head and confronted himself in the wall of mirror above the vanity. He looked different from his usual tightly controlled, immaculately groomed self. Not outwardly—the swelling where the edge of the tin had connected didn't show. It was in his eyes where the change lay. Instead of the customary cool calculation, they were filled with turmoil.

What had unnerved him? The sudden bond he found himself forging with Jennie? Or the angelic-looking nanny who'd woken the devil in him?

Nick wasn't sure he wanted to know.

A sharp cry woke Candace.

After silencing the baby monitor, Candace sprang out of bed and ran along the carpeted landing lit by night-lights until she reached the nursery. Lifting Jennie out of the crib, she rocked the baby in her arms.

"Hush," she murmured as Jennie's head swung up and butted her chin.

The red numbers of the counter clock on the dresser glowed in the night. Two o'clock. Not yet time for a feeding. Jennie fussed in Candace's arms. Walking silenced her momentarily, then the whimpers restarted. Candace laid Jennie down on the changing surface above the dresser, and reached for the thermometer in the first-aid kit on the shelf above. Talking a stream of softly whispered nonsense to Jennie, she deftly removed the diaper and inserted the thermometer.

"Sorry, sweetheart. I know you would've preferred a tympanic thermometer, but those ears might still be tender."

A few seconds later the thermometer beeped. The reading was above normal, but far from dangerous. Quickly, Candace put on a clean diaper, then picked Jennie up and started to walk, Jennie grumbling incessantly.

Candace suppressed a sigh. "So much for not losing any sleep tonight, huh, Jennie?"

A flash of memory hit her of the wild pleasure that had pierced her when Nick Valentine had kissed her…and the flare of absolute panic that had followed.

She must've communicated her unease to the baby because Jennie let out a volley of wails.

Seconds later, the door to the nursery burst open.

Nick stood there, a dark silhouette against the shaft of light that spilled in from the landing. A rustle of movement, then a switch clicked and bright light flooded the room.

Candace blinked against the glare. Nick wore only a pair of hastily donned pants, the top button still undone. His chest was bare, his hair mussed.

He'd told her he had no intention of losing any sleep over the kiss they'd shared…and had expected her to do the same.

Yet the sight of him caused her pulse to thud.

She was a fool.

Candace looked away as Jennie wailed more loudly.

Nick advanced. "Let me see if I can settle her."

Gut instinct caused her arms to tighten.

"Give her to me," he ordered, his face closed, exhibiting no sign of the passionate man who'd kissed her with such ravenous hunger.

Candace took herself in hand. *Forget about that kiss.* This hard-eyed man was her employer. Jennie's father. Soundlessly she surrendered the baby.

Nick took Jennie with more ease than he'd shown earlier. Instantly, Jennie's cries stilled. Her eyes widened as she stared up at the man who held her. The sight of the baby bundled up against the muscled torso caused pain to splinter deep inside Candace.

When Jennie looked down from her father's face and stared at the wall of chest in front of her with a puzzled expression, Candace's throat closed. The baby reached out and touched a ridge of muscle, her puny fingers closed around a sprinkle of hair. She tugged.

Nick didn't flinch.

Jennie gave a gurgle.

And Candace wanted to cry.

It was clear that the baby hardly knew her father.

So what am I going to do about that? Candace asked herself. *Can I leave Jennie with a man who doesn't have time for his own child? A man who didn't even care enough to call home from overseas when she was sick?*

Nick Valentine needed to take responsibility for Jennie. He was her father.

"I'm going to make an appointment to take her back to the doctor tomorrow," Candace told him.

"She doesn't appear that ill." Nick was studying the baby.

He'd seen Jennie for maybe an hour after a month away and now he was an expert on her health? As much as she itched to, Candace couldn't voice that reaction—Nick Valentine was her boss. The last thing she wanted was to annoy him enough for him to dismiss her.

Besides, if she was honest, he had a point. Right now Jennie didn't look that ill. But Nick hadn't seen her flushed with fever, her body limp after being contorted with convulsions. He hadn't experienced the fear—the helplessness—that had caused his sister to sob at the hospital. When Candace had taken the baby from Alison that day, she'd been terrified by the baby's burning temperature, the spasms that had shaken her little body. Nick couldn't possibly understand.

He'd been thousands of miles away, choosing furniture and carvings for upmarket gardens, focusing on making his next million.

But blaming him, working herself up, wasn't going to help the situation. Candace pulled herself together and said with forced calm, "I don't like the way she's fretting."

"Then make a doctor's appointment in the morning." He jiggled the baby in his arms.

"What time will suit you best?"

His head jerked up. "What?"

"When will you be free?" Did he imagine she'd make an appointment without consulting him? Even she knew he was a hotshot tycoon with endless demands on his time. "Or should I ask your assistant when you're available tomorrow?"

"I can't come—I've got too much to do tomorrow."

Of course he did. Poor Jennie. "You have to come. You're her father and she's been ill."

"What exactly was the matter?"

"Chronic ear infection. Her temperature rocketed until she had convulsions. She had to be hospitalized."

And that was how she'd come into Jennie's life. Candace hadn't stopped thanking her stars for whatever twist of fate had put her on duty for the shift when Jennie arrived.

"I'd have come if—"

If it had been important enough…

Candace cut him off with a wave of her hand—she wasn't interested in his excuses. Nick had no idea what havoc she was capable of unleashing—especially driven by her own guilt, her own very personal demons. "Jennie needs you with her. And I want to make sure there's been no resurgence of the infection, that her eardrums are clear. I'd hate for Jennie to lose her hearing for life."

He gave her an unreadable look. "Arrange the appointment, and get Mr. Busby to take you. Let me know the time and I'll meet you there."

"Good—Jennie will appreciate it."

The baby might be blissfully unaware of the importance of the moment. But in the years to come, at least Candace would have the comfort of knowing she'd gotten Nick involved in taking care of his daughter.

Something about the expression on the nanny's face bothered Nick.

Nurse, he amended silently. His sister had told him Candace was a nurse…not a nanny. Frankly, Nick didn't care what Candace called herself as long as she quit having this unsettling effect on him.

He was doing everything he could to pretend her proximity was leaving him unfazed. He'd forced himself to be cool and distant, but it wasn't working. He only had to catch a whiff of her sweet, spicy perfume to want to pull her close and bury his mouth against her scented skin.

It wouldn't do.

If only he could make himself think of her as the nanny—or the nurse—rather than Candace, the woman with tousled hair and translucent silver-gray eyes who was standing a short distance away from him wearing nothing but a pair of pink-and-white candy-striped cotton pajamas. Nick's gaze fell on the monitor that poked out the breast pocket of her pajama top, and he said with more than a little desperation, "I'm glad the system works—you must've sprinted up the stairs to have got here quicker than I did."

She gave him a peculiar look. "What do you mean? I'm in the room next door."

Next door? "You're not in the nanny's quarters in the basement?"

She shook her head. "The doctor and I agreed it made sense for me to be close at hand when Jennie was ill." Her gaze was very level. "Your sister agreed. The house has so many bedrooms—all of them empty. It seemed silly for me to stay two floors away from Jennie."

"Of course."

His lukewarm response caused her to say quickly, "I'm here to look after your daughter. As long as she's happy and healthy, does it matter where I sleep?"

Nick could hardly confess that the thought of her living here—on the same floor as him, a short distance from the master suite—was going to drive him crazy.

At least, he supposed, his mind would be at peace knowing Jennie was well looked after. Even if his body was on red alert.

He suppressed a groan.

So much for getting any sleep...

Three

The next day Candace glanced at her watch for the hundredth time in the past five minutes. The minute hand had crawled to twenty minutes past noon.

Where was Nick?

On her lap, Jennie gurgled and gazed avidly at the two identically dressed boys on the opposite side of the doctor's reception room, who appeared hell-bent on stripping the florist ribbon out of a flower arrangement. Their harried-looking father kept telling them to stop, to no avail. The twins had arrived half an hour after Candace, right on the heels of a little girl with a rash on her face.

That patient had already been sent in ahead, Candace having elected to miss Jennie's scheduled appointment time and wait for Nick to arrive. Who was now forty minutes late. With every passing moment, it was becoming clearer that Nick had no intention of keeping the promise he'd made.

Candace had tried to call him several times. Only to get his voice mail. She should've expected this. He'd told her he was busy. But she'd blissfully thought this time he would put Jennie first…before work.

Had he ever intended to come? Or had he sent her on ahead with the chauffeur simply to get her out of his hair?

It didn't matter what excuse he'd make later, it wouldn't take away the ache of…of…disappointment…in Candace's heart.

She told herself the emotion she was feeling had nothing to with her ambivalent relationship with Nick…or with the desire he'd awakened within her last night. She told herself it was all about Jennie.

By not arriving for the appointment, by not even bothering to let Candace know he'd bailed, he'd irrevocably let Jennie down.

With his round face and ruddy complexion, the snowy-bearded man seated behind the heavy antique desk twiddling a pen between his fingers looked like every child's vision of Santa Claus.

Nick had been taken in by the air of jolly bonhomie when he'd first met Desmond Perry—until he'd discovered that the devil himself lurked behind that merry mask. Now he couldn't figure out how he'd failed to notice the splinters of ice in the startling blue eyes.

"The final payment is done." It had given Nick enormous satisfaction to come here, into Desmond Perry's lair, to tell him that. He glanced at his watch and pushed back the chair he'd taken because Desmond had clearly expected him to stand. He rose now to his full intimidating height. "I won't have a cup of coffee—" the older man hadn't offered "—because I have an appointment."

Desmond carefully set the pen he'd been twirling between his blunt fingers down on the leather inset of the desk. "You should know I plan to sell my stock in Valentine's," he said.

Nick said very softly, "You what?"

"I will be selling my share of your business as soon as Jilly's estate has been settled."

His share? For a moment Nick could only stare at his father-in-law in disbelief. Then reality sank in. Desmond was talking about Jilly's stocks. The stock that in terms of their prenuptial agreement Nick had given to his wife. Stock that Jilly had then bequeathed to her father in her will.

With Jilly's sudden death brought on by a virus, Desmond no longer needed to pretend any loyalty toward the son-in-law he'd bought for his daughter—but never liked. Mostly his own fault, Nick knew; he'd been unable to kowtow to the man, be the obsequious puppet Desmond had expected. For seven years he'd worked night and day to maintain the astronomical payments to repurchase the garden center Desmond had tricked Nick's mentors, Bertha and Henry Williams, into selling.

By giving Nick a job, Bertha and Henry had saved Nick from sure trouble when he'd been a teen. And though he'd gone on to establish his own business, he couldn't stand by and watch them lose the garden center they'd loved...and the home they occupied on the premises. And wily Desmond had known that.

Desmond had set him up. The price for the center had not only been an unrealistic, extortionist amount, but also marriage to Jilly. Nick had considered refusing, but Henry's heart attack and Bertha's terror had caused Nick to grit his teeth and accept the terrible terms.

But once he'd signed the contract, and taken occupation of the garden center that had once belonged to his mentors, he'd given Bertha and Henry back their home. It hadn't been the end of it.

His new father-in-law had sat back, expecting Nick to fail to meet the punishing payment schedule, which would've put the property back under his control—and allowed him to triumph over the son-in-law he detested.

But Nick had done it.

The final repayment had been made. And he'd done it without jeopardizing the financial well-being of his own company. Sure it had slowed his expansion plans down, tightened his finances, but he was still a wealthy man.

But now, as the first glimpse of freedom appeared like a fragment of sky between dark city high-rises, Desmond had dropped his next bombshell.

Nick wasn't going to roll over. "The prenup stipulated that once the full amount of the sale price was repaid to you—" and Nick had worked himself almost to death to make sure of that "—then I would have right of first refusal on the shares if Jilly ever wanted to sell them."

He'd paid dearly for Bertha and Henry's retirement dream…

"My daughter is dead. You failed to pay the price before she died—the right of first refusal died with her. In terms of her will, the stock is now mine. And I have no intention of waiting until you can raise sufficient funds for the stock," Desmond sneered. "The growth of Valentine's garden centers has not been at all what I expected. I'm selling."

Nick forced himself to keep still. Not to defend the performance of the stock. Not to reveal his shock at Desmond's revelation. Instead, raising an eyebrow, he asked, "You already have a buyer for the stock?"

"Oh, yes."

Nick allowed himself a slight, disbelieving smile at Desmond while his brain worked frantically. Alison had said she and Richard had had an offer for their shares, too. Was he sensing a conspiracy where none existed?

Nick shrugged. "Well, they'll have to wait for Jilly's estate to be finalized."

"My buyer is not in a hurry."

"Who is it? Another chain of garden centers?" Nick tried to think which of his competitors might have the liquidity in the present economic climate to force a takeover.

"Why must the buyer be a garden center? The land owned by the company is worth a fortune."

That wiped the mocking smile clean off Nick's face. "A developer?" he asked dangerously. "You're planning to sell to someone who will hunt more stock until he has enough to close all the centers and develop the land?"

Triumph glittered in Desmond's pale blue eyes. "The developer I have in mind is prepared to pay a premium rate for the stock."

The Super Center, Valentine's flagship store, was located close to Auckland city, not far from the waterfront on a sizable tract of prime real estate. It was worth a fortune, and other stores in other cities were equally well situated. A developer would love to get his hands on the company's assets.

In the back of Nick's mind, there had always been the knowledge that he could sell off some of the land to raise funds, but that would be a last resort. It was something he'd never seriously contemplated—no matter how hard Desmond rode him.

Because that would mean closing those centers. Not only would his staff lose jobs, the community where the center was located would lose, too. Each center had landscaped gardens, a café where customers could socialize, well-equipped playgrounds for children and bandstands offering musical events. A Valentine's Garden Center brought pleasure to everyone who stopped by.

To hurt him, Desmond wanted to destroy the culture Nick had built.

Desmond knew him too well...

Narrowing his gaze on his adversary, Nick challenged, "You'd sell your stock, so your crony has a chance to make a fortune out of building high-density developments?"

Desmond placed his hands behind his head and smirked. "Sounds like a good plan."

Nick rocked on his toes, tempted—not for the first time—to slam a fist in his father-in-law's corpulent stomach.

The open green space with streams and lakes that Henry had painstakingly created and lost to Desmond seven years ago would be the first site to be bulldozed and developed—Nick had no doubt about that. With it would go the craftsmanship that Valentine's stores had brought to the lifestyle market. The handmade pots. The carved garden statues. The water features that were so carefully created. The plants that were so lovingly tended.

And it wouldn't stop there. The network of suppliers would lose contracts…and as for his staff, Nick didn't want to think about the layoffs that would follow.

His anger roared into fury. Nick took a step closer to the devil behind the desk. Then he checked himself, drawing on the control that had always served him well and helped him thwart Desmond in the past.

A glance at his watch caused him to grimace inwardly. *Damn.* He'd lost all track of time. He'd been due to meet Candace at the doctor's room fifteen minutes ago. He was going to miss the chance to talk to the doctor about how well Jennie had recovered. Hurriedly, Nick stuck his hand into his pocket searching for his cell phone.

It wasn't there. Cursing silently, Nick remembered placing it in the holder between the front seats in the Ferrari before he'd left his office.

"We can discuss an alternative plan."

Distracted by his thoughts, Nick turned his head. The triumph in Desmond's expression glowed even brighter. Whatever the alternative plan was, it boded ill—Nick had no doubt about that. He had no interest in bargaining with the devil.

He wasn't going to stay a minute longer. Already he'd allowed Desmond to consume too much of his time. A twinge of shame pierced him. He'd told Candace he would be at Jennie's doctor's appointment.

She was going to be furious—and how could he blame her?

If he left now, he'd make the tail end of the appointment and be able to speak to the doctor about Jennie himself. Snatching up his suit jacket from where he'd slung it over the chair back, Nick swiveled on his heel and headed for the door.

"Nick!"

He kept walking as Desmond's voice called out from behind him, "If you don't stop right now, I'll start negotiating the stock sale."

Nick cast a glance over his shoulder. Desmond had risen to his feet, his face red with frustrated anger. It gave Nick an immense amount of satisfaction to say, "Do what you must, but you'll have to excuse me, I have something more important to deal with right now."

Nick watched frustration and rage darken Desmond's face to the color of a tomato. Quite suddenly, the other man no longer resembled Santa.

Four

Candace *was* furious with him.

It wasn't apparent from what she said, but rather from the overly cool, calm manner in which she had greeted his arrival. Nick decided he would've preferred it if she'd raged at him. Instead he was conscious of the chasm of chilly disapproval that divided them.

After leaving the doctor's rooms, Nick had given the keys to the Ferrari to Mr. Busby to take home and loaded Candace and Jennie into the more conservative Daimler, which at least provided space for Jennie's car seat. Rather ironically, Nick planned to buy Candace coffee from the café at the closest Valentine's—which had been the topic of his recent argument with Desmond.

Nick hoped the parklike surroundings and pretty gardens would pacify her—and he figured he owed her some sort of explanation.

"I'm sorry," he said finally, stopping at a crossing to allow a group of boys to wheel their bikes across.

"Sorry?" She turned her head. The eyes that clashed with his radiated silver-white heat that her cool civility couldn't cloak.

Incongruously, the heat caused desire to leap in his gut.

"I mean it." He'd never apologized to Jilly in the seven years they'd been married. Not for arriving home when dinner had congealed on the plates. Not when he'd left her standing on her own at one of the society events that were so important to her. Not even when he'd missed Jennie's birth—although that had been the one time that he'd come close.

He'd figured there was no point apologizing for anything to a woman who'd charmed her father into trapping the bridegroom she'd wanted at all costs. Saying *sorry* would've been a lie.

This was different.

"I suppose you had some life-threatening crisis at work?" she said.

Nick thought of Desmond's threat to sell Jilly's stock in Valentine's as he pulled away from the crossing. "Something like that."

"That's what I expected."

It was the weary, defeated note in Candace's voice that caused Nick to throw her a quick, sharp glance before focusing back on the road ahead. "I got there, didn't I?"

"Halfway through the deferred appointment, if that's what you mean."

He'd cursed the city traffic all the way. Now she couldn't even thank him for almost killing himself to get there. "The baby is fine. The doctor couldn't find anything wrong."

"But what if she hadn't been?"

Her tone was full of suppressed anger and disappointment and…some other emotion he couldn't name.

Why was this so important to her?

There was no point arguing. Yet a twinge of shame twisted deep within him. Nick nosed the car into a side lane and turned into the parking lot beyond. After bringing the Daimler to a halt he switched it off and changed the subject. "This is one of my centers. There's a café that overlooks a lake. Let me buy you a coffee."

She wrapped her arms around her middle and turned her head away so he couldn't read those all-too-expressive eyes. "Nick, I don't need you to buy me a coffee. I needed you to be there for Jennie."

"Maybe Jennie would like to see the ducks."

That evoked a response, though not one that he wanted to answer. "Is that the real reason we're here? Because you want to show Jennie the ducks?"

Nick searched her frozen features for sarcasm, but couldn't find any. "My first thought was that I owed you an apology." He spread his hands. "But it *is* a good place to show Jennie some ducks. I can't wait to see her face. She's going to love it."

It was the truth. To Nick's immense surprise, he was looking forward to watching Jennie's reaction.

The baby's birth had unleashed a startling realization of all that was wrong in his life. Beginning with his sham marriage to Jilly. A deal to which he should never have agreed.

"Nick…"

The uncertain note in Candace's voice captured his attention. The stiffness had left her face, although her arms were still wrapped protectively around herself. "Yes?"

"You and I need to talk."

Her expression told him that she wasn't looking forward to whatever she wanted to talk to him about. After a second's pause, Nick instinctively knew what it was about.

Damn, he should never have given in to that wild, insane urge to kiss her. God knew what she was making of his bringing her here for coffee.

Dismissively he said, "You're making too much out of the fact that I want to buy you coffee to apologize. This isn't a date…or any attempt to change the footing of our relationship to anything more personal—you don't need to worry about that."

Nick knew he was lying through his teeth. Despite his promise that there would be no more kisses, he hungered to kiss her again, and see if she tasted as good as he remembered.

But she was good for Jennie…and he needed her for Jennie's sake. He couldn't afford to screw it all up and have her leave.

He could sense her stiffening in the seat beside him, and Jennie didn't help matters by letting out a squawk from the rear seat. "I never thought this was a date," Candace told him with an edge in her voice.

"Then what do you want to talk about?"

"You and Jennie—but now is probably not a good time. Jennie wants out of the car."

Candace scrambled from the Daimler as if she couldn't wait to escape the cocoon of the car's interior, and the passenger door slammed behind her.

Nick gritted his teeth. Okay, so he'd sure got that wrong. Badly. Sex was the last thing on her mind. Whereas he couldn't think of much else. All he could think about was repeating the "mistake" they'd made the night before.

Except Nick couldn't view that kiss as a mistake. Unprofessional? Hell, yes. But a mistake? No way.

Nick had always gone after what he wanted. And right now he wanted Candace. But he didn't want to spook her and lose her. Nor could he rid himself of the wriggle of discomfort over his ruthless desire to seduce someone who worked for him. He'd never been tempted to do anything like that before.

But then again he'd never experienced anything like this.

He wanted Jennie's nanny.

And what was more, he was certain Candace desired him, too, despite her cool annoyance. The challenge lay in getting her to admit her desire—especially after all the lengths he'd gone to in order to convince her that he wasn't interested.

Yet Candace wanted to talk about him and Jennie, the last thing Nick wanted. He *never* talked about Jennie—about his suspicions that she wasn't really his daughter.

By the time Nick had gotten himself firmly back in control, Candace had already taken Jennie out of the rear car seat. Nick pressed the key fob to open the trunk, hoisted the stroller out and unfolded it.

He took Jennie from Candace and lowered her into the stroller. She let out a howl of protest and went rigid.

"Hey," he chided her, "stop that."

The objection grew more vociferous.

Nick shot Candace a helpless glance. She was watching him through narrowed eyes—okay, so he was on his own. He transferred his attention back to Jennie; he wasn't about to let a baby defeat him.

"Come on, missy, be still. Let me buckle you in."

Jennie let out a yell of objection. It was clear to Nick—and to anyone who cared to listen—that she had no intention of submitting to being strapped into the stroller. Time to change tactics.

"After we show you the ducks I'll take you up to the café. You can have a treat—an ice cream," he said craftily.

Jennie greeted his bribe with the contempt it deserved and simply shrieked more loudly.

"You little hellion," he told her softly, his admiration growing in leaps and bounds.

The noise stopped abruptly. Eyeing him assessingly, Jennie cooed and blew a raspberry.

Nick couldn't help himself—he laughed, then leaned down and planted a kiss on her plump cheek. It was soft, like a peach. A wave of emotion rushed through him.

What did it matter if she wasn't his child? No one except he would ever know that Jilly had played him for a fool.

There was no point in maintaining the distance he'd been keeping from Jennie. She didn't deserve to suffer; after all, she was the only innocent party in the entire mess.

And if he wanted, she could be his. All his.

"You *are* a hellion," he said, impressed.

She gave him a gummy smile and capitulated, allowing him to put her into the stroller.

In that moment Nick felt his heart constrict and he fell irrevocably in love.

"You're also a wicked flirt," he scolded Jennie as the clip for the restraining strap locked into place.

A movement out the corner of his eye had him lifting his head. Candace was watching them. The look in her eyes was full of yearning, but as she caught him studying her, shutters dropped into place.

It was possible that Candace was as ready as he to take their relationship to its inevitable conclusion. Yet Nick suspected that Candace would want more than simply sex. And while he could never tell her the true reason why he'd held Jennie at a distance, it might help to divulge the precarious position he was in with Valentine's. It wouldn't be easy to share that knowledge; he'd always handled his problems by himself, in his own way. He'd never been the kind of man who shared his concerns.

Maybe it was time to let a little of his tightly leashed control slip.

The idea of letting his control slip became even more attractive as Nick followed Candace through the rose-covered archway and down the pathway to the landscaped parklands by the lake. He couldn't help but notice the pert curve of her bottom under the fitted, narrow black jeans. Her long legs picked up speed when the path dipped as they approached the water's edge, causing the stroller to roll faster and faster. In the breeze her blond hair streamed like a banner over her shoulders.

When he caught up to her at the edge of the lake, she wasn't even breathing hard.

"This is a wonderful spot." She knelt down and pointed at the water. "See the ducks, Jennie?"

At last he'd done something she approved of. Nick couldn't stop the surge of pleasure.

Jennie was sitting bolt upright, starfish fingers pushing on the arms of the stroller, her eyes wide with excitement.

For the first time since leaving his office, Nick started to relax. This might work. There was still a chance for them... for him and Jennie.

More than a chance.

Resolve set in and Nick's jaw firmed. He had a responsibility to Jennie. He'd agreed to donate his seed for the baby Jilly wanted, even though he knew, almost to the day, that Jilly had changed her mind. She'd stopped talking about *their* baby... started talking about *her* baby. Initially, it hadn't sunk in that she'd found another donor...a lover. Hindsight was twenty-twenty.

Yet after Jilly's return from the fertility clinic on the Southeast Asian island of Namkhet, he'd been sure of it. It wasn't his sperm that had impregnated Jilly....

But Nick no longer cared. All that mattered was the baby leaning forward in the stroller, her eyes gleaming with delight. So vital and full of life. The child everyone believed to be his daughter. He spared a glance at the woman kneeling beside the stroller. Candace had made her opinion clear—he didn't deserve Jennie. But what did her opinion matter? Jennie could be his daughter...all he needed to do was accept her. He'd already made a start. It was proving to be much easier than he'd imagined—and the rewards were pure pleasure.

And little Jennie didn't know it was a lie. To Jennie he was the only father she'd known.

Nick vowed that he would *make* it work. He would prove Candace wrong. He was the only family Jennie had.

A pair of black swans glided toward them, long necks gracefully arched. Candace started to smile as Jennie beat her arms up and down and let out a squeak. Even Nick grinned at the baby's antics.

"Sorry, no food." Candace spread her hands out as the swans slowed in front of them.

"Look, there are even eels," Nick said as an inquisitive nose poked out the water. "See?" Jennie was all eyes. "Want to take a closer look?"

Not liking the sound of that, Candace said quickly, "She's fine in the stroller."

But Nick ignored her warning and unclipped the restraint. "Come on," he told Jennie. "I'll show you."

Jennie hung out of his arms as he hoisted her up, her arms flapping frantically. Little breathless puffs of baby excitement filled the air, and Candace clambered to her feet. "Nick, this isn't a good idea—"

"Don't be such a killjoy!"

Ducks crowded around, craning their necks, beady eyes fixed on him. In the water, the swans paddled in one spot. Nick laughed, shrugging aside the cautioning hand Candace placed on his arm Jennie gurgled with unrestrained glee.

"Just look at her." With Nick reveling in the baby's amazement, Candace didn't have the heart to spoil the moment. "Next time we'll bring bread," he promised the baby.

More ducks were scrambling out of the water.

"Nick, that's probably close enough." Candace cast an anxious glance at the water's edge. "Those are geese coming— and they can be quite aggressive."

"Jennie's having the time of her life. And so am I."

There was no suitable response to that. Candace let out the breath she was holding and tried to stop hyperventilating about the way Jennie was hanging over his arm. He wouldn't drop the baby, she told herself. He really wouldn't...

So why couldn't she relax? She ought to be thrilled Nick was having such fun with Jennie, yet Candace couldn't stop fretting as she cast a wary glance along the grassy bank to the trio of advancing, honking geese.

In Nick's arms Jennie gave a squawk. The geese slowed. He chuckled. "That's my girl. Give 'em hell!"

Candace frowned, but forced herself to bite her lip and say nothing.

"Look—" Nick took a step forward and pointed "—more ducks."

Unable to stop herself, Candace hurried up beside him. "Careful, don't drop the baby!"

Nick returned his hand to Jennie's waist, anchoring her securely against him. To Candace's increasing annoyance, he ignored her and murmured to Jennie, "Those are woodland ducks. I used to feed ones just like that in the creek near my grandmother's cottage when I was a boy."

After a second, Candace's curiosity got the better of her. She knew so little about Nick, and what she'd read in the business newspapers and gossip pages mentioned nothing about a grandmother. It made him seem more human. "You lived with your grandmother?"

"Yes, she was a tough lady with a heart of gold. She never complained when I'd sneak a loaf out of the pantry to feed the ducks, even when times were tight." Hitching Jennie higher up against his shoulder, he said, "What about seeing if there's anything on the café's menu that's suitable for Jennie?"

Candace waved to the stroller where it stood surrounded by ducks. "I've got a tumbler with diluted juice she can have, and some apple slices...if the ducks haven't gotten to them. We don't need to go to the café."

"I still owe you a coffee by way of an apology."

Candace gave him a measuring look "Oh, all right then." Then realizing he might well be affronted by her lack of enthusiasm, she added, "That would be nice." And it would have the added bonus of getting them away from the water's edge where Jennie's flock of new feathered friends hovered.

She held out her arms for the baby. Nick hesitated for a fraction of a second, then surrendered Jennie. Candace stepped backward.

"Careful!"

Nick leaped forward as she stumbled. Candace teetered, grabbing at him with one hand, clinging to the baby with the other, her eyes fixing on Nick in fright.

"Jennie!" she pleaded.

For a split second Candace was aware of the solid warmth of his body, the heavy thud of his heart, before the sobs of her own panicky breath drowned it all out, and Nick's arms locked around Jennie. Jennie was safe.

To Candace's horror, Nick started to slide along the grassy bank down to the water, Jennie still clasped in his arms. He landed with a dull splash, feetfirst in knee-deep water.

The baby didn't even squeak. Instead, Jennie was hanging over his arm, reaching for the surface of the lake.

Nick was laughing. "None of that," he said as Jennie flapped her arms furiously, frantically trying to free herself from his grasp. "No swimming today."

Candace didn't think it was the least bit funny.

Yet looking down at Nick, water rippling around his suit pants, his Italian shoes totally submerged beneath the lake's reflective surface, she felt a stab of totally inappropriate desire. Jennie had almost landed in the lake, and she was lusting after Nick Valentine?

What was wrong with her?

"That was close!" she said, as her breathing slowed.

Nick chucked the little imp under her chin and Jennie gave him a toothless smile.

"She's fine."

She forgot that he'd swept the baby to safety. Anxiety and lust coalesced into anger. "It's not funny—she could've fallen in."

His smile faded. In a blink he was back to the distant, narrow-eyed businessman. "I wouldn't have you drop her."

She suppressed the flare of resentment at his suggestion that *she'd* almost dropped Jennie, when *he'd* been the one to take the baby out of the stroller in the first place. "You might not have been able to stop it."

"I would've done everything in my power."

Nick placed one foot on the bank, Jennie still squirming in his hold. "Hey, stop it, miss. You *will* end up going swimming if you carry on like that!"

"Nick!"

At her warning shriek, Nick glanced up.

"Look out!" Candace was almost incoherent with apprehension. *"The geese."*

He jerked his head around as Jennie's fingers jabbed in the direction of a goose who'd silently paddled up behind them. He swung the baby away, but it was too late. Jennie's wail rent the air.

Rushing to the water's edge, Candace blocked his way as Nick clambered back onto the bank.

Jennie was screaming, her face cherry-red with protest, her hand limp.

Candace reached for the pecked fingers. "Let me see!" Her head bent over Jennie's reddened finger. "Ouch."

"The skin's not broken."

His words set a torch to her already frayed emotions. "Don't be so callous!" Nick started to object, but she overrode him. "It's going to need cleaning. Heaven knows what might've been in that bird's beak."

"The café has a bathroom where you can clean it up, and I've got a first-aid kit with some antiseptic in the trunk of my car."

Candace glared at him. "I've got a rudimentary first-aid kit in the stroller—enough to deal with this." She drew a shuddering breath, stunned at how quickly everything had happened—and at the extent of her fear. "Jennie should not have been taken out of the stroller."

Nick stared at Candace in disbelief. *Now it's my fault? She wanted to get out.*

"She could see perfectly well from where she was."

"You're overreacting," he said tersely.

A fresh wave of anger flooded her. "She got hurt because of *you*."

"Oh, please. That kind of thing is a normal part of growing up. It happens." He was studying her in a way that made her grow tense. "You're shaken up. I'll take Jennie and clean her up."

What was he getting at? Was he implying she was too emotional to do her job, to look after Jennie? "I'll do it! You can bring the stroller and the first-aid kit."

To Candace's distress, Jennie's wails grew louder as they stormed along the winding pathway up the rise to the café. The little body huddled against her was rigid with outrage.

As he waited for Candace to return from tending to Jennie's pecked finger, Nick couldn't stop thinking about Jennie's puckered-up little face glaring at him accusingly over Candace's shoulder as she'd been borne away.

Candace was right.

Jennie had been hurt.

And he could've—should've—avoided it.

Sometime in the past twenty-four hours he'd connected with Jennie. Nick silently promised himself that in the future he was going to make sure he spent more time with the baby so innocent of the treachery surrounding her conception. And, as little as he wanted to admit it right now, he had Candace to thank for opening his eyes to the fact that his life—what was important in it—was getting away from him.

By the time Candace and Jennie joined him at the table in the sunny sheltered spot outside the café, Jennie had stopped crying. After Candace secured her in the stroller, the baby lay back and focused intently on the Micky Mouse Band-Aid wrapped around her finger.

Nick winced. "Is it very bruised?"

"A little red. But no bruising—and no blood."

"That's a relief."

A black-skirted waitress who'd been hovering while Nick waited took their coffee order. As an afterthought, Candace added a request for biscotti.

"Jennie will enjoy chewing it—the teeth coming through have been niggling her."

Nick glanced at the baby. The stroller had been angled so the hot February sun didn't fall on Jennie's face, but her eyelids were drooping. "The biscotti might have to wait. She looks sleepy."

Candace leaned forward across him and a hint of that sexy, spicy perfume wafted over Nick. It was becoming all too familiar—and so was the intoxicating effect her closeness had on his senses. He inhaled slowly and resisted the urge to stroke back the curl that had fallen over her face.

"She's already asleep." Candace couldn't hide her astonishment. "The shock and tears must've tired her out."

Nick sensed implied accusation. "It's been a long morning for her—an outing to the doctor, the ride in the car, the fresh air and the excitement of seeing the ducks. It all added up." He fixed his gaze on Candace, challenging her to mention the mishap with the goose.

Her lips pursed and she sat up straight. "There's something you need to know."

Folding his arms behind his head, Nick rocked back on his chair and gave her a lazy smile. "What is that?"

"I haven't been completely honest with you."

His smile disappeared. "What do you mean?"

Nick thought about Candace's alarm when the goose pecked Jennie. It had hardly been the cool composure he would've expected from a nurse. Alison had sworn her references had been top rate. Was she a fraud? Not a nurse at all? Had she taken his sister in? "Don't tell me. Not only are you not a nanny, you're not a nurse, either."

"I *am* a nurse—I'm fully qualified to take care of Jennie," she said quickly.

The way his stomach dropped forced Nick to take a steadying breath. How bad could it be? "Spit it out."

"I'm Jennie's biological mother."

Nick blinked. Whatever he'd expected, it wasn't this. It took a moment for him to absorb her statement, and once he'd digested it, the tension in his belly unwound like a compressed spring uncurling and he let out a shout of laughter. "Don't be absurd!"

"I'm not being absurd. I *am* Jennie's mother."

Nick took in the set of her pink mouth, the sparkle in her eyes—and lust, wholly unwelcome, surged in his groin. Giving her a slow smile, he lowered his voice and murmured, "Do you honestly believe I would've forgotten making love to you?"

"No!" A flush stained her cheeks. "I don't mean you…" Her voice trailed away.

"Yet you claim to be Jennie's mother."

Disappointment flooded Nick. The woman might look like an angel, but she was the worst kind of fraud. A fallen angel. He didn't know what she was after yet, but Nick was sure he would find out. All it would take was patience—and he'd always possessed plenty of that. He settled down to play her for all he was worth.

"Yes, but—"

"But? You're suddenly no longer so certain?" Nick raised an eyebrow to express his disbelief. As she rushed into speech, he raised a hand to cut her off. "Before you sink yourself any further, you should know that even though I was away on a string of business trips *while Jilly was pregnant*," he emphasized, "I certainly *never* messed around during my marriage."

"I'm not implying—"

"Then what are you suggesting?" he asked silkily.

"Jilly is not the baby's mother. I am."

She spoke Jilly's name with easy familiarity. As if she'd known her...

Nick's eyes narrowed.

Was it possible that the connection between the women was his late wife's lover—Jennie's father? Was that what this whole charade of pretending to be Jennie's mother was all about? This must be what she'd been hinting at when she'd told him earlier that she wanted to talk to him about Jennie.

"So let me get this straight. Are you trying to say that Jennie was switched at birth?" Nick drawled.

"No."

"What do you mean, 'no'?"

"I agreed to be a surrogate mom."

It wasn't possible. Candace had to be lying!

Nick's initial amusement had been replaced by impatience. He knew she was going to lose this battle. The sooner he got this crazy woman out of Jennie's life the better. "Look, I don't have time for this—"

"You don't have time for your daughter's mother?"

He'd had enough. Nick rolled his eyes and rose to his feet. Taking his wallet, he drew out a fifty-dollar bill and a business card. He held them out to her. "For a cab—when you leave. But first go to my office, it's in the block at the entrance. My assistant will have a check ready by the time you get there, together with severance pay. I'll call her now to arrange it."

Candace made no move to take the card or the money. He shrugged and dropped them on the table. A downward glance revealed that Jennie was still asleep in the stroller. If luck was on his side she'd remain that way until he'd gotten her home and called an employment agency to hire a new nanny—one he'd vet himself this time. If worse came to worst, he'd call his sister.

He wheeled the stroller to the cashier inside the café, greeted her by name and asked her to call a cab. Without question she reached for the phone. Nick smiled and waved to the manager on the opposite side of the coffee shop, and pushed Jennie back out into the sunshine.

"Wait."

A hand came down on his arm. Nick brushed her off and kept walking, stroller trundling in front of him. About twenty yards down the path, Candace rushed in front of him, blocking his way, and this time she grabbed his arm with enough force to ensure he wouldn't easily shake her off.

Her eyes were intense and angry, spitting smoke. "You're firing me? For being Jennie's mother?"

Nick glared back at her. "I might not have been there at Jennie's birth, but I sure as hell saw that Jilly was pregnant! I'm firing you for being a charlatan…a liar…a fraud. Take your pick. Just count yourself lucky you hadn't raised the issue of money yet or we could've added blackmailer to the list."

He glanced pointedly down at feminine fingers spread on his arm, but what she said brought his eyes back to her face in shock.

"DNA tests don't lie."

Five

"You have a DNA test proving you are Jennie's mother?"

"Not anymore," Candace said, and felt Nick's forearm tense beneath her fingertips.

"So you are lying!"

"I don't have them—they'll be in the doctor's file. One thing I'm not is a liar." Then she tacked on, "Or a fraud."

Candace could feel the heat in her cheeks as she belatedly snatched her hand off the fine wool of Nick's suit jacket. Even through the fabric she'd been uncomfortably conscious of the warmth of his body.

She drew a second deep breath, desperately trying to calm herself down. She couldn't let him keep Jennie. He wasn't worthy of being Jennie's—any baby's—father. But it wouldn't help to get his back up.

"Okay, maybe I handled this badly," she said slowly. "You made me mad."

"*I* made *you* mad?" He was frowning down at her. "Lady, I'm not the crazy one around here."

Crazy? Candace squinted up at him. "I'm not crazy."

Nick didn't bother to answer. Instead, he wheeled the stroller—with her baby—away. Candace rushed after him. "Where are you taking Jennie?"

"Home!"

"Home? That glossy mansion that's as cold as an icicle isn't a home." Nick kept walking away from her. In desperation she said, "You're not fit to be Jennie's father!"

At that his shoulders stiffened and he slowed.

Oh, no! So much for trying not to antagonize him. Well, she had no choice now but to soldier on. "Nick, you've been away for the past month, you didn't even return home when Jennie was desperately ill and you know nothing about caring for her. What else could I think?"

He turned. There was a white line around his mouth, and his face was leached of all color. "I've had enough of this. You will never get the chance to take her away—and even if I accepted a word of your insane claim, my first question would be where the hell were you when Jennie needed a mother?"

He'd homed in on the heart of her pain—her guilt. "That's not fair—I had no choice."

Nick glared. "I still don't believe a word of this."

Candace hesitated. She'd known from that first heart-in-her-throat moment when she'd met him that her name had meant nothing to Nick. Candace wasn't a common name, yet he hadn't even done a double take when he'd said, "You must be Candace."

For one wild instant she'd thought he was pretending. Yet even when she'd revealed her surname, his expression hadn't changed. And finally she realized that Nick Valentine had never bothered to find out the identity of his baby's egg donor and surrogate mother. And now he was making out as though he knew nothing about it all…

Jilly had made it clear that he was a busy man, and Candace had slowly pieced together the image of a driven, workaholic husband who cared more for his multimillion-dollar company than his wife. Jilly had assured her that was all going to change when the baby was born.

Yet Nick Valentine had shown no interest in Candace's pregnancy—unlike Jilly, who'd traveled all the way to the exclusive Namkhet Island clinic to be there while the IVF took place, who'd kept every prenatal appointment once they'd gotten back home to New Zealand, who'd visited Candace every week and bought her treats, and loved showing her photos of the nursery she was preparing for Jennie.

Right from the outset Jilly had explained that Nick hadn't wanted to meet the surrogate...that he wanted to imagine the child as his wife's. Candace had accepted the explanation. She'd so badly wanted to be convinced that she'd done the right thing—even after the stomach-churning second thoughts had started to creep in.

Now she challenged him. "You can't walk away—this is too important. You must listen to me."

"Okay, you've got my attention..." he glanced at his watch "...for one minute."

That was better than nothing. Speaking rapidly, she said, "Jennie's a baby. She needs a parent. I gave her to you and Jilly. I *trusted* you to look after her...to love her and—"

"You *gave* her to me and Jilly?" Nick hooted with derisive laughter.

Something wasn't adding up. "You and Jilly needed a surrogate," Candace said slowly.

"Stop this!" His brows jerked together and glared at her again. "I'm not listening to any more of your crazy creations. My wife was pregnant... I witnessed her debilitating morning sickness, saw the pregnancy develop. Jilly gave birth to Jennie."

Jilly hadn't been pregnant!

Candace couldn't help herself. "*You're* crazy." She advanced on the stroller that he'd let go and grasped the handles. "I'm not leaving Jennie alone with you."

He tussled with her and the stroller jerked.

"You're going to wake Jennie," she warned.

"If you think I'm going to let some deluded woman kidnap my daughter, you can think again."

"I have no intention of kidnapping her. I'm coming with you back to your home. I'm not letting Jennie out of my sight—and if you think you can brush me off, think again. I'll walk up to every customer in this garden center and tell them I'm your baby's mother and you're trying to pay me off."

He went very still. "Don't threaten me. I'll call the police."

"You think I'm bluffing? Do you really want to stage a scene here…and get the police involved?"

"We'll finish this discussion at the house." Nick gave her a killing glare, and Candace knew she'd won a temporary reprieve.

The drive back to the Valentine mansion passed in Arctic silence.

Once the tall, imposing electronic gates swung soundlessly shut behind them, Candace started to lose her nerve. What if Nick Valentine truly was crazy? What had she done to put herself—and Jennie—at his mercy?

The Daimler came to a stop behind a Lexus parked in the circular driveway edged by clipped boxwood hedging. The evidence that someone else was at Nick's house eased Candace's apprehension.

It would be okay; they would get this sorted out, she reassured herself. But whatever happened she wasn't abandoning her baby to Nick's negligent care. He might have all the money in the world, but she'd seen firsthand what kind of parent he was. She wasn't leaving Jennie alone with him.

A glance into the backseat showed that Jennie was still

sleeping. By the time Candace had gathered up the diaper bag at her feet, Nick had the rear door open and was carefully taking the baby out of the car. Watching him, Candace had to shove aside the momentary doubt that he was the uncaring, crazy man she knew him to be. Mr. Busby, Nick's chauffeur and handyman, had arrived and taken the stroller out of the trunk, and was carrying it up the white marble stairs to the front door.

Nick followed, cradling the baby. Jennie's mouth twitched in her sleep.

Mrs. Busby was standing inside the front door. "Mrs. Timmings is in the living room."

Relief filled Candace. Alison Timmings was a sensible woman—even if her brother was crazy.

"I'll take Jennie to the nursery." Nick's stare dared Candace to argue with him. To Mrs. Busby he added, "Tell my sister I won't be long, please."

"Nick?" In the archway that opened into the living room appeared the tall brunette that Candace had first met when Jennie was admitted to hospital while Nick was away. "I heard your voice. I tried your office, but Pauline said you'd left hours ago. Where have you been?"

Without waiting for an answer, Nick's sister came toward them, her high heels tapping on the marble tiles. She smiled a greeting to Candace before making a beeline for the baby in Nick's arms. "Hello, sweetheart."

Jennie woke and smiled at Alison, holding her short arms out wide.

Her aunt swept her up in a swarm of cooing sounds. Jennie immediately clutched a handful of pearls and thrust them into her mouth.

"Looks like she's teething, Nick." Alison rescued her necklace from the baby.

"It would appear so." He moved closer. "Here, give her to me."

"I'll take her." Candace came up on the other side of his sister.

"Thank you, Candace." Alison surrendered the baby gracefully. For a moment Candace thought Nick was going to object to her having possession of the child, but then his sister was saying, "It's not like you to swan out of the office."

"Hardly swanning—although we did see some black ones after I met Candace at the doctor's office for Jennie to be checked out."

"You took her back to the doctor? Is anything wrong?" Alison asked at once, glancing to Candace for a reply.

"No, Jennie's fine," said Candace soothingly. "She was restless last night, running a bit of a temperature, so I wanted to make sure there was no resurgence of the infection."

"You're so good to her."

"Thank you." She smiled at the other woman. "I'll take Jennie upstairs so you two can talk."

"Not so fast." Nick moved to obstruct her. "I'm not letting you go anywhere until we've finished our discussion."

What he meant was *I'm not letting you out of my sight,* Candace thought rebelliously.

His sister must've thought the same thing. "Nick, you're being rude—and you're frightening Candace."

Ignoring his sister's interjection, he gave her a mean stare. "She's not frightened enough."

"Nick!"

Even as Alison objected, Candace's heart sped up. She hugged Jennie tightly. "I'm not going to back down on the truth. You don't scare me."

Alison glanced from Candace to her brother. "What truth? Anyone care to fill me in about what's going on?"

"Candace claims she's Jennie's mother."

Nick's dismissive tone set Candace's teeth on edge. She still couldn't swallow that he hadn't known. "Claims? You *know* I'm Jennie's mother! You contracted me to donate the eggs and share my womb so you and Jilly could have the child she so desperately wanted."

"Contracted?" Nick gave a snort. "Why would I want to do that?"

Candace gave him a cold stare over the baby's head. "Because you and Jilly were unable to have your own child."

He stared. His features tightened. "IVF worked successfully for Jilly and me."

Jennie shifted restlessly in her arms and Candace unsuccessfully ducked her head sideways as Jennie grabbed a handful of her hair. When she'd extracted the strands from Jennie's hands she said, "Be honest. Jilly told me all about the struggles you were having—that IVF wasn't working. That's why the two of you decided to look for an egg donor, someone who could carry the baby for her. Which, of course, is where I came in."

Now both Nick and Alison were staring at her as if she'd grown two heads.

"What?" asked Candace. "Why are you looking at me like that?"

"It's true that the IVF didn't work in the initial attempts." Nick appeared to be picking his words with care. "But then Jilly tried a new procedure at an overseas clinic."

"What my brother is trying to say," cut in Alison, "is that Jilly was pregnant." With her arms she mimed a swollen belly. "Very pregnant. She gave birth—to Jennie."

Candace gaped at them both.

A vision of Jilly clad in black leggings and a belted long cardigan floated through her mind. Jilly had been reed slim when she'd excitedly assisted the midwife at Jennie's home birth in the cottage, and bore absolutely no resemblance to the rounded belly Alison had mimed.

Hitching Jennie higher against her shoulder, Candace said slowly, "That's not possible, because Jilly was *never* pregnant."

Alison stared at Nick and raised an eyebrow.

"She's crazy." Nick shrugged. "I've been saying exactly the same thing as you, Alison, but she won't let go of her delusion that Jilly was never pregnant—that *she's* Jennie's mother."

Confusion clouded Candace's brain, making it feel wooly. Was it possible that Nick Valentine and his wife had pulled off a spectacular deception, fooling even their own families that the baby was Jilly's? Had they gone as far as to fake Jilly's pregnancy? Placed padding beneath Jilly's clothing to fool everyone—even Alison? That was crazy!

Candace struggled to put her chaotic thoughts in order.

What would be the point of such a massive deception? Nick was a wealthy man, and Jilly had made it clear that Candace could name her price for her kindness, though, of course, Candace had refused all Jilly's generous offers. It was, after all, illegal in New Zealand to be paid to be a surrogate. She'd done it because Jilly had been so desperate. As a pediatric nurse, Candace had never met a woman more deserving of a baby. Her heart had gone out to the other woman as they'd become friends.

"Perhaps Mrs. Busby could make us all a cup of tea. I'll see to it." Alison cast her brother a look that Candace couldn't interpret. "I'll also call the doctor just to check that Jennie is really going to be okay."

Had Alison decided that Candace was unhinged? Was that the reason for the secret exchange of glances, for the call to the doctor?

"Yes, by all means let's call the doctor." Candace pressed a kiss on top of Jennie's downy head, then lifted her lashes and gave Nick her most dulcet smile. "And while you're at it why don't you call Jilly's doctor to clear up once and for all the small matter of who really is Jennie's mother. Ask for a copy of the DNA report that was done once the pregnancy was confirmed."

* * *

"The DNA report?"

Nick stared at Candace in disbelief. Was she going to persist with this? Of course there was no DNA report. An urge to snatch the baby out of her arms overwhelmed him. He quashed it. To do so would reveal how deeply her mad claims were unsettling him. Far better to play it cool.

Candace's eyebrows lowered. "All I want is for you to give me a chance to prove I'm telling the truth. The doctor should have a copy of the results of the DNA tests that were done after Jennie was born as part of the terms of the surrogacy agreement—" She broke off as he rolled his eyes skyward. "You still think I'm lying!"

"I don't know anything about postbirth DNA tests or a surrogacy agreement. Don't you think that's a little strange?"

She was chewing her lip. *That mouth.* Heat popped in his groin. God!

"You're not drawing me into another debate where you clearly have no intention of conceding anything. All I want is for you to see the test results."

Was that really all Candace wanted? After all, if she'd been telling the truth, it wouldn't be an unreasonable request. Except it was a lie—it had to be. Yet she was still gnawing her lip and her eyes were troubled. She didn't look like a fraud... or a crazy. She looked worried.

And he wanted her more than ever.

Nick sucked in a deep breath. He had to get over this.

She might look like a worried angel, but how could he trust his reactions? Sure, she was lovely. And sure he desired her. Right now his priority had to be Jennie.

Still, what if Candace was telling the truth?

He tried to think sanely. Why was he so sure that everything Jilly told him was the truth and Candace's claim was pure fiction? He'd witnessed Jilly's blossoming body...that was indisputable. Yet he'd never gone with her to the doctor. Never seen her naked or touched her burgeoning belly. He'd been so certain the baby wasn't his...

In the past, Jilly had gotten what she wanted at all costs. What if...

He shied away from the thought. Jilly didn't deserve this. She was dead. Yet the distress in Candace's eyes niggled at him.

"Call the doctor," she insisted.

Nick excused himself. It took only a few minutes for him to ascertain what he'd already suspected. There was no DNA report—and Jilly's doctor had never heard of Candace. Although he did remind Nick that Jilly had used a gynecologist and midwife for the birth, and they might know more.

Nick didn't need to call them. He already knew the truth. And he took great pleasure in returning to the sitting area and confronting Candace with it. "The doctor knows nothing about a test."

"There *was* a DNA test done." She lifted her chin. "But if you want, we can redo the tests...it doesn't take long to get a result." Nick narrowed his gaze as she said, glancing down at the oversize bargain watch on her slender wrist, "Too late today, but no reason why we can't have it done on Monday."

Over his dead body were they having DNA tests done on Monday—or any other day.

There was no way that Nick was going to allow Candace to expose the real lie he'd been living. He was not Jennie's father; his wife had taken a lover.

Nick was not about to let this woman—a woman who turned his body in knots—make him the laughingstock of the city.

At the same moment as he said, "That won't be necessary," Alison—who'd come back into the room without his noticing—chimed in, "A DNA test is the perfect solution. It will answer all our questions, won't it, Nick?"

The impulse to throttle his sister, which Nick hadn't felt since adolescence, rose. "I can handle this, Alison."

She threw her hands into the air. "Of course you can. And you expect me to butt out, right?"

Nick gave her a sharp frown. He didn't have time for one of his sister's diatribes about what she considered his fear of intimacy. "I said not now, Alison."

"Don't get impatient with me." She picked her bag up and stalked toward the archway leading to the lobby. "I'm off. If you want my opinion—which you clearly don't—I think you should have that DNA test done. It's the only way you're going to know whether Candace is telling the truth or not."

Nick spared a glare for the woman who'd caused all the trouble. To his great annoyance, Jennie had snuggled up against Candace and was resting her cheek against the black T-shirt she wore. The pair looked like a modern take on Madonna and Child. Nick gnashed his teeth. "Of course Candace isn't telling the truth—and I've got Jennie's birth certificate listing me and Jilly as her parents to prove it." But Alison had already left.

"DNA doesn't lie." Candace spoke into the silence that simmered after his sister's departure. "A birth certificate can be tampered with."

Annoyance rose within Nick. "Are you accusing me of tampering with the system?"

Candace muttered something about money talking, and Nick could feel his anger growing. She was boxing him into a corner, forcing him into a place where he was going to have to agree to the test to expose her as a fraud.

Yet watching her, her head bent over the baby's, caused his anger to dissipate. Only the raw throb of betrayal remained. He wanted her…hell, he'd been growing to like her. The combination had been so seductively powerful, so consuming, he'd been ready to open himself to her…more than he ever had to any other woman.

A sense of emptiness filled him. Why had she done it? Candace didn't appear unstable. In fact, she seemed heart-wrenchingly attached to Jennie. Nick abandoned his musing. What did it matter what her motivation was?

The test would prove her a liar. Conclusively. And then he would sever all ties with no looking back.

The house was still when the darkness of midnight was broken by the silver streak of light pouring through the crack of the opening door.

Nick moved restlessly.

She came to him, floating soundlessly across the carpet like a wraith in the night. He shifted, and miraculously she was beside him, naked, eager. Her mouth covered his. Hunger rose swift and sharp. *He needed this.* And she understood.

He took her mouth, plundered it. His fingers sank into her shoulders, holding her captive. She shifted against him with one of those little catlike moves he'd seen her do, and his body went crazy.

He forgot how long it had been…

He forgot that she was a fraud he was determined to expose. He forgot everything except that he had a woman in his bed, a woman he wanted with an unfamiliar desperation.

She twisted beneath him. A silent lover, no sighs or moans split the night. Her legs tangled with his. He grasped her thighs, pushed them apart and sank between them into the moist, waiting heat of her.

His spine arched, his body driving.

Gasping, Nick opened his eyes, blind to everything except the excruciating need that pumped through him as his seed spilled.

A band of bright light fell across the bed from the open door of the en suite. Nick tensed. He reached out a hand. The bed was empty. He groped further, his fingers encountering cool, smooth sheets. Not fabric rumpled by passion.

Where the hell had she gone?

He rolled over onto his stomach, burying his face in the silk fabric, his sleep-numbed brain trying to make sense of what the hell had happened. The sheet smelled of soap and lavender; no hint of her spicy, slightly exotic fragrance lingered. The only softness a plump abandoned feather pillow, damp and crumpled.

He swore viciously.

More asleep than awake, he swung his legs out and stumbled from the bed to the bathroom. In the shower cubicle, he turned the faucets on and let the force of the cold water crash over his overheated body.

He refused to yield to the desire that still raged through him. He told himself it had all been an illusion, nothing but a cruel trick played on him by his starved libido. No woman could ever be as good as a man's desperate fantasy.

Not even Candace…

Six

His arms folded behind his head, Nick leaned back in the leather chair behind the walnut desk in the study that was his only retreat in a house Jilly had created and furnished with help from an expensive design team. It was Tuesday evening, and Candace was still living in his home.

He hadn't figured out what her motivation was for lying about being Jennie's mother—nor had she given up on her insistence that she was.

The other thing that hadn't changed was that he still craved her with a hunger that made absolutely no sense. Nick couldn't believe he was fantasizing about a woman whom he should be kicking out.

The past few days had been hell.

Every now and then a flash of that crazy dream would creep insidiously into his brain before he could banish it. *Traitor.*

First thing yesterday morning Nick had ordered Busby to drive Jennie and Candace to his doctor, where the swabs for DNA tests had been taken.

Candace had shown no surprise when he'd bowed out, inventing a meeting to attend. Yet while being thankful that she wasn't suspicious of his reasons for absenting himself, Nick couldn't help feeling that he'd given Candace more ammunition for her belief that he was an unfit father for Jennie.

But he'd been eager to avoid questions about why he wouldn't give a sample. A call to his doctor had satisfied Nick that it wasn't necessary. Buccal samples taken from Candace and Jennie by mouth swabs would be sufficient to establish with certainty that Candace wasn't, in fact, Jennie's mother. Even though his doctor had suggested that the result would be more conclusive had his DNA been available to be matched, Nick had chosen to ignore that advice.

Now, with the samples taken and the results from the diagnostic laboratory fast-tracked and due any minute, Nick had been tensing every time his cell phone beeped.

He couldn't make up his mind what he wanted more: for Candace's claim to be true, proving she hadn't lied, or for it to be false so that he could be rid of her, once and for all.

Without a shadow of a doubt, Nick knew which would be the easier solution to deal with. Getting Candace out of Jennie's life—out of his own—and returning to the even keel of his existence was what they both needed.

So why did that leave him feeling so…flat?

Nick stared sightlessly at the two antique botanical watercolors that flanked the study door. They'd belonged to Henry. Instead of selling them, the old man had insisted on gifting them to Nick. Usually the pictures gave him an immense sense of satisfaction and accomplishment.

But today all he could think of was Candace. Of how she'd disrupted his life and turned his world upside down. He wasn't going to allow her to unravel Jennie's world, too.

When he'd called his assistant yesterday morning to tell her he wouldn't be in for the day, there'd been utter silence on the other side of the line before Pauline had asked if he was ill. Only then did Nick realize that in all the years Pauline had worked for him he'd never taken a day off—the only time he didn't go in to work was when he was out of the country on business trips. Hell, he hadn't even taken time off for a honeymoon after he'd married Jilly. Much to his new bride's tearful dismay.

But there'd been no need for a honeymoon and all the trappings of romance. He'd been nothing more than his bride's bought husband—and he hadn't intended to prop up the pretense with a fake honeymoon.

Jilly's expectations had been suffocating. She'd wanted a pet. A husband who came when she crooked her finger, who mated on demand—one she could trot out and show off to her friends. Her attempts to domesticate him had had the effect of driving him away to seek his freedom in the corporate corridors she avoided and the boxing gym she despised.

Despite his romantic surname, Jilly had made a horrible mistake. He'd never been cut out to be the trophy husband she'd mistakenly believed she could groom him to be.

The phone rang.

Nick rocked forward in the chair and picked up the handset.

Within seconds his hands were clenched around the instrument in a stranglehold. "Almost a hundred percent likelihood that she is Jennie's biological mother!" he exclaimed. "How is that possible?"

The laboratory didn't have an explanation—other than the unwelcome suggestion that Candace was, in fact, Jennie's mother.

Nick wanted—needed—answers. And there was only one person alive who was able to provide them.

Grim-faced, he ended the call, rose from his desk and strode toward the door.

* * *

Candace was in the bath, when the door to the en suite flew open to reveal the tall, male frame of Nick Valentine. One look into his blazing eyes and her objections to his uninvited presence died.

Nick was in a towering rage.

His eyes were a scorching shade of black, his mouth pinched into a tight line. His fury made him look twice his normal size—which was already substantial.

Candace swallowed. Then moistened her lips nervously as his angry gaze skimmed the bits of her wet, naked body that weren't hidden by the mounds of bubbles from the baby wash she'd snitched from the nursery. One hasty downward glance, following in the wake of the burning trail his eyes had left, revealed rosy tips peaked to hard nubs. Even as she instinctively covered her breasts with her hands, she knew her last-ditch attempt at modesty was futile.

She found her voice. "Get out!"

The flags of livid, burning color high on his cheekbones told her he wasn't immune to her nakedness. Strangely enough that knowledge gave her the confidence she needed to sit upright in the bath.

If he wanted to ogle, let him damn well look.

Candace was pretty sure her body would hold no surprises that he hadn't seen before. And she would have another reason to detest him when he feasted his eyes on her.

But instead of leering, Nick retreated to the doorjamb. "Get dressed," he muttered, jerking his eyes back up to hers, his color high. "I want to talk to you."

"It will have to wait until I've finished my soak."

Two long strides across the expanse of polished black-slate tiles and he was looming over her. "This can't wait."

The bathroom that had seemed so decadently glamorous only minutes earlier was now suffocatingly intimate.

"I want you out of here." Candace hoped she didn't sound

as shaky as she felt. "You're my employer and I'm entitled to some privacy."

When Nick bent forward, Candace tensed, snapping, "Do you want me to file a suit for sexual harassment?"

Then her breath rushed out her lungs as he scooped her out of the bath. Shocked by his action, she stared up at him. He was plastered against her, the water from her body streaming down his shirt. Their gazes clashed. Beneath his anger she detected a maelstrom of other pent-up emotions—heat and turbulence and a host of indefinable nuances that were impossible to read.

Candace decided the wisest course of action right now might be silence. Nick looked fit to explode.

He stepped back, grabbed a towel and wrapped it around her, pushing the edges into her nerveless hands.

"No harassment, see?" he snarled.

His actions had paralyzed Candace. "You can't just walk in here and—"

"This is my house. I can do exactly as I please. You have ten minutes—that should give you time to dry yourself off and change." Over his shoulder he tossed, "Don't make me come and fetch you. I'll be waiting for you in my study."

Nick halted outside Candace's closed bedroom door, his head in turmoil.

His ordered existence had been turned inside out. All that he'd thought was true…wasn't. And the only person who could give him the answers he sought was naked, only one flimsy wall separating them.

God.

Nick broke into a sweat all over again as the unwanted memory of the pearlescent gleam of Candace's wet, naked flesh flashed through his mind. He'd been tempted to strip off his clothing and get naked with her. Only her timely reminder that he was her employer had stopped him.

It had been hard enough to keep his imagination reined in before; now that he'd actually seen what previously he'd only fantasized about, his body was going into overdrive.

Yet everything had been complicated by the incomprehensible discovery he'd made. Candace wasn't his daughter's nanny…nurse, he amended. Candace was Jennie's mother.

Nick didn't understand it. The situation was too surreal to absorb. How had Jilly come to have Jennie? And what had happened to the baby his wife had been carrying? The baby who had been created at the Namkhet Island clinic.

He'd watched Jilly's body changing. Every time he returned from an overseas trip sourcing products, or returned from a visit to one of the cross-country garden centers, her pregnancy had advanced. The baby had been born while he was overseas.

Had there been a switch? So where was Jilly's baby? Or had the baby died? Was there something wrong with it? Where was it? And then when had Jilly arranged for Candace to be impregnated? Or had Candace already been pregnant and sold her child?

That was the scenario he liked least of all.

But Nick was struggling to make sense of it all. His feet had carried him outside the nursery. Softly he pushed the door open and went in.

Jennie was lying in her crib, in some kind of white jumpsuit with pink ears on the hood.

Nick found himself grinning down at her, and for the first time since the unwelcome call from his doctor, the coiled tension that had him strung tighter than a bow started to unwind.

"Ears…?" He shook his head. "Who on earth designed ears for the top of a baby's head? You're not a rabbit!"

Jennie flapped her arms, and Nick could've sworn her eyes gleamed with humor. He bent close to her and whispered, "I never understood why Jilly was so desperate for a baby—" Nick broke off and gulped "—until I met you."

It was a life-changing admission.

Only now, almost too late, was he coming to realize how much Jennie meant to him. He'd resented her. She'd underlined the emptiness in his life: the wrong wife, the wrong life. It had taken the realization that he might lose the baby to realize that he wanted another chance.

Fine time for that to happen.

He gazed down at the baby. The fluffy ears atop her round head made her look incredibly cute. Her mouth moved and she blew a raspberry, then her face broke into a smile.

A wave of emotion swamped Nick. Only one thing was certain. Jennie wasn't his. He'd known it when Jilly had stopped all the talk about *their* baby. Even though he'd never called her on it, and maintained the fiction that the IVF had been successful—with his sperm. So how had he allowed this to happen? How could this little imp have crawled into the empty space in his heart?

Naturally, Candace wanted Jennie back. What mother wouldn't?

A tight chill settled over him.

Well, he wasn't going to make it easy.

For whatever reason, Candace had chosen to give Jennie up. She might regret her decision, but she'd made it, she'd signed a surrogacy agreement and he could find the document and make sure she stuck with whatever terms it entailed. He was sure Jilly would've adopted Jennie…he'd need to check whether he could've been included in the adoption without his knowledge.

But Jennie had been living with him for the past six months and Candace hadn't shown any interest in the baby during that time. No court would ignore that.

A premonition of the battle to come flashed before his eyes. He'd find out all the facts, get top legal advice. As far as he was concerned, he had as much right to the baby as Candace. More, in his mind. Then there was the fact that he'd been misled...made to believe the baby was his wife's child. Surely that would carry weight, too?

Because he wasn't about to give Jennie up. Not without a fight.

Candace would have to live with the choice she had made.

Nick's study was a surprise.

Candace hadn't been inside Nick's private domain before, and it was a total departure from the highly polished and reflective black-white-and-acid-yellow decor of the rest of the house.

This space was welcoming...

Homey.

Under normal circumstances the deep-brown leather sofas would've invited her to sink down, and the rows of books on the wooden shelves would've tempted her to browse between the covers. But now the sight of Nick standing with his back to her—arms akimbo, looking out the window into the darkness beyond— caused her stomach to knot. She was all too conscious of the huge divide between them. She was a nurse, a working woman, accustomed to long shifts; he was a millionaire, a man with a fortune at his command.

But what did it matter that he wore three-hundred-dollar jeans while hers had cost thirty dollars at Kmart? Or that his loafers were made of the finest Italian leather, whereas her slippers had come out of the supermarket bargain box? What did wealth matter when it came to love?

He swung around. His face was sterner than she'd ever seen it. "I have some questions I want answered." He gestured to the nearest sofa. "Sit down."

Candace perched on the edge and her strung-out nerves almost gave out. She pulled herself together. "I assume you wanted to see me because you have the test results and you've discovered that I was telling you the truth—and now you're ready to apologize to me."

Nick made a choking sound. *"Apologize?"*

"You've been treating me like I was some lowlife liar instead of the Good Samaritan who agreed to help you and your wife."

"Hang on a mo—"

"Jilly told me you were both undyingly grateful for a chance to have a baby." Candace flinched as the word *undyingly* hovered between them.

Before she could say *sorry* for her tactless word choice, he'd settled himself on the other end of the sofa she was on, and Candace reminded herself that Nick Valentine's own behavior in this mess was certainly less than laudable.

"Jilly was—"

"—delightful." Candace glared sideways at him. "You should've taken a leaf out your wife's book. In all the months I was pregnant you never once came to visit."

His face went blank. "Why the hell should I have come to visit you?"

"To say thank you for the enormous gift I gave you both." Her throat thickened and she felt like she was about to cry. Damned if she would. "But no, your work was too damn important."

"Wait, I didn't know—"

"How long were you married?" She wasn't interested in what he thought, didn't want to hear his justifications. When he didn't answer she repeated, "How long?"

"Seven years." Nick muttered, clearly reluctant to admit it.

"Did you love your wife?"

"That's none of your business!"

Candace held his gaze bravely. "Of course it's my business. I gave you both my baby on the assumption that Jennie was going to a loving family." Her naïveté made her want to cry. She should've taken more care…

Rather than accept Jilly's logical explanation that Nick wanted to pretend the baby was his wife's, Candace should have insisted on meeting him. Instead, she'd been satisfied by a pile of newspaper and magazine cuttings—all of which had deified him as an eco-friendly tycoon. She'd let her worries be soothed.

Dumb.

Nick rose restlessly to his feet. "I did receive a call confirming that you're Jennie's birth mother. But you must be aware by now that I didn't even know about your decision to give your baby up—you made that all by yourself."

Pain stabbed at her. Then anger flared and she gave a snort of disgust. "You're going to heap all the blame on me?"

"Don't expect me to believe you did it out of the kindness of your heart. What was in it for you?" he badgered.

Candace bent her head and studied the rich colors of the Persian rug. Why was nothing ever simple? "In terms of New Zealand law, all I was entitled to recover were the expenses I incurred."

Nick waved a dismissive hand. "I'm aware of that, but there are any number of ways around the legalities."

At the cynical note in his voice Candace glanced sharply up at him. How could he suspect? She couldn't read his expression, but his lips were curled into an unpleasant sneer.

"So what did my wife offer you for the gift of Jennie?" There was an icy inflection on the word *gift*. "What price did you put on your baby?"

It hadn't been like that. "Nothing!"

Although that wasn't strictly true. But the financial assistance had come later—once she and Jilly had become friends. That had made the arrangement acceptable, one of friendship.

It had been an unlikely friendship, but during her pregnancy

Candace had grown to feel an incredible sympathy for Nick Valentine's wife. Jilly had appeared to have everything most women dreamed of. A husband she adored. Plenty of friends. Yet she had seemed lonely, her life empty. The baby she'd wanted more than anything in the world had been an impossible dream…until Candace had come to her rescue.

"You're sure?"

"Why do you think your wife would've had to pay me for a baby?" Candace countered desperately. "Are you so devoid of human kindness that you can't believe it's possible for anyone to be selfless?"

A strange expression crossed his face.

He came closer. Candace's pulse picked up speed as he leaned forward and placed his hands on the sofa back, trapping her inside the curve of his arms. "Are you telling me you're the real deal? A true angel?"

Her breath quickened. She couldn't look away. "I'm no angel. I'm all too human."

"Are you?" His gaze dropped to her mouth.

Candace's heart thundered in her chest. She felt dazed, disoriented. "I'm just like a million other women out there," she managed breathlessly.

"I don't think so." His head came closer still. "I must've met almost a million women in my life and you're unlike anyone I've ever met."

It hurt to breathe. "A million women?" she asked skeptically.

The side of his mouth kicked up. "Maybe that's an exaggeration."

"What's so different about me?"

One hand dropped away from the sofa back to cup her cheek, his gaze intense. "I thought it was only Jennie who had skin as velvety as a Queen Anne peach."

He hadn't answered her. She didn't press him. Maybe it was for the best not to know.

"Genetics." Candace tried to laugh his intensity off. "My mother's skin is soft, too."

The back of his hand brushed down the side of her throat to the top button of the fine cotton-knit cardigan she'd donned with jeans after she'd hurriedly gotten out the bath, fearful he might make good on his threat to return.

His index finger rested on the pearly button, above the hollow between her breasts, and her breath quickened.

The button popped loose.

Candace's heart stopped.

When Nick bent forward her lips parted. There was a moment before his mouth touched hers, a time when she could've told him to stop, that she didn't want this awful complication. Candace didn't utter a sound.

Instead, her eyelids fluttered down.

His lips were unexpectedly cool as he kissed her. Heat ignited, wild and raging. The hand on her jaw pressed her closer and the angle changed. Nick let out a hiss and his touch gentled, the kiss becoming increasingly intimate. Candace burrowed against him with small, hungry movements of a cat.

The pressure of the kiss deepened for a sharp instant, then eased. Candace opened her eyes.

Nick gazed down at the woman enfolded in his arms, shaken by the emotions that stormed through him.

Beneath his fingertips the cotton of her sweater was fine and delicate. He undid the next pearl button, heard her breath catch, and glanced down. The scalloped edge with its border of embroidered pink roses was almost too feminine against his square-tipped fingers. Her still-damp hair had been pulled back from her face with a hair tie, and from this angle he could see that she wasn't wearing a smudge of makeup.

Yet she was breathtakingly beautiful—like the angel he'd imagined her to be the first time he'd seen her.

Her eyelashes fell again, shielding the misty eyes from his. The dark lashes lay against the fine-grained skin, a faint flush giving her face a warm glow that caused his breathing to falter. Swallowing, Nick undid a third button. She didn't object. The sweater fell open, revealing the curves of her breasts.

His arousal was immediate.

Pushing the cotton knit off her shoulders, he watched her face. Her eyes remained shut. When he lowered his gaze to the skin he'd bared, he saw the prickles of arousal that had broken over her rose-flushed skin.

He suppressed a moan.

Nick dropped to his knees in front of the sofa and lowered his head to carefully tongue the dainty pink tip of the breast he'd exposed.

For a split second, time froze. There wasn't a sound in the room. After a pulse beat in which Nick thought his heart might explode, Candace let out a gasp.

He licked again. Lightly. Insistently. Her head whipped back, and her hands dug into the leather of the sofa on either side of her thighs. Immediately he closed his lips over the tight nub and felt the shock of reaction that went through her. Pulling away, he pursed his lips and blew. The nipple hardened. She made a mewing sound and her hands tangled in his hair, pulling him back to her.

Nick's head rushed down, his mouth wide, and he sucked her in.

This time her spine arched. Her breathing grew rapid, becoming harsh pants in the quiet of the study. Nick's fingers were clumsy with haste as he opened the remaining buttons. Rising up, he parted the edges of the sweater. His chest seized tight as he gazed at the sleek skin, the full curves of her bare breasts.

"Ah…"

He wasn't sure who'd broken the silence—him or her. His hands came up. Slowly, reverently, he framed the full ripeness of her breasts, the peaks popping hard. He bent his head toward the breast he hadn't yet touched and laved it with long sweeps of his tongue.

She convulsed against his mouth, her body superbly responsive, even though her eyes were still screwed shut.

His breathing was harsh and erratic, loud in the cozy intimacy of the study. Releasing her breasts, Nick sat back on his heels and tore his shirt open.

Then, taking both her hands in his, he pressed them against his naked chest under his rumpled shirt.

"Touch me," he commanded as her eyes shot open. "Feel my heart pounding."

As she stroked his chest, Nick was engulfed in the endless, misty depths. He felt himself sinking...drowning.

"Candace."

She blinked. But instead of the spell breaking, she came to life. Her fingers feathered down beneath his shirt...across his stomach...until lightning forked through him. Nick swallowed, his mouth parched dry.

"I can't think," he muttered hoarsely. "All I can do is... feel."

Sensation, wave on wave, broke over him as her fingertips swept lightly across his skin. His hands closed on her hips, the denim of her well-washed cotton jeans soft under his thumbs. Rising high on his knees in front of her, he yanked her off the sofa into his arms and hauled her up against him. Hard. He hugged her to him and claimed her mouth, and kissed her deeply.

When he'd finished, he loosened his arms a little until his hands rested on her shoulders. He sat back on his heels as they both gulped in air, their breathing audible in the overheated room.

"Wow." She sounded awed.

Nick suddenly felt about thirty feet tall. He gave a husky half laugh and let his fingers caress the rounds of her shoulders where her sweater had fallen away to expose tempting creamy skin.

"Again?"

"I'm not sure I'll survive if you keep kissing me like that," she said honestly. "My knees are weak."

"So what was it like with…him?"

The eyes that met him were wide and suddenly very, very wary. "Who?"

"Jennie's father."

She tore out of his arms with a force that caught him off guard. "Stop this, Nick. It's not funny!"

Her reaction startled him. "Hey…"

Perhaps his morbid curiosity had freaked her out. But he'd wanted to know, dammit. A surge of unfamiliar possessiveness swept through him.

Hell, he couldn't stop thinking about her—and he couldn't remember when last he'd had the hots like this over a woman.

He'd certainly never felt this way about Jilly in the seven years' famine that had been their marriage.

Candace was on her feet, rebuttoning the knit top, her color high, her gaze averted.

"Tell me about him." Nick stood. "I need to know."

She raised her head. Her mouth was set, her eyes flashed. "C'mon, Mr. Valentine. Stop playing games. You must know you're Jennie's father."

Seven

Nick looked pole-axed.

"I need a Scotch," he said, and crossed over to the liquor cabinet to pour two fingers of amber liquid into a heavy crystal glass. "Can I get you one, too?"

Candace shook her head and suppressed the instinctive urge to tell him that sugar water would be better for shock. Somehow she didn't think Nick would appreciate it.

His hand closed around her wrist and he gently drew her down onto the couch beside him. "Now run that past me again."

She simply wasn't ready to confront the fact that she and this man who caused such an emotional response in her had made a child together.

A perfect, wonderful little girl.

Jennie...

A child Candace had no intention of leaving in his care, a child she wanted back...whatever it took.

But she was starting to suspect that Nick might not

surrender Jennie so easily. And Candace was delaying the inevitable moment of confrontation, thinking about the best way to address it.

"Jennie is your child." Candace's stomach churned. "Your sperm was used for the IVF. And the DNA tests after her birth confirmed that you are her father."

At the time she'd signed the surrogacy agreement, she'd been affronted by the clause requesting a DNA test before the baby was delivered to the Valentines. But she'd understood that the couple had wanted to be assured that the baby was Nick's—not the child of some stranger she'd slept with.

"Frankly, I'm stunned that you believe Jennie is my child," he finally admitted, not looking at her, "and more than a little skeptical."

He hadn't known. Her suspicion that he and Jilly had worked together to pull off the pretense of a lifetime had been off the mark. She'd been so sure he'd known that Jennie wasn't Jilly's baby, that for reasons of their own he and Jilly had wanted to keep that secret.

Now it appeared Nick really had believed Jennie was his wife's child all along.

That stunned her.

Her attention shifted back to him as he ran his hands through his hair in a distracted manner. "I told you Jilly was pregnant—and my sister confirmed it."

"But..." Candace's voice trailed away.

He raised an eyebrow. "But?"

"Jilly couldn't have children," she said slowly.

"She told you that?"

Candace nodded, miserably conscious that every word was knocking the nails further into the coffin of her hopes. Oh, heavens, what had she done? Had she ruined her chances of securing custody of Jennie? "She said that the IVF wasn't working—that her doctor had established that she'd been one of those unlucky women who undergo menopause very early."

Nick blew out a pent-up breath. "Well, clearly my wife was lying to someone. She told me that the IVF had been successful. That she was pregnant." There was a strange note in his voice. "I watched her pregnancy progress over nine months...even though I was away a lot of that time. Hell, she spent a fortune on designer maternity wear."

"And, of course, you had no reason not to believe her."

Nick shook his head. "I had my doubts, but not for the reason you think. You see, I thought Jilly had a lover." His mouth kinked. "Someone who'd obviously been more successful at impregnating her than I had been."

Nick hadn't even believed Jennie was his child?

Candace suppressed the urge to howl with frustration at the injustice of it all. If she'd said nothing about him being Jennie's father, maybe he would've been only too glad to relinquish custody of the baby to her.

It was enough to make Candace feel seriously sick with regret.

Yet it wouldn't have been right. How could she have taken Jennie under false pretenses? Nick had been lied to enough already...

She drew a deep breath and said slowly, "That must've been hard to accept."

"Somewhat."

Normally the dry retort would've amused her, but Candace couldn't bring herself to smile. Not now. Maybe not ever... if she'd destroyed her chance of getting Jennie back. Yet she couldn't stop the flood of sympathy for Nick.

"So Jilly faked her pregnancy."

"Faked her pregnancy?"

This was awkward. "Only you know for sure whether it was possible. I have heard of women who hate their bodies when they're pregnant—don't want anyone to see them naked, move into a separate room. If Jilly had been like that…" Candace could feel herself coloring. She didn't want to be privy to this man's personal life with his dead wife. The thought of him and Jilly together caused her stomach to sink.

"It's possible," he said tightly.

"Jilly flew with me to the clinic where the insemination was done."

"You went to Namkhet Island?"

Candace nodded.

"Jilly said she was planning to be inseminated there. I consented to my sperm being used—and acted out the whole fiction. I even received bills," he said. "I never knew that she'd traded places with you nor that she never intended to undergo any of the procedures there herself. In fact, I came to believe she'd taken her lover with her and replaced my sperm with his."

"I can vouch that there was no lover."

"So the bills I received for the IVF procedures were your bills, not Jilly's as I assumed?"

Candace's discomfort increased. "Yes—that was part of the arrangement."

"Of course." Nick's mouth twisted. "There was also a bill for double accommodation and shared meals at the most glamorous resort on the island. Jilly told me she needed time alone to steel herself against the very real possibility that the IVF might again not work. Once the hotel bill was forwarded to me for payment, I knew instantly that she'd lied to me."

Candace felt sick. Clearly Nick had assumed Jilly had stayed there with her lover. "That was for me—I told Jilly it wasn't necessary." She hadn't needed a luxury holiday to convince her that she was doing the right thing. She'd done it for Jilly and her husband who had no other way of getting the child they craved. "Jilly said it was important to her that she get to know me. It felt a little weird, but I told myself she wanted to make sure the surrogate she'd picked wasn't a lunatic before she went through with the final insemination. I might've done the same thing in her place."

Nick laughed without humor. "Receiving the bill was a relief. The worst of it all was I didn't care that Jilly had taken a lover. I even hoped it might finally pave the way for a divorce."

Poor Jilly.

What he'd told Candace gave her some insight into the relationship—or lack of relationship—between Jilly and Nick. It appeared they'd drifted apart...so separate they might as well have lived in different houses, on different continents. No wonder Jilly had been able to fake a pregnancy while arranging with a surrogate to create a baby her husband had known nothing about.

"That's why you didn't go to the island with her," Candace said. "Because she convinced you she wanted time alone. And once you discovered she'd lied, it was easy to convince yourself that she had no intention of having your baby."

He nodded.

Jilly had told her Nick had been too busy. She'd accepted it at the time, but now Candace found that she desperately wanted to hear Nick's own version of how events had unfolded.

"But I never confronted her with it. We'd been through IVF before—several times. Unsuccessfully. Jilly told me I didn't have to be there. That the frozen embryos and sperm would be forwarded by the specialist we'd been dealing with here in Auckland."

He met her eyes. "I questioned how reputable the institution was—hell, I even did some checking. Everything seemed fine. There'd been some breakthroughs achieved, and I could understand why Jilly wanted to give it a try—why she thought it might be her last chance." Nick rubbed the bridge of his nose. "To be honest, my first reaction was relief that she didn't appear to want me along. Jilly could be very..." he paused "...demanding."

"She only wanted what any wife would expect—your time and your love."

Dropping his hand, Nick slanted her a mocking stare. "Not quite. She wanted a baby—a totally different thing. Clearly she had already put in place an elaborate plan to switch the recipient of…"

"Your sperm," Candace added helpfully.

"Exactly."

"It's hard to believe you didn't know." Candace's head was whirling as she tried to process everything Nick had told her. "I signed contracts…" Her voice trailed away. "You must've signed them, too."

His face said it all. "If there is a signature there, I'm sure an expert would pronounce it a forgery."

"Why did she go to such lengths?" It puzzled Candace. "Did she hope you'd spend more time with her if there was a baby in the house?"

"You know nothing about what my wife expected. And she's dead now, so it's all in the past. But, believe me, our marriage should never have taken place." Nick changed the subject. "But now I have to start accepting that Jennie came from your womb. Did the egg belong to you—" Nick paused "—or was there another donor I don't know about involved?"

Candace had to feel pity as she watched him grappling with the enormity of his discovery. "The egg was mine—and I carried Jennie in my womb. That's why I am her biological mother."

"Biological mother?" Nick swore. "Your egg was fertilized by—" He broke off.

"Your sperm." Candace added the words as clinically as she could. She was a nurse. She worked with babies all the time, knew where they came from. Nothing about this was foreign to her. So why did she feel as if she stood on the edge of a whole new dimension?

This time Nick said politely but with far more force, *"Hell."* He shook his head again as if to clear it. "I still can't believe Jilly *planned* this." He paused, his face hardening. "I should be thankful, I suppose, that she bothered to use my sperm."

Beneath his anger Candace could sense his hurt and confusion. She touched his arm. "Nick, I really don't think there was a lover. Jilly told me you were soul mates. She wanted your baby. Desperately. That's why I had to undergo DNA confirmation after Jennie's birth—she wanted to be sure the baby was yours."

An indecipherable emotion flickered across Nick's face— guilt perhaps?—and then it was gone. "Jilly certainly didn't ask my permission to take a sample for DNA for matching— assuming she took one."

"Oh, she had a sample, the test confirmed you were my baby's father. It could've been your toothbrush…a hair from your brush…as long as it had your DNA on it."

"Anything Jilly wanted Jilly got—and the hell with what it cost."

There was a savage note in his voice that warned Candace this was about much more than Jilly taking tissue samples without his knowledge. Candace got the impression that Nick was a man who had been pushed to the brink of his endurance.

And that conviction only grew when he added grimly, "I'm still going to need proof before I accept that I'm Jennie's father."

The axis of Nick's world had tilted.

He was grateful for the string of meetings that kept him occupied the following morning. Yet his mind kept buzzing with questions to which he had no answers: Why hadn't Jilly told him about her infertility? How could Jilly have arranged a surrogate and fooled him so easily? And, more importantly, what was he going to do about Candace?

There was one final question that was the easiest to resolve…was Jennie his daughter? Deep in his heart he knew it didn't matter, because either way she was his. The blood tie no longer mattered.

But there was something very seductive about the idea that part of him and part of Candace had merged to produce the little girl who was fast becoming the most important person in his life.

At midday, a break in his schedule gave Nick the opportunity to visit the doctor. Within twenty-four hours he'd know for sure whether Jennie was his child or not. Once a swab had been taken and bagged, he headed the Ferrari to Valentine's Garden Center and walked down to the lake. The grassy edge was crowded with preening ducks—the ducks that had so intrigued his Jennie—while the trio of trouble-causing geese stood in the lee of a nearby willow tree.

Damn birds didn't know what they'd unleashed. Nick knew he had his work cut out to convince Candace that he was perfectly capable of caring for Jennie. That he wasn't the unfit father she'd pegged him as.

The question of what he was going to do about Candace remained unresolved.

If Nick was honest with himself, he knew precisely what he wanted to do with Candace. He wanted to take her to his bed, slake this restless need that vibrated through him—the hunger and desire that sent his thoughts winging her way at the most inopportune moments. Thoughts that had him fantasizing about pulling her to him, covering her mouth with his and…

Hell, why not call it what it was? He wanted to cover her body with his, and he hardly cared whether he got her naked or not. All he cared about was possessing her—every inch of her creamy flesh. Touching her, tasting her, making her his.

Yet if he did that, he'd be left with the biggest headache of all. Nick wasn't certain that if he took Candace in every way he dreamed, he'd be left intact. Would the burning passion consume more of his sense of self than he was willing to risk?

Then there was the impact a hot, reckless affair with Candace would have on the baby. Would it jeopardize his relationship with Jennie?

Yet this was hardly the kind of question Nick could bring himself to ask his lawyer.

The call from Apple Orchards Rest Home came just after Candace had fed Jennie her lunch in the garden on a picnic blanket overlooking the ocean.

Candace's mother had suffered a fall, the kindly rest home director explained, once she'd allayed Candace's fears of the worst. Nothing was broken—the x-ray had confirmed that. But her mother had been badly shaken.

Candace promised to come at once.

Terminating the call, Candace considered Jennie, who'd crawled to the edge of the picnic rug, her hand reaching for a cluster of tiny white daisies that had sprung up in the immaculately kept lawn.

In principle, today was Candace's day off. She hadn't taken time off because she'd wanted to stay close to Jennie in the wake of the confrontation with Nick. To be truthful, despite the confirmation that she was Jennie's biological mother, an unreasoning fear lingered that if she left the property she might not be able to gain access again.

Candace knew she was overreacting.

Yet it was impossible to forget that bone-chilling moment outside the café when Nick had told her he was taking Jennie home and she could collect her paycheck from his office.

In her mind Candace had seen the tall gates of the Valentine mansion closing to her forever. She'd known it would be impossible to get back into Jennie's world once she'd been shut out…and that primal fear lingered. Enough for her to have decided against visiting her mother today. But now her mom had taken a fall.

The guilt was hard to shake.

Candace knew Mrs. Busby was more than capable of looking after the baby for a few hours while she checked on her mom. Yet she hesitated. Mrs. Busby had her own responsibilities. Wednesday was the day she planned the week's meals and did the shopping. Candace hated the thought of throwing Mrs. Busby's schedule off. Nor did she want to arouse the housekeeper's curiosity. To raise questions Candace didn't want to be forced to answer...

The alternative course was to leave Jennie with Alison. But that was quickly ruled out when she learned that Alison had gone with her husband to an urgent meeting. Turning her attention back to the baby, now with a fistful of daisies, Candace considered Jennie. A smear of apple puree on her chin had Candace reaching for a cloth. The baby laughed as Candace wiped it, and love for Jennie swept through her.

There was no other choice. She'd take Jennie with her to check on her mother, because she had no intention of asking her baby's father for help. Ever since yesterday, she'd been plagued by unwanted images, her body prickling with unwelcome awareness of the man who was starting to consume far too much of her thoughts. He was Jennie's father, for heaven's sake. He could never be her lover...

She could not allow herself to need Nick Valentine.

Eight

"Mrs. Timmings is here to see you."

Nick glanced up at his PA. Alison had been remarkably patient—he'd been expecting to hear from her long before this. His sister had always had an overwhelming interest in his life…and the bombshell he'd dropped about Candace announcing she was Jennie's mother would've been driving Alison crazy.

He knew he should've contacted her and told her the outcome of the DNA tests. Alison would've expected it of him.

With a mental sigh he said, "I'll be with her in a minute."

His sister appeared in the doorway behind Pauline. "Too late. I'm already here."

Nick mentally braced himself for the scolding to come. "How are you, Alison?"

She settled herself in one of the four chairs arranged around a table in a sunny spot in front of the glass wall looking out over the lake and parklands beyond.

Getting up from the black leather executive chair behind his desk, Nick crossed to the table where his sister sat and pulled out the chair beside her.

"Not good. Richard has received notice from the NorthPark Mall Group that our appliance stores have to move out of all their shopping centers."

Nick gave her a sharp look, his already overloaded brain whirling with this new setback. But at least Alison wasn't asking about Candace...or Jennie.

"Have you and Richard defaulted on a payment?" he asked.

Alison hesitated. "One..."

"You should've come to me, Allie. I would've helped you." *He should've offered.* But he'd never realized his sister and brother-in-law's chain of appliance stores was in quite so precarious a financial state.

"You know how proud Richard is—he wouldn't take help. But it wasn't that we couldn't afford to pay the rent." Alison looked utterly miserable. "Oh, Nick, it was all my fault. We changed banks because we managed to get a more favorable rate on our home loan, but part of the arrangement was that Richard had to transfer the business accounts there, too."

Nick nodded. "That's pretty standard."

"But I forgot to give the bank the authority to deduct the rent to NorthPark. I only found out when I checked the bank statements the day after the payment was supposed to go through that it had bounced." She gave a helpless shrug. "No one from the bank even called to let me know before they'd bounced the check. Our old bank would've called first."

"That's the price of change—it takes time to build a relationship with a bank." Nick thought about the irony of his observation. He had better relationships with his own bank than he'd ever had with his dead wife.

But Jilly wouldn't have been his wife if he hadn't been forced into marrying her.

Too late to dwell on that. Nick focused his thoughts back on his sister's predicament. "You spoke to the NorthPark Mall Group? Paid the late rent?"

"Of course." She nodded. "And I thought it was all sorted out. Then the letter came from their lawyers. I called and they told me we'd breached the contract so the group was exercising their right to terminate. Richard checked with our lawyers and they can do it."

"Seems odd that they'd be so eager to evict you," said Nick. "It's not easy to get new tenants for the kind of floor space you occupy. Especially in this economy. Is there something else you're not telling me?"

"No—we've been model tenants in all the shopping centers NorthPark owns."

"Hmm." Nick's mind was racing.

"Richard has started looking for new space in other malls, but it's going to be hard to match the deal we had and find premises that are one hundred percent suitable. It's scary—we might actually have to shut down some of the stores. Oh, Nick, I should've been more organized!"

There was nothing he could say to make Alison feel better. Rising to his feet, Nick went around the table and gave her a clumsy hug.

She hugged him back and sniffed. "You're being so nice— you're going to make me cry."

"I'm always nice."

"Not really—you're usually distant. No, don't withdraw and ruin it all," she said hastily as he straightened up. "I just want you to know I'm so grateful you didn't tell me it's all my fault."

"How would that help?"

She made a sound that was half laugh, half sob. "Oh, Nick, that sounds more like you." She looked up at him, a small smile curving her lips. "I'm glad you're my brother—you know that?"

He shrugged.

"How are things?"

Nick looked away. "Fine."

"You're not going to tell me about Candace…about her claim that Jennie is her daughter?" His sister was quivering with curiosity.

"Will you let me rest until I do?"

"Probably not. I've left you alone all week—I didn't want to be nosy." She paused. "Nick, did you have an affair with her?"

That offended him. "No! I suppose I'm going to have to get used to that kind of reaction. You're my sister, and if you thought that, then it won't be the last time it comes up."

"If you didn't have an affair with her, then she can't possibly be Jennie's mother."

"Wrong again." He smiled wryly. "Turns out Jilly faked her pregnancy and engaged a surrogate."

"A surrogate?" Alison's eyes popped. *"Candace?"*

Nick nodded.

"So Candace was telling the truth? She *is* Jennie's mother?"

"That's the way it looks." His tests hadn't come back yet, but Candace's voice had held a persuasive conviction when she'd told him that Jilly had made sure Jennie was his. But Nick wasn't ready to concede that until he had hard proof.

His sister placed her elbows on the table. "She must've planned to get into your home."

Nick considered his sister. As much as he wanted to agree, it was unlikely that Candace could've managed to orchestrate that. Nor did he believe that she was the conniving type.

Unlike his late wife.

"I don't think that would've been possible. Not unless she could've played a role in Jennie's ear infection—and I think you'll agree that's impossible."

"But she would've recognized Jennie's name when we came into the emergency room that night."

Nick nodded. "Granted."

"And she didn't hesitate to take advantage."

He didn't want to defend Candace, but he couldn't stop himself from saying, "Perhaps she was curious."

Alison considered him. "I imagine you're right. What woman wouldn't be? Her baby… A mother would want to know that she was okay. And I made it simple for her. The boys were giving me such a hard time that afternoon…"

She sucked in her cheeks, making her look even more harried. "She was so easy to talk to, so interested in the boys… and Jennie. I told her all about Margaret leaving us high and dry. That's when she said she wouldn't be averse to working as a nanny for a while because she didn't have a full-time job. I'm so sorry, Nick."

When he didn't respond, she dropped her head into her hands. "I don't seem to be able to stop screwing up at the moment, do I?"

"Don't worry about it." Awkwardly he patted her shoulder. Staring over his sister's head into the courtyard outside, he asked with studied casualness, "Did you mention that I was overseas?"

Her head came up. "I probably did."

That would've sealed Candace's conviction that Jennie needed her. But there was no point in telling his sister the problem she had unwittingly caused.

"So what have you decided to do?" Alison asked.

Trust her to get to the crux of his problem. "I don't know." Yet.

It wasn't like him to be indecisive. Vacillation went against his character. But he had Jennie to think about—what he wanted had to be best for Jennie, too.

"It could've been worse," Alison was saying.

"Worse?" What did his sister mean? As far as Nick was concerned, it had gotten as bad as it could.

"Jilly could've picked a real loser, like the kinds of friends she picked. Candace is cool—as my sons would say." Alison rose to her feet and gathered up her bag. "I might pop in on the way home to see how she's coping with all this. Thanks for listening to my woes, Nicky—I'm feeling a lot better already."

What his sister meant was that she was going to try to build a bridge with the woman who might prove to be necessary to Jennie. Nick knew he should be thinking like that, too.

But he was still struggling with the idea of Candace as Jennie's mother. All he could think of was Candace as a woman—the one he'd held in his arms, the one he'd kissed… the one he was dying to seduce.

A sexy angel he couldn't wait to see again.

Work be damned.

"You know what?" He forced a half smile. "I don't seem to be able to concentrate today. I might come with you—blow the cobwebs from my brain."

Nick ignored the shock on his sister's face. First Pauline, now Alison. He hadn't become that much of a workaholic, had he?

Her mother was already back from the hospital, relaxing in her room at Apple Orchards Rest Home when Candace and Jennie arrived. She looked pale and tired.

"How are you feeling, Mom?"

"I've had better days." Catherine Morrison's mouth twitched into a smile and Candace wanted to applaud her mother's bravery.

"I've brought someone to meet you," she said instead. She bent over the stroller and unclipped the straps. "This is Jennie."

Catherine turned her head on the lace-edged pillow that matched the handmade quilt Candace had bought as a housewarming gift after her mother had moved into Apple Orchards five months ago. The room was cozily furnished.

Candace had bought a compact love seat covered in pretty fabric where Catherine could sit in the sun by the window on days when she felt a little stronger. The dressing table where her mother's favorite perfumes and toiletries were stored and the bed's headboard were her mother's own. So were the collection of knickknacks and photos on the bookshelf in the corner. The homey touches had transformed the institutionalized space.

"Hello, Jennie," her mother said to the granddaughter she didn't know existed.

A lump thickened at the back of Candace's throat. "I'm looking after her."

"But what about your work at the hospital, darling? I thought you were going back to a full-time post once you had me settled."

"I'll go back to that when I'm ready. I needed a break."

For the last four months of her pregnancy, Candace hadn't seen her mother. She'd established a fiction that she'd decided to travel overseas—Jilly had even generously offered her the funds to make the story a reality. It hadn't taken the needy expression in Jilly's eyes to affirm what a sacrifice she was making with the offer. Candace had known Jilly would miss visiting her, seeing Jennie grow as Candace's pregnancy progressed.

Candace had declined. She hadn't felt comfortable accepting the gift. Instead, she'd dropped out of sight, renting a cottage on the rugged West Coast, an hour's drive from Auckland, where she'd lived quietly while her family and friends assumed she was on the other side of the world.

There was a certain irony in the fact that during the time Candace had been living that deception, Jilly had been practicing her own deception with a surreal fake pregnancy.

Perhaps that was why Jilly had visited the cottage so often—sometimes even spending the night in the cramped second bedroom that was little more than a closet. It would have been the only time Jilly could break out of her lie because it was only with Candace that she wasn't pregnant. The charade must've been exhausting, waiting for someone to catch any slip...

Yet now Candace knew that those visits to the cottage, the nights away, would only have added fuel to Nick's belief that his wife was having an illicit affair.

By the time Jennie had been born, Candace had been drained. The strain of the imminent parting from her baby had taken its toll. After nine months spent caring for her unborn baby, suddenly there was a dark, black hole of loss that threatened to swallow her.

Her mother had known instantly that something was wrong. She'd assumed—wrongly—that her daughter must've fallen in love with someone across the ocean.

Of course, Candace hadn't been able to confess the enormity of what she'd done. The only way to survive was not to think about Jennie. To get back to work. It hadn't taken her long to realize her days as a pediatric nurse were over.

She couldn't bear to work with babies and children. Every time she looked into a little girl's face, Candace wondered about her baby girl. What she was doing. And, most important, if she was loved.

The decision to switch to working in the emergency room—as far away from young babies as she could get—had been inevitable.

Then her mother had almost died.

Catherine had fallen off a ladder while packing winter blankets into storage and cracked her skull. It had been touch and go—and had taken a week for her to regain consciousness. The doctors had feared she would be permanently brain-damaged.

Looking at her mother now, Candace marveled over the amazing changes time had wrought.

Her mother wasn't out of the woods yet and she still

suffered memory lapses, but with every month that passed, Catherine grew stronger. The chances of the stroke that the doctors had initially feared were lessening.

"I'd like to go sit in the garden," her mother said suddenly. "And I'm sure Jennie would like that far better than being cooped up in an old woman's room."

"You're not old," Candace said automatically, though her mother had aged since the accident. Being outside would lift her spirits and the vitamin D would be good for her, too. "Are you sure you're up to it?"

"Oh, yes. The sunshine is beautiful."

Candace helped her mother into a wheelchair and planted Jennie on her lap. Then she pushed them both out into the sunlight.

"Let's go to the rose gardens," Catherine suggested.

Halting the wheelchair in her mother's favorite spot, Candace said, "Here, let me take Jennie from you. She must be heavy."

"She's fine." Catherine gave her a faint smile. "It's been a long time since I held a baby. She smells just as I remember you did…of that special fragrance babies have. Clean skin, well-laundered clothes and something else—" she bent her head and inhaled "—lavender?"

"And tea tree."

"Lavender will help her sleep." Her mother looked startled. "I'd forgotten that."

"It has good antiseptic properties, too." Candace didn't want to look too elated at the tiny breakthrough in her mother's ability to recall information.

"But the lavender doesn't always work." Reaching out a hand, Candace touched the baby's head tenderly.

"She doesn't sleep?"

"Most of the time she's an angel." That instantly reminded her of Nick. He'd called *her* an angel…

"There's a rocker in her room that I sit in when I give Jennie her nighttime bottle. That sends her to sleep most nights."

"But what about her parents?"

Candace looked up to find her mother watching her, a frown wrinkling her forehead.

"Where are her parents?" Catherine asked again.

Drawing a deep breath, Candace said, "Her mother is dead."

"Oh, poor little tyke. What about her father?"

"He's a businessman—he owns a string of garden centers that keep him busy."

"That's a shame." Her mother's brow wrinkled. "I used to visit Valentine's Garden Centers. I loved buying plants—particularly my roses."

Candace stared at her mother. "I work for Nick Valentine," she said slowly, the air that had been so summery suddenly chilling her. She shook the eerie sensation off.

Her mother wouldn't—couldn't—know that Nick and Candace were Jennie's parents. It wasn't possible. Catherine only remembered the centers because she'd been an avid gardener before the accident.

"In fact, we recently took Jennie to one of the centers—she loved the ducks."

"There must've been swans, too."

"Oh, there were." Was her mother starting to remember? Months ago the doctors had said that her mother might never remember things from the past, so each recollection was a moment to treasure and be grateful for. "There were geese, too—one pecked Jennie." That memory was one Candace would sooner forget.

But there would be other memories to replace that. Like the sight of Jennie in her grandmother's lap. This was a moment Candace would treasure forever.

* * *

By the time Candace pulled the station wagon up in front of the Valentine mansion, the late-afternoon rays of sun had taken on a golden hue. The light warmed the stark lines of the residence, softening the hard, sculpted angles of the design.

She—and Jennie—were exhausted. But in Candace's case it was the exhaustion of deep satisfaction, the feeling of a mission accomplished.

The glow didn't dissipate when the front door opened and Nick appeared.

"So you've decided to come back," he said from the bottom of the stairs as she clambered out of the car.

A quiver of apprehension fluttered in her stomach. Nick Valentine always looked crisply immaculate, but the man who faced her appeared nowhere near as well-put-together as usual. He was wearing suit pants, his jacket had been discarded and the white striped business shirt hung out, giving him an unusually rumpled look. She noticed that the top two buttons were unbuttoned, revealing a triangle of golden skin at his throat. Candace jerked her gaze upward, and clashed with a stormy pair of navy-blue eyes.

"Where have you been?"

She couldn't have found her voice even if she'd tried.

"I've been calling you for hours," he bit out.

Oh, no! Candace scrabbled in the side pocket of her tote and extricated her phone. Switching it on, she was met by a chorus of beeps signifying missed messages.

"My phone was off." Remorse filled her. "I'm sorry, Nick. I didn't realize."

A vague memory of switching the phone off before entering her mom's room surfaced. She'd been so preoccupied she'd forgotten to turn it back on.

She could hardly blame Nick for being irate.

Though normally he would never have noticed her absence. He never left the office early—that was one of the golden rules of Nick Valentine's busy life. Everyone agreed on that. Jilly, Mrs. Busby, his chauffeur. Their schedules had all revolved around his very set hours.

Yet today that had changed...

"Was it something urgent you were calling about? Is everything okay?"

The tumble of questions was met with a short terse nod. Candace took in the way his hair stood up, as though he'd been running his fingers through the almost black strands.

"If everything's okay, then why are you home?"

As the words left her mouth, it occurred to her that those were not the words of an employee. She sounded like a wife.

Flushing uncomfortably, she muttered, "Sorry, that's none of my business."

"It is your business all right. You're the reason I came home. I canceled a meeting with a new supplier, because my sister wanted to see you."

"She wanted to see me?" Candace frowned.

Why?

"Alison's been concerned about you."

"Oh." So much had happened it seemed like a century since that awful confrontation that his sister had witnessed. "I'm sorry we were out." Candace started up the stairs, Jennie firmly clasped in her arms.

Nick's hand came down on her shoulder, halting her. "Where were you?"

With her standing two steps above him their eyes were level. Seeing the dark blue this close up was strangely intimate... and incredibly disconcerting. Candace sought a distraction. "Is your sister still here?"

"No, she left hours ago. I was about to file a missing persons report."

She hitched Jennie up higher in her arms and smiled uncertainly. "You're joking, right?"

The brooding scrutiny he subjected her to made her heart skip a beat. "Except I wasn't sure that you were missing...I thought you might have taken Jennie into hiding."

"Kidnapped her?" Astonishment caused her to blink. "I'd never do something so stupid."

His mouth relaxed imperceptibly. But all he said was, "Good."

"If I did something like that, I'd kiss goodbye to any sympathy I might get from the courts when I challenge your custody of Jennie."

Nick glanced over her shoulder, and Candace became aware of Mrs. Busby hovering in the lobby.

"I'll take the baby, shall I?" she asked.

Reluctantly, Candace surrendered Jennie to the housekeeper.

"Come into the sitting room." Nick stood back, allowing her to pass into the stark room that Candace had decided she hated.

She halted in the middle of the cold space and wished, for once, that the immense flat-screen television was on so it could break the taut silence that vibrated between her and Nick. Candace could see the tension humming in his tall lean frame.

"I'd advise you to think long and hard before deciding to drag this through the courts," he murmured. "You have everything to lose."

Instantly, she started to panic. "What do you mean?"

He came closer, and the breathless fear changed into something else...something more dangerous, rooting her to the spot.

"It would be foolish to threaten me." He spoke through his teeth. "I'm being as patient as I can. Don't push me too far."

"Or what?" Candace challenged boldly. "What will you do?"

"I might be tempted to pursue court proceedings myself

and have you prohibited from coming within a hundred feet of Jennie."

The impact of his words jolted her. Candace stared at him, stunned by his reaction. If he made good on his threat, her baby would disappear behind high walls and electronic gates. Then she'd be forced to go to court to challenge the legality of his custody of Jennie. That would take money. A great deal of money. Money that she didn't have.

A vision of a future too bleak to contemplate faced her. She'd be standing on the outside—in a world that would become a desert if she was without her baby.

"You can't do that."

"Is that a challenge?"

"No...*please*." Tears spilled out her eyes. "I couldn't bear never to see Jennie again. Please, not that."

"Oh, Christ, don't cry!"

The rough brush of his mouth against hers came as a shock. Yet instead of shoving him away Candace found herself yielding...leaning into the warmth of his body as he kissed her again. And again.

She tasted the salt of her tears, a hint of mint. Then she closed her eyes and her body slumped against him, his heat and hunger filling the empty numbness. His arms steadied her, pulling her more firmly into his embrace.

One hand stroked her hair, and he whispered, "Steady on."

She rested her head against his shirt and sniffed.

His hands cupped her nape, tipping her head back. She shut her eyes, refusing to let him see the hopelessness, the hurt flooding through her.

"Look at me, Candace."

Finally, she opened her eyes.

There was an expression on his face that caused her throat to constrict.

"I shouldn't have said that."

"You're such a bastard." She discovered she was crying in earnest now. "How could you do that to me?"

"Candace—"

"Don't touch me."

She wrenched herself away and rushed from the room before he kissed her again...and she lost what little of her heart still remained intact.

Nine

In the summery morning light that streamed into his bathroom and sparkled off the white tiles, Nick stared at a face half covered in shaving cream in the mirror.

His eyes were bloodshot from lack of sleep. Through the long hours of the night he'd been unable to shake from his mind the hurt, shocked look in Candace's eyes. Her pain had haunted his dreams last night.

He didn't much like what he saw; he wasn't proud of himself.

Without flinching, he thought about how the women in his life might have reacted if they'd been caught in the same position as Candace: Bertha Williams, his grandmother, his sister...even his devious wife. And he came to one conclusion.

Every one of them would have fought to keep her child. And every one of them would've been stunned that he could threaten to cut a woman off from the child she'd given birth to.

Even if she had agreed to give that baby up...

Nick lifted his hand and carefully brought the razor down in a long sweeping line. In minutes the white foam was gone, the shave complete. His skin glowed, clear and unsullied by stubble.

Yet Nick suspected the same wasn't true of his soul...

Once showered and dressed, Nick paused on the upstairs landing. Glancing at his watch, he saw it was already well past breakfast time.

Instead of heading for the stairs, he checked himself and went the other way. To the wing that held the nursery—and Candace's room.

Where the landing widened into a sitting area, he stopped.

Candace had pushed the glass table aside and was lying flat on her back on the carpet. A DVD showing a group of mothers doing exercises with babies was playing on the television screen that hung on a wall. Candace's arms were fully extended as she swung Jennie above her.

Both of them were laughing.

The shorts Candace wore were white and very, very brief. The ice-blue tank top fitted snugly over her curvy breasts.

Hell. The hollow in Nick's chest contracted into a tight, hard ball.

Desperately he looked away, scanning the room. The place looked—sounded—like a home. In a way that the perfectly decorated space never had before.

It even felt like a home.

He dithered on the periphery, not wanting to break the mood.

But a movement must've given him away because Candace turned her head—and saw him. Her laughter stilled. She lowered the baby and started to sit up.

"Don't stop," he said. "It looks like Jennie's having the time of her life."

Candace smiled hesitantly, and Nick felt as if the room had been flooded with more sunshine.

His cell phone chose that moment to ring.

It was his doctor confirming that he was almost certainly Jennie's father.

Nick thanked him for his help and killed the call. Staring at the woman on the mat, a heavy beat thundered in his ears.

Candace had told the truth. He hadn't believed her. Once again the sense of his soul being less than pure struck him. He shook off the thought, strode forward and sank onto the floor beside her, his legs awkwardly long in the confined space.

Jennie reached a hand toward him, and he gave her his. She grasped his thumb with a grip that was surprisingly strong.

"You'll get wool from the carpet all over your suit," Candace warned, folding slim, bare legs under her and resting Jennie in her lap, still attached to his finger.

Nick forced his eyes away from her smooth limbs.

Down, boy.

So this was how she was going to play it. As if that ugly scene between them last night had never happened.

For a split second Nick considered forcing the issue, trying to explain his confusion—what Jennie was coming to mean to him. Strangely enough, he hadn't needed the doctor's call to care about the baby. That had happened all by itself in some miraculous way.

The hesitation stretched into a pulsing pause, became overlong, and the moment passed.

Finally, he took the conversational olive branch she'd offered. "A bit of lint on my trousers hardly matters."

Everything that mattered in his life sat right in front of him. Jennie, snuggled into Candace's lap, holding on to his thumb like there was no tomorrow. Candace, her cheeks flushed with exertion, her eyes sparkling.

"Candace—"

Her eyes were bright, inquiring. "Mmm?"

"That was my doctor."

The brightness faded a little.

"And?"

"The tests are back. You were right. Jennie is my daughter."

Ominously, she didn't say that she'd told him so. She tightened her arms around the baby until Jennie objected. Her stillness was starting to concern him.

He needed them...both of them.

Jennie perched on Candace's lap looking comfortable and at ease. Both had been so utterly absorbed in each other until he'd come along and ruined it. They didn't need him at all.

That realization made his heart miss a beat.

For the first time he had some inkling of how Jilly must've felt in those long years she was married to him.

He'd behaved like a bastard, resenting the fact that Jilly had trapped him into a marriage he hadn't wanted...yet couldn't refuse. It had been a choice between the devil and the deep blue sea, and he'd been determined not to drown. So Jilly, the agent of his downfall, had borne the brunt of his anger.

Nick was starting to like himself less and less...

As if she sensed his thoughts, Jennie dropped his thumb and turned her attention to tugging at strands of blond hair that had escaped Candace's hair tie. Instead of pulling away, Candace simply laughed.

Nick cleared his throat. "Look, every year there's a carnival at the Super Center on the Sunday closest to Valentine's Day. That's this weekend. It's very festive." God, he was starting to sound desperate. With studied casualness he asked, "Would you like to come with me this year?"

"You're asking me on a date? To be your Valentine?"

Damn.

He couldn't read her expression. What the hell was he supposed to say now?

Nick forced a laugh. "No, no. Nothing like that."

"Oh…"

God, he was screwing this up badly.

"Candace—" He broke off and reached out the hand Jennie had held and covered Candace's with it. She flinched.

He withdrew swiftly and brushed a nonexistent piece of fluff from his jacket, trying to face up to the fact that he wasn't behaving with very much subtlety or grace.

"I just thought you might want to join us—spend the day with Jennie."

The joy that lit up her eyes was blinding. "Thank you. I'd love that."

So spending the day with him held no appeal, but spending it with Jennie was something else. He should've expected that. He might be driven by lust, but clearly Candace didn't reciprocate.

Ah, well. "Valentine's…growing happy families. A loving home begins at Valentine's."

"What?" Confusion clouded her eyes.

"Those slogans are part of our latest advertising campaign," he explained.

"Oh, yes." Her face had cleared. "I've seen the television ads."

She didn't think he'd lost it.

Yet.

Just as well she couldn't read his mind—she'd have run screaming from the room.

"It's a day for families," he said awkwardly. "For Jennie's sake, you should be there."

This time Candace didn't say a word.

Nick wondered if that had been overkill. Too late to wish he hadn't been quite so heavy-handed on the whole family angle. There was nothing for him to do but rise to his feet and say, "Well, I'd better get moving or I'll be late for work."

"You're the boss, what would it matter?"

"It matters," he said. "I've always believed a boss should

lead by example. And lately I've been sneaking out quite a bit."

Though what worried him most was how much he'd enjoyed playing hooky.

The temperature rose swiftly, turning into one of those glorious summer days that lingered.

With Nick at work, Candace decided to take advantage of the weather and take Jennie swimming. The water in the pool was silken and cool—and Jennie was in her element, hanging over Candace's arm, smacking the surface of the water with fat palms while Candace laughed.

All through the day she'd been kicking herself. Why hadn't she told Nick that Jennie should live with her, not him? She'd had the perfect opportunity this morning…

Instead, she'd chickened out.

Perhaps it had been the look on his face. There'd been something—a vulnerability—that had tugged at her heart. He'd looked…lonely.

Candace told herself that she was being ridiculous. Men like Nick Valentine weren't lonely. They married wealthy trophy wives, lived in glossy architect-designed mansions, owned multimillion-dollar businesses.

Except Nick's wife was dead…

He couldn't possibly be missing Jilly, Candace told herself. Hadn't Nick told her he'd suspected Jilly of having an affair? The extent of Jilly's deception over the baby signaled to Candace that theirs had not been a healthy marriage.

A footfall scraped the deck and Candace turned her head. The sight of Nick coming toward her, threading his way between the lounging chairs, caused a flutter in her belly.

This made it two days in a row that he was home early… maybe being the boss had its perks after all.

"You're early," she commented, squinting up at him as his highly polished Italian shoes halted at the pool's edge.

"I secured a contract to do the landscaping and supply the plants and garden furnishings for two coastal resorts. It's a coup. I called it a day." Nick glanced at his watch, then met her gaze and raised a quizzical eyebrow. "Half past six is not much earlier than normal."

"Half past six?" Candace squawked. "Already?"

"Time flies when you're having fun."

Candace ignored his quip. "Gosh, Jennie will turn into a prune."

"She looks fine to me." Nick squatted down on his haunches and wiggled his fingers at the baby. She gave him a delicious smile and chuckled. "I might go change into swim trunks and join you."

The notion of being trapped with a good-humored, nearly naked Nick in a pool on such a balmy summer's evening was more than Candace could handle.

"I should get Jennie out. She must be starving."

His face went wooden, and she felt suddenly small and mean. "You know, a little while longer won't kill her. You go change…we'll wait for you."

It took Nick only five minutes to change into swim trunks, grab a towel and hurry back to the pool.

Candace and Jennie were still in the water, the baby squealing with pleasure as Candace swung her back and forth, skimming the pool's surface.

After dropping his towel on the lounger, Nick launched himself into the water. Jennie's eyes popped out as he surfaced beside them. Her face puckered in distress and for a moment it looked like she might cry.

"Hey, hey," he murmured, mentally kicking himself. "It's only me…not some sea monster."

When he looked up, Candace was watching him, but she was smiling.

"She wants you."

Jennie had her arms out, and she rewarded him with a gurgle as he swam closer.

Nick's insides melted. "Come here, you."

Taking her from Candace, he scooped her to him and made little growls against her neck.

Jennie giggled, and bounced excitedly in his arms. Her fingers hooked around his hand as she bumped up and down.

"Hey, take it easy. I'll be in trouble if I drop you," he whispered. The memory of the day she'd been pecked by the goose and he'd nearly fallen in the lake still made him shudder.

That wasn't happening again...

Jennie stuck out her fingers and closed them around his. Gold glinted on his left hand in the slanting rays.

"You wear a wedding ring."

He glanced at the wedding band, then across to the woman who'd asked. Her gaze was still trained on his hand. "Yes."

"A lot of men don't wear a ring."

"Jilly bought it for me." She'd bought her own rings, too, Nick remembered with a touch of discomfort. But wearing a ring had saved him plenty of explanations at inopportune moments—not that some of Jilly's acquaintances had paid much attention to the band of gold that had marked him as her property.

"You're still wearing it."

"I hadn't thought about taking it off." There hadn't been another woman in his life so it hadn't entered his mind. Except now there was Candace...

Their eyes meshed—and held. Her pupils, so black against the misty gray eyes, expanded. Trapping him.

"Ouch!"

He gazed down at Jennie's fist clutching at the dusting of hair on his arm. "That hurt."

The baby dimpled up at him, showing a gleam of pearly white.

"She's got a tooth." He stared at Candace.

"One. Lower incisor. The next one should cut any day now…"

"Wow." Nick transferred his attention back to the wriggling bundle in his arms. "You're growing up fast. I hadn't even thought about braces yet."

"Soon she'll be dating."

But Nick didn't laugh. Instead, he squeezed his eyes shut. "Jeez, that idea really hurts. I don't want to think about it." When he cracked open one eye, he found Jennie watching him. She cooed.

It made Nick feel like the most important man in the world. Hell, he *was* the most important man in his daughter's world—at least until she turned sixteen and started dating— and he wasn't about to screw up again.

"I'll have to lock you up," he told her. "Vet all the boys who come visiting."

He peeked across at Candace, but she wasn't laughing. Instead, he was surprised by the strange expression on her face. Then she turned away and made for the pool end nearest the house and gracefully exited the water.

As he watched her pick up a white towel and dry her face, it struck Nick that Candace must be thinking about the coming years without Jennie. He would be there for their daughter. Candace would be gone. His daughter would have no mother to guide her through the minefield of teen-girl years.

Hell.

Of course he'd lean on his sister for help and, in time, Candace would have a family of her own. A husband. Babies…

Emotion flared inside him. He couldn't imagine her with some other, faceless man. It hurt to think of her with a child other than Jennie.

The intensity of his response took him by surprise. What the hell was going on?

The answer came at once.

Nick didn't need to watch Candace towel off those tantalizing legs to know he wanted to stroke her skin, kiss her lips, make love to her. He didn't want some other man sharing the moments he dared not even admit to fantasizing about.

Jennie chose that moment to protest and look around, an expression of bewildered panic on her face.

"You want Mommy?" Bending his head, Nick whispered against her ear, "Me, too. But that's our secret, 'kay? Because it's an impossible fantasy."

Jennie grumbled.

Nick knew exactly how the baby felt. For now he could be generous. "It's all right, I'll take you to her."

With the baby in his arms, Nick waded over to the steps. When he reached the top step, Candace was waiting. Jennie almost leaped out of Nick's arms and Candace swaddled her in the thick towel.

The bond wasn't all on Candace's side—Jennie was equally drawn to her biological mother.

The gold rays of the sun caught her face as she gazed at the baby in her arms, her expression content and happy. "I'd better get her some supper. She'll be hungry after that swim."

"Why don't you feed her out here?" suggested Nick. "It's such a beautiful summer evening—no point wasting it by being closeted inside."

Candace hesitated only for a second. "Okay. I'll take her upstairs to whip her swimsuit off and put a dry diaper on, then bring her dinner out."

Nick watched her saunter to the glass doors, her hips swaying, the content, gurgling baby in her arms. Everything worked so well now. Yet Nick knew Candace's time with

Jennie was limited. And, for him, becoming involved with Candace was an impossible fantasy.

Because of their daughter.

Nor could Candace continue to live with them. It would only cause heartache for Jennie in the long term. The longer it lingered, the greater the hurt would be. Nick knew the situation could only end in tears.

Candace was going to have to leave. Sooner would be better for Jennie; and the woman who had him tied up in sexual knots was going to hate him even more when he suggested it.

Candace had been right, Nick realized twenty minutes later. Jennie was hungry, and it didn't take long for the baby to devour her dinner.

Sitting across the table from Candace, with Jennie in a high chair between them as the sun's sloping rays reflected off the mirrored surface of the water, the mood felt almost domestic.

Nick watched Jennie's eyelids droop. He'd opened a bottle of crisp Sauvignon Blanc and poured both himself and Candace a glass, but hers was still full.

Candace followed his gaze. "She's almost asleep."

"Why don't you put little madam to bed and come back and finish your wine? I'll see what Mrs. Busby has planned for dinner."

Nick suspected that he was playing with fire and Candace looked as though she might object. But she surprised him by saying, "A sandwich would suit me fine. I shouldn't be long."

Adrenaline rushed through Nick's veins as he smiled at her. "Don't be."

He told himself nothing was going to happen.

He and Candace were going to share a glass of wine together, have a light meal…and that would be the end of it. He was capable of controlling his emotions…his desires. After all, he'd been doing it for years.

True to her word, Candace was back within fifteen minutes. To Nick's everlasting regret, she'd donned a pair of navy sweats and a white T-shirt. No sign of the aqua one-piece swimsuit remained. Pity…

But very much safer.

"Good timing," said Nick. Mrs. Busby had just left after placing a tray of sandwiches on the table.

"Jennie is exhausted." Candace set the baby monitor on the table and sank into the chair opposite, then pulled a plate toward her.

"It's the water. She should sleep well."

"Until two o'clock." Candace grimaced. "That's the drill."

"She wakes up every night?" He hadn't known.

"Like clockwork." Peeling back the protective food wrap that covered the platter of sandwiches, she said, "These look delicious."

"Smoked chicken and avocado on this side. The others are Swiss cheese and salad."

"Yum." Candace helped herself. It didn't take long for them to demolish the contents of the tray, eating in companionable silence. When the platter was empty, Candace raised her wineglass. "To Mrs. Busby. She's a wonder."

Leaning forward, Nick clinked his glass against hers. "I'll drink to that."

Tilting her head to one side, Candace studied him. "She tells me she's worked for you for ten years."

Had it already been a decade? Nick thought about it. He'd been married to Jilly for seven years, and Mrs. Busby had been with him for several years before Jilly had had this house designed, built and decorated. "It's possible. I first employed her when I lived over on the North Shore. I owned a drafty old Victorian house with an enormous garden."

Jilly had hated the house as much as he'd loved it. It had been the first casualty of their marriage.

"Mrs. Busby told me about it—she said it had been built by one of the pioneers of the city. She misses it."

"I never knew that."

"She told me about the gardens—about the ferns you planted behind the house. She said it was like a secret world—she thought that Jennie would've loved playing in there, that it was the kind of place where a child could imagine fairies and elves."

"Goblins, too." Nick couldn't suppress the tide of nostalgia that the memory of the house brought.

"Don't you miss it?"

Candace's question brought him back to the present. He dismissed the momentary sense of loss, and his customary mantle of control dropped into place. He lived in the present, not the past. What happened now he could control. The past had already happened; nothing could change it.

"No." To soften the brusque reply, he shrugged and said, "It was time to move on."

Candace glanced up at the white structure behind them. "You moved on to something a lot more modern. This house is a completely different proposition."

"It's a good investment—it's everything the market wants. Great architectural style. Location." He gestured to the sea shimmering in the setting sun. "The value has more than doubled."

There was no point saying it had been Jilly's house, not his. It had never felt like home.

Candace brushed a strand of hair behind her ear. "You want me to believe that you sold the Victorian house to upgrade to something that needed less restoration and was a better monetary investment?"

He met her gaze levelly. "What other reason could there be?"

She made an impatient sound in her throat. "Mrs. Busby thought you lived here because Jilly loved it."

After a pause, Nick said, "Sounds like Mrs. Busby and you had a real heart-to-heart chat."

Leaning forward, Candace touched his arm. Lightning forked along his skin. "She wasn't gossiping," she said earnestly. "She's very fond of you."

"That surprised you?"

She looked startled by his question. Finally, she said, "Truthfully?"

"By all means be truthful."

Nick braced himself, and hoped she wouldn't be too truthful.

"Yes, it did surprise me. You come across as being very distant and remote. Not the kind of man who would be easy to work for. Yet she's adamant that you're the best employer she's ever had—even though she seems to have found Jilly..." Candace hesitated "...trying sometimes. Not that she said it in so many words. It was more in what she *didn't* say—and how much she raved about you."

"Mrs. Busby deserves a raise—for loyalty at the very least. Because Jilly *could* be trying." And demanding. And insecure. And like the house she adored, with its plethora of glass and mirrors that needed constant shining, she'd been high-maintenance.

"Do you miss her terribly?"

Nick didn't hesitate. "No."

Candace's eyes widened and her mouth formed an *O*.

"Did you want me to lie to you?"

"My impression was that you were everything she'd ever wanted."

Nick looked away. He fumbled and drew the gold wedding band off his finger. "It's long past time to take this off. What Jilly and I had could hardly be called a marriage."

The sound of Candace's sharply drawn breath filled the sudden silence.

"Nick—"

He didn't look at her. "Jilly is dead. I don't want to conduct a postmortem over a marriage that never even got off the ground."

Her hand stroked along his arm. "I never meant to—"

Man, she was killing him. The worst of it was she had no clue. Finally, he looked at her. "I should never have married Jilly."

Her eyes were so soft he could've sworn she understood what he felt. The confusion. The guilt. The frustration at the lost years.

The yearning for a woman like her.

Her hand released him, and he felt the loss. Picking up her wineglass, Candace took a deep sip.

Nick knew how she felt. Except she had no idea how bad he had it—the whole damn bottle of wine wouldn't ease the desire that heated him, it would only inflame it. And Nick had no intention of losing sight of the most important aspect of his existence—his control.

However much he wanted Candace.

He knew the time had come to retreat. Before he lost his head and did something he might later regret. Rising to his feet, he said, "I have a long day tomorrow. I think I'll turn in."

"Nick…"

He paused, his pulse thudding. "What is it?"

Candace shook her head. "Don't worry about it."

"Tell me," he insisted.

She hesitated, then said, "Do you still want me to come with you and Jennie to the carnival on Sunday?"

Nick was sure that wasn't what she'd planned to say, but he didn't challenge her. "Of course." The coward in him added,

"Alison and her husband, Richard, and her boys will no doubt be there too. It's a great day out."

Nick didn't want Candace guessing how pleased he was that she'd agreed to go.

Ten

A welcoming banner festooned with hearts fluttered over the arched entrance to Valentine's Garden Super Center.

"How did you manage to arrange for so many roses to be in bloom for today's carnival?" Candace asked Nick as he pushed Jennie's stroller under the arch covered in cascades of red, pink and white.

Nick's mouth slanted. "Good planning—I leave nothing to chance."

Candace gave him a narrow-eyed glance. Before she could react, a cloud of red, heart-shaped balloons floated toward them. A teenager wearing a T-shirt proclaiming *Valentine's... Gardens of Love* emerged from behind the bunch and held a balloon out to Candace.

"Thank you." Candace smiled and accepted the red heart. Bending forward, she tied it to the stroller. Jennie's eyes lit up and her hand reached out. At her touch the balloon bobbed away, and Jennie squealed with pleasure.

Nick laughed. Straightening, Candace met his dancing

eyes. There was a moment of pure, joyous accord, before she came to her senses and walked away quickly, leaving Nick to follow with the stroller.

She couldn't allow herself to forget that Nick had wanted to get her out of her daughter's life. Candace knew the battle wasn't over yet. Nick was a hard-nosed businessman; he'd simply be choosing his time to regroup and attack again. She dared not let her guard down.

Inside the garden center, a lively sight met her eyes. The area around the coffee shop had been transformed, with extra tables and chairs arranged on the cobbles, and red-and-white petunias cascading out of planter boxes. On the wooden adventure playground children swarmed down rope ladders and over wooden battlements, and beyond the playground red, blue, and yellow canvas booths had been set up. In the nearest booth three young women were painting toddlers' faces, while the booths beyond housed hook-the-fish, a skittle lane, a balloon twister and an assortment of other festive activities.

"Goodness, it *is* a carnival."

"Close enough." Taking one hand from the stroller, Nick placed it under Candace's elbow and guided her through the crowd while deftly maneuvering the stroller with his other hand. Instantly, shivers skittered across the bare skin where his hand rested. Candace forced herself to pretend she hadn't noticed.

In the farthest corner a table had been cleared, and a waitress descended on them, brandishing menus. Nick's hand released Candace, and he drew out a chair for her and then parked the stroller with a suddenly heavy-eyed Jennie in the corner beside them.

"There are pony rides and more booths down by the lake—even a kissing booth," said Nick.

Candace sat, determined not be drawn into a discussion about kissing. The lingering sizzle from where his hand had rested was more than enough. She didn't need any mention of kissing to heighten the constant warmth that enveloped her whenever Nick was nearby. So she changed the subject. "It's all too much for Jennie to take in. Look, all the excitement, and she's almost asleep!"

Nick laughed, then greeted the waitress by name, took the menus and passed one to Candace. "What would you like? I recommend the berry smoothies."

"A smoothie sounds lovely." Candace was relieved that Nick hadn't pursued the topic of kissing booths.

The waitress gathered up the menus and departed. Candace glanced around. A little way off, an old-fashioned gazebo swayed with a trio of musicians. Plenty of older customers—and some younger couples—sat on the benches scattered throughout the carnival scene, enjoying the music. Her mother would've loved this…

But the days for this kind of pleasure were past for Catherine Morrison. "You've catered to everyone—all ages," she said, trying not to let regret take hold at the thought of what her mother had lost.

Nick nodded. "Our Valentine's Sunday carnival is part of the annual social calendar for many of our customers. Some have been coming for years. Old couples. Young families. At the heart of it all, everyone wants love…a family…and a home."

She liked him in this gentler mood. It wasn't the controlled—and controlling—Nick Valentine he usually presented to the world. This was a different Nick—nothing like the uncaring businessman she'd pegged him to be.

A much more likable Nick.

Fixing her attention on his face, she said, "You sound like you believe in that, too."

"Of course I do. Our centers provide a chance for people to build fantastic gardens they and their families can enjoy—irrespective of age…or of how many people are in their families."

The passion Nick was talking about was absent from the soulless perfection of the sculpted pool deck, flat lawns and clipped boxwood hedging of his own home. Candace couldn't keep from saying, "But what about your own garden?"

"What do you mea—"

"Nick! I almost didn't spot you hiding back there in the corner." A stooping, angular woman with salt-and-pepper hair and a weather-beaten face stopped beside their table.

He got to his feet and gave her a great bear hug. "Bertha."

Once Nick had pulled away from her embrace, the old lady's sharp green eyes inspected Candace, then dropped to Jennie sleeping in the stroller. "This is that newborn baby I came to your house to see?"

"This is Jennie."

Could that be pride in Nick's voice?

"My, but she's grown." The woman fixed an accusing stare on Nick. "I can't even pick her up because that would waken her. I keep telling you to bring her to work so I can see her."

"I'm sorry."

Nick Valentine actually sounded humble. Who was this woman?

Candace realized she was attracting equal interest. "I'm Candace." She hesitated, then added, "Jennie's nanny."

Not the whole truth, but a version she could live with. For now.

"Candace, meet Bertha Williams."

"This young man used to mow my lawns."

"Bertha and Henry gave me a job in their garden center and taught me to grow vegetables, generate cuttings. They ignited my love of gardening and then convinced me that my dream to enroll in a landscaping course at night school could be turned into reality."

"We owned it for forty years, before losing it. Nick had to wrest the center away from the businessman who was ready to build houses on the property. Henry and I might have been fine gardeners but we couldn't keep the money straight." Bertha's brutally honest account made no apologies for their shortcomings. "Nick set it right." The old woman gave him a fond smile. "So after Nick moved us back into the manager's house seven years ago, I insisted that he hire me."

Nick grinned at her. "It was a good investment."

"Good for us, too. Since you took over the business it's given Henry and I time together. Even despite his heart attack, freed from the strain of running the business, the years have been wonderful."

For once Candace couldn't believe that Nick's decision to employ Bertha had been driven solely by profit. Even though her eyes were bright with life, Bertha's hands were crippled with arthritis, her back hunched. Seven years ago she would've already been over sixty. Nick must really care about the old woman.

Yet he hadn't brought Jennie to visit her...

Because he hadn't believed that Jennie was his child?

Before she could speculate further, Bertha said, "Giving Nick a summer job all those years ago was the best business decision we ever made."

"Flattery gets you everywhere," Nick told Bertha, lifting his napkin as the waitress delivered the smoothies to the table.

Candace smiled her thanks to the waitress, placed her straw in the deep pink drink and sipped. Despite being so driven, it appeared Nick did have some redeeming qualities. Bertha clearly thought he was wonderful. Mrs. Busby had extolled his virtues as an employer and now Bertha was implying that he'd single-handedly saved their garden center. Would taking Jennie from her father be the best thing for the child?

Candace found herself wavering.

Then she forced herself to take stock. Jennie's well-being came first. She gazed at the man who had thrown her into such confusion. Could Nick Valentine match the kind of love she could give her daughter?

"Would you like to join us for a cup of tea, Bertha?" Nick was asking as he picked up his own smoothie.

Bertha glanced from Nick to Candace. A crafty expression crept across her time-wrinkled face. "I think I've kept you young people long enough." Patting Candace's shoulder, she added, "Nick works too hard, my dear. Do an old lady a favor and make sure he takes it easy today…and has some fun."

Satisfaction settled over Nick.

Down near the lake the carnival was in full swing. Two black ponies led by a woman with long braids plodded along the path beside the lake, their young riders clutching at the reins.

Things were finally going better, he decided as Candace slowed the stroller, in which Jennie was still sleeping, and brought it to a halt.

Changing Candace's belief that he was a poor parent hadn't been as easy as he'd thought it would be. For one thing, Nick found it difficult to talk about himself. For another, while he'd vowed to spend more time with Jennie and to behave more like her father, that meant changing habits of a lifetime. He would do it. He'd already made great strides in spending more time at home. Hell, even Pauline and his sister had noticed. Nick had every intention of honoring the promise he'd made to Jennie the day she'd almost ended up in the lake—except he'd never been the kind of man who wore his heart on his sleeve.

Fortunately, his plan of inviting Candace to see firsthand the family-friendly empire he'd built had been nicely jump-started with Bertha's zealous endorsement. He could've kissed the woman who'd played such an important role in his life.

How could Candace not reconsider her low opinion of him?

A little way down the rolling bank, he caught sight of his sister waving frantically. "There's Alison," he told

Candace. "Come on, if Jennie wakes up she can play with her cousins."

They reached the lake, and he introduced Candace to his sister's husband, Richard, while their two sons crowded around—the four- and six-year-old both talking at once.

"Can we go see Princess Piggy?"

Nick shuddered theatrically.

"Scoot," their father ordered.

"Can we have money to get some cotton candy?"

Alison rolled her eyes. "I'm sure your dad will give you money…be back in ten minutes."

"I might go with them," said Richard. "Just to make sure they don't get into trouble."

As the boys and their father disappeared around the bend in the path, Alison turned to Candace and shook her head. "Kids! You're lucky you don't have any."

As Nick glared at his sister, Alison immediately realized her mistake. "Oh, I'm so sorry, Candace, that was tactless, I wasn't thinking."

"Who's Princess Piggy?" asked Candace in what Nick was sure was a brave attempt to distract his sister.

Alison brightened up. "Haven't you seen the kissing booth? You ought to get Nick to take you—it's his favorite booth." Alison grinned.

Candace shot Nick a wary glance. Nick could've rung his sister's neck. "That's not very nice."

Alison hooked her arms through his and Candace's and bore them both along with her. "See? There's Princess Piggy."

Inside a fully enclosed booth was a pink pig sporting a strapped-on glitzy rhinestone crown and a passion-pink satin sash. Nick grimaced and his sister giggled.

"Look at Nick's face," she whispered to Candace loudly enough for Nick to hear.

He watched as Candace glanced up at him and her gray eyes started to smile. Nick fought to keep his face impassive and not give away the effect she had on him. "The funds we raise today will be donated to charity," Nick explained. "Princess Piggy's stall is often one of the most successful."

"People pay to kiss a pig?" The doubtful look Candace cast the Kiss-the-Princess banner above the stall told Nick what she thought of the idea.

Nick pointed to a row of glass jars with names written on the front in black marker, each containing money. "See those jars? People pay for someone else to kiss the pig. Around midday the contents are tallied up, and the person with the most monetary 'votes' in his jar is tracked down and forced to kiss the Princess." Nick gave the porker a sour look.

"I take it you've had to do that in years past?"

"My staff seem to think it's extremely amusing."

"The proceeds go to charity and Nick's a good sport." Alison pointed at the first jar. "I think I see your name there again this year."

Nick groaned.

Beside him he heard Candace laugh, which almost made the prospect of kissing Princess palatable today.

"And here I imagined everyone was queuing up to kiss the prettiest woman at the fair." Amusement lingered in Candace's voice.

Had she been jealous? Nick found the notion curiously heartening. But Candace bent forward over the railing, preventing him from reading the expression on her face.

"Princess Piggy's quite cute," said Candace.

"Sure," said Nick unenthusiastically. "Alison certainly thinks so." He gave his sister a mock frown.

"Hey," said Alison. "To make up for the fact that I'm certain you'll have to kiss the darling again today, I'll babysit for you tonight…if you want to take Candace out for dinner?"

Nick's heart flipped. But Candace was flushing as she said quickly, "No, no, that's not—"

Before she could turn down the offer, Nick cut in. "That's a great idea. Thanks, Ally." He touched Candace's arm. "Don't forget, Bertha told us to have fun."

Candace's bottom lip jutted out endearingly, causing Nick to fight the impulse to kiss it.

"I'm sure you'll both enjoy some time out," said Alison, looking around her. "Speaking of which, I've been left alone far too long. I'd better go and check where those boys of mine have gotten to."

Before Nick could ask his sister to wait so they could finalize Jennie's sleepover arrangements for the night, he spied a familiar snowy head in the approaching throng.

Putting an arm around Candace, he braced himself for the inevitable clash of wills with his father-in-law. "I didn't expect to see you here, Desmond."

"As a future stockholder in Valentine's, I wanted to investigate my investment. What better time than today?" The grim smile didn't light up his glacial eyes. "Aren't you going to introduce me to your woman?"

Nick felt Candace tense.

Resisting what was rapidly becoming a familiar urge to land his fist in Desmond's stomach, he said, "This is my father-in-law. Desmond, this is Jennie's nanny, Candace." He chose the explanation she'd offered Bertha, and thankfully Candace didn't contradict him.

"I see."

Without sparing the sleeping baby in the stroller a glance, Desmond looked Candace up and down, making his opinion of what he saw very clear. Nick resisted the urge to let his hand fall from where he'd rested it protectively in the small of her back.

"I doubt it," said Nick levelly.

"I see a pretty woman living in your home—"

Candace tensed under Nick's touch.

"A woman *my sister* employed while I was overseas on

business." Nick spoke from between gritted teeth, furious with his father-in-law's implication, and even more furious because he couldn't in clear conscience tell Desmond to get his mind out the gutter.

Because the irrefutable truth was that Nick was lusting after Candace. The spark of attraction that had flared that first night had raged out of control. Now that he'd discovered they'd created a daughter together, Nick couldn't get the picture of making love to Candace—the real, passionate way, not the clinical IVF way—out of his mind. It was driving him crazy. *She* was driving him crazy.

Even now he caught the scent of her perfume as the wind lifted tendrils of her hair off her nape. He was intensely conscious that only one layer of cotton fabric separated the fingers resting on her back from her bare flesh beneath. And the idea that Desmond had spotted what Nick was so determined to conceal turned his stomach.

He dropped his hand from where it rested.

"Was that your sister who rushed past me?" asked Desmond.

Nick's hackles rose. He was sure that Desmond knew it had been Alison. "Why? Did you want an update on how her husband is progressing on finding new premises?"

It was a shot in the dark. But the slight widening of Desmond's eyes gave him away even before he blustered, "I have no idea what you're talking about."

"I'm sure you do." Nick lowered his voice. "Leave Alison and Richard out of it. This is our fight."

Desmond glanced away, then back. "I see someone I need to talk to—I'm sure you'd agree with me that people would line up to buy an apartment on the lake's edge."

"It's not going to happen," Nick said, "and that's a promise."

Desmond glared at him, and the rush of anger that his father-in-law so often provoked rose fast and hard in Nick. He stepped forward.

"Nick," said Candace, "let's move on. I'd like to wheel Jennie around to keep her from waking."

Nick suspected that Candace's timely concern had more to do with stopping him from flattening Desmond than from worry about Jennie's waking. His initial surge of annoyance ebbed to be replaced by a more complicated emotion as he glanced across to Candace.

An unspoken connection leaped between them.

"I found my boys," Alison said from behind them, bringing Nick abruptly back to earth, and then she added, "Oh, hello Desmond."

Muttering a greeting, Desmond gave Nick an ugly look and stalked away.

"What did I just interrupt?" Alison let go of her sons' hands.

For a moment Nick thought his sister had spotted that instant of electric intensity between him and Candace. How could he explain something he didn't understand himself?

Then Alison grabbed her younger son as he drifted away. "Don't you disappear again. Your dad is coming any minute." She rolled her eyes as both boys grumbled and she shot Candace an apologetic smile. "They're little rogues." Turning to Nick, she asked, "Now, what's Desmond doing here?"

Relief filled Nick. Alison's sharp eyes had missed that moment of secret connection he'd shared with Candace. "I suspect he's responsible for much of the misery you and Richard are experiencing at present."

"But why?" asked Alison.

From the corner of his eye Nick caught the flicker of shock on Candace's face. "He wants to hurt me—and hurting you is a very good way of accomplishing that."

"You know what?" Alison stuck her hands on her hips. "I'm going to drum up support to have that jerk be the one to have to kiss Princess Piggy today. I'm going to get a jar with Desmond's name in big bold black letters started."

Alison's vehemence was enough to assure Nick that today Desmond would be the one kissing the pig.

"Don't do anything foolish," he warned. "We're going to win this battle against Desmond." Then, turning to Candace, he said ruefully, "Sorry we're dragging you into something you don't deserve to be part of. But take note that my sister may be the most dangerous woman in the whole world."

Then he realized that was totally true. It had been Alison who had engineered his date with Candace tonight—and, given the connection that was growing between them, that was going to be a truly risky occasion.

Eleven

The restaurant Nick chose for dinner was located in Auckland's highly fashionable Viaduct Basin.

A valet had taken the Ferrari away to park it. And, despite the restaurant's being heavily booked, the manager had found them a table on the edge of the terrace outside, overlooking the water where the reflection of the evening sun shimmered in shades of rose, orange and gold between berthed luxury yachts.

The beauty of the scene tugged at Candace's heart. "This is glorious."

"Isn't it?"

Nick pulled his chair up around so that he could sit beside her and they both could look out over the water. Instantly, Candace's senses started to sing with subtle tension. He was so big, so overpowering in a black long-sleeved shirt and black trousers. To distract herself from the effect he was having on her, she smoothed the simple ivory cotton sundress that was the only thing in her wardrobe remotely suitable for tonight's outing.

"Bertha will be pleased that I've taken her advice," said Nick leaning toward her. "Go enjoy yourselves. That might as well have been her and Henry's life motto."

Conscious of Nick's shoulder only inches from her own, Candace murmured, "It sounds like they were happy together—they had each other."

"Yes, they have each other."

Nick shifted, stretching his legs out, and Candace couldn't help but notice the way the fabric of his dark trousers rippled as his thigh muscles bunched. She looked away quickly, feeling her cheeks warm. At least with Nick sitting next to her, thankfully he wouldn't notice.

He gave a contented sigh. "This is the life. From now on, I'm going to listen more to Bertha. I haven't done enough enjoying—or living—in the past dozen years."

"In those years you built up a successful business, married a woman who loved you, fathered a baby. Isn't that life?"

Nick didn't answer. Instead, after a long pause, he slung his arm around the back of her chair, and said, "So what do you do to enjoy yourself?"

Now it was her turn to fall silent.

"My sister told me that you'd recently come back from traveling abroad when she met you at the hospital."

There was a certain irony that she'd been caught in a lie by his sister. The convenient catchphrase to explain away the months of absence while her pregnancy came to term. Now that easy fiction had come back to haunt her.

"I wasn't traveling," she said at last. To her relief, just then a waitress arrived with pen and pad to take their orders. Nick's hand slid off the chair back, and rested on Candace's shoulder. She was very conscious of the warm weight against her skin. The shoestring shoulder strap of the ivory sundress offered no protection from his touch as his fingers played idly, brushing against her, causing shivers of desire to ripple.

After the waitress left with their orders, Candace changed the subject. "Bertha seems very fond of you."

"She's known me a long time. Henry, her husband, employed me when I landed in trouble as a teenager for playing hooky from school."

"I got the impression you lived nearby?"

His fingers stilled, and Candace breathed a sigh of relief.

"Yes," he said with clear reluctance. "I lived with my grandmother—she had a vegetable garden and used to send me to buy seed from the center."

Getting personal information out of Nick was like trying to get blood from a stone. "And your parents?"

He shrugged. "They moved to live in Kenya when I was ten years old. They took Alison with them because she was only a baby. My grandmother thought it would be better for me to stay with her and get an education. It might've been better if I'd gone with my parents—I would certainly have gotten into a lot less trouble. Henry's offer of a summer job probably saved my grandmother from shipping me off to Africa to avoid expulsion from school."

He must've missed his parents. Candace's heart ached for him. "Did you see them often?"

"No, they've never been back to New Zealand—they still live in Kenya," he added as she started to ask. "But Alison came back for my grandmother's funeral, and she chose to stay on."

Candace wasn't letting him off the hook. She wanted to know more about what made Nick Valentine tick. "You're very close to Alison."

Lifting one shoulder, he let it fall. "She's my sister."

No confessions of endless devotion. But what had she expected? Yet she'd seen the way they teased each other and the clear bond of affection between them.

"Nick, why do you always want me to think the worst of you?"

A flush crawled along the side of his neck.

There was a long pause before he replied huskily, "Perhaps it's safer that way." He dropped his arm off the back of her chair, moved his chair around until he sat opposite her, then added, "Here come our appetizers."

"That's right, change the subject," she muttered, incredibly annoyed for some reason that she couldn't fathom.

The waitress set down their orders, then moved an ice bucket beside their table and placed the bottle of wine in the ice. Candace refused the offer of wine, and dug silently into the bowl of chowder she'd ordered.

When she'd finished, she set down her spoon and asked, "Do you ever talk about important stuff?"

"What important stuff?"

Candace gave an impatient sigh. "You're a master at this, aren't you?"

"I don't know what you're talking about."

But the wariness in the indigo gaze told her Nick knew precisely what she meant and he was equally determined to avoid the issue.

"You know, I might have thought you were a bad father—"

"Hey, wait a min—"

"—but I never had you tagged for a coward."

Anger flared, turning his eyes that blacker shade of midnight and his head went back. "A coward?"

"Yes, a coward. You're afraid of talking about anything that matters."

"You've been gossiping with my sister," he said tonelessly.

"No, I haven't. But how interesting that we agree." Candace drew a deep, steadying breath. Ah, well, she'd started this; there was no turning back now. "You're afraid of intimacy."

"You know nothing about me!"

"Because you don't allow anyone to get close?"

His face had tightened into an expressionless mask. "You don't know what you're talking about."

"Your wife loved you—you didn't let even her inside."

Nick bent forward and spoke in a soft, forceful voice. "My wife never loved me. She wanted to own me, possess my every waking thought, my soul. That's not love."

For the first time, the facade had cracked and she'd glimpsed anger and a ferocious passion that caused the tiny hairs on her arms to prickle.

"Nick…" She placed a hand on his arm.

"Don't touch me." His tone was dark and raw. "Unless you're prepared to reap the consequences."

Excitement licked at her, taking Candace by surprise. She'd never been reckless. The spreading desire warned her that was about to change. She forced herself not to be distracted. To focus. She wanted to know what kind of man Nick Valentine was.

"So tell me, *make* me understand."

The look he gave her was hostile. "Okay, you want to hear the story of what you consider great love? I'll tell you."

Candace was no longer so sure she wanted to hear whatever he was about to tell her. Lifting her hand from his arm, she said, "Nick—"

"You accused me of being a coward. You can damn well listen, *then* you can judge."

Nick took the wine out of the ice bucket. Before he could pour any into her glass, Candace shook her head. She suspected that she needed to be one hundred percent sober for the coming conversation.

Instead of pouring himself wine, Nick placed the wine back in the bucket. "My wife was a photographer. She took photos of flowers and had them blown up onto canvases—"

"Yes, I know. They're very popular. I bought one of her

works at a gallery exhibition." For her mother's birthday—the last one they'd celebrated before the accident. The photograph had been expensive, but it had been worth every cent. Her mother still loved it. "That's how we met."

Then they'd met again when Jilly had bumped into her at the hospital visiting a friend's premature baby. That was the first time Candace had glimpsed the other woman's yearning for a baby. They'd bumped into each other several times after that and Candace had been touched by Jilly's concern for her friend's baby.

"Well, we have that in common. It's how I met her, too. I was contracted to landscape her father's garden—I'd already built up a successful string of garden centers. Jilly was taking photos of some of the flowers when I came to check the landscaper's plans for the garden. She started to talk to me, and before I knew it I was being invited to lavish parties at the Perry residence with promises of securing more lucrative landscaping work, and somehow I became her regular date."

Candace could visualize the scene. Nick, strong, handsome, so full of drive and energy. "She fell in love with you."

He shook his head. "You're making romantic assumptions. She fell in love with the vision of what she thought she could mold me into."

Mold Nick? He must be joking! Anyone could see that this was a man who knew his own mind. This man was no one's toy.

"She couldn't get what she wanted, so like a spoiled little girl she told her father I'd seduced her and refused to marry her. Desmond and I had an angry stand-off and I told him that he, and his daughter, could go to hell. He told me that he would make sure I would marry his Jilly."

The white line around Nick's mouth warned her there was more. "What happened?"

"Bertha and Henry's bank loan was called in. Desmond

stepped in and bought the center. Then Henry discovered that Desmond, the bank manager and a developer had cooked up a scheme to establish a high-density housing development on the land. He and Bertha were devastated."

She stared at him aghast. "You're joking!"

"I wish I were. He'd found my Achilles' heel. Desmond is a very wealthy man. The banker involved was an old friend of his who held all Desmond's bank accounts."

"You could've reported the banker."

"For what? Bertha and Henry were too old to still be in debt for such a large amount, even though the value of the land more than covered the debt. But it could be argued that it was a sound business decision."

"It was immoral."

"Sure."

He smiled at her, and a chill settled in Candace's stomach. "There's more to the story, isn't there?"

"Bertha and Henry were evicted from the house on the property. The shock caused Henry to have a heart attack. I went to see Desmond full of sound and fury. Desmond told me that I could stop it all."

"How?"

"By marrying his daughter. But he didn't intend to make it easy for me—he wanted me to pay for not marrying her earlier. In return for agreeing to marry Jilly, he would sell Bertha and Henry's garden center to me at a ridiculously inflated price. He resented me. He made it quite clear that things would only get worse for Bertha and Henry if I didn't accept his deal. They would lose not only the garden center, but also the home where they'd lived for forty years. Desmond also intended to humiliate the old couple by having them declared bankrupt. The center would be sold and developed—" Nick stopped, an agonized expression on his face "—God, he's so predictable."

"Oh, Nick…" Candace could see it all. Jilly desperate for

the man of her dreams, Desmond wanting to get his way at all costs, and Nick wanting the best for the elderly couple who had given him a chance in life. "How tragic."

"I had no choice... I couldn't risk Bertha's happiness and Henry's health. It brought Henry and Bertha a future together. It was worth it. Now she has her job in the garden center—which she loves." He shrugged. "So I married Jilly. Part of the deal, in addition to a brutal repayment schedule, was that I gifted stock in Valentine's to Jilly in our prenuptial contract—a tangible hold over me for good behavior." His mouth slanted. "I had right of first refusal on buying those shares back once the full price for the Williamses' business was paid or Jilly and I had a baby—whichever came first. But she died before I made the final payment."

"But you had Jennie..."

Was that why Jilly had been so desperate to have a baby? To secure for the husband she'd trapped into a marriage he'd never wanted some degree of freedom? Candace wanted to believe Jilly had regretted the way events had played out.

Nick was shaking his head. "That is no help because, remember, I was sure Jennie wasn't mine—and now I've discovered Jennie is not Jilly's biological baby. She's yours."

"But Jilly adopted her," Candace argued. "Jennie is very much Jilly's baby. That stock is yours."

Nick shrugged. "I have a team of lawyers looking into that right now."

"What did you do after you accepted the deal?"

"I started to work like a dog so that I could repay Desmond."

"And you employed Bertha?"

"At first I tried to get her and Henry to stay in the house on the property. She's a proud old woman, and she wouldn't accept what she regarded as charity. Now I owned the garden center that had been hers and Henry's. So I offered Bertha a job and in return she and Henry got to stay in the house while working for me for four mornings a week. The rest of the time she spends with Henry."

"No wonder Bertha adores you."

"She doesn't know the half of it—" he gave her a warning glance "—and I trust she never will."

"I won't say a word."

It wasn't surprising that he didn't trust love. It was clear that he'd never loved poor, needy Jilly. In her desperation, Jilly had driven him away before any relationship between them had gotten off the ground.

"Given the state of your relationship, why the decision to start a family?"

"Jilly had always wanted a baby." Nick looked away. "She'd made that clear from the moment I placed a wedding band on her finger. I wasn't spending a lot of time home…I think she was lonely."

At the mention of their wedding Candace felt an unexpected stab of jealousy. Yet their union hadn't yielded a child. Maybe that was never meant to be. But the flip side of that coin was equally hard to accept: she and Nick couldn't possibly be meant to be, either.

Or could they?

"But something changed." Nick interrupted her thoughts. "When Jilly stopped talking about *our* baby, I became convinced she had a lover, someone she preferred to father her baby."

"Maybe she stopped thinking of the baby as *hers*," said Candace slowly. "After all, the eggs and womb were mine. It had nothing to do with your role at all."

"That would make sense." Nick shook his head. "God, what a mess. I drew the wrong conclusion. But I didn't care enough to confront her. I was relieved—all I could think about was paying Desmond back. In the back of my mind I knew I would eventually divorce Jilly. It suited me that her child wasn't mine. It was an easy way out for me."

She touched his hand where it lay on the table. "I'm sorry, Nick."

He held her gaze. "It's not a very nice story."

"No. But you must've felt terribly trapped."

"Like my back was against the wall," he admitted.

"Yet you never took it out on Jennie."

"I wouldn't be truthful if I didn't confess that I did resent her a little—I believed she was another man's baby. But it didn't take me long to figure out she's the innocent in all this—and it's not hard to love her. She's very special."

Her fingers were still resting on his hand. It was a masculine hand with scrapes and calluses. A strong, capable hand. His fingers closed around hers. Her gaze flicked to his, only to be snared in the blazing heat.

After that, Candace couldn't have said what she ate when the main course arrived. The intensity of Nick's gaze, the way her stomach bottomed out every time their eyes met—all left her with an edgy feeling of expectation that grew as the evening wore on. She couldn't help thinking that Nick had depths she'd never expected. He'd suffered so much, worked so hard…and proven himself to be a man of honor.

A man worthy of being a father to Jennie.

Once back home, Nick followed Candace up the marble stairway.

She paused on the landing where it widened into a sitting area. "Thank you for dinner—it was lovely to get out."

There was a moment of awkward silence, then Nick muttered, "The hell with it." He stepped closer, gave her a brief chance to escape.

Candace murmured huskily, "I'll go to my room now."

Yet she didn't move.

The silence between them stretched out. Two beats. Then three. At last, when Nick was quite sure she'd had all the time in the world to make her decision, he reached for her. Candace never hesitated. She flew into his arms.

It wasn't a gentle kiss—Nick was far too aroused for that. The tension that had been rising in him for days had reached a breaking point. By the time it ended, he was breathing heavily.

Their eyes met. Something shifted, subtle, impossible to recognize.

Nick's hands came up to tangle in her silky hair, holding her so that when he lowered his head a second time his mouth slanted across hers, creating the perfect kiss.

Candace didn't object. She kissed him back with enough eager intensity for him to know that the blazing attraction was mutual.

Hunger twisted inside him, hot and wild.

When the kiss ended this time, Nick had to battle for control as tremors of anticipation quaked through him.

Slowly…

He'd thought he could leash the power, but Candace quickly proved him wrong. It didn't take much. Her hands crept up, along his shirtfront…up…until they rested on his shoulders. Rising on her toes, her tongue tip tantalized his bottom lip, shredding what little restraint he still possessed.

His hands shaking, Nick unfastened the frustratingly small buttons of the chemise-style front of her dress. The edges parted, and his fingers found the soft skin of her breasts. She wore no bra. Heat exploded in him.

Nick groaned.

"I don't know how much of this I can take," he muttered hoarsely, his hands closing over the curves.

She leaned closer, her body pressing up against his. Nick released the soft flesh, and his arms slid around her. He let his hands wander down her back, over the cotton jersey that fell in soft folds over her hips. He clasped her hips, pulled her close to him, so she could feel his body's hard response.

Candace moved in little restless circles against him. Nick's erection leaped, straining to be free.

This was more woman than he'd ever held...even in his dreams. Nick groaned again.

She nibbled his bottom lip. Nick yanked her closer so that she was plastered up against him, her softness yielding to him. The shoestring straps of her dress slid down her shoulders. He bent his head and pressed openmouthed kisses along the crest of her shoulders tasting her...inhaling the hauntingly familiar sweet, spicy scent of her until Candace shuddered in his arms.

Nick's heart pumped furiously, the blood pounding in his head.

He became aware of the chandelier blazing above them, of the backdrop of arched windows illuminating them to the deserted garden outside.

Scooping her off her feet, he headed past the closed doors of Jilly's rooms to his suite beyond. He kicked the door shut, and four long strides took him to the king-size bed with its pile of casually arranged pillows. Muted light pooled from the two bedside lamps, warming the dull gold cover. He let her slide down his torso onto the bed with excruciating slowness, tormenting him, prolonging the pleasure. By now he was shaking inside, the desire he'd been suppressing spilling over.

"God, but you're beautiful."

With the straps already half-down her arms, and the bodice open, Nick pushed the dress over her hips. Underneath she wore tiny lace panties. Those went next. Grabbing the collar of his shirt, he yanked it—still buttoned—hurriedly over his head. Undoing his belt, then his pants, he shucked them off. They landed in a heap on the carpet.

Then he followed her down onto the bed among the mountain of dull gold and black cushions.

Her skin was pale and creamy. *Luscious.* He touched her

with a trembling hand. So soft. So warm. Impatience clawed at him. He stroked her, his fingertips exploring the rise of her breasts, the valley between, the flat plain of her stomach. Driven by increasing desperation, he sought out the sweetest, most responsive spots.

By the time his hand found the moist skin between her inner thighs, she was damp and superbly responsive. He slid two fingers into the moist channel. Her hips came off the bed, and Nick almost came apart.

He couldn't do this. He couldn't wait…

There was a moment when he thought about the new pack of condoms in his bedside drawer, then he abandoned it. What did it matter if he impregnated her? He was going to marry her. Nick wasn't conscious of making the decision—he simply knew that it was the right one.

"I'm sorry," he whispered, drawing his fingers out. She shuddered, her hips undulating. "I can't wait."

Nick shifted over her, covering her.

"Are you okay? I'm not too heavy?" He caught a glimpse of her incandescent silver eyes as she shook her head forcefully, her hair whipping around her face.

Then her legs tangled with his for a moment before they parted, granting him the access he'd only fantasized about before. He pressed into the space, his heart thundering.

She'd borne his child.

"Take me," she murmured.

All thought dissolved as her hands slid into the tight space between them and closed around the length of him.

Nick gritted his teeth. "I can't hold back."

Surging forward, the blunt length of him pushed into her readied softness. Nick fought against the strength of the sensations that shook him as her heat swallowed him; he fought to hold on, to give her time to catch up.

"I've never been this hot," he whispered, and licked the soft skin behind her ear.

She arched up beneath him and gasped.

Nick clutched her buttocks and drove deeper. Pleasure ripped through him.

One. Two. Three thrusts.

Candace gasped again and flung her head back.

It was enough to send Nick spinning into oblivion. He shot deep inside her womb, where his child had lain, and then the passion and heat consumed them both.

Nothing had ever felt more right to Nick.

Candace opened her eyes—and the sight of the dark gold bedcover caused her to freeze. She didn't need the shafts of sunbeams or the sinking sensation in her stomach to tell her she'd fallen asleep in Nick Valentine's bed.

She jerked fully awake.

Jennie…did Jennie need her?

Then she remembered. Jennie was spending the night with Nick's sister. She rolled over, and gazed straight into Nick's lazy eyes.

"Hello," he said softly.

His hand came up and brushed a strand of hair off her cheek. She managed not to flinch as heat arced through her. Shifting, her legs brushed against his naked ones beneath the sheets.

A fiery tide of embarrassment swept over her. Candace swallowed and anchored the silk sheet under her arms so that it wouldn't shift. "This is so awkward."

"Why?" His lips curved up. "Don't feel that away. After all, we have a daughter—this should've happened a long time ago. We've done things the wrong way around."

Oh, help!

A tender, teasing Nick Valentine was more than she could handle. How could she ever have thought those beautiful indigo eyes remote and inscrutable? The warmth and fire and emotion that filled them now tore at her heart.

She remembered how his passion had grown to a strange, very moving desperation last night.

He'd made her feel so special.

But now in the light of the morning after, it felt…wrong.

His fingers trailed down her cheek and came to a rest in the hollow of her throat. He caressed the sensitized, bare skin, and Candace was conscious of his square-tipped fingers touching her…slipping closer to the edge of the sheet trapped above her breasts.

And under the sheets his body was naked.

So was hers…

What had she done? All she could think of was that it was going to be impossible to keep working in Nick's home. How could she have jeopardized everything? Her relationship with her daughter, her position in Nick's house? Stupid. Stupid. Stupid.

And for what?

One night of desperate passion? That was forever going to lurk between them; they would never be able to put it to rest. She was going to have to leave. Leave Jennie.

Her heart clenched in pain.

And leave Nick.

The cold ache that numbed her chest was as unexpected as it was unwelcome.

No.

It couldn't possibly hurt to think of leaving Nick…

No. No. *No.* He meant nothing to her.

Yet the denial did nothing to ease the ache as she remembered how he'd listened to Bertha yesterday, how he'd laughed when his sister had tormented him about having to kiss Princess Piggy, how he'd ripped her heart out when he'd told her about his hollow marriage at dinner last night.

She couldn't possibly have—

No, she didn't want to think about it. Falling in love with Nick would be the stupidest thing she'd ever done.

"Come here." He pulled her into his arms.

For a split second, Candace resisted, then she let herself be drawn up against him. Shivers of delight raced through her as his bare skin brushed hers. He kissed her. Her mouth blossomed beneath his, opening, taking him into her, drawing him deep.

With a shock she realized how easy it would be to succumb.

Candace tore out of his arms, putting the length of the bed between them.

"Nick—no." Her breathing was ragged. She paused for a moment. "I don't want to make love again."

"You don't mean that—"

"I do," she said with a firmness she was far from feeling. "It's not going to happen again. This was the one and only time."

The soft light went out of his eyes. "Don't dismiss something you might regret losing later."

"Believe me, I won't regret this. We can't be lovers. It won't work." She said it with a finality that she hoped was convincing. And prayed he wouldn't recognize the undertone of desperation in her voice.

Twelve

The throaty roar of the Ferrari coming up the driveway caused the tension that had been lurking in the pit of Candace's stomach since Nick had made love to her two days ago to tighten another notch.

Run. Hide.

The anxiety that had been gnawing at her resurfaced. *You're not in love with him.* Candace sharply pulled herself together. There was no need to run, and she wasn't retreating to hide in the nursery. She was going to stay seated right where she was—on the carpet of the upstairs sitting room, playing with Jennie.

"You're losing it," she admonished herself. "Nick's home. So what?"

The memory of the time he'd kissed her here in this very place after she'd held the ice pack to his head flashed through her mind. Oh, God. Nowhere was safe from him, from the emotions he aroused in her.

Then Jennie gurgled, and, as always, Candace's heart warmed.

The baby's smile put everything in perspective.

She'd done nothing wrong. So she'd slept with Nick Valentine—a foolish mistake. Hardly the love of a lifetime. She had to keep telling herself that. Despite the starbursts of intense pleasure the experience had released, despite the sense of inevitability about what had happened, it was an error of judgment she bitterly regretted.

But there was no reason for it to cause her this much distress.

Except if there were consequences...

Candace told herself there wouldn't be. It was the wrong time of month. But she'd been reckless. *Stupid.* It was time to come to terms with what had happened, take the necessary steps to deal with any unfortunate circumstances and move on. She couldn't allow every thought of Nick to keep causing her heart palpitations.

The only problem was that Nick was making it incredibly difficult to put that night behind her.

Every look, every comment, seemed to be calculated to throw her into a state of confusion, where desire warred with good sense.

Even now, the sound of his footsteps coming up the marble stairway made her pulse go wild.

Nick was coming!

For one panicky moment Candace wished she'd retreated to the nursery when she'd had the opportunity. Then she steadied herself.

Get over it.

But the sight of his grim face knocked her off the frivolous emotional seesaw of her own dilemma.

"What's wrong?"

Something terrible had clearly happened.

Nick crossed the carpet, tossed a large envelope on the coffee table, and reached for Jennie.

"Nick…" The cold, set expression on his face as he lifted the baby into his arms unnerved her. "What's *happened?*"

He turned his head and gazed at her over the baby's head. There was a blank opacity in his eyes that made her heart stop. "Talk to me," she said. "You're scaring me."

"Desmond—" He broke off, burying his face in Jennie's neck.

"What about him?" What could his father-in-law have done to evoke this kind of reaction?

"He wants Jennie."

"What do you mean?" Chills goosed over her skin. "What's going on?"

"He's launched legal action." Nick raised his head and nodded toward the envelope he'd cast onto the table. "He wants custody of Jennie."

Candace covered her face with her hands. "Oh, my God." Spreading her fingers, she raised her head and stared helplessly at Nick. "Will he get it?"

"Not while I breathe." Determination turned his voice to steel. "He has money and power, but so do I. And this time I'm going to fight him."

"Why is he doing this?"

Nick hesitated, then said reluctantly, "He claims that I am a womanizer, that Jennie is neglected. It appears it was sparked by seeing you with me at the carnival—perhaps he thought I'd defiled his daughter's memory. That I'd already replaced her…with you."

That only made her feel so much worse. Because Desmond hadn't been wrong. By the end of the day she had been in Nick's bed. Jilly's bed. Oh, darn…

How sordid.

So much for putting it all behind her. It was proving to be impossible.

"Surely he won't have a case? He'd have to prove you grossly neglected Jennie." Anyone could see that wasn't true. Jennie was exploring the buttons of his chest, so at home in his arms that it brought a lump to Candace's throat.

Nick's mouth slanted up. "Even you thought that was true at one time."

"But not anymore." And that was true.

"He'll call Jilly's friends as witnesses to say I never cared for her, that I ignored her while we were married. Emotional abuse, they'll call it."

"But it was understandable," Candace defended him. "And it doesn't relate to Jennie."

"The same people will say that I wasn't interested in Jilly's pregnancy, that I wasn't even present for the baby's birth, that I went away for long periods for work and didn't even return when my child was ill—and it's all true."

He sounded so wretched that Candace's heart went out to him.

Nick settled down on the carpet beside her. Jennie stretched her hands out to the toys scattered around Candace, and he set her down. Both of them watched the baby as she tried to crawl toward the nearest blocks.

"How could I ever have known that she would wrap herself around my heart?" His gaze met Candace's. "I won't lose her. Desmond doesn't realize what he's started. I've already instructed my lawyers to oppose it. I think his suit is based on a pack of lies, but I'm not prepared to risk losing." Nick shifted closer. "Candace, we're going to make it clear he has no claim to Jennie—no biological tie exists between Jennie and Desmond."

"But Jilly adopted Jennie."

"I'm still waiting for proof that the adoption went through. You and I are Jennie's biological parents—and we both love her." His hand settled on hers where it pressed into the carpet.

"I don't think this is about Jennie—I think this is about clinging on to Jilly. He can't accept that she's gone."

Candace shifted her weight to enable her to turn her hand palm up, and laced her fingers with his, drawing immeasurable comfort from his touch. She'd been so careful to stay out of Nick's reach for the past couple of days in case she gave away her newly discovered feelings to him. The tender emotions were so precious, she had to shelter them from the bruising and battering that were inevitable.

But this time his touch wasn't about sex. It was about so much more.

"It must be hard for Desmond to have lost his daughter." Watching Jennie playing, she couldn't stop a twinge of sympathy for Jilly's father from stirring within her. How terrible to lose a child. "Poor man."

"Don't waste too much sympathy on him. I'm sure he only came up with this idea after seeing you with me on Sunday."

"You don't suppose—" She broke off, not wanting to voice the unkind thought.

"I don't suppose...what?"

"You spoke about Desmond trying to hurt you through Alison on Sunday. You don't suppose he's only doing this to hurt you again? That it's not about Jennie at all?"

Nick didn't respond, but the grip of his fingers grew tighter. Jennie was gnawing at a block. Her gums had been swollen, the next tooth would be through very soon.

"Such an overreaction would be insane," she said finally, hoping her response wasn't misplaced.

"Not for Desmond," said Nick slowly. "He's more than capable of that kind of malice. I simply hadn't considered that he might want to hurt me that much."

She turned her head and met his gaze. "Why would he want to do such a thing?"

"It's a power thing…he couldn't get me to bend to his will. Perhaps he thinks Jennie would be my breaking point."

"And would she be?"

Candace held her breath as she waited for his answer. This was crucially important, far more important than the throwaway tone of the question suggested.

There was a flash of something…vulnerability?…in the navy depths of his eyes. "It would kill me to lose Jennie."

The simple intensity of his response rocked her to the foundations of her existence. *He cared.* Candace wasn't sure why it mattered so much, only that it did.

He loved Jennie.

She placed her other hand over his, cradling his hand between both of hers. Her love for him flowed through her fingers, and she hoped it would give him the strength he needed to do what was right.

Without taking his eyes from her, he raised her hands and placed a kiss very carefully, first on the back of one hand, then on the other.

A rush of emotion overtook her.

Currents electrified the space between them. A compelling need to defuse the sudden tension vibrating between them made her say with forced lightness, "Boy, you certainly picked the family to marry into."

Nick shook his head. "They did the picking."

She remembered what he'd told her about how Jilly and her father had all but blackmailed him into marriage, and his suppressed frustration became totally understandable.

At last she said, "What are we going to do?"

We?

Nick stared at the woman sitting, legs outstretched, on the floor beside him, while their baby inched forward half crawling, half sliding as she tried to reach for a brightly colored ball. The firm hold of Candace's hand warmed him.

"It's not your problem," he said automatically.

Her eyes sparkled. "Of course it's my problem. I'm Jennie's mother. You're not going to leave me out in the cold on this."

"It would weaken Desmond's crazy suit to announce that Jennie is not Jilly's child—she's yours." It was a dangerous move. And it would give Candace an advantage that he would never be able to regain. Still, it might be a risk worth taking. "That way Desmond can claim no biological tie with the baby."

"It will cause a scandal."

"I don't care." But he hadn't thought about how it would affect her, and he discovered that he didn't have any desire to see her hurt or humiliated. "Will it matter to you if I announce it to the world?"

"Of course not!" A luminosity lit her gray eyes that made her more beautiful than ever. "I can think of nothing more wonderful than being publicly branded as Jennie's mother."

The moment of truth had come—if he announced that she was Jennie's mother, there would be no going back, there'd be no more talk of her leaving…

When she'd first told him that she was Jennie's mother, he'd wanted her out of the baby's life at all costs. But she'd called to something deep and dark and primitive in him, something he didn't fully comprehend.

All Nick knew was that he wasn't going to let her go.

The decision he'd come to the night he'd lost his senses returned from where he'd buried it at the back of his consciousness…it was a plan. A plan that might even work.

Thinking about it, he realized it was a team solution. *We.* He was starting to like the sound of that.

"Then marry me," he said simply.

"What?"

Her eyes darkened with disbelief.

"If you marry me, then as her biological parents we will be

able to show any judge that living with us is the best solution for Jennie. Together we will refute any evidence that Desmond might choose to present that Jennie is neglected. She has a father and mother who love her, and a safe and secure home. What more could any child need?"

And best of all, not only would he get to keep Jennie… Candace would never be able to leave.

"It's the best solution for Jennie," said Nick.

The best solution for Jennie? If she married him, Candace knew she would get hurt. Marrying a man she was falling in love with, living with him day by day, but never loved by him in return…

It sounded like hell on earth.

In her shock she couldn't think of anything logical to say, so she stated the obvious. "I'm not the kind of woman a man like you marries."

"What is the kind of woman a man like me marries?" One dark eyebrow arched up. "Someone like Jilly?"

Help.

"She'd be better suited to be your wife than me."

"I have to disagree." One of his hands let hers go and he cupped her face, his thumb stroking her jawline. "I don't think anyone would make a better mother for Jennie than you would."

Her insides melted.

"You might even already be pregnant with a sister or brother to Jennie. I didn't use protection the other night—or are you on the pill?"

Unfair.

"No, I'm not. But it's highly unlikely…I've already worked it out. So don't feel you have to marry me for that reason."

"I don't have to do anything. But marrying me will be the best thing to do."

Why was he suggesting this? Nick had spent seven years

in a loveless union. Last time he'd been trapped into it. This time he was volunteering it of his own accord. What was he thinking by proposing such an arrangement?

The answer came to her at once.

He was doing it for Jennie.

Nick was prepared to sacrifice himself. Out of his love for his daughter.

For Jennie.

Candace glanced down at the baby playing obliviously with blocks...and her heart ached. Tears pricked at the back of her throat. She'd come here to work as Jennie's nanny because she'd been convinced that Nick was neglecting her baby. She'd known he didn't love Jennie with the same depth of emotion that she did. She'd been ready to take Jennie away.

Now he'd just proved conclusively how much he loved their daughter.

Drawing a deep shaky breath, Candace returned her attention to the man who had turned all her assumptions about him upside down. "But what about you?" It was a cry from her heart. She didn't want him to give up so much for his daughter. "It's certainly not the best solution for you—you'll be trapped in a marriage you don't want all over again."

"This time it will be different."

Her heart leaped. Was it possible that he was starting to feel the same way about her as she felt about him?

Candace was almost afraid to ask. Her heart was beating so hard she was sure he must hear it, sitting so close to her. "How will it be different?"

She tensed, wired, every nerve ending expectant as she waited for his answer.

One finger trailed down her cheek, leaving a trail of fire in its wake. "This time I will have a lover."

So he hadn't said he loved her. But *lover* was good, wasn't it? Candace wavered. No, she decided, she wanted more; she needed him to tell her he loved her. Choosing her words carefully, she asked, "But how will this be different? Jilly was your lover, too."

The teasing finger stilled. "I never made love to Jilly."

Was he saying that he'd only had sex with his dead wife, that he'd never loved her? Did that mean he loved her, Candace?

"I know you didn't love her."

"I didn't love her, nor did I *make* love to her."

"What do you mean…?" Voice trailing away, she waited. Was Nick saying something else altogether…something she could hardly believe was true?

"You've seen my bedroom. It was mine alone. Jilly had her own suite, her own bed. I never shared it. We never slept together." His mouth compressed at her incredulous look. "There was no sex. Not for seven long years."

"You once told me there were no other women—" Candace broke off unable to finish.

"That's right."

My God.

No wonder he'd been so…*desperate.* Now he was telling her that he expected their marriage to have sex. Yet he'd never said he loved her.

Stupid! He wasn't marrying her because he loved her. He was marrying her to gain Jennie a set of biological parents—a set of parents who loved their daughter and would make it clear to any court.

Nick was making the same mistake of going into a loveless marriage with the best intentions for the wrong reasons all over again. Except this time, instead of saving Bertha and Henry, he was trying to save Jennie. And this time sex would be part of the deal.

The pain below her heart grew more intense.

Nick Valentine deserved to find a woman he could really love. For all his life. Candace wished that woman were her. But it wouldn't be her. Even though he was the father of her baby…and the man she loved.

Nick would never be hers.

Shaking her head, she said slowly, "I'm sorry Nick, I can't marry you."

Not even for Jennie.

Nick had retreated to the sanctuary of his study, where he'd poured himself one measure of single-malt Scotch, then collapsed onto the burgundy love seat.

He'd been so certain she would say yes.

If Candace married him, it would've been a tidy solution, and Jennie would've been safe. He couldn't fathom why she'd refused the most sensible course of action under the circumstances.

There'd been flashes of time over the past few days when he could've sworn she desired him almost as much as he craved her. It had been there in the way her gaze flicked to him, then quickly away, in the soft flush of color that followed, in the slight stutter she developed when he stood too close.

But she'd turned him down flat.

Well, he supposed it served him right for being so sure of her.

He raised the heavy crystal glass to his lips and took a sip, savoring the smoky flavor.

It wasn't over yet. Nick was determined to escalate that reciprocal passion he'd sensed in her. He was convinced he could change her *no* to a *yes*.

He knew he didn't have a lot of time. He'd have to move fast if he wanted a marriage to thwart the thorn in his side that Desmond had become. He had to move now.

If he wanted to keep Candace.

Thirteen

Nick had rarely entered Jilly's suite of rooms during their marriage.

Now as he crossed the threshold he noticed that it smelled... empty...like a hotel room long deserted. The curtains were drawn, dimming the room. He flicked the light switch, picked up a remote and activated it. The curtains opened and sunlight filtered in through the lacy blinds beneath.

The bedcover in Jilly's signature gray and white and lime lay smooth and uncreased. Two crystal perfume bottles stood on the dresser, and a Lalique vase stuffed with silk tulips occupied a writing desk beside the windows.

Feeling like an intruder, Nick crossed to where a dressing room opened off Jilly's en suite. Her clothes had already been packed up and given to charity. The wall safe was empty. Nick had placed Jilly's jewels in a bank deposit box in trust for Jennie, the day after the funeral.

Any hope that he might discover secrets that had not died with Jilly was fading rapidly. The bathroom cupboards held only unopened toiletries, clean towels and a hairdryer. Impersonal items waiting for the next occupant. The personal items Jilly had used were long gone.

Back in her bedroom he checked the dresser drawers, her bedside table...all empty...as he'd expected. He'd gone through them himself. Nick moved on to her writing desk, already knowing what he'd find.

The first drawer revealed her wallet, a checkbook, an expired passport and a folder of canceled credit cards. The next drawer down contained Jilly's lime-green laptop and an iPhone. The final drawer held a box of Jilly's gold embossed stationery, envelopes, her address book...exactly as she'd left them. He lifted the stationery box out and opened it. Letterheads with *Jilly Valentine* surrounded by tiny pink hearts. He smiled. How Jilly. There were thank-you notes, too. He put the box back and started to close the drawer, then paused.

Taking out the stationery box again, he lifted the large black address book, and pulled out a second black volume. Jilly's appointment book. Next he opened the drawer above and extracted her laptop with its power cable.

Seating himself on the padded desk chair, Nick flipped open the cover of the five-year appointment book. Finally he booted the laptop up. In less time than expected he'd found a file labeled *Journal*. Opening it, Nick started to read.

The following morning, Nick strode past an unsuspecting receptionist and, at the end of the corridor, entered the corner office unannounced.

Desmond Perry sat behind his desk, puffed up as an angry toad. Red-faced, he demanded, "What's the meaning of bursting into my office like this?"

Nick took a seat in one of the two chairs in front of the desk, and leaned back. "If you prefer, I can arrange to see you another time with my lawyer in attendance. Or you can listen to what I have to say now."

Desmond stopped blustering. "What do you want?"

"I want you to stop harassing my sister and brother-in-law and tell your crony at NorthPark to withdraw his eviction notice." Nick paused, while Desmond stared at him. "I want you to forget about trying to acquire enough of a stake in Valentine's to force a takeover—yes, I know about your plan to develop the land, not for high-density apartments, but for a shopping mall in partnership with NorthPark."

"How did—"

Nick held up a hand. "And you're going to halt all legal action to get custody of Jennie."

"Why should I do anything you want?"

Nick started with what was most important to him first. *Jennie.* "Jennie isn't Jilly's daughter."

"I know that."

It appeared that Candace was right; Desmond was only trying to hurt him though his daughter, enough to make him pursue a frivolous legal suit purely to frustrate Nick. But did he know who her real mother was?

"Then you know you have no right to her."

The older man picked up a pen and tapped it against the wooden edge of the desk. "My daughter adopted her—she's my grandchild."

Nick's first reaction was to lean over the desk and punch Desmond, as he'd been dying to do for weeks. Instead, he said, "I intend to challenge that adoption. I don't want my daughter growing up like Jilly did, with a guardian whose only way of showing his love is to buy her whatever she wants."

Desmond blinked, and Nick regretted his hotheaded reply. The man had lost a daughter. Then he remembered the pain that had poured out in Jilly's diary. It was no wonder that the only way she knew to respond to being in love was to try to buy the loved one.

It had been a disastrous course of action; but spoiled, emotionally starved Jilly had been too insecure to know any other way.

Nick held his father-in-law's gaze, until Desmond looked away first.

"I found the journal Jilly kept. It made for very interesting reading." That jerked Desmond's attention back to him, Nick noticed with satisfaction. "She poured everything into it—even the reason why the IVF was done offshore—she knew she would never get her harebrained scheme past the ethics committee that approves surrogate arrangements in New Zealand. When I gave the necessary signature for my sperm to be transferred offshore, I had no knowledge that it wouldn't be used to impregnate my wife, but rather the surrogate she had chosen."

Jilly had written of her overriding need for a baby to fill the emptiness of her life. That had caused Nick a pang of guilt. He'd been so busy resenting Jilly for forcing him into an untenable situation that he'd never tried to figure out what had been behind her desire for a child. Jilly had also written about her craving to experience pregnancy firsthand. Nick could only assume that longing had triggered the fake pregnancy she'd enacted—together with the desperation for Jennie to be seen as *her* child.

Watching Desmond carefully, Nick added, "New Zealand law requires the baby's real mother to be listed on the birth certificate. Jilly bribed the midwife who tended to the baby's birth to state that Jilly was the baby's mother." When Candace had first claimed to be Jennie's mother, Nick had known it was impossible. According to the birth certificate, Jilly was Jennie's mother. Jilly's journal had solved another piece of the puzzle.

Heaven knew what else Jilly had done.

It was time to play his hand. "The baby's birth certificate will be corrected." He hoped to attend to the change quietly.

Jennie's status as Candace's daughter was something he intended to handle as tactfully as he could. "Do you want your daughter's fraud to be made public? The fact that she lied to me, her husband, about being pregnant while forging my consent to a surrogacy arrangement? About bribing medical practitioners to go along with fertilizing another woman's egg and implanting it offshore into that woman without my knowledge and consent? About paying off a midwife to falsify a birth certificate? Do you want people to know how mentally frail she was? How your years of emotional neglect affected her?"

Desmond started to object, then he stopped.

"You've worked to build a media image as a philanthropist, a devoted father to Jilly. Desmond, do you want that tainted?" Nick pressed on. "Do you want the real story of your troubled relationship with your daughter made public? The facts of how she manipulated the surrogate system exposed, along with how she bribed medical officials?"

Holding his breath, Nick waited. Would it be enough to persuade Desmond to back down?

"No," Desmond conceded at last. He tossed aside the pen he'd been fiddling with, and spat out, "I'd rather she was remembered as the beautiful, happy woman she was before she married you."

Nick nodded. "I was not the right man for her—there can be no doubt about that." He regretted the years he and Jilly had both wasted. From Jilly's journal he'd learned that in her way she did love him, and she'd come to realize her mistake in forcing him into a union he didn't want. That had been one of the motivations for a baby. To bring them closer together. She'd thought that Nick needed a child—she'd viewed him as a great prospective father. That had deeply touched Nick, giving him a way forward to remember Jilly in a kinder way.

And Jilly had done more…

"Inside Jilly's journal, I also discovered a codicil Jilly

added to her will, leaving her stock in Valentine's to me."
The codicil was dated shortly before Jennie was born. Nick
was grateful she'd taken time to create it.

Desmond picked up the pen again. "My lawyer told me Jilly
had instructed him to draw up a codicil, but he didn't have the
signed document. We decided she'd had second thoughts."

"She signed it. And it's witnessed. It's valid. I've sent it to
my lawyer," Nick said. "He'll communicate with the lawyer
handling Jilly's estate."

After a long moment, Desmond gave a sigh. He looked less
arrogant—and much older—than when Nick had first entered
the large corner office. "It looks like there's not much for me
to say."

"You'll drop the suit for custody?"

Desmond gave a terse nod.

"You will agree to speak to NorthPark about having Alison
and Richard's eviction notice revoked?" Again a nod. "And
you will stop pursuing Valentine stock?"

"I'll do what you want." There was still anger on the older
man's face.

Nick reminded himself that Desmond had lost his daughter
tragically, unexpectedly, and whatever their convoluted father-
daughter relationship, he'd loved Jilly in his own way.

Although Nick wanted as little as possible to do with
Desmond in the future, he didn't want the man to be an enemy,
forever scheming how to hurt him. There'd been a moment
earlier when he'd itched to hit Desmond; he was relieved that
he hadn't.

It would've made him less of a man in his own eyes—and
he knew that Candace would've hated to hear that he'd used
violence against a father who must still be grieving.

Bottom line: he wanted the feud with Jilly's father to
be over. To that end he said, "I plan to build a children's
playground at the flagship Valentine's in Jilly's memory."

Desmond studied him warily. "I'd like you to open it—I'll make sure the event has plenty of publicity."

"Jilly would've appreciated that. Thank you." The anger started to fade from Desmond's face. "Perhaps you could build a bench somewhere with a plaque dedicating it to her. She loved flowers."

"I could do that. There's a rose garden where Jilly often took photographs, with a sundial in the center. A bench would fit in perfectly. Many people could sit and enjoy the surroundings."

Desmond nodded slowly. "I might come and sit there myself."

"Good." He could tolerate that, Nick decided, rising to his feet. He held out his hand. "I'm glad we've resolved our differences." He only hoped the coming confrontation with Candace was going to proceed as smoothly.

Nick knew Desmond Perry would no longer present a threat to his family.

Candace was reclining on a lounger in the shade under the poolside umbrella, rubbing the fluff that was Jennie's hair dry after a lunchtime swim in the pool, when she heard the scrape of the sliding doors and looked up.

Her pulse picked up as Nick emerged from the house. He'd left early for work this morning, and Candace discovered that she'd missed him. She'd gotten used to the three of them— Nick, Jennie and her—sharing breakfast on the deck on the sunny early mornings but he'd kept himself away since she'd turned down his proposal.

It had left her feeling restless.

Sitting up, she set down the towel and pulled the T-shirt Jennie wore straight, then checked to see that the sarong she'd donned over her own damp swimsuit hadn't parted to reveal her tummy or legs. Since she'd made love with Nick, she'd taken great care not to allow any opportunity for those burning moments of awareness to arise.

"She's a real water baby," she remarked, stroking Jennie's head before glancing back up to Nick.

"The signs were always there," said Nick. He barely glanced at Candace's scantily clad body as he pulled up a chair from the table arrangement where they ate in the morning. "I need to talk to you."

His face was stern.

"Yes?"

"Desmond has agreed to withdraw the application for custody of Jennie."

She couldn't stop the huge grin that lit up her face. "That's fabulous news. Nick, I'm so relieved. When?"

"As we speak. My lawyers are talking to his."

"Oh, I could hug you." Then she wished she hadn't added they last bit as his face remained set. Nick didn't even joke in response. Something was wrong. "There's more isn't there?"

"I found Jilly's journal and I've been reading her appointment book."

He paused.

Candace waited, feeling puzzled at the withdrawal she sensed in him. On her lap, Jennie grew restless.

"Do you know that you're not named as Jennie's mother on the birth certificate?"

She frowned at the switch in subject. "You said that when I first told you I was Jennie's mother. I thought you'd simply never seen it." It had seemed typical of the remote, uninvolved father she'd pegged him to be. "That can't be right."

She didn't like the way he was watching her, like a dark panther waiting to pounce on the first slip she made. She swung her legs to the ground so that she was perched on the edge of the lounger. Spreading the biggest towel on the deck in front of the lounger, she placed Jennie on it and handed her a teething ring. Immediately, Jennie started to chew.

"You had a midwife at the birth."

"Yes—Jilly wanted the home experience, she thought it would give you and her a better chance to bond with the baby than a hospital birth, where your involvement would be minimal." Candace paused. "She even said you'd decided not to be present because you would be overseas. Thinking about it now, you wouldn't even have known about the birth, right?"

He shook his head. "I didn't. Jilly told me she was three weeks off her due date, that it would be a good time to take a trip to meet three new suppliers…and on the way home I attended a gardeners' conference. I thought there was still plenty of time."

"Oh." It put paid to another assumption she'd made. "It was fortunate for Jilly the timing worked out."

"Yes." He was still watching her, but the flat line of his mouth had softened.

Candace found she was breathing easier. "When you failed to turn up at Jennie's birth, I started to grow truly worried about what kind of father you would be. I told Jilly I wished I hadn't signed away my right to stay in contact with the baby after the birth. Jilly was quick to point out that she'd always made it clear that you didn't really want to know about the surrogate, that you wanted to pretend the baby was Jilly's. But I couldn't understand how any father would want to miss such a momentous occasion."

"It certainly wasn't part of Jilly's plan for you to stay in the picture. I discovered from my reading that Jilly bribed the midwife to list her as the mother on the birth certificate."

"I never knew that." Candace thought about it as she watched Jennie toss the ring down, then pick it up again and shove it back in her mouth. "But it makes sense. That's why she wanted a home birth with a midwife?" Sadness swept her.

"I would've been happier at the hospital, given that Jennie was my first child and anything could've gone wrong. But it was so important to her that I gave in."

"Is there anything else you want to tell me?"

Even over the two yards separating them, she could sense his tension.

It was hardly a good time to confess the one aspect of her behavior she wasn't proud of. It would be better to wait for a time when Nick was more open to discussion. Candace knew she was putting it off. When would there ever be an easy time?

She drew a deep breath and squarely met Nick's indigo gaze. "Yes. Jilly gave me money."

Nick's almost black gaze bored into her. "You lied to me. You told me you weren't paid for being a surrogate."

"I wasn't," she said automatically. "You—I mean Jilly— paid for the medical expenses and she covered my other expenses. The one thing she did pay for that I didn't want was the stay in the resort when the IVF was done. And she spoiled me with gifts when she visited during the pregnancy…I didn't have the heart to refuse because it gave her such pleasure. But this payment was different."

"How?" He gave a snort.

"It was a large sum."

"Okay." He nodded. "So when did she give you money? Did you call her?"

"No! I wasn't ever supposed to make contact again." Candace glanced down at Jennie again, remembering how the despair in the empty days after Jennie's birth had sapped her. "After I'd given Jennie up, she called to see how I was."

Then she lifted her gaze to Nick's, hoping he couldn't sense her inner shaking or recognize the fear and vulnerability. "I was a mess. Jilly came around to see me—she didn't bring Jennie. When I first heard her car pull up, I hoped with a desperate yearning I can't even begin to describe to you that she'd reconsidered, that she was prepared to relax the noncontact clause in the surrogate contract. But she was alone. I told her that my mother was in the hospital after falling off a ladder in the pantry. She was unconscious, and brain damage was suspected. I started to cry, I couldn't stop. I didn't know what I was going to do. You probably won't believe me, but Jilly gave me comfort."

"I do believe you. Jilly liked to be needed. Too many of the people in her life didn't need her at all," Nick said slowly. "It may be part of the reason she was so eager for a baby."

"When it became clear that my mother was going to need care, Jilly offered to pay for her place at Apple Orchards."

"So in the end you did accept payment for Jennie."

Candace shook her head frantically. "*No.* It was never meant to be like that! How could you think that I'd accept a womb-for-hire arrangement?" It hurt that he'd assumed the worst. "I kept saying no, but Jilly insisted. I gave in, because it made my life, and Mom's, easier."

Nick didn't say anything. He just stared at her with a blank expression, the muscle high on his cheek pulsing furiously.

"You know what?" The shaking had taken over her whole body. "I'll tell you something I haven't even admitted to myself. I felt so guilty later. Because deep down I feel like I traded Jennie for my mother's comfort. And even telling Jilly I would try to pay her back didn't help ease the guilt. We both knew it was far beyond my means."

"I'm sorry." Nick rose to his feet and settled himself beside her on the lounger, and groped awkwardly for her hand. "I found reference to the payment she'd made—and I jumped to the conclusion you'd taken money in exchange for Jennie. Jilly liked you," he added after a small silence. "There was an entry after one of the times she'd spoken to you at the hospital, saying how sympathetic you were. She worked hard to become friendly with you."

Candace gripped his hand, and the trembling started to

subside. "I liked her, too. But I felt a little sorry for her…she was so desperate for the child she couldn't have."

"She sensed that she could manipulate you…I suspect she might have helped your mother because she felt remorse about it."

"How awful."

"Not that awful." Nick tipped his head in the direction of the baby sitting on the towel in front of them. "It gave us both Jennie."

The distance she'd sensed between them when he first came out had gone.

"And I met you." Nick gave her a bittersweet smile. "That would never have happened if not for Jilly."

Before Candace could respond, he'd risen to his feet.

"I'd better get back to work. I have several appointments this afternoon about the company's expansion into the South Island and the sooner I get them over, the sooner I can be home again." He paused, and then said, "Perhaps we can go and see your mother on the weekend. I'd like to meet her."

Fourteen

"Oh, you've brought Jennie back for a visit." Catherine Morrison stood in the open doorway of her large sunny bedroom. "Come, bring her stroller in."

The first thought Nick had on meeting Candace's mother was that Jennie had been here before. The second was that he could see where Candace had gotten her lovely gray eyes. And that led him to realize that Jennie would, in all probability, be blessed with a pair of angel eyes, too.

His final realization was that Catherine had no idea Jennie was her granddaughter.

"Jennie fell asleep in the car, and we managed to get her into the stroller without her waking. Mom, this is Nick Valentine," said Candace.

Catherine inspected him curiously, and then smiled, a lovely gentle smile that reminded him immeasurably of Candace. "I'm pleased to meet you."

"Sit by the window, Nick." Candace pointed to a sofa covered with roses. "Mom can sit next to you. I'll sit on the bed."

"We could go down to the lounge," suggested her mother. "There's a lot more space down there."

Candace wrinkled her nose.

"The lounge was full of people playing bingo." Nick grinned conspiratorially at Catherine. "It will be too noisy to talk."

Catherine nodded slowly. "I'd forgotten about the bingo."

"We'll take a walk down to the roses a bit later." Candace perched herself on the bed, Jennie's stroller beside her.

"You like roses," Nick said to the older woman.

Her eyes lit up. "Oh, yes…but you could've guessed that from my room."

Glancing around, Nick took in the design of the sofa, the creamy white roses in the vase on the dresser and the photo of a pale pink, old-fashioned damask rose printed onto a canvas block that hung above the bed. Jilly's work. He studied it. The photograph revealed all the best sides of Jilly. Her femininity. Her passion for beauty. He could see why Candace had chosen it for her mother.

"That was my birthday present. Candace chose it for me."

"Yes, I know."

"Do you know Candace well?"

"Mom—"

"Are you…" Catherine's voice trailed away and she glanced at Candace. "What does one call it these days? He's too sophisticated to be called a boyfriend."

Candace had gone bright red, and Nick started to smile. Then he took pity on her. "You can tell your mom if you want."

"He *is* your boyfriend." Catherine looked delighted. "You were so sad when you came back from your trip, I thought you'd had your heart broken." She clapped her hand over her mouth. "Sorry."

Nick quickly reassured her. "I didn't break her heart."

"Mom—" Candace got up from the bed and crossed over

to perch herself on the arm of the sofa beside her mother. "I have to apologize to you. I've been keeping a secret from you. There was no trip. I agreed to help a woman—have a baby. I agreed to donate my eggs and carry the baby for her. Part of the agreement was that I'd keep it a secret. I should've told you."

Catherine made the connection immediately; she glanced at the stroller and back to Candace. "Jennie is your daughter."

She touched Candace's hand, and Nick's throat closed at the tender empathy in the gesture. How different Jilly's life could've been with a mother like Catherine.

"It must've hurt terribly to give her up," she was saying.

Candace's eyes glimmered with unshed tears. "It did. But she had parents who wanted her."

Nick thanked her silently for that.

"But you're looking after her...is that a good idea, darling?"

"Her mom died. She needs me."

The simple words rang out in the room.

Nick faced the truth of them. Jennie needed Candace. So did Catherine. And so did he. Candace brought light and sunshine into all their lives.

He loved her.

The knowledge settled over him without any sense of shock. In his heart he'd known it all along. The special qualities she possessed—her loyalty, her patience, her generosity—made her easy to love.

But he'd been too afraid to face up to it and admit it. So he'd hidden behind emotions he'd called desire and passion, want and even lust...

But he loved her. And that admission freed him.

Catherine was watching him with gentle understanding in her eyes. "You will make sure Candace doesn't get hurt?"

"Mom!"

"Of course," Nick assured Catherine, ignoring Candace's horrified expression.

"You will take care of her if anything happens to me?"

For a split second, Nick glimpsed stark fear in the eyes so like Candace's. "I'll take care of her—and Jennie. But be assured nothing's going to happen to you. Not for a very long time."

"Thank you." The smile was sweet. Then Catherine looked down at the baby in the pram. "Look, Jennie's waking up—"

A cross gurgle of complaint made them all laugh.

"I think the time has come for that walk in the garden," said Nick.

They'd gotten back to the house—Candace didn't think it could ever be called a home—and she'd bathed and fed Jennie. Nick walked into the nursery as she was putting a sleepy Jennie into the crib.

Restlessness seized Candace. Excusing herself on a pretext, she'd gone downstairs to make herself a cup of chamomile tea and had just settled down in the upstairs sitting room with the hot drink and a magazine when Nick came out of the nursery.

"She's fast asleep." He sat down on the love seat opposite her and stretched back, folding his arms behind his head.

She shifted, aware of him watching her, conscious that night was falling and that the two of them were alone with so much unspoken between them.

"I liked your mother," he said at last.

Candace set the magazine down on a lamp table beside her cooling tea. "Thank you."

"But I will admit that I was surprised today," he added.

"Why?"

"Your mother had met Jennie before."

"Once. She had a fall and the staff called me to come and see her because she was badly shaken." She looked at him through her lashes. "It was the day you thought I'd kidnapped Jennie—and you almost filed a missing persons report."

"Ah, that day."

"I didn't want to call you for help…so I took her with me. I'm sorry, Nick, I should've told you."

"But then you would've had to explain about your mother."

Nodding, she agreed, "Exactly."

There was a long pause.

"You're going to marry me," he said with such a lack of fanfare that for a second Candace thought she'd misheard. But the leap of her heart, coupled with the determined resolve in his eyes, told her that she'd heard right.

"Nick…" She sat forward on the edge of the love seat, and searched for the right words.

This was exactly what she didn't need. She might love Nick until it hurt. But she wasn't marrying him, because she wasn't prepared to confine him in a trap he would come to resent.

Sex would never be enough…

If there was one thing Candace was certain of by now, it was that Nick had an overdeveloped sense of responsibility. He'd done everything in his power to save Henry and Bertha's garden center because they'd offered a young rebel a job; he'd been prepared to do everything in his power to help Jilly have the baby she desperately desired, even though he'd never loved her.

Now Candace couldn't rid herself of the memory of the expression on Nick's face when he'd all but promised her mother he would take care of her, too.

"You can't just say things like that," she said at last.

"I'm not just saying it…we're getting married."

"Why? So that you can take care of me?"

His eyes grew slumberous. "Among other things."

"I don't need you to take care of me!"

Candace wasn't going to allow him to distract her. Sex would never be enough. Not without love. And she wasn't about to fool herself that her love would be enough for both of them. Nick had been down that road once before, and it had brought nothing but unhappiness to everyone concerned.

Finally, she had no choice but to tell him the truth. "I have no intention of trapping you into a loveless marriage."

"You're not Jilly." Nick got to his feet and came around the glass coffee table to sit beside her. "You wouldn't be trapping me. I want to marry you. Trust me to know the difference."

He was too close.

Help!

If she said yes, all her problems would be solved. It would be so easy to throw herself into his arms and accept his proposal. She'd be able to live with her daughter; she'd have Nick at her side, her partner by day, her lover by night.

It was too tempting.

Fear that he'd talk her into a marriage she wanted so badly made her say, "You're only doing this because my mother said I needed to be taken care of."

He took her hand.

"Not true." Nick tugged her toward him. "I've already asked you to marry me once, so I certainly didn't need Catherine to come up with the idea."

She let him draw her closer, inch by breathtaking inch. "I hadn't forgotten. But last time you asked me for Jennie's sake…because you love your daughter."

"Clearly I've been doing it all wrong." Nick had maneuvered her right next to him, now he bent his head and kissed her. Her lips parted. But instead of deepening the kiss, he murmured, "What I should have been saying was that you need to marry me for *my* sake."

Candace was too scared to breathe. "What do you mean?"

Then he kissed her. This time it was deep and dark and sexy, none of the light butterfly wings that he'd been tormenting her with for the past few seconds.

When he'd finished, he raised his head and his eyes met hers. "Haven't you figured it out yet?"

His expression was gentle, and Candace could feel her throat tightening with emotion.

But she didn't dare hope...so she waited.

"I love you."

It felt like her birthday and Christmas had come at the same time. Candace closed her eyes and offered a prayer of thanks.

When she opened them again, he was still gazing down at her, his expression quizzical. "If you marry me, we would be a family. You, me and Jennie. Then there's Catherine and my sister and her family." He smiled at her. "That's more family than I ever dreamed of having."

"Oh, Nick. I love you, too."

"So you will marry me?" Uncertainty flickered in his eyes, and then it was gone. "I'm not going to allow you to say no again."

"I have no intention of saying no." Candace found herself smiling. "All those noes...it sounds ridiculous. So I'll just have to say yes."

He punched the air. "Yes!"

That made Candace burst out laughing, but she stopped abruptly as he kissed her again. Her arms crept up around his neck, and she leaned into him.

"Let's go to bed." Nick's heart was thudding against her chest.

She pulled away and gave him a demure smile. "Why not?"

Rising swiftly, Nick helped her to her feet. Then, arm in arm, they made their way to his suite.

This time they made love with slow intensity. Every touch counted. Every kiss brought a burst of new emotion. By the time Nick finally pulled her over him and they united, both of

them were ready for the hot glow that waited. The heat built
and built until the world spun.

Afterward, Nick pulled her into his arms, and pressed a
kiss on her forehead. "That was fantastic."

"I'd have to agree," she said.

"One more thing." Nick shifted the pillows before leaning
back, and arranging her into the crook of his arm. "There's a
house that's come up for sale that I want to show you."

She turned her head, and looked up at him. "Oh, good,
does this mean you're going to sell the marble mausoleum?"
A weight she didn't know existed lifted.

"Mausoleum?" he sounded affronted.

"It's not a home," said Candace. "It's too cold."

"Cold? The heating system is spectacular."

"I don't mean the temperature—it doesn't have a heart."

Nick gave her a secret smile. "Wait until you see what I
have to show you. I think you'll want to call it home."

"You might have to consider trading the Ferrari in for a
family model," Candace told Nick as he throttled the Ferrari
back and slowed down. They'd left Jennie with Alison and
her sons while Nick took her to see the secret house he'd been
so tantalizingly closemouthed about.

A Realtor's For Sale sign leaned drunkenly against a large
pohutukawa tree.

"Is this it?" she asked.

Nick swung the sports car into an overgrown tree-lined
driveway. "It's a jungle in here," he commented. "Let's see
what state the house is in."

Puzzled, Candace turned her head to look at him, and her
heart constricted at the sight of his beloved profile. He would
forever have this effect on her. She must be the most fortunate
woman in the world. She pulled her thoughts together and
tried to remember what she'd wanted to ask. It came to her.
"I thought you'd already seen the house."

"A long time ago. Seven years ago to be exact."

And then she knew. She placed her hand on his thigh, and dug her fingers in. "Nick!"

Laughing, he trod on the brake. The car came to a stop. "Careful where you grab me, woman."

"I don't care what state the house is in, this is where I want to live."

"Hang on, we need to take a look first. The house might no longer be a good investment."

Candace said a rude word. "I don't care if it's a bad investment, if you still love this place we're living here."

His eyes softened. "You'd make that great a sacrifice?"

"Nothing compared to the sacrifice I thought you were willing to make." Candace shot him a cheeky grin. "At least I know you love me—a house can be fixed."

"Okay, let's go see."

The Ferrari nosed through the trees, and Candace's breath caught as she glimpsed the grand old structure rising ahead. This was the house Mrs. Busby had told her he'd loved and sold when he'd married Jilly. "Oh, it's beautiful."

"It needs painting for starters."

"What's a little paint?" When Nick pulled up outside the homestead, she jumped out. "Hurry up…and don't forget the keys."

It took them half an hour to wander through the place, Nick showing her nooks and crannies she would not otherwise have found.

"It was built back in the 1880s when trading ships used to stop off not far away. The floors are made of kauri wood."

"I can see why you love it. It reeks of heritage. I think I've fallen in love." She slanted him a glance as she slipped her hand into his. "Again."

* * * * *

THE PREGNANCY CONTRACT

BY
YVONNE LINDSAY

New Zealand born, to Dutch immigrant parents, **Yvonne Lindsay** became an avid romance reader at the age of thirteen. Now, married to her "blind date" and with two fabulous children, she remains a firm believer in the power of romance. Yvonne feels privileged to be able to bring to her readers the stories of her heart. In her spare time, when not writing, she can be found with her nose firmly in a book, reliving the power of love in all walks of life. She can be contacted via her website www.yvonnelindsay.com.

To Anna Campbell and Trish Morey, the funniest
"went to the cheese shop" and French champagne
buddies a girl could have!

One

"He's *dead?*"

Wade watched her carefully. Oh, she was a good actress all right. Anyone would think she was shocked, or even sorry, to hear her father had died. But if that was genuinely the case, maybe she'd have been at his side in his last hours instead of partying her way around the world these past eight years. He fought back the rawness of his own grief for the man who had been his mentor—his best friend. He should have been able to share that grief with the man's daughter. But he knew better than to share any part of his feelings with Piper Mitchell again.

"Yeah. Four days ago. This—" he gestured behind him to the throng of people circulating through the lower floors of the house "—is his wake."

"No, he can't be dead. You're lying." Piper took a shuddering breath. "You *have* to be lying!"

"I wouldn't waste my breath lying to you."

His words slowly sank in, digging beyond her disbelief.

He could see the exact moment the reality hit her. Her face paled beneath the healthy tan that had gilded her cheeks only moments ago. Her light-colored irises that glittered like the palest blue topaz all but disappeared as her pupils dilated and the shadows under her eyes hollowed and darkened. She took an unsteady step backward, and instinctively Wade shot out a hand to stop her before she toppled down the tiled stairs behind her.

She tilted her head to look at his hand, curled around her arm.

"I...I don't feel very well," she said, her voice trailing away into nothing as her knees buckled and her eyelids fluttered shut.

Silently cursing her for both her timing and her reaction, Wade scooped her up into his arms and carried her through the front door.

"Mr. Collins, is everything all right?" Dexter, the butler, for want of a better description, came hurrying from the ballroom where the bulk of the mourners had gathered over drinks and canapés.

"It's Miss Mitchell, she collapsed when she heard the news about her father," Wade replied, clamping his jaw on the more colorful adjectives he'd have preferred to use to explain her reaction.

"Should I call a doctor?" Dexter asked.

"No, I don't think that's necessary. Let's see how she feels when she wakes. Is her room still prepared?"

"It was one of Mr. Mitchell's express wishes that Miss Piper's room always be kept ready, sir."

"I'll take her up, then." Wade nodded at the pack Piper had dropped on the front porch. "Could you bring her things?"

"Certainly, sir."

Wade powered up the wide sweep of stairs with his late boss's daughter in his arms. Despite her height, she barely weighed enough to register on his breathing, and when he lay her down on the frilly comforter that adorned her bed, he noticed how thin and frail she was beneath the jeans and bulky sweatshirt she wore.

"Perhaps it would be best if I called Mrs. Dexter to attend to her," Dexter said smoothly as he deposited the grimy backpack on the polished wooden floor of the room.

"Yes," Wade said, watching for any signs of consciousness from the still inert form on the bed. There was no way he wanted to have his hands on her any longer than necessary. Not anymore. "That would be best."

Why now? he wondered. Why had she come back now? He stood to one side of the bed, watching the shallow rise and fall of her chest beneath the well-worn sweatshirt. He shook his head. He'd seen the bank statements and knew how she'd burned through her trust fund over the past eight years. What the hell had she spent all her money on? Certainly not clothing if what she wore now was anything to go by.

A noise at the door alerted him to the presence of the housekeeper-cum-cook he'd inherited along with Dexter when he'd bought the house from Rex Mitchell a couple years ago.

"Ah, lovey, what have you done to yourself?" Mrs. Dexter muttered under her breath as she pressed a hand to Piper's forehead. "And your beautiful hair, what on earth is this?"

"I believe they're called dreadlocks," Wade said dryly, his lip curling with derision.

Trust Piper to arrive on his doorstep looking like some refugee from another country. It was just the kind of plea for attention they'd all come to expect from her during her late teens.

Mind you, why should he be surprised? It amazed him to realize, deep down, he'd still hoped that she might have changed. But, no. In typical Piper fashion, she'd proven time and again that there was only one person who she cared about in this world, and that person was herself. And nothing and no one would ever get in the way of her pleasure. Not even her dying father.

Not even the baby she'd almost had.

Dexter reappeared in the doorway to Piper's room.

"Mr. Collins, your guests?"

"Yes, thank you, Dexter. I'll be down immediately."

Walking away from the woman on the bed, he returned to the gathering below. The gathering that was supposed to be a celebration of the life of the man who had given Wade every opportunity to shake off the dregs of his upbringing and excel. Rex Mitchell had been an ornery bastard at times, but he'd had a heart bigger than most and believed in rewarding hard work. And he'd loved his daughter, who had repaid him for that love by walking away from him without a backward glance. Sure, he'd tried to control Piper, but she'd been headstrong and needed a firm hand to guide her. For all the good that had done any of them.

Wade joined the throng in the ballroom of the stately home that was as much a part of Auckland's history as the families who had lived within its walls. He carried on, going through the motions, accepting messages of condolence, sharing stories that brought bittersweet smiles to everyone there. Finally, though, it all had to end and he was alone. Alone except for the Dexters, still clearing away glassware and dishes, and for the woman who'd remained upstairs.

Just when would she show her face again? he thought. Well, he wasn't in a hurry to force a confrontation. The outcome was bound to be less than pleasant.

He crossed the hall into the library, and made his way straight to the sideboard. The cognac gurgled satisfyingly from the neck of its bottle, the amber liquid splashing within the bowl of its receptor. Continuing the ritual he had enjoyed most evenings—before Rex's illness had left him weak and bed bound—Wade settled into the wingback chair beside the fire and lifted the glass in a silent toast to the empty chair on the other side.

"I see you couldn't wait to hit Dad's cognac."

Wade stiffened at the sound of Piper's voice from the entrance but he wouldn't give her the satisfaction of knowing how much she got under his skin with her choice of words. She, better than anyone, knew how he felt about alcohol and its disrespectful consumption.

"Care to join me?" he drawled in response, not even bothering to turn his face toward her.

"Sure, why not."

He heard her pour herself a measure then move across the hand-knotted carpet that covered the floor between them. With a tired sigh she settled into the chair that had been her father's. The fresh clean scents of soap and a light fragrance teased his nostrils. He cast her a glance. She'd showered and changed into a clean pair of jeans and a finely woven sweater. Beneath the fabric he could make out the lines of her bones. Even her face was more angular now. Harder, more experienced. A far cry from the spoiled young woman who'd taken his heart and crushed it beneath the soles of her feet when she'd walked out eight years ago.

"I can't believe he's really gone," she said softly.

He knew what she meant. Even he'd found it hard to face facts when Rex had handed the business reins over to him eighteen months ago. And before that, when Rex had negotiated the sale of his ancestral home to Wade to prevent it from sliding into a developer's hands after his death.

"Yeah, well, he is."

"I never thought he'd die."

"Neither did he, at first. The success rate for beating testicular cancer was in his favor."

"Cancer? I thought he died of a heart attack."

"What made you think that?"

"I don't know. I had no idea he was sick. I just assumed it was his heart. He always worked so hard."

Wade watched as her eyes washed with tears. He hadn't agreed with Rex's decision to withhold the details of his illness on the rare occasions Piper had made telephone contact. In recent months, the older man's stubbornness on the matter had been the only contentious bone between them. Rex hadn't believed Piper was strong enough to handle the stress of his illness, but with Piper as Rex's only living issue, Wade knew Rex deserved to have her there in his final days. And Wade hadn't really given a damn if she was strong enough for it or not.

Piper continued, "I'd have come home sooner had I known."

"Maybe that's part of why he didn't tell you," Wade retorted, her words just adding fuel to his frustration. She hadn't seen fit to share those last years of her father's life with him. Was it supposed to pacify Wade that she'd have been willing to come for Rex's death?

She bristled under his words, her eyes clearing instantly and the tears being swiftly replaced with a spark of anger.

"What do you mean by that?" Piper demanded.

"Exactly what I said. You know what your father was like. I'm not denying he wanted you home. He wanted that every day you were gone. But I think that deep down he still wanted you to come home because you wanted to, not because you had to."

"So you're saying I disappointed him—again." Her words were as defensive as the closed expression now on her face.

"Don't put words in my mouth, Piper." He expelled a frustrated huff of air, refusing to rise to her bait, and transferred his gaze to the fireplace. "Above everything, Rex always wanted to shelter you from the big bad world. In this last instance, that included his illness. He didn't want to put you through everything he was going through. Besides, it's all relative now, isn't it?"

"I think it's safe to say that we can take my father's continuing disappointment in me as a given," she said bitterly before taking a sip of her drink. "You, however, have remained the golden boy."

Piper fought back the urge to scream at Wade, to do something, anything to provoke him into a fight. After all, they'd had quite enough practice at it in their time together. It had always been that way between them. Passions running high, emotions deep. All of it crashing madly on the surface. A fight was something she could handle.

What she couldn't handle was the irrefutable truth that she'd never see her father again—never hear his booming voice through the home that had been in her family for generations, never feel the warmth of his arms clasping her to his barrel chest. The gaping hole that had taken up residence somewhere near her heart widened.

She would never have the chance to make it up to him for all the stress and emotional hardship she'd caused ever since, at the age of fourteen, she'd realized the power of her femininity. She knew he'd been sorry to see her leave for overseas shortly after she'd turned twenty, but she'd have been an idiot not to realize that his sorrow was tempered with relief at not having to deal with her, at times, appalling behavior in close quarters anymore.

Piper put down her glass on the small side table and pulled up her feet onto the seat, her knees tucked under her chin and her arms wrapped around her lower legs. How could he have kept his illness a secret from her like that? She'd had a right to know. He'd sounded tired the last time she'd called. When was that? Maybe three months ago? He should have told her.

A shaft of jealousy speared through her. He'd obviously shared everything with Wade. The two men had been close ever since Rex had taken on Wade as an intern at his export company. Wade had quickly become the son Rex had never had. The mythical son she'd never measured up to as Rex's only child.

She'd envied their closeness and done her level best to disrupt it—failing miserably in the process and irrevocably hurting the only two men she'd ever loved.

She hazarded a look at the man seated opposite her and felt that old familiar punch of desire. Even with that glowering expression on his face, he still had the power to make her nerves hum and her heart skip a beat. He'd certainly grown up since she'd been away. His face had settled into far more serious lines, and there was an edge to his jaw that the beginnings of a five o'clock shadow only enhanced. He filled out his designer suit with more breadth than he'd had before—it looked good on him. Clearly hard work and good living had served him well.

She flicked a glance to his left hand—no sign of a ring she noted—then castigated herself for even caring. He'd made his antipathy toward her quite clear. Besides, the new Piper Mitchell had determined to make amends for her past transgressions. Transgressions that included how she'd treated Wade, how she'd let her love for him make her selfish, demanding—wanting more from him than he was willing to give. She was so sorry now for the way she'd behaved, the choice she'd forced him to make between her and her father. Those amends needed to start now.

"I'm sorry," she said. "I know how much Dad meant to you, how close the two of you were. It must have been tough for you."

Wade looked at her, genuine surprise on his face. "Thank you," he answered.

There were fine lines of strain around his slate gray eyes that had never been there before. He looked thoroughly worn out.

"Did he suffer?"

Wade shook his head sharply. "Only inasmuch as he couldn't do what he wanted to do. The medical staff worked hard to keep him comfortable. He stayed here, at home, right to the end. We installed a hospital bed in the morning room and he had round-the-clock professional care."

"Thank you for being there for him."

"He'd have done it for me," Wade answered simply. "Besides, there was no place else I would rather have been."

And there it was again. The subtle slap. The reminder that she hadn't been there. Piper clamped down on her instinctive need to justify herself, her choices, her behavior. She was past that now. There was no way she could turn back time and rewrite history, but she could make a new beginning and that started here and now.

"I'm really grateful to know that he had you there. It must have meant a lot him. He always respected you."

"The feeling was mutual."

"So what happens now with the company?"

"What do you mean?" Wade looked surprised that she'd even asked.

"Well, you know, without Dad at the helm. Will everything be okay?"

"Yes, everything will be fine. Rex and I had a stable management plan in place before we knew he wasn't going to beat the cancer. I basically took over operations about a year and a half ago."

"Really?" Piper was surprised. "He let go that early?"

"It was a case of having to. The treatments, both here and overseas, left him pretty wiped out. But he maintained a keen interest in everything almost until the end. You know what Rex was like."

And where had she been a year and a half ago? Somalia? No, Kenya. She'd been helping at a women's clinic there. After that had been flood relief in Asia, then volunteering to help reconnect victims with their families after an earthquake in another devastated land. Everywhere but where she'd really needed to be. The one place where she should have made a difference.

Piper was suddenly hit with a massive weariness. She fought back a yawn and failed miserably.

"Still tired?" Wade asked.

"Yeah, when I got here I'd been traveling for about thirty-six hours. I don't think my body clock has caught up with the fact that I'm stationary yet."

"Why don't you go on up to your room? I'll get Mrs. Dexter to bring you a tray if you're hungry."

Despite all her good intentions, Piper bristled. This was her home, so who'd appointed him to the role of gracious host? If anything she should be offering him her hospitality under her father's roof. Reminding herself of her determination to be a better person, she swallowed the retort that hovered on the tip of her tongue. Instead she unfolded herself from the chair and stood up.

"Don't bother Dexie. I'll grab something from the kitchen on my way up."

She stretched slowly, easing out muscles that had been unused for far too long with all the travel she'd endured. She halted midstretch, suddenly aware of Wade's eyes locked onto her body. A long-suppressed, yet still familiar, tingle started deep inside and tendrils of heat began to unfurl from her core, radiating out to her extremities. She swallowed against the lump of tension that formed in her throat.

That old attraction was still there. Just as strong as ever. Did he feel the same way, too? Her eyes met his—for a moment seeing the same heat that had infused her body and now painted a faint flush against her suddenly warm cheeks. Then in an instant his eyes were the cool gray of indifference that had met her at the front door only a couple hours ago.

Stung by the clear rejection, Piper summoned every last ounce of dignity and offered him her hand.

"Thank you for everything you've done today."

Wade stood, his six feet two inches eclipsing her barefooted five feet eight. He took her hand in a brief clasp.

"I did it for Rex."

"I know that, and I appreciate it. Really."

He let go her hand as if the idea of holding it for a moment longer than necessary was abhorrent to him.

"Well," she said, gathering courage to her like a cloak, "I'll see you out and then I think I'll have an early night. No doubt I'll have plenty to do with the legal side of things tomorrow."

When Wade didn't make a move for the door, she speared him with a glance. "Is there something else you wanted to discuss?"

A slow smile, somewhat lacking in humor, spread across his handsome face.

"No," he replied. "I'll say good-night, then."

She watched as he left the room, but rather than heading toward the front vestibule he turned and made for the sweeping staircase that led to the upper floor.

"Where are you going?" she asked.

"To my room."

"To *your* room?"

His response was short and sweet. "I live here."

"Look, I appreciate that you probably stayed here for a while with Dad but that's not necessary now and, quite frankly, I'd really appreciate a bit of space and privacy to come to terms with everything."

"No problem. You're welcome to stay as long as you need to."

His answer left her baffled. "I beg your pardon?"

"I think you heard me, Piper. Despite your current appearance I'm sure you're not entirely stupid."

"How dare you!"

Better person be damned. That was quite enough. She'd already had to bear facing Wade for the first time since she had left him, not to mention hearing the news about her father's death. She wasn't about to stay and listen to him put her down, too.

"Look," she sputtered. "I think we both know there's enough history between us that your staying here is not a good idea."

"Probably." He shrugged. "But I think you may have misunderstood what I meant when I said I live here. Piper, I own the house. You're here as *my* guest."

Two

"You what?"

He owned the house? How could that be? The house had been built by her forebears in the mid-1800s. Passed on, generation by generation. Had Wade somehow finagled the property from her father while he was weakened by his illness? It seemed unlike him, but what else was she to think? His voice broke through her chaotic thoughts.

"Look, now probably isn't the best time to go into it. It's been a tough day all round. We can discuss this tomorrow."

"Like hell," she countered. "We can darn well discuss this right here, right now."

"If you insist," Wade said, closing the distance between them and gesturing toward the library. "Care to take a seat?"

With tension vibrating through every nerve in her body, Piper preceded him back into the room. She threw herself into the chair she'd only recently vacated, watching Wade as he lowered himself into his with far more elegance and grace than she'd exhibited. It only served to rankle even more.

"So, tell me. How is it you've come to be the owner of my father's house, and his before him, and his bef—"

Wade cut in. "Don't get melodramatic on me, Piper. It won't work."

Melodramatic? He thought *that* was melodramatic? That was nothing compared to how she felt right now. But before she could speak again, Wade continued.

"Your father and I came to a financial arrangement early on in his illness. The doctors here could offer little hope and he wanted to embark on some radical alternative therapy being offered overseas."

"What kind of arrangement?" she demanded. "And why on earth did he have to come to any kind of arrangement, anyway? Our family has always had money."

"*Had* being the operative word," Wade said, lifting his eyes to clash with hers.

"What? You're blaming me? I have my own trust fund. I was never a drain on my father's finances."

Wade's lips thinned and she saw a muscle clench in his jaw before he pushed a hand through his dark brown hair, sending the short cut into charming disarray. Despite her anger, her fingers itched to smooth his hair down—to feel if its texture was as smooth as she remembered it to be. Piper curled her fingers into her palms and squeezed tightly, ridding herself of the urge as quickly as it had surfaced. This wasn't the time to be thinking of any kind of touching.

"Not everything is about you, Piper. When you calm down, you'll see that what we did was supposed to be for the best, at the time."

"At the time? Explain it to me."

"Rex was single-minded about beating the disease and wouldn't take no for an answer, not even when his situation was very clearly laid out to him by his doctors. He was determined to fight, regardless of the cost—and the cost was very high. I've no idea what rock you've been hiding under for the past eight years but there has been a global recession out there. Our business was hit just as hard as everyone else's. Despite everything, there was a stage where we were bleeding money and Rex used a lot of his own funds to shore that up."

"You didn't use yours?" she asked pointedly.

"He wouldn't let me. Mitchell Exports was always *his* baby, you know that."

She probably knew it better than anyone. She'd always known that Rex's devotion to his business came well before his devotion to her.

"So he needed money for this treatment?" she probed.

"Yes, and he wouldn't take the money from me, even though I offered it freely. He was, however, happy to enter into a loan agreement with me, registering a mortgage in my name over the property."

"But this place is worth millions."

"He was very determined to live, Piper. He was prepared to pay whatever it took to beat the disease. At that stage, he never believed for a minute that he wouldn't live to pay me back."

"And he knew you already loved the property and would look after it."

Wade nodded slowly. "It was a more palatable solution for him than putting it on the open market to raise the funds, and seeing the land be gobbled up by developers, or risking borrowing the money through some financial institution and watching it go in a mortgagee sale if the treatment failed. When he knew he was going to die, he signed the property over to me in its entirety, provided he had a lifetime right to stay here. I had no problem with that."

Piper blinked back a new rush of tears. What Wade had said all sounded plausible. She knew how much her father had trusted Wade. Moreover, she knew—just as her father had known—how hard Wade's upbringing had been, how much he had wanted to prove he was better than his roots. If he'd been given the chance to demonstrate his friendship to Rex while simultaneously establishing himself in both the home and the business he'd always admired, then of course Wade had taken it. He was *right* to have taken it. But knowing that didn't take away the sick sense of loss Piper felt at the evidence that her father had given his entire legacy away to someone other than her.

If she'd been more determined to prove to her father that she was just as good as the son he'd always dreamed of having, if she'd stood by his side through the hard times instead of running away as soon as she didn't get her way, maybe she'd have been able to help him. But with her having remained overseas for as long as she had, often without any contact until she'd run out of money, again, and needed another advance from her funds, it was no wonder her father had sought a suitable custodian not only for his business but also for the house.

It didn't make it hurt any less, though. She'd never known another home and now she couldn't even call it hers anymore. Hopelessness hit her with a vengeance. Here she was, twenty-eight years old, no fixed abode, no job and no prospects. Sure, she still had her trust fund, but she didn't want to dip into that unless absolutely necessary. What on earth was she going to do?

"I meant what I said before, Piper," Wade said, his voice breaking into her tortured thoughts. "Rex asked me to look out for you. You're welcome to stay as long as you need to."

As long as she needed? How was she to know how long that was? She'd come back to New Zealand, back home, to restore the relationships she'd damaged so very badly with her selfish decisions and past behaviors. The past four years, volunteering with aid relief in less privileged countries, had been a major eye-opener. One that had systematically changed her focus and made her realize just how empty her life had been and how much she continued to owe the people who'd been a part of it. People who she'd only later realized had tried to give her the love and stability she'd always craved. People she'd cast off in her anger and hurt for not loving her the way she'd wanted, oblivious to the fact that she was hurting them with her actions, too. People like her father, and Wade.

"Thank you," she said softly.

What else was there to say? She was at his mercy. He had every right to turn her out of the house.

"If there's nothing else, I'll say good-night," Wade answered.

He rose from his seat and started to leave the room, hesitating a moment at the door as if he had something more to say. But then, with an almost imperceptible shake of his head, he continued into the hallway.

Around her, Piper heard the wooden timbers of the hundred-and-sixty-year-old home settle in the cooling night air. A sound she'd never even stopped to listen to before, yet a sound that was a solid reminder of all who'd been before her and left their mark on her world. Their expectations lay heavy in the atmosphere that filled the room. What mark had she left?

The emptiness around her invaded the hollows of her body and echoed through to her soul.

Nothing. She'd left nothing.

She drew a shaky breath deep into her lungs. Then another. She'd made a conscious choice to change her life. No one ever said it was going to be easy or that she'd have all the things at her disposal that she'd always taken for granted. Maybe this was one of the lessons she needed to learn along the way. Take nothing, and no one, for granted.

Piper moved down the hallway, her bare feet making no sound on the faded carpet runner that lined the polished wooden floor. She hesitated outside the morning room, unsure of what she'd find there. What remnants of her father's illness and care from during his last days would linger? And what of the hospital bed and equipment Wade had said they'd set up in here?

She wasn't surprised he'd chosen this room. It had purportedly been her mother's favorite. Not that she remembered her mother beyond a vague sense of being enveloped in soft arms and being showered with butterfly kisses. Sometimes, as a child, she'd come in here and curl up on a chair with her eyes shut tight—trying to gain a sense of the woman who'd borne her. But try as she might, she had never felt any more than that elusive memory.

Her hand hovered over the brass doorknob until with a sudden resolution, she closed her fingers around the cold metal and gave it a twist. The door swung open before her revealing a room unchanged from the last time she'd seen it.

The chaise longue still resided in front of the French doors that opened onto the wraparound veranda. The side tables and comfortable furniture she remembered as far back as her childhood were all still there.

She sniffed the air carefully. No, not a hint of hospital or illness, or death, remained. It was as if her father had never been in here at all.

A solid lump of grief built in her throat as she stepped back and closed the door again. She desperately wanted some connection with him. Some proof that despite everything he'd still loved her.

Noises from the kitchen at the back of the house reminded her that Dexter and his wife were hard at work cleaning up after her father's wake. She should go to them. Offer to help. But the need to be alone with her thoughts was stronger. She turned and made her way back along the hallway and then up the stairs that led to the bedrooms on the next floor.

Rex's room had been at the opposite side of the house from hers. When her mother had died when Piper was three, he'd hired a nanny who'd slept in the room next to hers. But he'd kept his distance for many years, physically, emotionally and socially. It was only when she'd begun to bring certificates of achievement home from school that he'd really begun to acknowledge her existence, spurring her to do better, reach higher—whatever it took to garner his approval.

But that approval was always short-lived as his work took the bulk of his attention. She'd always wanted for him to see her as more than a child to be spoiled, her every whim indulged. She'd wanted him to acknowledge that she had a brain, that she could achieve, even that she might be worthy one day of working with him in the family business as he would have expected a son to do. Instead, no matter how high she flew academically, it was as if her achievements never really mattered to him. After that, behaving like the spoiled little princess he expected had become second nature—in fact, she'd almost turned it into an art form. For all the good it did her.

Piper bypassed her own room and headed toward the rooms that had been his. The door to his suite was open. She stepped into her father's domain and was instantly enveloped by his personality. The room was neat and tidy, typical of the ordered way he'd liked things, but here and there were the memories she'd always associated with him. The books he had loved to read, the sweets he had kept in a porcelain jar beside the bed for "just in case."

Pulling open his wardrobe, Piper was assailed with the faint reminder of the cologne he'd always worn. She reached for the dressing gown that hung on the hook on the back of the door and dragged it to her, burying her face in the velvet softness of the fabric and inhaling deeply.

"Is everything okay?"

She spun around to see Wade framed in the doorway, the light from the hall behind him, leaving his face in shadow. He looked as if he was in the process of getting undressed. Gone were his jacket and tie. His shirt buttons were now open halfway down his chest, his shirt untucked from the sharply creased trousers that encased his long legs, the cuffs undone and loose around his strong wrists.

Longing for what-might-have-been hit her in a surge of confused emotion. She shook her head slightly, trying to dislodge the sensations that clouded her mind. Comfort. She craved comfort, that most basic of needs. But she could no more ask that of Wade than she could ask for the moon, not after what had happened between them. Not when she still had so much making up to do. So much to prove—to him and to herself.

"I'm fine. Just…" What? It was impossible to put into words. Instead she settled for the benign. "I miss him. Why didn't he give me the chance to come back earlier and say goodbye?"

In the doorway, Wade shifted on his feet. She sensed there was more he wanted to say but that he was holding back.

"Like I said before, he didn't want you to have to go through it all. To have to watch him deteriorate. Maybe it was a bit of pride, too, wanting you to remember him as he was when you left rather than when he was so ill."

"He never really expected me to come back, did he?"

Wade shook his head slightly. "No, I don't think he ever did. Didn't stop him wanting you here, though."

The light from the hall shone into the room, bathing Piper in a stream of golden light. She looked so vulnerable there, holding her father's robe to her as if it was some form of security blanket. As if it was the last remaining thing she had left in the world. Well, truth be told, it pretty much was. Still, she didn't need to know that now. Time enough for that. Even he could see she was struggling with the reality of Rex's death. Hell, he'd been here, through it all, and he still struggled.

He clamped down on the sympathy that came as naturally to him as breathing. The past few days he'd doled out his fair share to Rex's friends and business associates. Offering solace to Piper should have been just one more drop in the bucket. But, he reminded himself, she'd made choices that made it difficult to dredge up any consolation for her. One choice in particular he could never forgive was that she'd chosen to end the life they'd created together before he'd ever known it had existed. He'd sworn she'd pay dearly for that choice. She owed him now in ways she couldn't begin to imagine.

Even with that mental reminder, his hands itched to reach out to her, to touch her, comfort her. He'd been so in love with her once, and as angry as he still was with Piper, those old instincts dominated. Wade curled his hands into fists and thrust them inside his trouser pockets lest he give into them. He had no doubt she'd take what he offered—before throwing it right back in his face all over again.

She'd made it monumentally clear during their last bitter and very final argument, before she went overseas, that she needed nothing from him. Even her demeanor downstairs when she'd joined him in the library had been targeted to make him feel inferior, an outsider.

He leaned against the doorjamb, marshaling his thoughts and reminding himself that her vulnerability was little more than a facade. Piper Mitchell was more than capable of handling herself in any situation. She'd suckered him in once before and he'd vowed he would not be a fool twice over her.

He shook his head slightly to clear his mind of the errant thought. He'd been under a lot of pressure. That was all. He just needed time to get his bearings again, to sort through what still needed to be done about Rex's estate and to put a lid on his grief until it no longer had the capacity to render him weak, or open to confusing thoughts about Piper.

Wade cleared the thickness in his throat and took one hand from his pocket and gestured toward the room.

"I've been charged with clearing out your father's things. Do you want to help with that?"

She nodded, a mere incline of her head. The action typical Piper, too wrapped up in her own thoughts to give anyone her full attention. But in the gloom he heard a noise that sounded suspiciously like a choked sob.

"Look, it's been a tough day," he continued. "Why don't you head off to bed? There's no hurry with your dad's things."

"Okay, but don't get rid of anything before I can see it."

Ah, so despite that faint wobble in her voice she was back to giving orders. That hadn't taken long. "Sure," he said, denuding his voice of its last threads of empathy. "By the way, I have an appointment with Rex's lawyers in the morning for the official reading of the will—you should come along. I'm already conversant with its contents but you should probably take the opportunity to find out exactly how you're placed."

She nodded. "Sounds like a good idea."

Wade stepped aside as she approached, but Piper's foot caught on the edge of the carpet square, making her stagger. Instinctively, as he had already done once today, he put out a hand to steady her, shifting his body to block her fall. Again, her weight bore against him, seeking support. She looked up at him, her eyes dull with sorrow.

"Thank you. I'm going to have to stop making a habit of this, aren't I?"

"Might be an idea," he conceded, even as his body warmed instantly to the feel of her.

He put his hands to her shoulders. It would be so easy to attempt to recapture that old spark simply by lowering his mouth to hers. Her lips were already parted on a hitched breath, their softness moist and enticing. Her pupils rapidly consuming the pale color of her irises.

The firm roundness of her breasts pressed against his chest and his body surged to aching life. Wade silently cursed himself for being all kinds of a fool. His hunger had been tamped down and controlled for far, far too long. Beneath his hands her body stiffened, freezing in response to his very obvious physical reaction to her nearness.

His hands tightened, his breath catching in his chest as he fought his demons. She had always been temptation incarnate. But he was stronger now. Stronger and more determined to succeed—in all things.

Even though his entire body pulsed with wanting her—wanting to push aside the shabby clothing she wore and to rediscover the creamy smoothness of her skin, the warm recesses of her body that held incalculable delight—he pushed her gently from him. It was sobering to realize that passion had threatened, albeit briefly, to blot out his every reasonable thought.

Piper pulled farther back, her arms still wrapped around that damn robe. It occurred to him that throughout their entire embrace, she hadn't voluntarily touched him with any part of her body. He shoved one hand through his hair.

"So, until tomorrow then?" she said, the lightness in her voice sounding forced in the heavily charged air between them.

"Tomorrow?"

"The lawyer? What time should I be ready?"

"The appointment isn't until midmorning. No need to rush."

"Okay, I'll probably see you at breakfast, then."

She slipped past him and down the hall to her room. He watched her every step—the graceful posture, the gentle sway of her hips.

They said that revenge was a dish best served cold, but he preferred his steaming hot. Hot and sexy and totally satisfying on all counts. He *would* be vindicated. And, when the time was right, he would savor every moment.

In her room, Piper sat heavily onto her bed and raised her fingers to her lips. She'd been so sure he was going to kiss her.

She'd have almost staked her life on it. The flare of desire in his eyes had been so endearingly familiar that it had shaken her to her core—had awakened her senses, her own needs— in a way she hadn't experienced for a very long time.

She knew he'd wanted her—she'd felt the undeniable evidence against her. So what had made him stop? One minute he'd been conciliatory, the next cool and commanding and then he'd been on fire for her. A fire she'd all-too-readily reciprocated. Even now, her skin felt too tight. Her nerve endings too close to the surface. She pushed up from the bed and paced her room, suddenly filled with an excess of energy that begged for some form of release.

Who was she kidding? She knew exactly what form of release she craved. And with whom. But it wasn't going to happen. Wade had always had the power to turn her inside out, right from the first time she'd laid eyes on him. The instant physical attraction had rapidly morphed into one that went infinitely deeper. She had no doubt they would be as compatible now as they'd been before, but she couldn't allow herself to go down that path. It would undoubtedly lead to broken promises and broken hearts all over again and she had resolved to put things right when she came home. Put things right and prove herself to be the kind of person she most wanted to be. Not the selfish creature of the past who sought satisfaction for her every desire, but someone who could genuinely contribute to the world in which she lived and moved.

It hurt deep, deep down that she'd never be able to prove to her father that she was capable of being more than what he'd pigeonholed her to be. What she'd shamefully allowed herself to become in the face of his opposition to her gaining a career that could amount to something. He'd loved her, but he'd never had any understanding or appreciation for the person she had the potential to be. It was too late to show him otherwise. But she could prove it to herself.

She shook her head. How was she ever going to prove herself if she couldn't control even her most basic urges around Wade?

Piper stopped pacing in front of the built-in bookcase that lined one wall of her room. It was still adorned with the things she'd grown up with. Her previous life had been sealed in a time capsule, waiting for her return. She looked around, seeing everything with new eyes.

Her gaze stopped on one of the collections of porcelain dolls her father had insisted on buying for her, but had never let her play with. What a perfect analogy for her life, she thought bitterly. Look but don't touch. Learn, but whatever you do, don't use that knowledge. Be beautiful, but don't actually *be* anything.

She drew in a deep breath and squared her shoulders. Well, all that was going to change. As much as she'd loved her father, and had strived for his attention, she could see that they were equally to blame for her past behavior. But she had changed and she planned to continue to change and grow a whole lot more. Including going back to university and finishing her degree.

It had taken quite a bit to make her eventually grow up. Being overseas alone, facing her darkest days and subsequently her brightest moments as she'd reawakened to who she needed to be.

Still, she had to attend to her father's estate first, and that meant getting up on time to see the lawyer tomorrow morning, which in turn meant getting a decent night's sleep.

She went through the motions of getting ready for bed, finding solace in routine and joy in the things she used to take so much for granted. Simple things, like a tube of toothpaste, running water from a tap, a flush toilet. She laughed at her reflection in the mirror. Who'd have thought that Piper Mitchell would ever have been reduced to this? Finding joy in modern plumbing. Frankly, she didn't care, not anymore.

The toll of the news she'd borne today, and the travel she'd undertaken to get here, swamped her and the lure of fresh clean sheets and a proper bed became stronger than she could resist.

The next morning, Piper woke as the sun began to filter through her window. To her surprise she had tears on her cheeks and her pillow was damp beneath her face. She'd been dreaming about her father and the sense of forever being left reaching out for him, yet not being accepted by him, still filled her. She swiped a hand across her face. Tears wouldn't solve anything, she knew that with an entrenched awareness she'd learned the hard way. No matter the loss, you had to learn to get through it.

She rolled to the other side of her bed and stretched, luxuriating in the sensation of fine cotton sheeting against her bare skin. Her father's robe was spread over the top of her bed and she grabbed it to her, pulling it on as she sat up and slipped from between the sheets to make her way into the adjoining bathroom.

Eschewing a shower for the decadence of a deep bath, she bent over and turned on the faucets. Watching the water fill in the ancient claw-footed tub gave her an illicit sense of pleasure. She would never take something like this for granted again. Despite everything that had happened since her return, it was so incredibly good to be home.

Hard on the heels of that thought came the reminder that the house was no longer her home. She was a guest here. Wade's guest. The news had come as a shock last night and her reaction had been instinctive and out of sorts with her new resolve. She hoped that would be the last unpleasant surprise she'd have to bear.

She was in a painfully tenuous situation. She had no qualifications to speak of, unless bartering with local rebels or militia for medical supplies and trading with cash from her trust fund was anything worth mentioning. Nor did she now have a roof over her head to call her own.

Piper slipped the robe off her shoulders and, letting it drop to the floor behind her, stepped into the almost full bath. She sank into the water, letting its warmth seep into her skin all the way through to her bones. After the heat of some of the countries she'd lived in, she didn't think she'd still crave warmth the way she did now. But with her father dead and her prospects perched on a very precarious ledge, the world around her felt very cold indeed.

Piper let her hair fall over the back of the bath and rested her head against the edge, closing her eyes and trying to concentrate only on the warmth and softness of the water enclosing her body. She'd found the exercise of isolating herself to be an invaluable tool in coping with some of the hardships she'd witnessed in the past few years, but for some reason she couldn't find quite the degree of separation she needed now.

Where she was going to live, how she was to support herself, all took precedence over her relaxation ritual. It wasn't as if she didn't still have the trust fund her mother had left her, she rationalized. Her father had been angry with her when she'd gone overseas, especially when she'd tried to get between him and Wade, but he hadn't cut her off completely. Whenever she'd applied for an advance from the funds she'd come into when she'd turned eighteen, the money had duly appeared wherever she'd needed it. By her reckoning she should still have sufficient capital left to get herself on her feet, certainly enough to finish the degree she'd partially completed before running away.

She grimaced. *Running away* sounded so infantile. And yet, her reactions had been those of a spoiled brat. She wasn't proud of the person she'd been then. Not at all. But that was changing. Slowly, surely and in the right direction. And with the balance of her funds behind her, the rest would be a piece of cake.

She felt a pang of grief tug deep inside her. How she wished her father was still alive. Maybe he could finally have been proud of her, *really* proud. She missed him with a sorrow that went soul-deep. When she'd set out on the journey home, she'd been looking forward to seeing him again. She'd hoped with all her heart that today could be the first stage of a new relationship with her dad. One where he would finally see who she was and what she was capable of.

Well, she still hovered at the edge of that first stage. One she'd have to embark on for herself, not for anyone else. It was what she should have realized all along.

Piper pulled the plug on the bath and stepped out as the water swirled down the drain with a satisfying gurgle. She shook her head at the decadence of it. It would make better sense to find some way to utilize the waste water from this sort of thing on the property. Maybe she could make some suggestions to Wade and see what he thought. He'd probably have a hard time believing she could even care about something like waste water.

Piper dried herself off and padded naked into her bedroom. She extracted some clean underwear from her drawer, a small puzzled frown fracturing her brow when she couldn't find the stuff she'd brought in her backpack. The pack itself had been emptied at some stage yesterday, its clothing contents now nowhere to be found. Maybe Mrs. Dexter had taken it all to be washed, she thought. She wondered what the housekeeper would think of the wardrobe that consisted mainly of jeans, camo-patterned trousers and an array of T-shirts that would probably better serve as polishing cloths than anything else.

She looked at the underwear she'd taken from the drawer. An exquisite shell pink, the matching bra and panties were a brand she'd never bought before, even though they were all in the size she'd worn before she went away. She slipped into the panties, thankful that at least they fit without threatening to fall off her hips, then adjusted the straps on the bra and started to put it on.

She turned and looked at herself in the mirror. She'd lost weight in recent years. Hard work and a limited diet had a way of doing that. The bra, while beautiful, was far too big for her, even on the tightest fitting. She could pad it up, she supposed, but then what if something slid free while she was wearing it? No, far better to go without, she decided and turned to her old wardrobe for something to wear.

A swimming sense of déjà vu enveloped her as she opened the doors. There, arranged by color and functionality, hung every article of clothing she'd failed to pack and take away with her. According to the dry cleaning tags on the garments, everything had been freshened recently. But why, when no one knew when she was coming home?

Piper selected the least flippant items and pulled on a pair of charcoal gray trousers with a neat matching jacket that used to nip in perfectly at her waist. Eight years ago, it had been form-fitting enough to wear without a top beneath it, but it certainly wasn't now. She flicked through the hangers until she found a crisp white blouse to team with it.

An old belt threaded through the loops in her trousers cinched them in a little tighter at her waist, and when Piper pulled on the jacket and studied her appearance, she thought she'd scrubbed up quite well—aside from the hair. She grabbed a black and white long silk scarf from her dresser and tied her dreads into an approximation of a ponytail before nodding at her reflection. Well enough to see the lawyer, anyway.

Her feet had always been long and narrow and she pulled on a pair of stocking socks before pushing her feet into a slim fitting pair of black patent pumps. No longer used to the heels, she teetered a little before regaining her composure.

How had she ever walked in these things on a daily basis? she wondered as she made her way down the stairs.

Wade wasn't in the breakfast room, nor the kitchen, when she got downstairs.

"Looking for Mr. Collins?" Mrs. Dexter said with a smile as she bustled about pouring a fresh cup of tea and placing it at Piper's old place at the huge worn kitchen table.

"Yes, we have an appointment together this morning."

"He had to get away early to the office. Some problem or other. He said if he couldn't get back on time, he'd send a car for you so you could still meet with Mr. Chadwick in his rooms."

"Oh, thanks."

Piper fought back the unreasonable feeling of disappointment that he wasn't here. He had a business to run so she could hardly expect him to wait upon her hand and foot. Strangely, though, she had been looking forward to his approval that she'd made an effort to "scrub up," for want of a better term. Which reminded her. Her clothes.

"Dexie, can you tell me what you did with my clothing from my backpack?"

"Oh, that lot." Mrs. Dexter wrinkled up her nose in her rosy cheeked face. "I gave it all to Dexter to incinerate. Your father would never have stood for you dressing like that."

Piper bit back the retort that her father hadn't had the right to dictate her appearance for many years now. Swallowing the words she'd wanted to say didn't come easy. Those items of clothing were virtually all she'd had to her name in the way of physical possessions. She'd come back here to take control of her life and yet, even in something as simple as her clothing, she'd been railroaded.

"Besides," the older woman continued, "you have a wardrobe full of beautiful things to wear. I must say, lovey, it's wonderful to see you looking more your old self. Apart from the hair, that is."

A wry smile formed at Piper's lips. "You don't like it?" she teased.

"Humph, as if Mr. Mitchell would ever have tolerated such a thing."

Piper's smile died on her face. No, her father wouldn't have tolerated it. He wouldn't have understood the sheer practicality of wearing her hair this way in the circumstances in which she'd lived. Now she was home she supposed she'd better do something about it, but first there was the appointment today to get through.

"Get through" being the operative words, she realized later that day as her father's lawyer sat opposite her at his highly polished desk, a sobering expression on his face.

"What do you mean I have no money?" she demanded. "When I left, my trust fund was healthy. It had been operating since my mother's death, earning interest all the way. Surely I didn't spend it all?"

"No, Miss Mitchell, you didn't. But you didn't exactly use the funds wisely, or reinvest, either, did you?"

It felt as if she'd been victimized from the instant she'd arrived home. First Wade, then Dexie's disapproval, and now this.

"They were mine to use," she said, a defensive note in her voice.

"Of course, of course." The old man made a shushing sound in a vain attempt to placate her.

But Piper would not be placated.

"So where is it?"

"It?"

"The money," she clarified, holding onto her temper by a thread.

"You know that with your father as a Trustee, the funds were managed very carefully. Over the years he frequently diversified the investments, but as you must be aware, financial markets worldwide have been hit very hard. Even investments that appeared to be sound suffered, and you subsequently lost some rather large sums."

Piper shook her head. She couldn't believe what she was hearing. Her father had always been the most prudent and cautious of investors.

"So, I have nothing?"

"I'm so very sorry."

"But what about my father's estate?"

"Miss Mitchell, what your father didn't use to carry Mitchell Exports through some tough times, he used to fund alternative treatments for his illness. There really is very little left. The investment losses your fund endured hit him, also."

Everything Wade had told her last night had been true. She wished she could blame him, hold him responsible for her father's weak financial position at the time of his death, but it was clear Wade had conducted himself the same way he always had. With honor and loyalty to the man he revered above all others.

Mr. Chadwick continued, completely unaware of the turmoil in her mind. "I must say that Mr. Collins has been most benevolent. When he realized the situation your father was facing he personally acted to assist him. Rex was fortunate that Mr. Collins was compassionate enough to give him a lifetime right to reside in the house."

The sick taste of bile rose in Piper's throat.

Piper swallowed. "And my mother's art collection? That should have been left to me in my father's will. What has happened to that?"

At least if she had that, all was not lost. As much as she hated the idea of selling a single piece, she'd be able to liquidate some funds.

"All with Mr. Collins now. I understand the collection is on loan to the Sydney Art Gallery at the moment."

"But it wasn't my father's to give. It was supposed to be mine."

She fought to keep the panic from her voice. Without the collection, she really had nothing.

"Under the terms of your mother's will, it was your father's to dispose of at his discretion. While she stipulated her preference that it be given to you when you reached your majority, it was still left to your father to decide in the end. Some years ago, he mentioned to me that he had some concerns that you might feel compelled to break the collection up and he wanted to avoid that at all costs. Moreover, he wanted to be certain you were settled before entrusting it to you. In all fairness to your father, he honestly expected your trust fund to support you for your lifetime. Hardly anyone foresaw the long-term ramifications of the global financial crisis until it was too late."

Piper slumped in the chair. Her life couldn't get any worse, could it?

"There is one other thing," the lawyer said carefully, making all the hairs on the back of her neck stand on end.

Piper sat up. She didn't like the way he'd prefaced what was coming next. There was something in his posture and tone that warned her that what she'd learned already was small-fry compared to what was coming next.

"Tell me," she demanded. She may as well get it straight on the chin now.

"Your trust fund. With your withdrawals and the depreciation of the investments' value over time, it became overdrawn. Mr. Collins had taken charge of your father's affairs by that point, and personally advanced money to the fund to cover the shortfall when he was made aware of the situation."

"Just how much money did he advance?"

The lawyer named a sum that caused black spots to swim before her eyes.

"So you're saying he advanced several hundred thousand dollars to my trust fund?"

Wade had been the one responsible for the money she'd used to finance schools and health clinics, food and clothing and farm supplies in the counties she'd visited in the past four years? She was struck with an urgent need to understand the conditions of the loan and expressed as much to Mr. Chadwick.

"The loans were rather open-ended. As your trustee, your father entered into deeds acknowledging the debt between the fund and Mr. Collins. Obviously Mr. Collins has the right to recall those loans, with interest, at any time."

"So no repayments have been made to date?"

"None, Mr. Collins hadn't requested such repayment."

"Not at all?"

She was confused. How could anyone afford to make such huge sums of money available like that and not expect something back in return?

"No, not at all." Chadwick hesitated a moment, his mouth twisting into a moue of regret. "Until now."

"Now?" she gasped. "He wants me to repay the debt now?"

"Yes, Miss Mitchell, I'm afraid so. And he has specified it must be repaid in full."

Three

In full? Piper vibrated with ill-concealed anger, earning a look of concern from the elderly man across the table from her. No wonder Wade had arranged to not be at the appointment with her, the rat.

"Thank you," she finally managed to say through gritted teeth. "Could you tell me exactly *when* Wade Collins made that specification?"

"We received his instruction this morning."

This morning? It was unbelievable. While she'd been sleeping in, or even while she'd been lazing about in her bath, he'd been demanding she clear a debt he knew full well she had no ability to repay.

Forcing a smile on her face, she stood and offered her hand to the man who'd been her father's longtime legal counsel.

"Is there anything I can do for you, Miss Mitchell?"

"Short of conducting a miracle, I doubt it."

She kept her composure until she got outside the office and saw the car Wade had ordered for her waiting in the loading

zone outside. Every instinct within her urged her to turn in
the opposite direction and to keep walking. To put as much
distance as possible between herself and the awful truth about
her financial position. But where would she go?

The driver of the car got out and came around to the passenger side, opening the door for Piper and waiting until
she'd settled herself in the soft leather. The drive back to
the house passed in a blur. She couldn't have said whether
they'd taken one route or another but when they drove into the
long driveway that led to the imposing stairs and entrance to
the house, Piper found her eyes locked on the building she'd
grown up in.

The immaculate white painted woodwork, the wraparound
verandas on the ground and next story, the green-capped
pinnacles that marked the four corners of what had begun
as a two-story farmhouse. She'd taken every part of it for
granted. Its history, its shelter, its place in her life.

She had thought she'd changed, but she hadn't changed at
all. Even without a home to call her own, she'd still assumed
she had the money to make a new one. But now she didn't
have even that. And all because she'd been so stupidly pre-
sumptuous as to believe her security would never end.

So what now? She didn't even appear to own the clothes
on her back, and Dexter had destroyed what little she had
owned.

Piper slowly moved up the stairs and let herself in through
the front door. She started as a tall shadow materialized from
the formal parlor on her left.

"Wade," she said. "I wasn't expecting you here."

"I managed to clear things up at the office earlier than I'd
anticipated."

Her eyes raked his face for any sign of the man who'd
deliberately advanced money to her only to recall it when
he knew she was at her lowest ebb. Just how long had he
been prepared to go on making money available to her? she

wondered. If she hadn't come back when she did, how much would she have ended up owing him?

It didn't make sense. She had no way of paying him back. Why would he want to have such a hold over her when it was outside the realm of possibility that she'd ever earn enough money to settle the debt?

"Is that right?" she replied, fighting to keep her voice level when all she wanted to do was bombard him with angry questions.

"I take it the news at the lawyer's wasn't good?"

"You take it correctly."

"We should talk."

"No kidding," she said with an insolence she was incapable of hiding.

Wade gestured for her to precede him into the parlor and waited until she was seated before he lowered his body into one of the fabric-covered armchairs. The blowsy cabbage rose pattern on the chair was at complete odds with his controlled appearance. Not a hair was out of place on his head. His striped tie, a perfect match to the steel gray of his suit, was immaculately knotted at the equally immaculate fold of the collar of the white shirt he wore. He was altogether formidable, and he knew it.

Piper decided to take the bull by the horns.

"It would appear I owe you some money," she said, lifting her gaze to meet his squarely. There was no way she would show him that she was quaking inside.

To her surprise, Wade laughed. His even white teeth flashed in his face, his eyes crinkled in genuine mirth and the sound, a deep belly laugh that in any other circumstance would have been infectious, rang out to fill the room.

"I have to hand it to you, Piper. You're the mistress of understatement today."

She refused to be drawn to respond. He could think what he liked. He knew, as well as she did, that he held all the cards very firmly in those beautiful hands of his. While he composed himself she waited patiently for the bullet to come.

"Mr. Chadwick made you aware of the sum of money you owe me," he finally said, his voice no longer holding any hint of the humor that had just consumed him.

"He did."

"And he made you aware that the debt has been recalled."

"With interest, no less," she said, aiming for flippancy.

Maybe if she could make him angry she'd feel anything but the numbness that had pervaded her entire body since she'd heard the news.

"No less," he agreed.

He sat back in his chair and rested his hands on the arms of it, his rangy body relaxed even though his eyes were sharply focused on her face.

"I need time," she stated flatly.

"Is that a fact?"

"Of course it's a fact," she snapped, rising to his bait in spite of her best intentions. "I need time to find a job, get established. It's completely unreasonable of you to insist on repayment in full when I have no means to meet that commitment."

"Yes, indeed. Thing is—" he paused and flicked an imaginary piece of lint from his trouser leg "—I don't feel particularly reasonable right now."

A chill ran down Piper's spine. "You don't?"

"No, I don't. You never finished university, despite every opportunity to do so. You never sought gainful employment while in New Zealand. And if your current lack of funds is any indication, I'd say you've never actually worked a day in your life. Why should I believe that you could find a job now? The employment market is tough, Piper. Tougher now than it ever was. Even the local supermarkets have had more than two and a half thousand applicants for each of the new stores that have opened recently. What makes you think you're

better than all those skilled, and unskilled, workers desperate
to find a job?"

"I never said I was better than anyone else."

"No, you didn't. At least not recently, anyway."

Piper felt hot color flood her cheeks. She remembered
exactly what he referred to. She'd been an utter bitch to him
when he'd refused to drop his internship with her father and
travel with her overseas. She'd wanted him to prove that he
loved her—that she mattered to him more than her father
and his own future. When he'd refused, she'd said things
that didn't deserve remembering, let alone repeating. That
he hadn't forgotten them was quite clear.

"I'm sorry for all that, Wade. I really am. I was young,
headstrong and entirely stupid. I couldn't see past what I
wanted back then."

"And you've changed so much now?"

Wade watched her carefully. He didn't believe she'd
changed a bit. Not where it mattered. She could have swallowed her pride years ago. Come home before choosing to
terminate the pregnancy that was the lingering proof of the
love he'd thought they'd shared. But, no. She'd destroyed his
son or daughter as callously as she'd cast away everything in
their relationship. And she hadn't even bothered to contact
him—then, or in the eight years that had followed.

"I have changed," she insisted, the color in her cheeks
rising. The sound of her voice becoming even more impas-
sioned. "I used that money for good purpose."

"All of it?"

"No, not all of it. I was an idiot when I left here. I had some
serious growing up to do, but I did grow up. I have changed."

"Admitting your faults all sounds very impressive, Piper,
but again, none of it solves your current problem, does it?"

"I just need time."

"Time isn't an option." He put up a hand before she could

protest. "I do, however, have an alternative for you. A suggestion that takes into account your lack of credible work experience and probably accommodates the one thing I *do* know you're good at."

She leaned forward on her seat, clearly eager to hear what he had to say. He doubted she'd be as eager once she knew what he had planned for her.

"What sort of alternative?"

"I worked hard for your father over the years. And with your father gone, my workload has doubled at Mitchell Exports.

"As a result, I have neither the time, nor the inclination, to devote to a relationship with the type of woman I may want as a wife. Settling down just isn't possible for me right now. But I do have one thing, above all else, that I wish for.

"I've accumulated quite a legacy of my own, now, and it'll be all for nothing unless there is someone special in my life to leave it to. You know about how my mother died when I was ten and how my father refused to support me. You know how determined that made me to have children who will receive all my love and protection. I want to be the kind of father Rex was to you. When you were a toddler and your mother died he never let you go. It would have been far easier for him to have done so. Yet, no matter what, he always provided for you—sometimes too much."

"Our circumstances are completely different, Wade. Sure, Dad supported me, but not in all the ways that really mattered to *me*. I had to fight for his attention."

"He wasn't always the easiest of men to impress, but he never stopped loving you, Piper. Never. Have you stopped to wonder why your room was still exactly the same as you left it? Why you have new clothing in your drawers and why the things in your wardrobe have been regularly dry cleaned for when you eventually returned home? Keeping everything in readiness for you was probably the only way he knew to show you how much you meant to him. But you never came home."

Wade sighed and rubbed his eyes with one hand. "We're diverting from my point. What I wanted to say is that family is *everything* to me. I want to have a child to make all this hard work worthwhile. Someone I can leave my legacy to."

To his surprise Piper shot to her feet, coming to stand a bare meter from him.

"And I suppose this legacy includes all those things that were supposed to be mine. Things like my mother's art collection?"

"Things I have legitimate bills of sale for, yes."

"Where do I come into all of this?"

He remained silent, waiting for the penny to drop. It didn't take long.

"You want me to have your baby?" she cried, staggering back as if she'd sustained a physical blow.

"You're rejecting my suggestion?"

"Damn right I'm rejecting it."

"It's not what I'd call an ideal situation but I'm prepared to waive the considerable debt you owe me, if you give me a child."

He stood and closed the distance between them. A pulse fluttered frantically in her throat and her breath came in short bursts. Beneath her jacket he could see the unfettered rise and fall of her breasts against the fine linen of her blouse. A rush of heat swelled from deep within him.

He continued, "We're not completely repulsive to one another. It's not likely to be any hardship to do what needs to be done to meet your end of the deal."

"You're talking about a baby! A living, breathing human being. Not just some pawn in a game of chess."

"I know exactly what I'm talking about, Piper. The thing is, are you up for the challenge?"

Piper stared at him in horror. Did he have any idea what he

was asking of her? It was wrong on so many levels she could barely gather her wits. She wasn't ready to have a baby. Not now—maybe not ever. The word "no" echoed through her mind. In fact, it was on the tip of her tongue, ready to burst forth, when he spoke.

"I don't intend to be unreasonable about access to our son or daughter, Piper."

"Access?" she said, feeling completely dense.

"I don't expect to restrict your interaction with our child."

Oh, my God, she thought. *He's acting as if this is a done deal. As if I've said yes already, or worse, as if I have absolutely no choice in the matter.*

"Access won't be an issue," she said flatly.

"I'm pleased to hear you're prepared to be reasonable about this."

"I think you misunderstand me. Access won't be an issue because there won't *be* any access—there won't be any baby."

Rather than argue with her, Wade surprised her with a smile. A smile that held not an ounce of humor in the curve of his beautiful lips and which didn't so much as light his piercing eyes with a spark of warmth. Instead, it gave his face the look of a predator. One well used to winning.

Piper took another step back from him and crossed her arms instinctively.

"What are you smiling about? You can't make me change my mind. What you're suggesting…it's ridiculous. No, it's more than ridiculous. It's impossible!"

"Impossible? I think not." He hesitated a moment, his face settling into serious lines far more in keeping with the expression in his eyes. "Unless, of course, you're in a position to repay the money you owe me?"

His words hit her straight to her chest. Of course she wasn't able to repay him anything. She didn't even have enough money to stay in a hostel for a night. He had it all. Everything that had ever been hers and then some.

"You know damn well that I can't pay you back, you bastard. You have already taken everything that should have been mine." She flung her arms out. "This—my home, my history—not to mention my mother's art collection. You already own all that. You even had my father!"

As soon as she said the words she realized exactly where her pain and anger were centered. Her father. It was the final blow to know that he'd loved her so little that he'd sold everything to Wade. Every last thing in her world that had meant anything to her whatsoever.

"For what it's worth, I loved Rex like a father. At least I was there for him when he needed someone," Wade commented softly.

"I'd have been home if I'd known." Piper turned and faced out the window, speaking to the room rather than the man behind her who held the power to reshape her future. "I bet you even discouraged him from letting me know he was ill."

She felt, rather than heard, him close the distance between them. Felt the heat of his body pierce the cold that wrapped her in its solitary grasp. His touch on her shoulder was surprisingly gentle. The heartless businessman from a moment before seemed to have vanished, replaced by the devoted, fiercely protective man she'd fallen in love with years before. The man who'd always made her feel so safe and cherished.

"You probably won't believe me but I urged him to tell you. Especially when he knew he didn't have much longer. Rex was nothing if not stubborn. A trait you both shared." Even his voice was softer, more caring—and the wry fondness in his tone was so familiar that she felt the last wall around her heart crumble, setting all her emotions free.

The sob that been building in her chest escaped. After today's revelations and Wade's demand, she could no longer keep a lid on the anguish inside.

He turned her body and enveloped her in his arms, her

face against his chest. One hand, fingers splayed, rubbed big circles across her back. The other held her head gently against the rock hardness of his body.

It shouldn't feel so good, she told herself. She should pull away, refuse his offer of solace—he was the enemy—but instead, she found her fingers knotting in the fine cotton of his business shirt, felt the wrenching sobs that came from deep within her. Welcomed the warmth of his embrace.

Eventually she managed to bring herself under control, her sobs settling to the occasional snuffle. Beneath her hands she became aware of the tension that drew Wade's body as taut as a bow, felt his indrawn breath before he spoke.

"Would it be so bad, Piper? We were good together once."

His voice was pitched low, the coercion a subtle thread in his tone—compelling her to agree. Piper shook her head. Her tear-stained face leaving tracks of moisture in an untidy streak across the pristine whiteness of his business shirt.

"Please," she said, her voice strained and small as she drew away from the treacherous comfort of his arms. "Give me some time to work something out. At least give me time to think about what you're asking."

For a second she thought he'd refuse. That he'd press her for an immediate answer before either throwing her physically out the door or, alternatively, tossing her over his shoulder and taking her upstairs.

A zing of heat spiked through her core at the thought of the latter and she felt her empty womb clench tight in anticipation. Dammit, even her body was letting her down. It still remembered the way he used to make her feel, how good they'd been together. But that was all in the past now, she reminded herself. The man she'd loved had changed into someone she barely recognized. She couldn't love this stranger, and he certainly no longer loved her. It was all wrong to think of a child coming out of this. She could no more deny her intense physical attraction to him than she could stop breathing, but there was no way she was going to have another baby with him under these circumstances.

Another baby? Who was she kidding? She'd failed with the last one. Why would this time be any different? She couldn't go through that again. Wouldn't. Hadn't she lost enough already? Her fear must have shown on her face because Wade eventually gave her a short nod.

"You have until dinner tonight."

Four

Piper was too stunned to react to his words. She could only watch helplessly as Wade left the room. She heard him let himself out the front door and make his way down the front steps and across the crushed-shell-covered driveway to his car. The muted roar of his sleek gunmetal gray Porsche and the spray of shells signaled his departure and allowed her to release the breath she hadn't realized she held captive in her chest.

Her mind scattered on the monumental task ahead of her. She cast a quick glance at the antique carriage clock on the fireplace mantel. It was hard to believe it wasn't yet past midday. But that in itself was a bonus. At least it gave her time to see if she could raise the kind of money she was going to need to put Wade's appalling suggestion to bed.

To bed? What was she thinking? She rubbed at her face with both hands as if she could erase the thought once and for all.

She had to find some money from somewhere. Anywhere.

Banks were out of the question—she had no collateral to speak of. There was only one thing for it. She had to try to garner favor with her father's cronies. Surely someone, somewhere, would step up to help her.

Piper spun on her heel and stalked out of the room and across the hall to the library and settled at what had been her father's desk. Her hand shook slightly as she eased open the right-hand drawer to extract Rex's personal address book. She flipped open to the letter *A* and ran her finger down the list of names. It was a start. All she had to do was drum up the courage to actually make the requests.

The sun was waning in the autumn sky as she hung up the handset for the last time. Her ear ached from the amount of time she'd held the phone pressed to it, but nowhere near as much as her heart. It appeared that when she'd left, she'd burned all her bridges. Her perceived abandonment of her father had blacklisted her among every last person he'd called a friend. She hadn't been able to raise a single dollar.

She cast a glance at the untouched sandwich and cup of tea that Mrs. Dexter had brought to her a few hours ago. She hadn't felt like eating it then and she certainly didn't feel like it now. Just the thought of food was enough to tip her stomach, but that was nothing in comparison to what the concept of her rapidly diminishing alternatives gave her.

"Ah, lovey, you haven't eaten."

Mrs. Dexter bustled into the library and tutted her disapproval as she removed the tray from the corner of the desk.

"You won't get your bonny figure back if you don't take better care of yourself, Miss Piper."

"I'll be fine," Piper said quietly.

"Fine, humph! You'll be needing a bit of flesh on those bones of yours if you're going to attract the interest of a fine young man like Mr. Collins again."

Piper lifted her head and stared at Mrs. Dexter in horror.

"Why would I want to do that?" she couldn't help herself from asking.

"Why wouldn't you?" Mrs. Dexter gave her an uncharacteristically sly wink. "After all, it's not as if you're strangers to one another, is it?"

"I really don't think—"

"Oh, dear, listen to me. Here you are, only a day home and I'm already on at you. Why don't you go upstairs and get changed into something pretty for dinner. Mr. Collins will be home in an hour or so and I'm sure he'll be wanting you to look your lovely best. Although what we're going to do about that hair I just don't know."

"Mrs. Dexter!" Piper raised her voice, earning a look of chastisement from her old family retainer. "I'm sorry, Dexie," she amended, softening her tone. "It's been a while since I've had any looking after. I'm a bit rusty."

"Of course you are, lovey. But you're home now, where you belong. So why don't you run along and do as I said and when you're all finished, Dexter will serve drinks in the parlor before dinner."

It was all Piper could do to stop herself from shaking her head. She was twenty-eight years old, for goodness' sake, but in Dexie's mind she'd always be a little girl. Between the Dexters and her father, no wonder she'd never learned to grow up. That said, the prospect of taking a little distance from her failed attempts to raise *any* funds, let alone the kind of money she needed to clear her debt with Wade, did hold some appeal.

"Dexie, do we have any boxes in the house?"

"What? Storage boxes, you mean? Whatever do you want those for?"

"I'd like to clear some of the things from my room."

The older woman looked stricken. "Change your room?"

Piper forced a smile to her lips. "Yes, I'm not a little girl anymore, Dexie. I think it's time a whole lot of the things in there were packed up and moved away somewhere."

"But Mr. Mitchell—"

"Isn't with us anymore. And even if he was, I can't imagine he'd have any use for my old porcelain dolls. I don't mean to be harsh, but it really is time to move on."

Mrs. Dexter folded her lips in a straight line of disapproval and sniffed audibly.

"Well, if you insist. I'll see that Dexter brings some up for you, along with some packing foam and Bubble Wrap. We still have the boxes Mr. Collins brought when he moved in but I can't say I ever expected to see them used again so soon."

Piper held back the words she longed to say, words along the lines of wishing Mr. Collins would pack those boxes once more and move right back out again. Instead she opted for a civilized thank-you and made her way upstairs.

She quickly slipped into an old T-shirt and pair of sweatpants, the brand name imprinted across her buttocks in all its labeled glory. She shook her head. For what it had cost for both items, she could have fed a family in North Africa for a month, probably longer. The thought brought the enormity of the amount she owed Wade front and center in her mind again.

What the hell was she going to do?

An hour later she was no nearer to finding a solution but at least she'd had the chance to busy herself, and her mind, with clearing the shelves in her room of the remnants of her childhood. She'd individually wrapped the dolls in Bubble Wrap then laid layers of packing foam in between until each one was put away. As soon as all the glass-eyed empty faces were hidden behind the lids of the boxes, she felt something in her body begin to ease. As if she was no longer under constant scrutiny. No longer being held up in judgment against some impossible, unattainable ideal of perfection.

She stiffened as she heard the sound of a heavy measured tread outside her bedroom door. Clearly Wade was back from the office. No doubt he'd be changing and then returning downstairs for a predinner drink. The footsteps slowed before continuing along the landing toward his bedroom.

He'd expect an answer from her shortly and she still had no idea of what she was going to say.

What *could* she say? She had no means to pay him back, of which he was fully aware, which left her very little option for anything else. She was exactly where he wanted her. But why her? Why a baby?

She didn't believe for a minute that he didn't have time for a relationship. There were umpteen women who would happily have his child for the chance to have a piece of him, no matter how small. Was that what it was? Did he think the old animosity between them would stop her from being a problem? Prevent her from wanting a proper relationship with him?

A twinge deep inside reminded her how she'd destroyed the relationship they'd had through her petty selfishness, her unwillingness to share any part of his love. That had to be why he was prepared to offer her the deal he had. Deal? Who was she kidding? The word implied something reciprocal, but she still stood to be the loser even if she did agree to his outrageous suggestion.

So she wouldn't have a debt to him anymore. She certainly wouldn't have anything else, either. She'd be beholden to him for everything. Hell, she already was.

But what of the baby he said he wanted so very much? There was no doubt in her mind he would love his son or daughter with a single-minded devotion that only a parent could give. But would that excuse the lack of any kind of warmth or affection with which the child would be created? She couldn't help thinking back to her last pregnancy—to the child who had been conceived without conscious intention, and yet with so much deep, genuine passion.

Piper sat back on her bed and placed both her hands over her belly. The miscarriage of his baby had been one of the hardest things she'd ever had to go through in her life. When she'd first discovered she was pregnant, she'd considered coming home. Facing Wade with the truth that their lovemaking had given them both something they'd never dreamed they deserved. A child to love together.

But, in her mind, had been the bitter reminder that he'd chosen her father over her. That he'd made a conscious decision to further his career rather than be with the woman he'd said he loved. To her, back then, his decision had been all about putting her father and, most especially, his work before her. Something her father had always done all her life. It had been the final nail in the coffin that bore their dead relationship.

She'd finally resolved to go through the pregnancy alone. A decision that, in the end, proved futile when she'd suffered a miscarriage at fourteen weeks. Brokenhearted all over again, Piper had responded the same way she had every other time her hopes for love or happiness had fallen apart. She'd picked up her life anew. Partied hard, then partied harder still. No matter what she'd done, even though the hurt didn't show, the pain lingered inside her—and it was as fresh today as it was when she'd realized there was nothing she could do to prevent the infinite sense of loss. Their baby was gone—and Wade's rejection all those years ago meant that he still didn't even know she'd ever been pregnant.

Of course time and distance and even a little maturity had shown her that Wade had taken the right course. To have left his job back then would have been foolish in the extreme, and Wade was anything but foolish. It was why her father had taken him on in the first place—initially as an intern, then subsequently as a junior executive. She knew his loyalty to Rex Mitchell was absolute and came from a deep-seated respect and gratitude toward her father for taking a chance on him. And now look where he was. Head of the biggest export company in the country.

She'd been too young, too foolish and much too selfish to ever have been good for him back then. But what about now? While a part of her argued she should never have come back, logic also made a solid case that she'd needed to come home. Needed to finish healing. Needed to make amends for not being the daughter her father had wanted, for not being the woman Wade had needed. Maybe, just maybe, being that woman for him now.

Months ago as she'd cradled an undernourished toddler on a continent half a world away, she'd acknowledged how precious life was, how important the relationships within that life, and she'd promised herself she'd make it up to Rex and Wade, if they'd let her. That she could now never reconcile with her father was a cross she was going to have to bear the rest of her life. But Wade was another story.

Could she do what he'd asked of her in an attempt to make amends? The very thought sat uncomfortably with her. She'd be using a child, *their* child, as a tool to salve her own conscience. Everything inside her rebelled at the idea of being so manipulative—it was wrong on so many levels she couldn't even begin to count. Her arms still ached for the baby she'd never gotten to hold. Until that moment when she knew the tiny life inside her had died, she'd have entered into an agreement like Wade was suggesting without so much as blinking, if it got her financial freedom. She'd learned not to be that kind of person anymore. The past few years had taught her so very much about life, loss and even love.

Love. What if they stood a chance of reigniting their old relationship? Of building something worth saving and, this time, getting it right? The idea was both daunting and exhilarating at the same time and, for the first time since she'd arrived home and heard the news about her father, she felt as if she genuinely had a purpose again. It was a complete shot in the dark but she had no other alternatives to consider.

She glanced at her clock and noted she had better get ready for dinner. He expected her response and she didn't want to keep him waiting.

She got up off the bed and opened wide her wardrobe doors, seeking a dress that she knew had to still be here. It felt a little weird to know that her things had been maintained the whole time she'd been away but she pushed the thought aside. Her father had believed he'd been doing the right thing by her. Loving her in his way. It was a pity that she hadn't understood that at the time. She'd only been able to see that he hadn't loved her the way she'd wanted. For Piper, once she'd closed the front door behind her, all she'd wanted was distance. Her father had refused, yet again, to allow her to work within Mitchell Exports, in any capacity—telling her instead to do what she was good at, being beautiful and dressing well. In short, being a symbol of his success.

The response had been so typical of him. He had simply refused to believe she could be anything but ornamental. So she'd left home in defiance. Swearing she'd never come back until he'd see she was as strong and capable as any woman and asked her to return. She should have known better. Rex Mitchell asked nothing of anyone. If he couldn't make it happen by himself, it wasn't going to happen in his world. Wade was that way now, trapping her in a situation where he could force her to do what he wanted. Would she give in to his demand? She still wasn't entirely sure. She was scared at the thought of getting pregnant again, especially considering what had happened last time. But maybe this was her chance, as twisted as it seemed, to finally make things right. For her. For Wade. And for their baby.

Her hand finally settled on the dress she sought. Made

of dark blue and silver patterned silk, its lines were soft and flowing and would accommodate her more slender figure without looking too big on her.

If anything, she thought as she examined herself in the mirror a few minutes later, the dress looked even better on her now than it had the last time she'd worn it. The three-quarter sleeves showed off the tan she still bore on her arms, while the soft flowing lines of the skirt lent her a femininity she hadn't indulged in for far too long. She slid her feet into a pair of dangerously high-heeled silver pumps that picked out the threads of silver in the fabric of her gown and tied her dreadlocks back with a silver scarf.

She had no makeup with her, hadn't even worn any for several years now, so she was pretty much ready to join Wade downstairs. She hesitated at her bedroom door, her hand on the old-fashioned brass knob, her teeth worrying at her lower lip. What would she say to him? She couldn't simply capitulate to his wishes, no matter what. She certainly wasn't about to turn into a baby factory to salve his need to be a father. There had to be some ground rules. Some guidelines. What about custody? He'd said he would be reasonable about access but what was his idea of reasonable? And where would she and the baby live?

She tightened her fingers around the doorknob. She wouldn't be a pushover, even though he had her back against the wall over the money. There was no way she'd set up a child of hers to be a bargaining chip for the rest of its life. If he wanted them to have a baby together, there would be some conditions he'd have to agree to. Ultimately she had the power to say no. She could walk out that door tonight and find shelter somewhere until she could get back on her feet. Sure, things would be tough, but if he wasn't prepared to acquiesce on certain points then this plan of his was not happening. At least not with her.

* * *

Wade stared out over the subtly lit expansive emerald green lawn and tried to convince himself he wasn't nervous. He knew Piper was still upstairs, he'd heard her moving about in her room when he'd arrived home. She'd had ample time to come to her decision. But what would it be? She'd always been such a mercurial creature and he'd seen nothing in her that changed his mind on that score since her arrival home yesterday.

He took a sip of the sauvignon blanc in his glass. Had it really only been yesterday that she'd come back? She still had the capacity to turn his world upside down and inside out. He felt as if they'd gone several rounds against one another in the past twenty-four hours. In fact, as he'd clutched at sleep toward dawn this morning, he'd had to acknowledge a hard truth. Despite everything, she still had the ability to inveigle her way past his defenses. He'd thought he was completely over her, over what she had done to him—but he'd been so very wrong. She still had the capacity to hurt him and there was no way on this earth he was going to hand that back to her on a platter. He doubted his mentor would have approved of his tough love attitude. The older man would have been only too happy to see her arrive on the doorstep, and would have bent over backward to make things easy for her. Time had softened Rex's irritation with her for what he'd seen as nothing more than a temperamental spat.

"Look after her for me" had been Rex's dying words and, fool that Wade was, he'd promised. But Rex had said nothing about Wade putting in a few conditions of his own when it came to providing for Rex's prodigal daughter. She owed him far more than some trifling sum of money, and he *would* be repaid.

He wasn't oblivious to the fact that she might flat out say no to him and leave him to his own devices in attempting to recover the financial debt. But he was counting on the fact that she was enough of Rex's daughter to find an outstanding loan an anathema to her. There was also the slow burning spark of attraction that still simmered between them. She'd never been able to turn away from him before, he doubted she had the fortitude now. When Piper Mitchell wanted something, or someone, she'd usually do anything to get it. What she did after that was a little more obscure.

A sound at the door made him turn from the window. The sight of her was a visual punch to his solar plexus. He remembered the dress she was wearing in vivid detail. Remembered removing it from her body just as explicitly. Instantly his body grew rock hard at the memory of the indulgent and sybaritic night they'd spent together.

Piper's blue eyes met his across the room and in that instant he knew she'd chosen this dress on purpose. He bowed his head in a small nod of acknowledgment. He'd give her this point but it would be the only one she'd score tonight. He wasn't above conceding a strategic advantage here and there but it would be a brief concession, that much was certain.

"A glass of wine?" he offered, crossing the room to the sideboard.

"Thank you, that would be lovely."

Wade lifted the bottle of wine from the frosted silver cooler on the sideboard and poured a measure of the wheat-colored wine into a crystal goblet. He lifted the glass and took it over to where Piper had settled in one of the chairs.

"Had a busy day?" he inquired as she took the glass from his hand, painstakingly avoiding touching his fingers, he noted with some degree of satisfaction.

He rattled her on a physical level if not on an emotional one. Knowing that gave him an immense sense of satisfaction.

"You can quit with the pleasantries, Wade. We both know you couldn't care less what I did with my day."

"Now, that's not true. Not at all. I have it on good authority you were extremely busy this afternoon, making calls."

Piper stiffened in her chair. "You know?"

Wade shook his head deprecatingly. "I have to admit, I admire your resourcefulness, and your ability to stow away every last ounce of pride you once had, to have made those requests. It can't have been easy."

She took his veiled insult with surprisingly good grace.

"I learned that pride comes before a fall a long time ago. Thing is, have you?"

He laughed in response. "I never did let my pride get in the way of my success."

"Really? Maybe you should check yourself out again. Seems to me you have an inordinate amount of it now."

The smile stayed plastered on his face. She had no idea what he'd sacrificed to get where he was now. Beginning with her, in fact. But that was about to change.

"So did your calls elicit the response you wanted, Piper?" he asked as he sat down on the chair opposite hers.

"You obviously know exactly what kind of response I got. You can't tell me Dad's old friends weren't on the phone to you the instant they hung up with me."

"Actually, some of them were on the phone to me before you rang them," he conceded. "The rumor mill was busy this afternoon."

"And I suppose you told them not to lend me the money I need?"

There was a thread of steel in her voice that spoke of her frustration, but looking at her he'd never have guessed how angry she must have been to be thwarted in her attempts. Her expression remained serene, her eyes clear and bright. Even her lips were full and soft, not drawn into a line of tension as he'd have expected.

He shifted in his seat and tore his gaze from her mouth. His body still hadn't quite cooled down after that hit when she'd come into the room.

"Actually, I didn't have to. Your reputation preceded you."

His words scored a direct hit this time, he could see it in her eyes. He was suddenly sick of the game playing. He wanted to get right to the point of their meeting tonight.

"Have you reached a decision?" he asked.

"I thought you said I had until dinner," she replied, looking at the mantel clock with exaggerated interest.

"Don't beat around the bush, Piper. Will you or won't you have my child?"

Five

She rose from her chair in a fluid graceful movement. She always had the poise of a dancer, he remembered. Her limbs were supple and lithe…and there he went again. Hard, hot and wanting her. She strolled over to the deep sash windows and looked outside for a moment before turning to face him.

Her face was composed but he could see the anxiety in her eyes. Feel the tension that rolled off her in waves.

"I've been giving the matter some thought and it seems to me that I do not have all the facts I need to make a decision one way or the other. I have some questions," she said, lifting her chin ever so slightly in challenge.

"Ask away," he replied, holding his ground.

"If I were to agree to your proposal, there would need to be a written agreement between us. I don't trust you not to renege on your offer to expunge the debt you tricked me into."

Tricked her into? It wasn't worth arguing, so he let it go. "Okay, so you want a written agreement. What else?"

"How am I to support myself if I agree to have your baby?"

"By getting a job just like anyone else, I expect."

"So you don't think it would be your responsibility to provide for me?"

"You won't go hungry, Piper. Mrs. Dexter will make sure of that."

"You want me to stay here? Living under the same roof as you?"

"Until the baby's born, at least. That way I'll be sure you're taking the proper steps to look after our child prior to its birth. What you decide to do after that really doesn't interest me. If you choose to make your own home elsewhere, that's your prerogative."

"You'd let me take the baby and live away from here?" Incredulity made her voice rise.

"You misunderstand me. I said if *you* choose to make your home elsewhere. My child will stay here. He or she will be raised in this house, surrounded by their birthright."

"But the baby's care, feeding? What if I want to be a part of that?"

"You're saying you do?"

"I'm not confirming anything just yet."

"Piper, the baby will miss out on nothing. I will have nannies round-the-clock if necessary. Care will not be your responsibility."

She averted her head from him momentarily, but when she turned back her eyes were blazing.

"If I have a baby with you, you can be damn sure that its care will be my responsibility."

He shrugged, determined not to reveal his surprise at her latent maternal instinct coming to the fore. The prospect of her already being protective about a child who hadn't even been conceived was contradictory to what he knew about her and he found it unsettling. He hadn't expected her to be so...*feral,* about it, for want of a better word. Why now? Why this baby?

"Whatever you say. We can discuss that element further if you concede to my request."

"Request." She made a face, her mouth twisting in a line of disapproval. "As if you give me any real choice in the matter."

"You can still say no, Piper," he reminded her.

Her pride aside, he doubted she'd give up everything to live rough and fight her way in life starting from absolutely nothing.

"What if I want to stay here and be a part of my baby's life?"

"We could come to some arrangement."

"And what about payment?"

Ah, now we come to the truth, he thought. The real Piper Mitchell is in the building. "Money, to have our baby? Is wiping clean the sum you owe me not sufficient for you, Piper?"

"I'll need to buy things, for myself and for the baby. And if I do go ahead with this, I'd like to be under the care of a specialist."

"While you're under my roof, I will cover your medical costs."

"How generous of you," she said bitterly. "What if I choose not to live under your roof?"

"Not an option. As I said, I need to be able to ensure the baby's health and well-being until the point of delivery. After the baby is born, that would be your choice, of course. We would need to come to some arrangement regarding your visitation rights. Quite frankly, with your position, I don't see myself having any difficulty in gaining full custody, do you?"

"You're forcing me to stay here?"

"I didn't say that," he replied smoothly. "As I've said, once our baby is safely delivered you'll be free to leave whenever you like."

"How convenient for you. You expect me to walk away and never look back."

"It's what you do, isn't it?" he challenged softly.

She paled in response, uncharacteristically lost for words. Wade felt a sharp wave of regret for what he'd said, a wave he swiftly quashed. He couldn't afford to show any weakness. Not when so much hinged on her agreement.

"Is there anything else?" he asked.

"Yes, I want my mother's art collection back. It was her express wish that it be mine and it should have been mine all along."

He stood silent for a while, the seconds stretching out interminably between them. Of course she'd want the collection. He was well aware of Rex's concerns that she'd split it up to sell off individual paintings and then fritter the money away on her extravagant lifestyle. Still, it wasn't his place to say what she did with it.

"So let's get this right. Basically all you want from me is your mother's art collection, along with your outstanding debt being forgiven?"

"There's one more thing."

Of course there was. "What is it?"

"I want a job at Mitchell Exports."

A job? She was full of surprises today, wasn't she? he thought. Despite her very weak position, she could still make the kind of outrageous demands that had characterized the Piper he'd once known. A man had to admire her for her tenacity, he reluctantly admitted to himself.

"What would be the point in that? You're not trained in anything except spending money."

"I don't care what I get to do, but I deserve a place in that business. If you aren't prepared to find me work there, the deal is off."

"Minimum wage, then. I don't see why you should be paid

any more than that." He doubted she'd even be worth that much. "Do we have a deal?"

"If you give me a job we're certainly a step closer to coming to an agreement. I deserve a way to earn some money to support myself later on—why shouldn't I trade in on the family connection to the business?"

Wade momentarily struggled to control the exhilaration that swelled through him. They might be closer to an agreement, but at what cost? Her demand for a role at Mitchell Exports had thrown him somewhat, especially coupled with her uncharacteristic protectiveness toward a child they had yet to conceive. He had her right where he wanted her, yet at the same time he felt as if he was being manipulated, and that feeling put him very much on the defensive. He quelled the sudden rapid thrum that had lifted his pulse several notches—reminding himself that he didn't have her full agreement yet.

"If I agree to your terms, there are some of my own that I expect you to adhere to."

"Name them."

"First, I want you to undergo a full medical checkup. While you look healthy enough, given your lifestyle choices, I want a guarantee that you're fit to bear my child."

"My lifestyle choices?" she choked.

"Your antics in recent years have been cloaked from the media, unlike your behavior when you left here which was well documented in the tabloids. Who knows what you might have picked up?"

Two bright spots of color lit her cheeks. "What I might have picked up? And you? Where have you been finding *relief*? Might I ask the same of you? I have no desire to catch anything from you, I'm sure you understand."

Again, he found himself fighting to hide his admiration at her response. Here she was, most definitely the underdog, and yet she still didn't hold back, instead giving back as good as was dished out to her.

"In the interests of fairness, I have no objections to providing you with a clean bill of health. I'll make arrangements for us both in the morning."

Piper brushed past him and picked up her wine glass from the table and held it in the air in a bold salute. "Do we have a deal then?"

Wade covered the distance to where he'd left his glass and picked it up, touching the rim of the crystal to hers. "We do."

Piper fought to control the tremor that rippled through her body. She'd done it. She'd agreed. They were going to have a baby together. She didn't know whether to feel excited or simply terrified, although the latter fought for supremacy.

When would he want to begin the baby-making process? she wondered. Obviously at least not until they both had the all clear from the doctor. She'd felt so insulted, so dirty, when he'd made his stipulation. She had never been promiscuous. Sure, she'd partied along with the rest of them, but she'd never indiscriminately slept with other men. After the first two times she'd allowed anyone close enough to actually go to bed with them, once she'd left New Zealand behind, she knew that no man would ever compare to what she'd shared with Wade. It was simply easier to stop looking for it in every man she met, knowing that none of them ever had that special spark that was in constant evidence between her and the man standing opposite her right now.

As anxious as she was about their agreement, a tiny burst of excitement tinged with a healthy dose of apprehension began to unfurl from deep down inside. He'd changed in so many ways since they'd last been together. He was far more dominant now and appeared far harder than he'd been before, as if he tolerated nothing that tried to stand in his way—had he changed in other ways, too? Would he still be the caring and considerate lover she'd known, or had she irretrievably destroyed that person when she'd left him?

Would they make love, or would the conception of their baby be a clinical thing? Sex for the sake of it, or even conception achieved by artificial means? The sure knowledge that she would find out eventually was no consolation.

Piper realized with damning clarity that, as usual, she'd leaped into this thing without seriously thinking through all the consequences. Dread filled her belly. It was too late now. If she wanted to be taken seriously, she had to stand by her word. And, more than anything, she had to prove her worth— to herself and to Wade.

Later on she had no idea how she'd managed to get through dinner with Wade in the formal dining room. The table, which comfortably seated twelve, was spread with crisp white linen and glittering tableware and looked innocuous enough until you noted the place settings. One at the head of the table, the other intimately to its right.

While she had no doubt the food had been delicious, Dexie wouldn't have had it any other way, she could no sooner remember what it was she had eaten than she could say what it was they had talked about during the meal. It had been a time to be endured, while the reality of what she'd agreed to do sank in deeper and deeper.

Sleep was elusive that night, fractured with dreams that vividly included Wade in various states of undress. Beside her, beneath her, within her. She woke at dawn to the sound of rain beating against the windows, driven past the deep eaves of the upper balcony by a biting cold southwesterly wind. Overheated by her subconscious, she rose from her bed and pressed her face against the cool glass pane of her window, finding relief in the heat being drawn from her skin.

She was chilled to the bone by the time she crept back between the sheets of her bed and fell into yet another disturbed sleep, waking only when Mrs. Dexter knocked firmly at the door to tell her that Wade awaited her downstairs in the library. A quick glance at her clock confirmed that she'd slept far too late—it was ten o'clock already—and doing so had left her feeling groggy and out of sorts.

Piper grabbed her father's robe and wrapped it around her, and shoved her feet into a pair of slippers before going downstairs. The door to the library was closed and she hesitated, her fist raised and ready to knock at the ancient wooden surface, but then her usual streak of independence asserted itself and instead she reached for the handle, twisting it sharply and shoving the door open.

Wade sat at her father's desk—*his* desk now, she supposed. He looked up as she entered, a small frown appearing momentarily between his dark brows.

"Trouble sleeping last night?" he inquired, his voice cutting through the air with an astuteness that instantly rankled her.

Piper bit back the acerbic response that rose on her tongue, choosing instead to smile and to seat herself in the chair opposite his desk with as much grace as she could muster.

"I slept fine, thank you. And you?"

The shadows under his eyes matched her own but his response was a curt yes before he bent his head to flick through a sheaf of papers on his desk. Papers he then put in a folder and handed over to her.

"This is our agreement. Take some time today to read through it. Either of the Dexters will serve as an adequate witness, unless you'd prefer to use Mr. Chadwick. I can always see if he's available."

"He didn't draft up the agreement?"

"No, I used my own solicitor for that."

"You certainly didn't waste any time, did you?"

Wade leaned back in his chair and steepled his fingers. "Getting cold feet, Piper?"

Cold everything, if the truth were to be told. She'd thought it would be a good idea to show him how little he affected her by coming downstairs in such a state of dishabille but she should have taken the time to assume an armor of propriety at the very least. She felt at a complete disadvantage right now compared to his immaculate tailor-fitted suit, his cheeks smoothly shaven and his hair combed back off his face. The scent of his cologne, while not overpowering, tormented her with every inward breath. Spicy, exotic, alluring.

She straightened her shoulders and dragged in a deep breath before speaking. "No, not at all. We reached an agreement and I will honor that." If only to prove to you I *can* be honorable, she thought privately. "And when can I start at Mitchell Exports?"

She squirmed a little as Wade rose one eyebrow and cast an inquiring glance over her attire.

"You were expecting to start today?"

A tiny smile quirked at the corner of his mouth, as if she had presented herself in no less a state of readiness than he'd expected.

"Of course not. Tomorrow will be soon enough."

Piper allowed her gaze to meet his across the highly polished walnut desk. She wouldn't back down, not an inch. She could be honorable and still keep her pride, couldn't she? Somehow?

A surprising glow of approval shone in Wade's eyes, a glow that sent a spiraling warmth deep to her core. It shocked her to realize that his approval meant so much to her.

"Do you think you can be ready to come into the office with me at eight tomorrow?" he asked, tilting his head slightly to one side, the smile now spreading into a full grin. But it seemed less judgmental than before, as if he was teasing her instead of truly mocking her.

When he put that smile into action, he really was something else, she decided. She'd bet anyone—man, woman or child—would be putty in his hands in the face of it. Shamefully, she was no more immune to his charisma than anyone else.

"Of course."

"Excellent. And I assume you still remember how to drive a stick shift?"

If wrestling a bouncing jeep over potholed, unsealed roads was any claim to success, she figured she could cope with Auckland city traffic.

"I do," she replied.

"Your appointment for your physical is today, at eleven. It might pay for you to change before you go." A teasing smile played around his lips. "Here's the address."

He flicked a card across the desk toward her. She lifted it up and saw the name of a private medical clinic tastefully printed across the top of the plain white card. A doctor's name beneath it in black script. A female doctor, she noted.

"Thank you. Is that everything?"

"For now."

He reached into his jacket pocket and pulled out a key ring and offered it to her. Piper stood and reached for the keys, but started as his fingers closed around hers as she went to remove them from his palm.

"My keys. Drive safely, okay?"

"I didn't know you cared," she said as flippantly as she could manage even as her heart began to race at his touch.

"You will be having my baby, of course I care."

The words hurt her far more than she'd expected. She knew she was a vessel for him to have that which he most wanted, but it shocked her to acknowledge that she wanted to be so very much more than that.

"Don't worry, I won't do anything to jeopardize the merchandise," she said, aiming again for lightness but knowing she fell short when he didn't release her hand straight away.

"I can always arrange a driver for you if you'd rather," he said.

"No, I'll be fine. Seriously. And you'd best let me go if you want me to be on time."

She looked pointedly at their hands and snatched hers, and the keys, away the second he released her.

"I'll see you this evening then?" she said, heading toward the door.

"No, I have an appointment this evening."

She stopped and turned back to face him. "Oh, a hot date?"

"Something like that," he replied.

He still planned to go on seeing other women, even as he got her pregnant?

"I thought you didn't have time for relationships," she pushed. It was like pressing on a bruise. You knew, no matter what, it was going to hurt.

"This definitely doesn't fall into that category." He smiled again.

"Oh, so it's just sex then?"

Oh, God. When would she learn to haul back on her runaway tongue?

This time he laughed out loud. "Would that bother you, Piper?"

It did bother her. Far more than she was prepared to admit to *him*.

"Well, in the interest of keeping clean, maybe it should," she challenged. "When is *your* appointment with the doctor?"

"Don't worry, there'll be no chance of me catching anything tonight that you should be worried about."

She sniffed audibly. "I should think not."

Then, with as much decorum as she could muster, she headed through the door. She was at the foot of the staircase when she heard his voice behind her.

"Piper, you could come with me if you want to."

"To spend an evening with one of your women? I don't think so."

She had some pride left.

He shrugged at her response. "No problem. I just thought I'd give you the option."

The option. She clutched the folder containing their agreement to her chest and fought not to laugh out loud. Options were in scarce supply for her these days.

"It's okay. I want an early night before starting work tomorrow, anyway."

"Your choice," Wade said as he turned and went back into the library.

For a moment Piper was tempted to follow him back in there. To tell him that she'd changed her mind. She knew it would eat her up all evening, knowing he was with another woman. Wondering whether he was kissing her, whether his hands would push aside her clothing to bare her skin to his touch. Whether her hands were touching him.

She shook her head fiercely. She had to stop torturing herself this way. But even as she ascended the stairs she knew there'd be one amendment to their agreement that he may not be too happy about, and that was going to be an exclusivity clause.

Six

Piper swiftly discovered that driving Wade's Porsche 911 Carrera GTS was a world away from the rackety old jeep she'd driven last month. Her hands settled on the three-spoke steering wheel, the covering of which felt like suede beneath her touch, and she took a deep breath before letting the engine roar to throbbing life.

Man, this car was like a hard-on with wheels. No wonder men loved things like this so much, she smiled to herself as she slowly cruised down the crushed shell driveway and out through the iron gates of the property. It seemed almost criminal not to detour to the nearest motorway and let the car show its paces, but she wasn't that flippant devil-may-care individual anymore.

The car handled like a dream and by the time she pulled into the designated patient parking at the health center she almost wished she had escaped into the countryside. Nerves assailed her. What if the checkup disclosed something that would jeopardize her agreement with Wade? She sucked in a deep breath and let it go slowly. She just had to get out of the car and visit the doctor and see for herself.

The clinic's rooms were spacious and elegantly furnished. A far cry from what she'd become used to during her volunteer work abroad. She doubted a fly or a speck of dust would so much as dare to enter here. After giving her name to the receptionist, she sat in one of the comfortable waiting chairs and listlessly flicked through a magazine. She hadn't been there long before she heard her name called.

A woman, a little older than herself, stood waiting for her with a smile. As Piper approached, the woman thrust out her hand.

"Hi, I'm May Ritter. Wade asked if I could see you today."

So he was on first-name terms with the doctor? Piper gave her a surreptitious once-over as she shook hands and smiled in response. The woman was definitely attractive, with well-tamed, deep red hair, and a clear complexion any supermodel would die for. Bright green eyes sparkled behind frameless lenses.

"Come on through," May said.

She led the way down a short corridor and into a treatment room and gestured that Piper take a seat beside the desk that was pushed up against the wall.

"Now, tell me a bit about yourself," the doctor said, settling comfortably in the chair behind the desk and angling the computer screen toward her.

"What do you need to know?" Piper hedged. Where should she begin? The reality that she was here for a pre-pregnancy health check was all too real.

"Let's start with your full name, age and stuff like that, then we'll go into your medical history."

Piper felt a cold chill run down her back. Her medical history? That would mean disclosing her previous miscarriage. There was no way on this earth that she ever wanted Wade to find out about that. It wouldn't take much for him to put two and two together and realize that she'd been carrying his baby. And that she'd lost it.

"This information remains confidential, doesn't it?" she asked, her voice a little pitchy.

"Definitely. Wade wanted me to make sure you're in good shape to start a family, but any details you tell me will stay entirely between us. Wade's a friend, but that doesn't trump doctor-patient confidentiality."

"You know Wade personally?"

Could this get any worse?

"Oh, yes. He and my husband have been friends for about five years now. They have this ridiculous competitive thing going between them over weekly squash games. You'd think they'd have known each other a lifetime they're so close. Wade's the godfather of our three-year-old daughter. In fact, he's even babysitting for us tonight. Hopefully, part of my thank-you to him will be giving you a clean bill of health."

Ah, thought Piper, so that was his reason for not being home tonight. No wonder he'd looked so amused at her reaction. A flush of anger and embarrassment heated her cheeks. Why couldn't he simply have told her the truth rather than let her think he was seeing another woman? She dragged her attention back to the matters at hand.

Piper nodded. "All he needs to know is that I don't have any communicable diseases and that I'm healthy, right?"

"Sure, once we've run all our tests, etc., that's all he needs to know."

"Well, obviously I need to tell you this won't be my first pregnancy. Eight years ago I lost a baby at fourteen weeks." Piper swallowed against the lump that formed in her throat.

"I'm sorry to hear that. Were there complications with the pregnancy?"

Piper shook her head. "Just one of those things, they said."

May got up from her seat and sat in the chair next to Piper, taking one of Piper's hands in hers. "I'm sorry, Piper. It's never easy losing a baby, especially when there is no apparent reason. Did you have support at the time?"

"I was on my own. Aside from the medical staff, no one else knew."

May's fingers closed more tightly around Piper's in silent support. "That can't have been easy."

Piper blinked back the tears that burned in her eyes. "It wasn't. It makes me scared about this, though. About doing it again. What if—"

"Piper, there is probably no reason why you shouldn't have a perfectly normal pregnancy. That's why you're here today."

Piper nodded. "There's one other thing," she continued. "I've been working overseas for the past few years, volunteering with aid organizations. I contracted malaria a while back."

May reached across her desk for the folder in which she'd been making notes before and made a few notations. "How far back?" she asked.

"Just under four years ago."

"Any recurrences?"

"Not so far."

"Okay," May said, making a few more notes. "What sort of work were you doing?"

"Grunt work, for the most part. I'm not skilled in anything but you don't need a degree to help where it's needed. I basically just did what I was directed to do. Sometimes it was handing out food, other times holding an infant whose mother had just passed away."

"It sounds like heartbreaking work."

"It was at times, but at least I felt I could make a difference."

"I can see why that would have been important to you. Right," May said, standing up and putting her pen and folder back on the desk. "Let's get you up on the examination table and check you over."

To Piper's relief the rest of her check went smoothly,

inasmuch as something so intimate could go smoothly. May remained efficient and professional as she examined her thoroughly, occasionally asking questions and making notes as she went. She printed off a lab request and gave it to Piper.

"Take this through to the lab so we can complete these tests and then you're all done. I'll give you a script for some prenatal vitamins and folate. As soon as you've had the blood and urine tests done, you can fill the prescription and start taking them."

"So you don't see any problems with me falling pregnant fairly quickly?" Piper asked.

"Every case is different, but you've been pregnant before and there really isn't any reason why you should have any worries this time around. The only thing that could be a concern is the malaria. Should you relapse while you're pregnant, it could make treatment difficult and cause problems for the baby."

Piper swallowed. She'd contracted the illness in Africa, early on in her volunteer work. It was her own fault in blithely ignoring the warnings and not keeping her antimalaria routine up-to-date. The wake-up call had been a harsh one. She'd been fortunate not to experience a severe relapse since, but there were no guarantees she'd continue to be so lucky.

"Problems?"

"Many of the drugs used in the treatment of malaria are contraindicated during pregnancy. Have you experienced a relapse since your infection?"

"No, I haven't."

"Then let's hope that continues, hmm? We'll monitor you carefully, though."

May continued on with some further instructions for Piper on maintaining a healthy lifestyle. By the time Piper found herself back in the car park, her newly filled prescription clutched in one hand, Wade's car key in the other, her head was spinning. What had she let herself in for? The ramifications of what she'd agreed to were suddenly all too real and with that reality, fear of failure stole anew into her heart.

During the drive back home she considered their agreement in-depth. This was a monumental thing she had consented to. She had to make sure that this worked, for everyone's sake, but most importantly, for that of their child.

Wade let himself in through the front door later that night and heaved a sigh of relief to be home. As cute as May and Paul's daughter Maggie was, a whole evening with her was enough to wear out the hardiest of men. She was going to be a heartbreaker when she grew up, though, that was for sure. A feeling of intense protectiveness swamped him—as if he'd ever let anyone near enough to Maggie for her to break their heart.

It worried him sometimes, this fierce need to protect a child who wasn't even his. If he was this bad now, how would he feel about his own? He knew, better than most, how hardy children were. How they needed to push boundaries and find their paths in the world. But right now the idea of wrapping little Maggie in cotton wool and tucking her away somewhere safe for the rest of her life was inordinately appealing.

He couldn't wait to be a father. His own had been no role model and he was determined to prove that he could not only be more successful than the man who'd refused to continue to raise him, but he would be a far, far better parent. No child of his would ever be discarded. Not for any reason.

He cast a glance upstairs. From here he could see the door to Piper's room. The landing was dark with not so much as a glimmer of light from beneath her bedroom door. He was relieved she was in bed already—goodness knew every interaction they'd had so far had been fraught and contentious. After the day he'd had in the office where nothing had seemed to go right, and the evening with Maggie, who'd been way more demanding than usual, he was in no mood to go another round with Piper.

He turned toward the library so he could put his briefcase and laptop by the desk for an early start in the morning. As he opened the door he was surprised to see a movement in the darkened room. Only a slight glow from the fireplace lent illumination, casting a golden light across the very last person he wanted to see right now. She was dressed much as she'd been this morning, in her nightgown and her father's robe. Except the robe had fallen open as she'd dozed with her feet drawn up under her on the wingback chair, revealing smooth tanned skin and the slight swell of one breast exposed by the open buttons of her pristine white cotton nightgown.

She must have sensed him in the room because she shifted in the chair, her eyes opening, searching for him. "Wade?"

She sounded drugged with sleep.

"You were expecting someone else?" he countered, dryly.

And just like that she was wide awake. "Don't be ridiculous. I wanted to talk to you about the agreement. There's an addition I've made."

"An addition?"

When was she going to understand that she really didn't call the shots in this situation? He shook his head wearily.

"Piper, the agreement was drawn up in accordance with our earlier discussion—including your specific conditions. You cannot keep on amending it."

"It's just one change."

"Well, spit it out."

"I'd rather you read it, actually."

Piper walked over to his desk and picked up the folder she'd obviously put there. She opened it and took out the agreement, flicking through the pages until she found what she was looking for. He reached across the desk and flipped on the lamp, the sudden illumination revealing just how sheer the cotton of her nightgown was and how exquisitely shaped her nipples were as they pressed against the fabric.

His mouth dried and, if he hadn't known better, he would have thought all the blood in his body had just headed south. Wade tore his gaze from her and forced himself to accept the document. He leaned down over the desk, fighting his awareness of her standing next to him, desperately trying to ignore the alluring shadows of her form. As if she was aware of the torture she was putting him through, she grabbed the edges of her robe and wrapped them tightly across her body, tying the sash firmly at her slender waist.

Wade felt a momentary tug of regret before forcing his mind to the matter at hand. Her closely formed handwritten notes used clear and succinct language. *Very* clear and succinct language, he thought with an inner smile. So she didn't want him seeing other women. Given her response this morning it shouldn't surprise him. She'd been prickly when she'd thought he had a booty call rather than a babysitting assignment.

Knowing she was jealous of his other women was strangely satisfying, but the knowledge was, at the same time, a little unsettling. How did he really feel about that? Did he honestly want to pursue an exclusive relationship with Piper? Relationship should be the wrong word, but just the thought of it was enough to fill his chest with an unexpected warmth. He quelled the feeling almost immediately. This was Piper Mitchell he was talking about. He'd learned his lesson once, the hard way. He wasn't masochistic enough to involve his emotions with her again.

He straightened from the desk abruptly. Piper took a step back in reaction.

"Is that all?" he asked quietly.

She looked startled. Had she expected him to argue with her? To refuse to sign? Did she have no concept of what this child meant to him? Or how important it was that he regain from her what she'd taken? He'd have all but signed away his soul to get what should have been rightfully his all along.

"Y-yes," she stammered.

"Fine, I'll get my PA to witness my signature at work tomorrow and we can get down to business."

Even in the muted light he could see how she'd paled at his words.

"Business?"

"Yes, Piper," he said, stepping closer to her. So close he could see moisture glisten on her lips where she'd nervously swiped them with her tongue. "The business of making a baby."

She swallowed, dragging his attention from her lips to the long graceful sweep of her neck.

"Right. But we'll have to wait for the health check results to come back first, won't we?"

"Piper, seriously, if I didn't know you better I'd think you were nervous."

She swallowed again. "No, I'm not nervous exactly. I was just thinking today that we hadn't really gone into the mechanics of how we were going to create this child."

"Mechanics?" He smiled. "Well, it's been a while but I'm assuming people still do it the same way they have always done. You know—"

"So you don't want to go for artificial methods?" she interrupted.

Her voice had pitched even higher. She sounded a little scared. Such a change from the fearless girl he remembered. He was starting to feel bad about winding her up so much. It had always been so good between them, why would she be scared of that? Maybe she needed a reminder.

"Now, why would I want to do that, when we can enjoy this," he replied.

He reached forward, cupping one hand at the back of her neck and drawing her toward him. He bent his head, catching a glimpse of shock in her eyes before his lips captured hers. Her eyelids fluttered closed as he traced the seam of her mouth with his tongue, her lips parting on a gentle sigh. He deepened the kiss, pressing home his advantage and trying not to remember the last time he'd touched her like this. The last time he'd wanted her like this—with a force that threatened to consume him.

He swept his tongue along her lower lip before suckling it between his teeth, scraping softly on the tender membrane before releasing it again. Her body sank into his, the softness of her breasts crushing against his chest. The curve of her hips, her mound, aligning with his painfully hard erection. He craved her with a need he'd thought long suppressed. Wanted nothing more than to sweep the contents of his desk to the floor and to take her on that hard polished surface—to push up her nightgown over her waist and to sink between her glorious long legs, to her inner heat where he could lose himself, lose this overwhelming burning desire.

But, with a control borne of years of practice, he reined himself back, focused instead on nothing but their kiss, on inciting her to want him as much as he most definitely wanted her. Because when he took her to his bed, he wanted her to be a full and willing partner—physically at least. He would settle for nothing less.

Seven

Piper struggled to gather her thoughts, but they spun out of reach until she could only feel. Wade's kiss was a mastery of seduction. His lips a tantalizing tease across her own. His tongue a hot wet rasp of torment. She wanted more than this, more than a kiss. She wanted to feel his mouth on her body—her breasts, her belly, lower.

She squeezed her thighs tightly together against the swell of longing that ached at her core and wrapped her arms around his neck so she could press even more firmly against his length. His body felt different from how he'd been before. More heavily muscled through his torso, his legs stronger. But one thing remained the same. She recognized the feel and shape of a specific part of him as if it were only yesterday.

She trailed one hand down his chest, to the waistband of his trousers where she fumbled with his leather belt, desperate to test the weight and size of him in her hand. To feel his silken hardness, skin to skin.

He groaned into her mouth as her fingers pushed past

the elastic of his briefs and brushed the head of his penis. His erection jumped against her palm before she closed her fingers around his width and stroked. She felt the shudder go through him, heard him groan again as he tore his mouth from hers and fastened it anew in the curve of her neck.

And then the firm grip of his hand was at her wrist, gently pulling her away from him. Pushing her away from him. She fought to control her breathing, to get some semblance of control over her wayward behavior. Her body felt heavy, lethargic—aching with longing.

Her reaction to him—to the feel, the taste, the sheer craving she had for him—made her realize something that she hadn't wanted to consider in a very long time. She still had feelings for him—very deep feelings. The thought was a sobering wake-up call. That Wade desired her, she had no doubt. She'd felt the throbbing heat of his passion in her own hand only seconds ago. But could she hope that his feelings for her would ever again be more than the disdain he'd so clearly expressed?

She took a step away from him on legs that felt about as substantial as threads of cotton. Piper looked up to Wade's face. The light from the desk lamp cast shadows across his features. For a split second she thought she'd glimpsed something there, something from when she knew she'd held his heart in her hands as he had held hers. Before she'd systematically destroyed everything they'd had between them without realizing how much she would ultimately hurt them both. But that glimpse gave her a tiny shred of hope. Maybe they could make this work. Maybe, just maybe, they could build something new out of the ashes of their old relationship.

"I think we've proved we won't have any trouble on the compatibility score, don't you?" he said.

And there it was, back in full Antarctic chill. That aloofness that told her that while she might be able to affect him on a physical level, there was no way he was going to let her back inside on an emotional one.

She nodded, lost for a response.

"So there'll be no more talk about artificial conception?" he pressed.

She shook her head.

"Then I think you'd better get off to bed, don't you? You have a long day tomorrow at the office to look forward to."

Finally, she found her tongue. "Will we travel in together?"

"No, I need to be in early. I'll leave the car for you if you like."

"Or I could use Dad's," she said.

"Rex's Daimler was sold last year. There's the hatchback the Dexters use but they'll probably be busy with it tomorrow. What's the matter, didn't you like driving the Porsche? I can easily book a driver to take me into work."

She shook her head again. "That's not the point. What will everyone think if I turn up in your car? They'll assume the only reason I got a job there is because I'm sleeping with you."

He gave her a piercing look. "And that bothers you, that people might think—" he reached a hand out to trace her cheekbone "—we're on intimate terms?"

She jerked her head back but it did nothing to stop the tingling awareness on her skin.

"Yes, it bothers me. I meant what I said about learning to work there from the ground up. I need to learn to stand on my own two feet. I don't want any dispensations just because of who I am."

He chuckled but the sound lacked humor, and made the fine hairs on the back of her neck prickle in reaction.

"No dispensations like walking in off the street to a job even though you have no experience and no qualifications? Why does that not surprise me?" He rubbed his eyes with one hand. "Go to bed, Piper. I'll make sure you have sufficient means to get to work tomorrow. Means that ensure no one will think any the worse of you, I promise."

"Thank you," she said stiffly. "Good night."

"It's night all right," she heard him mutter as she walked past him and out the door. "Not that there's anything good about it."

Piper woke the next morning to the sound of Wade's car purring down the driveway. She stretched and rolled over to look at her clock. 6:00 a.m. He certainly wasn't kidding about heading to the office early. She rolled back into her previous position, seeking oblivion for perhaps another half hour, but the moment was gone. She couldn't get back to sleep. She was starting work today and the prospect thrilled and terrified her in equal proportions. What if she made a total fool of herself? What if everyone hated her when they found out she was Rex Mitchell's daughter? Would anyone still remember her or her reputation?

There were so many "what ifs" her head started to spin. She pushed aside her bed covers and flicked on the overhead light. Her eyes caught on the clothes she finally decided to wear for work. A plain pair of tailored navy trousers, teamed with a cream-colored blouse and a matching camisole underneath. She really needed to do something about getting some new bras, she thought. She couldn't go braless forever. She'd considered, again, the idea of padding up one of the bras in her drawer with tissue paper but had discarded it as quickly. She didn't want any other worries to occupy her mind while she started to learn the ropes of this next stage in her life.

Piper gathered her things and went through to her bathroom, a bubble of excitement beginning to form in her belly. She was starting work, paid employment, for the very first time in her life.

She stopped and looked at her reflection in the mirror. She'd changed so much since she had left here. Reinventing herself several times over from capricious daughter to single party girl to tireless aid volunteer. Now she was on the cusp of reinventing herself again.

She found exactly what she was looking for in the bottom drawer of her bathroom vanity. The scissors weren't unwieldy, but they weren't exactly the compact fine-precision steel of a hairdresser's instrument, either. Well, they'd have to do, she thought as she reached behind her and grabbed a dreadlock firmly in one hand. A swell of nausea rose from the pit of her stomach as she positioned the scissors and closed her eyes. Snip. There it was. The first real step toward the new Piper Mitchell.

By the time she stepped in the shower cubicle of the bathroom, she already felt different. Lighter. She laughed out loud. Of course she felt lighter. At least five years' hair growth lay scattered on the bathroom tiles. She lifted a hand to her head, feeling the wisps of hair that now clouded in a pale golden halo. She'd have to get it professionally shaped once she had some money but for now it would have to do.

After her shower she blow-dried her hair, combing her fingers through the unaccustomed short lengths. For someone who'd had long hair all her life it felt drastically different. She didn't doubt she'd get used to it, though. There, she was done. She stepped back and looked at herself in the full-length mirror on the back of the bathroom door.

Piper eyed herself critically. The new hair was certainly different, she decided, the makeup not too bad, and the overall effect with her clothes gave her what she hoped was a smart professional finish. Going back into her bedroom she took another look at her clock. Good heavens! She'd spent the better part of an hour and a half getting ready, it was almost seven-thirty. She'd better hurry or she'd be late for her first day and she couldn't bear to see the censure or, no doubt, the satisfaction on Wade's face if she wasn't there by start of business at half past eight.

Mrs. Dexter was in the kitchen when she arrived downstairs.

"Oh, my, what have you done to your hair?" she cried.

"Do you like it?" Piper asked, putting up a hand to touch her hair.

"Well, it beats what you arrived home with. I imagine it'll grow out soon enough. You always did have lovely hair. By the way, you'll be needing a raincoat," the woman remarked as she put a plate of scrambled eggs in front of a place setting on the kitchen table.

"Thanks for breakfast," Piper said, picking up a fork and sampling a mouthful before Mrs. Dexter's words sank in. "A raincoat? Whatever for?"

Mrs. Dexter pointed to a couple sheets of paper and a stack of coins on the table next to Piper's place setting. Piper slid the note out from under the coins. It didn't take long to read.

Here's the bus timetable. The nearest stop is about 800 meters from the house. Enjoy the ride.—W. P.S. I'll instruct the pay office to deduct the bus fare from your wages.

Piper almost laughed. The bus? Did he really think she'd shy away from catching the bus? Mrs. Dexter did, too, by the look of her. They had no way of knowing she'd traveled on far worse than Auckland's transport system. She carefully put the note on the table and lifted the timetable. She'd really have to hurry if she was going to reach the office on time. With little care for finesse, Piper shoveled down the last of the eggs and swiftly drank the coffee Mrs. Dexter had poured for her.

She rose from the table and put her dirty dishes in the sink then gave the older woman a smacking kiss on the cheek.

"Thanks, Dexie. I've got to go."

"Are you sure you'll be all right catching the bus?"

"I'll be fine, don't worry about me."

"You'll find a coat in the hall cupboard, and an umbrella."

"Perfect, thank you!" Piper cried as she raced upstairs to brush her teeth before leaving.

She knew what Wade was up to and she wouldn't give him the satisfaction of beating her down. Not now, not ever. She might have agreed to have his baby but there was no way he was going to call all her shots.

Wade walked to the reception area on the dot of eight-thirty.

"Any sign of Miss Mitchell?" he asked the receptionist.

"Oh, yes, sir. She's been here for ten minutes. Jane is showing her around, as you asked."

She was early? He hadn't expected that. No, to be completely honest, what he'd expected was a tantrum over the phone that he'd expected her to take public transport. The Piper he'd known would never have dreamed of such a thing. Still, he probably hadn't given enough consideration to the steel vein of stubbornness that ran down her spine.

"Thanks, I'll go find them."

"They're probably in accounts," the receptionist offered far too cheerfully.

Wade tried to keep his bewilderment in check as he headed toward the accounts department. He'd wanted Piper to start there, as a junior. If anything would break her ridiculous desire to work here, that would. He had no doubt she'd never so much as balanced a checkbook. Invoicing would definitely be her undoing. At least, he expected so.

He heard laughter as he walked down the corridor, not an uncommon sound in his workplace—he prided himself on the atmosphere he and Rex had built here—but this was more than usual. He entered the accounts department and saw a crowd of staff around one desk.

At the computer terminal a young woman sat with her back to him. Who, he wondered, before his body instinctively recognized what his own eyes had not. Piper. A very different Piper than the one he had kissed last night. What had she done to her hair? It had transformed into a short choppy multilayered cut. Far shorter than he'd ever seen her wear before. It emphasized the slenderness of her neck and the delicate line of her throat.

The laughter and bonhomie he'd heard suddenly fell silent. Piper looked over her shoulder from what she'd been doing. Her eyes locked onto him for a startled moment before dropping. He had the brief satisfaction of seeing a flush rise in her cheeks before she turned away.

"Everything under control?" he asked, irked to feel as if he was an intruder in his own firm.

"We're doing fine." Jane separated herself from the group and gave him a smile. "I think Piper will fit in extremely well here."

"That's good," he said, feeling completely the opposite. He looked around at the assembled group of staff. "But does it really take all of you to train her?"

One by one people muttered something and peeled back to their work stations, leaving just Piper and Jane with him. Jane gave him a speculative look. She'd worked here at Mitchell Exports the past five years and knew him well. She'd certainly never seen him speak to his staff like that before. The knowledge he was behaving unreasonably made him even more irritated.

"I'm glad to see you managed to get in on time, Piper," he said, gleaning a kernel of satisfaction as he saw her ears turn a little pink as his comment sank in.

"Did you think I might have a problem—" she hesitated a moment before adding "—sir?"

Well, that was telling him, wasn't it? He acknowledged her barb with a small, grim smile.

"Proof will be in your consistency, and your performance. It's not a popularity contest, you know."

"I'm aware of that, sir."

"And we don't stand on ceremony here, Piper. Just call me Wade."

She smiled back at him. The silence stretched out between them, with Jane standing at his side looking from one to the other as if she was at a tennis match.

"Well," he said uncomfortably, "I'd better not keep you from your work."

Piper merely continued to smile. He gave Jane a sideways look which wiped the smile from her face, then he turned and stalked out. Damn if she hadn't held the upper hand there all the way.

Once in his office he began to calm down, seeing his behavior for the ridiculous stunt it was. Were his expectations of her really so mistaken? Had she truly changed? He thought again about the bus ride she'd endured to get here on time, and the effort she'd obviously made to change her appearance and to fit in. He'd been unfair, he had to admit. She'd stepped up to the plate without so much as a murmur, and he at least owed it to her to acknowledge that.

He couldn't fault her. Not in anything she'd done so far today. With a sigh of resignation he reached across his desk and picked up the phone, dialing from memory the number of his car dealer. Some points were best made by gesture, he decided.

Piper gingerly walked up the driveway toward the house. As hard as her feet had become in the work boots or runners she'd habitually worn the past few years, spending a day in high heels was something she'd happily forgotten. The balls of her feet were almost raw, she was sure of it. Her first paycheck would have to go toward a sensible pair of shoes, she thought. The Piper she used to be would never have dreamed of doing such a thing, but she was most definitely more practical now. And if she was to bus to and from work each day, with the walks from the house to the bus stop and again at the other end to the office, then doing it all in reverse order each day, she'd need something sensible on her feet just to survive.

Huh, and she'd thought relief work was tough. While it had been demanding physically and emotionally, it had never left her this mentally exhausted. She certainly hoped that Wade wasn't planning on any more verbal rounds because she really wasn't up to it.

She lifted her head as she approached the house. Oh, great, she thought, noting a different car parked in the driveway. Visitors. She certainly hoped she wasn't expected to make an appearance. All she wanted to do right now was take off her shoes and give her feet a soak.

Piper veered along the pathway that led toward the back entrance of the house, hoping that she could avoid Wade and whoever he might be entertaining. But her hopes were dashed as she heard the big wooden front door swing open and Wade called her name as he stepped onto the wide veranda.

She stopped in her tracks and looked at him as he walked toward her.

"I owe you an apology," he said, the words stunning her with their simplicity.

"You were a jerk this morning," she replied stiffly. "I accept your apology."

She turned and started to walk away but his large warm hand settled on her arm and halted her in her tracks.

"Which part of this morning, particularly?" he asked.

She paused before answering, pretending to give the matter consideration. "Oh, pretty much all of it really," she finally replied.

He laughed, a genuine laugh that made his eyes crinkle at the corners and shaved years off his face.

"Well, that's telling me."

"Is that all you wanted?" Piper said, pointedly looking at his hand which still lay warm and heavy on her arm.

"Actually, no." With his spare hand he reached into his trouser pocket and withdrew a set of keys. "These are for you."

She avoided taking them from him. "What are they for?"

He nodded at the car parked in the driveway. "That. It's yours."

Inside she silently rejoiced and her feet agreed with her. A car. It would give her the independence and the degree of separation she needed, while removing the inconvenience of having to catch the bus—especially on days like today when it had been raining on and off. But she didn't want him to think she was asking for a handout. If she had to take public transportation every day from now until kingdom come to prove herself to him, then that was what she'd do. She lifted her chin and looked him straight in the eye. "What's wrong with the bus?"

"I thought you might prefer the comfort of a car of your own. Especially once you're pregnant."

The words brought home the reality of their situation to her with sudden clarity. Up until now it had all been a war of words, but hearing him say it made it a great deal more real.

"And will you deduct its value from my wages, too?" she said, fighting for some measure of control.

His mouth quirked on one side in that half smile he was inclined to do around her these days. "No, I won't. It's a gift. There's an account for you at the local gas station, too."

"Thank you," she said simply, accepting the keys from his hands and going to look at the car.

It wasn't the newest vehicle on the block but it certainly wasn't the oldest, either.

"I didn't think you'd want anything showy or expensive," Wade said from right behind her.

"I appreciate it. After your performance this morning, Jane's already looking at me funny."

"She'll get over it." Wade shrugged. "Want to take it for a spin around the block?"

Piper thought for a moment of the soak she wanted to give her feet but the temptation to see how the car felt to drive was too tempting.

"Sure, you coming?"

In answer he opened the passenger door of the car and slipped inside, securing his seat belt. "Well, come on," he urged.

She walked around the car and settled herself in the driver's seat, adjusting it and the rearview mirror slightly before clipping her seat belt and starting the car. She was pleased to see it was automatic. She could drive a stick shift well enough but in Auckland's rush-hour traffic, constantly riding the clutch would be a pain.

Wade's presence seemed to fill the car, not surprising given its compact size, but it was more than that. It was as if, by his very presence, he consumed her, too. Not just his presence, she realized, but his happiness. He was smiling and seemed genuinely content to drive around with her. She was struck by how much she'd missed this Wade—the Wade who enjoyed just being with her, as if he couldn't imagine anything better than an afternoon with her. Could she keep him like this—or would he revert back to his colder self at any moment?

"Everything okay?" he asked.

"Fine," she answered with a nervous smile.

She slid the car into gear, released the hand brake and drove the car down the driveway and out of the gates. The car handled beautifully. Certainly not in the same league as Wade's Porsche, or the snazzy little BMW her father had given her for her eighteenth birthday, but it certainly did the job. And it wouldn't make her stand out in the workplace car park, either.

When they returned home, Wade directed her to the new five-car garage at the rear of the house and indicated where her automatic door opener was. As they walked back to the house she thanked him again.

"No problem," he said. "I *was* being a jerk this morning. You manage to bring out the worst in me, Piper." They stopped under the porch by the kitchen door. "And I'm wondering, what are we going to do about it?"

Eight

"Just learn to be civil, I guess," she hedged in response.

But she knew exactly what he was talking about. They'd been circling each other like angry cats from the moment she'd arrived a few days ago. Antipathy was there, for sure, but beneath the surface lay something else. Something thick and heavy and powerful. Something neither of them wanted to acknowledge. It itched beneath their skin with a constant presence. An itch that she knew, without doubt, only one thing would assuage.

"Civil," he repeated. "You think that's the answer?"

She opened the kitchen door, letting out the warmth and golden light from within, dispelling the gloom outside.

"Maybe not, but it's the only one I can think of right now."

He took a step nearer, and rested a finger on her lips.

"Is that what you feel toward me now, Piper? Civility?"

Oh, God, no. She felt anything but. Given the opportunity, she'd open her mouth right now, draw his finger in and lave it with her tongue. She'd drive him crazy with wanting her and then eventually they'd do something about it, and maybe, just maybe, some of the tension between them would ease.

"Ah, so there the two of you are. What do you think of your new car?" Mrs. Dexter's voice broke the spell that bound them in the moment. "Come along inside and shut that door before you let all the warmth out. Dinner is almost ready."

Piper didn't know whether to be relieved at the interruption, or annoyed that she and Wade weren't going to pursue his question any further. In the end, she opted for relieved. It had been a demanding enough day so far already. She had no wish to complicate it further by exploring her feelings for him on a physical level right now.

Dinner was a mostly silent affair, punctuated only when she thought of questions to ask about Mitchell Exports that only Wade could answer. She wanted to return to the easy comfort she'd felt with him in the car, but ever since he'd stopped her outside the house, she'd been far too aware of him physically, tuned in to the tension rising between them.

Though the conversation was stilted, it was still instructive. She was beginning to feel a reluctant admiration for how he'd held everything together through her father's illness. Despite what he'd already told her, the other staff at the office today had informed her that Rex Mitchell had been forced to withdraw from business a whole lot earlier than she'd originally thought.

Not many of them made the connection that she was his daughter, thank goodness—and those who had, had also had the common courtesy not to bring it up in front of everyone else. She was lucky that Mitchell was a relatively common name. Most of her coworkers hadn't given it a second thought.

As Piper readied for bed that night, after setting out her clothes for the next day, she thought also of the university degree she'd never achieved. It would be both incredibly satisfying and useful to complete the papers she needed to finish her degree. What she'd learned before she left for overseas was a little rusty in the back of her mind. She could see how having the educational background would help her to grasp the running of Mitchell Exports a whole lot faster.

Wade might not realize it yet, but she planned on being an integral part of the company. It was something she'd always wanted to do at her father's side from when she'd been a little girl and finally understood what it was that kept him from home, from her, for so many hours a day. She'd wanted to be a part of it, a part of *his* world, a part of him. But Rex had never believed she was competent to do more than spend his money. Beating her head against his chauvinism for so many years had eventually done her in and driven her to behave stupidly. Now, inasmuch as she was capable, she was bound and determined to prove to Wade she could be something, someone, worthy of working there.

As she slipped between the fine cotton lavender-scented sheets, she resolved to find out what she could do about furthering her studies. She fell asleep happy in the knowledge that she was finally on the right track with her life. And if she could make this thing, the constant simmering heat between her and Wade, into something real and lasting along the way, to build a real future for herself and Wade and their baby, then all the better.

The days began to blur into routine. She'd wake and dress for work, always leaving the house after Wade, and usually getting home before him. She knew he was keeping an eye on her in the office but so far, aside from one invoicing incident, so good. Thankfully, Jane had picked up on the mistake before it had gone any further but Piper imagined that it otherwise would have resulted in a warning, and she didn't want to give Wade any reason to end her employment.

The prospect of earning her own wage was exhilarating. It was the first time in her life that she'd been gainfully employed. While she'd worked herself to exhaustion with her volunteer stints, and had gained a deep satisfaction in her achievements, this was quite different.

It was Friday afternoon, at the end of her first week of work, when she was asked to join a group of the staff at a nearby pub for a quiet weekend wind-down drink. Wade had been out of the office all day with clients. No doubt he'd be wining and dining late into the night and since it was also the Dexters' night off, Piper didn't relish going home to an empty house. But when she joined her new colleagues, she also didn't feel as if she fit in. They were full of gossip about boyfriends and mutual acquaintances. It left her feeling on the periphery of what her life should have been all this time. In the end she made her apologies after only half a glass of wine, and shot away home.

There were a few lights on in the house, she noticed as she rolled along the driveway. Wade's bedroom lights were among them. She parked her car in the garage and walked along the covered walkway that led to the back entrance of the house. More lights were on in the kitchen. Maybe the Dexters hadn't gone out after all. But the instant she set foot inside she knew they weren't home.

There was a very strong male presence in the room, a very singular strong male presence. Wade stood at the stove top, dressed casually but all in black, and with a plain white apron slung around his hips. A rich aroma redolent with tomato, garlic and a hint of spice filled the air. Instantly her mouth watered.

"What's this?" Piper asked, deliberately pitching her voice to be light and airy as if his mere presence wasn't enough to send her pulse racing. "Your take on *MasterChef?*"

He looked up from the pot he was stirring and flung her a smile. "No, I wish. In fact you might wish so, too, when you taste it. I like to cook but rarely have the time."

"I imagine Dexie doesn't let you over her threshold much,

anyway, at least not to do anything but eat," Piper commented dryly.

Mrs. Dexter's proprietary manner over her domain was legendary. Wade chuckled in response to her comment.

"No, you're right. I only get to play on her nights off. Why don't you go upstairs and get changed. I'll have dinner ready in about half an hour or so. Here, take this up with you."

He reached for an open bottle of wine on the kitchen table and poured her a glass of red. She sniffed the bouquet appreciatively before taking a sip.

"Mmm, that's lovely. Is it a new label? I don't think I've seen that one before."

"You won't have. It's from a new winery down in the south island near Wanaka. I've been in meetings with the owner and winemaker most of today. We'll be handling their exports into the South Pacific."

"Well, I sure hope they'll be keeping some stock for domestic sale." She took another sip. "You said half an hour. Any chance we can stretch that out a bit?"

He shrugged. "I suppose so, why?"

"I just thought I'd like to take a bath before dinner, help me get the kinks out after sitting at a desk all day."

"Regretting it, Piper?" he asked, his face inscrutable as he watched for her response.

"No, of course not. I'm just not used to being in one place doing one thing all day long."

"Go on, take your time," he said, taking a sip of his own wine. "Everything will keep."

She ducked her head in acknowledgment and left the room, full of surprising anticipation. This felt like a date. And she had to admit, she liked it.

Wade watched her go, and wondered if she'd have been so relaxed if she'd known exactly what he had in store for her tonight. He turned the heat down on the pots on the stove and settled at the kitchen table absently swirling his wine in his glass as he played with the paper—the medical report—he'd left on the table.

They were all systems go. The news had left him with mixed feelings. Gaining some sort of dominance over Piper, making her regret her actions when she'd left New Zealand, how she'd treated both him and Rex—those had all been driving motivations for him. But she'd surprised him since her return. Sure, she was still as feisty as ever, but it had a purpose now. While she hadn't been above making her demands about him creating a job for her at Mitchell Exports, she had impressed him with her fight for independence over getting to work and starting from the ground up. Not to mention her aptitude in the workplace.

Maybe Rex had been wrong about her. He'd often wondered why the older man had been so adamant that she be wrapped in cotton wool and never be allowed to experience the ugliness of the big wide world they lived in. He could understand the urge to protect her, to smooth away hardship from her path, but had Piper felt dismissed by her father's unwillingness to let her into the business side of his life?

Wade thought back to the first time he'd met her on a day when she'd come to the office to coerce her father out to lunch. Rex had refused, suggesting instead that she take Wade. He'd seen the flash of hurt in her eyes. Hurt rapidly followed by an equally swift flash of anger.

That lunch had been interesting. Piper had been equal parts amusing, tempting and terrifying. And underneath it all he'd sensed a vulnerability in her, almost a need for approval. He'd laughed often at her clever conversation and couldn't fail to notice how she'd bloomed at the attention he gave her. Looking back, it was as if she hadn't trusted that her intelligence would be enough to snare him, so she'd had to use her physical wiles to ensure she had him where they both wanted to be. How had he never noticed that before? Of course, he'd been younger then, and he'd have been blind and stupid not to have been attracted to her on a physical level, or to have ignored her blatant flirtation. A flirtation that had rapidly led to other things. "Things" that he hoped to resume tonight.

He still wanted a child, wanted all he'd demanded when he'd laid out their agreement. But he was finally allowing himself to admit how much he'd missed having her in his bed.

Piper soon returned downstairs. She topped up his glass and refilled hers before taking a seat at the table.

"Is there anything I can do to help? Set the table, maybe?" she asked.

"No, everything's all ready. You can take our glasses through to the dining room, though. I'll bring the tray with our meal."

"We're eating in the dining room?"

"Sure, why not? Why? Don't you think my cooking will be worth it?"

May as well aim for offhand, he thought, because the evening was going to get serious before very long.

She flicked him a glance but grabbed their glasses and the bottle and did as he suggested. He quickly took a pair of covered dishes from the oven where they'd been warming and placed them and a bowl filled with freshly tossed salad onto the large butler's tray and followed her.

He heard her gasp as she entered the room, and smiled a secret smile. The scene was set, and he wanted her to enjoy it. Wanted to make this night so much more than just fulfilling an agreement.

"This looks amazing," Piper commented as he laid the tray on its stand and transferred the dishes onto protective mats on the mahogany table.

Wade cast a glance at the highly polished silverware, the

ornately embellished candelabra gleaming under the glow of tall crimson candles and the sparkling crystal.

"Thanks," he answered simply as he crossed to where he'd laid her place setting and pulled out her chair.

"You've gone to a lot of bother," Piper said.

"I think the end of your first week at work calls for a celebration, don't you?" he asked as he settled into his chair at the head of the table.

"Yes." She nodded, as if surprised to be reminded. "It does. Thank you."

Wade gestured to the hot dishes in the center of the table. "Would you like me to serve or would you prefer to help yourself?"

"Oh, let me do something. I'll dish it up for us."

She leaned forward, the action exposing the curve of one breast inside the deep V-necked top she wore. The color, a deep blush pink, suited her but he thought the color better matched the tip of the one pink nipple he'd glimpsed as she'd moved. Instantly he was rock hard for her. His mouth dry and his skin stretched taut across his body. He wanted to dispense with the formalities. To forgo the niceties of dining together, of slowing wooing her, but he'd promised himself he'd take it slow.

"Wade?"

Piper's voice dragged him back into the present. She gestured to his plate. She'd served him and he hadn't even noticed, he'd been so wrapped up in his reaction to her.

"Thanks," he said, although his voice sounded strained even to his ears. He reached for his glass and lifted it in her direction. "Let's make a toast. To your first week at Mitchell Exports."

"And to many more," she amended as she clinked her glass with his. She sipped her wine before putting down her glass and lifting her fork. "This is beef stroganoff, right? Did you make it from scratch? It smells divine."

Wade pretended to be mortally wounded that she would think he'd resorted to a packet. "Of course, I made it with my own fair hands," he insisted. "What do you think?"

He watched as she lifted the fork to her mouth and tasted the rich mixture of beef and sauce. She chewed slowly before closing her eyes on a moan of pure pleasure. He swallowed. This evening wasn't going to get anymore comfortable any time soon. He'd better hunker down to weather it out.

"This is fantastic. And you really made it from scratch?" She gave another appreciative moan. "No wonder Dexie keeps you out of the kitchen. You're fierce competition."

He felt his cheeks heat a little under the compliment. "She's got no fear of me treading on her toes. I have a few dishes I do well, that I enjoy preparing, but for the rest I'm quite happy to be fed by someone else."

"Well, at least you'd never starve if you were on your own. I'm hopeless in the kitchen."

"Maybe you just need someone to take the time to teach you," he remarked.

For a minute she looked pensive. "I often wonder what my life would have been like if my mother had lived. Whether I'd have had the chance to learn things like cooking, keeping house properly. Dexie is so capable at everything but she doesn't tolerate fools. She's always been inclined to shoo me away when I've wanted to help her."

Piper had been so much younger than him when she'd lost her mother. At least he'd still had memories to cling to when the going got tough. It couldn't have been easy for her—a distant father and older family retainers meant no loving arms to welcome her each and every day.

"Do you remember your mother?"

"Not really, just hints of things. Like the smell of her perfume or the sound of her laughter. Sometimes I wonder whether they're real or if they're just related to other things and people from when I was growing up. I know Dad loved her dearly. Sometimes I wonder if he didn't die inside when he lost her."

"It certainly can't be easy losing a partner."

"You lost your mother, too. Do you remember her well?"

"Sure, and I count myself lucky for that if nothing else. Life was different when she was around. She made every day fun."

His voice trailed into silence. The fun had irrevocably ceased when his mother had passed away suddenly from an undiagnosed heart condition. Life after that had become very dark indeed, especially when the Family Court and Children's Services had become involved. He shook his head.

"Listen to us, we're supposed to be celebrating, not getting all maudlin."

Piper smiled back at him, but he noticed her smile didn't quite reach her eyes. Wade devoted himself to ensuring the rest of the meal continued in a far lighter vein. It was important to him to chase the shadows away for her, for reasons that no longer involved his agenda for their evening.

Nine

They'd cleared the table and put the plates in the dishwasher. Piper was amazed at how comfortable and domestic it all felt with just the two of them, alone. Wade had been fabulous company throughout the evening, showing a side of himself that she'd missed from their earlier months together—the months before she'd ruined everything by setting herself in total competition against her father for Wade's attention. She'd loved Wade with a passion that had frightened her at times with its intensity and she hadn't known how to handle it, or him. And to her shame, she'd resented anyone else who'd had a place in his heart.

She'd been so immature. She could have had them both, instead she'd ended up with neither. And now, she had Wade in a legal contract that had nothing to do with emotion or love.

Sometimes she wished she could simply turn back the clock and make better choices. But then she'd temper that with what she'd learned along her journey. It was a rite of passage she'd had to, *needed* to, go through on her own to really learn what was important in life.

"Do you feel like a nightcap?" Wade asked as he straightened from loading the last of the plates in the dishwasher.

"What were you thinking?" she asked.

"How about a twenty-year-old tawny port?"

"Sounds lovely. In the library?"

"No, I was thinking about in my sitting room."

Piper raised her eyebrows. "Your sitting room? I didn't know you had one."

"When the property was signed over to me I did some remodeling of the guest suite upstairs."

The guest suite. That had originally been her parents' suite until her mother's death, at which time her father had relocated farther down the hall.

"I'd like to see what you've done," she said, even as anticipation mingled with unease curled in the pit of her stomach.

It was one thing having an intimate dinner together in neutral territory, but being in an area that was solely Wade's domain, that really was something else.

"Come on, then," Wade said, holding the kitchen door open for her and gesturing for her to precede him.

They ascended the stairs together and as they walked the length of the landing that led to his suite, Piper felt her apprehension develop even further.

"Have a seat and make yourself comfortable," he said as he opened the door for her.

Piper was taken aback the moment she stepped foot inside the door. The room wasn't as she'd expected. Somehow she'd imagined he'd have gone for dark, heavy furnishings, similar to what her father had done in his rooms. Yet there was a comfort and lightness about the room that made it instantly welcoming. Welcoming, and yet there was also something else. An ambience that suggested a very particular kind of welcome. She sat down on one of the comfortable caramel-colored leather sofas arranged in front of the fireplace.

Even the air in the room suggested an atmosphere of sensuous luxury and well-being. Wade stepped forward and lit a series of candles that decorated the wide mantelpiece over the fireplace. Behind the antique fire screen, embers glowed warm and inviting in the grate. He added another log to the fire, sending a shower of sparks flying up the chimney.

"I had the fireplace redone and the chimney cleared when I took over these rooms. It seemed a great pity not to make the most of it, especially on cooler nights like this," he said, dusting his hands lightly.

Piper moved to the end of the sofa, closer to the fireplace, and put out her hands to the warmth from the flames that were already licking the log. To her surprise her hands were trembling. She clenched them into fists and thrust them back into her lap. She was just here for a nightcap, so why was she so nervous? Behind her she heard the clink of crystal against crystal as Wade poured a measure of port into each of the glasses he'd had prepared on a tray.

She hadn't missed seeing them there as they'd entered the room, as if he'd known all along he'd be sharing a drink with her, here, tonight. She turned to face him, accepting the drink he'd poured her and fighting to ignore the quiver of awareness that sparked up her arm at the casual touch of his fingers against hers.

"Wade? Is there something else behind tonight? Something you're not telling me?"

"What makes you ask?" he answered, his gaze meeting hers unwaveringly.

"It's just…oh, I don't know. I just feel as if you have some kind of agenda going on here."

"Agenda," he repeated, as if testing the word on his tongue. "I suppose you could say that," he admitted.

She froze as he shoved one hand deep into his trouser

pocket and pulled out a crumpled sheet of paper. He handed it to her. Piper put her drink on a side table and took the paper, smoothing it out on the arm of the chair. Her eyes blurred a little as she attempted to read the words printed upon the sheet. She blinked and tried again. This time they made total sense.

She lifted her face to look at Wade who had seated himself opposite her on the matching sofa, his legs outstretched, his feet crossed at his ankles. He looked as relaxed and as comfortable as a man could get but she could see the lines of tension around his mouth and eyes. He was waiting for her to respond.

"So we're all systems go, then," she said, her voice cracking on the words and making a total lie of her insouciant shot at delivery.

"Yes, we are."

She waited for him to say something more but instead he just sat there, watching her. She felt her skin prickle under his regard, but it wasn't an uncomfortable sensation. More stimulating than unpleasant. She shifted on the sofa, trying to ease the tension building inside her. She should have known it would be futile. The movement made her thighs brush together, causing her inner muscles to involuntarily clench.

She swallowed and reached for her glass of port, taking a sip before putting the glass down again.

"And when do you suggest we begin to…?"

She couldn't bring herself to say the words. Not out loud. Wade, it transpired, had no such compunction.

"Make our baby?" he asked. "No harm in starting right now."

She froze in her chair. "N-now?"

"What's the matter, Piper? Do you have any objections?"

He rose from his seat then settled his body down on the sofa next to hers. Instant heat emanated along her side. Heat that spread across her shoulders as he draped one arm casually across the back of the sofa, behind her.

"No," she denied, even though everything inside her screamed yes.

"Then you won't mind me doing this," Wade said softly.

He lifted one hand and turned her face toward him, then moved forward to seal her lips with his in a smooth movement that spoke volumes as to his determination. His lips were gentle against hers, teasing, coaxing. Not the ravishment she'd expected. Inch by inch she felt her body relax. The man certainly knew how to kiss.

His fingers traced lightly along her jawline, before sliding behind her ear to cup her head.

"I've wanted to do this for days," he groaned against her mouth.

She was lost for a reply. Part of her was insanely glad he'd been suffering the same desires as she had—with the emphasis on suffering. But the other part of her was in a state of chaos. She had known all along this day, or night, would come. But now it was here, she knew she was most definitely not ready. Oh, yes, on a physical level there was no question she was up for this. In fact it would be a relief to actually get down and dirty with him. But on an emotional level? She didn't know if she could come out of this without some serious harm.

Wade's lips began a new onslaught, this time down the fine cord of her neck. Oh, she thought—as fire raced through her, sending all her senses aflame and clouding the thoughts that tossed around in her mind—he remembered. Her neck had always been a major erogenous zone for her. Especially that part just behind—

"Oh!" she gasped as his lips found the tender skin behind her ear.

"You still like that?" he growled softly.

In response she let her head fall to the other side, exposing her sensitive spot and giving him unobstructed access. He didn't let her down. He used his tongue and his lips in an alternating assault, while his hand lifted the edge of her top and his fingers traced a steady path to her breasts. She squirmed as he allowed his hand to linger on its journey, her body all but screaming out for his touch in other tender places.

"Let's get rid of this, shall we?" he said, now gripping the bottom of her top with both hands and beginning to pull it off for her.

She assisted as much as she was able, her breath catching in her throat as he paused and allowed his eyes to feast upon her naked breasts. The stark appreciation evident there sent a flood of heat to her core.

"And you," she said, her voice shaking. "Let's get rid of yours as well, hmm?"

He helped her pull off the black sweater that had clung to his muscled shoulders and coasted over his upper torso. And what a torso. If a man could ever be described as beautiful, Wade was very definitely that man. While not bulked up with muscle, there was no denying the latent strength beneath his pale golden skin. A light smattering of hair sprinkled from the middle of his chest, before thinning out into a line that arrowed down to the waistband of his trousers.

She reached for his belt buckle and murmured a tiny sound of protest when he grabbed her hands in his. But the protest turned to a deep-throated sound of satisfaction when he pulled her to her feet and continued to undress her. Skimming the elastic-waisted yoga pants she'd worn down her legs, then removing the tiny scrap of sheer satin and lace panties with equal grace.

He even moved beautifully, she registered as she watched him undo his belt buckle and zipper and remove his pants and briefs in one smooth motion. Next came his socks and then he was standing there before her, male perfection in all its glory. Wade bent and gathered the soft cushions off the sofas and cast them on the floor in front of the fireplace before guiding her down onto them.

She expected him to join her but he crossed the room and flicked a switch, turning off all the lights so that she was bathed only in the illumination of the fire and the golden glow cast by the candles above it. She stretched against the pillows and smiled as he walked back toward her.

Without saying a single word, he lay down beside her and began to touch, at first featherlight caresses designed to titillate and tease. And tease they did. She felt her nipples tighten into hard buds, felt moisture gather at the apex of her thighs. Felt her need for him, for his total possession, increase in steady increments until she was mindless for anything else.

And then he changed his tactics. He shifted his body over hers, stretching up her arms above her head and securing her wrists with one hand while supporting his weight with the other. The torture began with his tongue and his mouth, with the hot, heavy weight of his arousal against her body.

"Let me touch you," she whispered. "I want to touch you."

"Not yet. A man can only exert so much control, Piper, and I want this to be good for us both."

The knowledge that he was holding on by a fine thread only ignited her more. She squirmed against him, feeling his erection at her entrance and wondering just how hard she'd have to push to drive him over the edge of control and into abandon. She didn't have to wonder for long. His entire body shuddered as she moved sinuously against him.

"You're not making it easy for me," he said.

"I don't want it to be easy for you." She smiled up at him. "I want you to feel everything just as much as I am."

"Oh, believe me, I do."

He caught her mouth with his and gave her a deep wet kiss that left her in no doubt as to how close he was to capitulating. She gave back as good as she got, taking his tongue into her mouth and suckling it, using every trick she could to get him to give in. And then, oh, glory, he let go of her hands.

Immediately she reached out to touch him, to stroke his shoulders, his chest, to pull lightly at his nipples. He retaliated in kind, with his teeth and his tongue against her own, drawing her nipples, one then the other, into his mouth and releasing them, over and over. She drifted her hands lower, past his waist, to his hips and then, to his groin. His penis was hard and hot, a drop of moisture already pooling at its tip. She stroked him, holding him firmly in the grip of her fist, and felt him shudder against her again.

Piper let her legs fall open and guided him to her entrance, rubbing his blunt head against her moisture. His hand covered hers, positioning himself just inside her. His entire body shook as he waited there, his eyes, glittering chips of granite, meshed with hers. She lifted her hips and felt him slide a little farther within her. A tiny cry spilled from her lips. She surged against him again, wanting to take him deeper still—yet his hand over hers prevented it. How could he just stay there? She was desperate now. Desperate for his full possession.

"Wade, please?" she begged, her hips still riding him as much as he allowed.

"Yes," he answered, the single syllable a raw sound on the air between them.

He took his hand away and she grabbed at his hips with both of hers, angling her pelvis and waiting for his full possession. When it came, it drove the air from her lungs and thought from her mind as her body clenched around him. His length surged within her, again and again, driving her to higher peaks with each thrust. She couldn't keep her eyes open any longer, sensation took over her body, starbursts of light danced behind her eyelids. Wave after wave of pleasure built inside her. Wave after wave that grew until her entire body exploded from sheer intensity. Expanding ripples of ecstasy undulated through her, finally easing in force until her body fell back against the cushions filled with a delicious lassitude that invaded every cell in her body.

Wade collapsed against her, his back slick with perspiration, his buttocks and thighs still clenched beneath her touch. She could feel him pulsing rhythmically within her, feel the heat of his climax against her womb.

She'd never before felt this level of synchronicity, of bliss— not even with Wade eight years ago. What had just happened between them fell on the scale of cataclysmic. Even through her pleasure-hazed stupor, she was aware of her heart beating erratically in her chest and her pulse skipping through her veins with the speed of a madly galloping stallion. And he was no different. His breathing was ragged, and she could feel his body throb with the velocity of his own pulse.

"I didn't hurt you, did I?" he asked, his voice muffled against her neck.

Piper laughed softly. "Hurt me? You have to be kidding."

He went to lift himself off her but she wrapped her legs around his and her arms about his waist and held him close, keeping him trapped inside her at the same time.

"I'm too heavy for you," he protested.

"No, you're not. Stay, I don't want to lose this feeling just yet."

Wade sighed in response, his breath warm and moist against her sensitized skin. Her inner muscles tensed, pulling against him one more time as an aftershock of pleasure fluttered to her very core.

She hadn't felt this good, this satisfied, in her living memory. She wasn't about to do a single thing to change that right now. Her eyes slid shut and she continued to hold Wade to her, reveling in his heaviness and warmth, and hoping against hope that they'd conceived their baby with all their barriers down—with nothing between them but perhaps the hope that things might just work out after all.

* * *

Piper woke much later to the sound of rain once more hammering against the windows. The candles on the mantelpiece had long since gutted in their containers, the last of the embers in the fireplace now casting the only light in the room.

Wade's weight kept her pinned to the cushions and rug beneath her. Not the most comfortable position she'd ever slept in, she thought, but far from the worst, either. She trailed a hand down his back. Oh, how she loved the feel of his skin, especially where it touched hers. He was strength and hardness combined with an intrinsic thread of gentleness woven through at the same time. A man of contrasts.

He'd make a great father.

The thought shocked her. She'd never thought of Wade in terms of being a dad. She'd heard him talk about it, allowed herself to be locked into this agreement between them. Allowed? She wrinkled her forehead as she considered the concept, and forced herself to acknowledge that which she'd been trying to avoid all along. She could have just said no to him. Left him to see what the worst was that he could have done to her. She had no money. She had no home. No court in the land could have made her pay what she didn't have.

So why had she allowed him to bully her into signing?

Could it be that she still loved him? As the thought blossomed, she forced herself to acknowledge the real truth. The truth that resounded through her mind with a single word.

Yes.

Ten

She must have made a sound or a movement that disturbed Wade.

"Are you okay? I didn't mean to fall asleep on you like that."

"It's all right," she answered, still reeling from the certainty she'd only just acknowledged.

Wade shifted his weight off her and traced the bone structure of her face with one hand as he lay on his side next to her.

"I'd better get to my bed," Piper said, moving away from him.

"Why?" he asked.

"Well, we've…you know." She waved her hand futilely.

He laughed. She seemed to have that effect on him a lot lately.

"What's so funny?" she said, prickling at his response.

"That you think I'm going to let you go."

He got to his feet in a single movement and reached out a

hand to help her up. Keeping her hand captive within his, he guided her to a door that led off the sitting room. He swung it open and drew her toward a massive four-poster bed. Swags of heavy fabric, pointed with gold tassels, hung from the four points.

"Very Lord of the Manor," Piper commented as Wade pulled back the covers and ushered her within the sheets.

"Very." He smiled in return and followed her into the bed.

The contrast of his warm body and the cool sheets against her skin sent a tingle through her nerves. A tingle that intensified as Wade's arm curled around her and one hand began to play with the short thatch of hair at her groin, every now and then slipping a little lower to graze against the taut bud hidden there.

"Hey, that's not fair," she said when she could catch a breath.

"Indulge me," came the command from behind her.

His erection slid between her legs and she hitched herself up a little letting him enter her fully.

"Since you're so persuasive, I think I will."

His penetration hit just the right spot and she could feel the rising pleasure begin to radiate with every drive of his hips. She moved with him, wanting more with every stroke. His fingers didn't let up their offensive either and it was only a few minutes before she began to feel her body coil tightly as her orgasm built and built.

"Too much," she cried into the pillow.

"Never too much," he replied, his hips now picking up the pace and driving her over the edge until her body spasmed in paroxysms of satisfaction.

Wade held on as long as he could, but his body had other ideas. The force and strength of Piper's orgasm was his complete undoing and he gave over to the gratification his body demanded.

He continued to hold Piper long after she'd fallen back into an exhausted sleep, his fingers tracing tiny circles on the smooth, soft skin of her belly. Who knew? Maybe they'd already started a new life tonight. The mere thought was enough to make something in his chest clench in anticipation.

One thing was certain, though, he would do everything to ensure this baby made it. He would be there through every single step of this pregnancy and thereafter. A virtual slide show ran through his head of his child's life, with him there for him or her at every pass.

He chose to ignore the quirk of his mind that placed a smiling image of Piper right at his side.

Wade woke late that morning, surprised to find his arms and his bed bereft of Piper's warmth. He flicked a glance at his bedside clock and was amazed to see it was already nine o'clock. He couldn't remember the last time he'd slept that late, not even with an unhealthy dose of jet lag.

He hurried through his shower and getting dressed and went downstairs. Piper was seated at the kitchen table, the remnants of her breakfast on the plate pushed to one side, her attention focused on the bundles of paper scattered on the surface in front of her.

"Good morning," he said as he came in.

"Morning," she replied, not even lifting her head from her perusal of what looked like a prospectus of some kind. "I put your breakfast in the oven to keep warm."

"Ah yes, the Dexters are away this whole weekend, aren't they?"

Piper nodded. Obviously not up for a huge amount of morning-after conversation, he observed wryly as he lifted his plate from the oven.

"Hot!" he yelped as he rapidly transferred the plate from his hand to the placemat opposite where Piper sat.

"I did say I'd put your breakfast in the oven to keep warm," she said, finally looking up to meet his eyes.

"So you did." He lifted the foil off the top of his plate and grinned appreciatively. "I see you haven't lost your touch with a good old-fashioned breakfast."

"I was hungry this morning," she admitted, a flush of color lighting her cheeks.

"So am I," he answered, but kept his gaze very firmly upon her.

To his delight her blush deepened and spread and she quickly averted her eyes, transferring her attention back to the booklet in her hand.

"What's that you have there?" he asked as he poured himself a cup of coffee before sitting down opposite her.

"Nothing much," she hedged.

He reached across the table and with one finger pushed the booklet up in her hands until he could see the front cover clearly. A university prospectus?

"Looks like a bit more than *nothing much* to me. Are you thinking about going back to Uni?" Wade fought to hide his surprise.

She nodded. "Do you have a problem with that?"

"Not if it doesn't interfere with your current commitments."

"My work at Mitchell Exports? I don't think you need to worry about that. It's hardly taxing what I'm doing there."

"True, but I was talking about your commitment to me." More particularly, her commitment to their possibly already conceived child. He didn't want her to overtire herself or to put herself or their baby at risk.

She gave him a hard look and pushed her chair back from the table. "Trust me, you won't have anything to worry about."

Wouldn't he? He certainly hoped she was right. He didn't want to stand in the way of her bettering herself, if that was what she really wanted. "Perhaps you should let me be the judge of what I worry about." He forced a smile.

"What are you looking at enrolling for?"

"I thought I'd find out how I can supplement what I did

before I went overseas. I would like to finish my business degree, if possible."

Finish her degree? "But you only completed a couple papers before and that was eight years ago. What makes you think you can just pick up where you left off?"

"I don't know if I can, that's why I'm looking into the courses and pre-enrollment information now."

"Piper, you were hardly an A-grade student. This is really going to take time and perseverance. Don't you think you're biting off more than you can chew?"

"Well, thanks. It's nice to know where you stand. I would have thought you'd be happy to see me doing something so that I can eventually support myself."

"Is that what this is about? I already told you that, as long as you're under my roof, I will cover your expenses."

"Good, then you can pay for my tuition."

Piper rose from her chair and gathered her papers.

"That wasn't what I meant," Wade said firmly.

"Fine, so I'll apply for a student loan."

Before he could reply she'd left the kitchen with her nose very firmly in the air. Wade watched her go with narrowed eyes. Piper? Back at Uni? She looked, and sounded, as if she was serious about this. If she was, then of course he'd make sure she had the financial support she needed to make it happen. But he still struggled to reconcile the girl he'd once thought he knew so well with the determined young woman of today.

Piper fought back the tears that smarted in her eyes. She felt so stupid. She'd have thought that maybe Wade would understand why it would be a good thing for her to complete her degree but he was no different from her father. It seemed they were cut from the same cloth after all. Both determined to pigeonhole her. And no matter what she did to try and prove her worth—to garner their love and respect for her as a person—they wouldn't see it. No wonder the two men had gotten on so well. Perhaps leaving them both had been the best decision she'd ever made. Certainly better than the one she'd made to come home.

It had been nothing but heartache, and challenge after challenge since her return. Drawing water by hand from a well or clearing away a mudslide so a medical team could pass a road suddenly looked like easier options.

She let herself into the morning room, the room that had been her mother's, and threw herself onto the chaise. Why did everything have to be so hard?

In a perfect world she'd be able to declare her feelings for Wade, and of course he'd reciprocate and they'd both live happily ever after. A cynical laugh bubbled in her chest. As if. No, there was one thing and one thing only that Wade wanted from her and it was definitely not her lifelong devotion.

She rubbed one hand absently over her lower stomach. She'd felt him do the same last night. Had he been wondering, as she did now, whether they'd conceived the child he so desperately wanted?

A sound at the door drove her to her feet. Wade came inside the morning room and stopped just one step from the door.

"Are you absolutely serious about finishing your degree?" he asked, an inscrutable expression on his face.

"Of course I am, why else would I have gone to the bother of getting all this?" She waved the clutch of papers she held in her hand at him. "I need this, Wade. I need it for me. I know I bummed around the last time. I was in a different head space then. I didn't appreciate any of what I had, I just knew I wanted it all." She shot him a glance that she hoped reiterated that he had been among those things she'd wanted so very much. "When I couldn't have what I wanted, I behaved like an idiot. I know that. I just think I deserve a second chance. I really want to get it right this time."

She'd said more than she'd wanted to, far, far more than

she'd wanted to. Right now she wouldn't blame him if he out-right laughed in her face and walked away but to her surprise he held out his hand.

"May I see the courses you're looking at taking?"

Silently she handed over the information and watched as he settled into a chair and flicked through it all. Finally he looked up again.

"You *really* want to do this?"

"I really do."

He leaned back in his chair and looked up at her. Despite her having the physical advantage, it certainly didn't feel that way. For a long moment he said nothing and the silence stretched out painfully between them. He cleared his throat before speaking. "If you're absolutely serious about this—"

"Oh, yes. I am," she interrupted.

"If you'll let me finish," he said with a small but genuine smile.

"Sure, go on. I'm sorry."

"As I was saying, if you're absolutely serious about this then you may be eligible to do these papers through Mitchell Exports. We run cadetships, much like your father used to do unpaid internships, but this way you get to earn as you learn. We have strict entry criteria and a panel made up of management personnel at Mitchell Exports has the final decision. Are you prepared to be scrutinized and assessed to see if you're deemed worthy?"

Scrutinized? Assessed? It sounded daunting. The old Piper would have laughed in his face then run a mile in the opposite direction. But she'd had to change and she really needed to prove to herself that she could do this.

"Yes," she answered simply. "I'll do whatever it takes."

"It's not going to be a walk in the park, Piper. You will have to apply yourself at work and here at home in the evenings. The study load is huge. Are you sure you will be able to cope with that?"

"Don't underestimate how much this means to me, Wade. I am determined to do this."

"And when you fall pregnant?"

"I don't see why I can't continue to study. I remember pregnant women and young mothers at Uni when I was there. I'll find a balance. Look, I don't expect to achieve this overnight. I'm being realistic. I know it won't be easy for me to get back into a learning mind-set, let alone a lecture environment. But I will do it."

Her earnestness must have convinced him.

"I'll discuss it with the team on Monday and we'll go from there, okay?"

"Thank you," she said.

It was far more than she'd expected of him. Far more than she deserved given her track record.

"Just don't let me down on this."

"I won't."

As autumn slid wetly into winter, Wade found himself having to reassess his opinion of Piper on a regular basis, both in the office and at home. Her application to her work had seen her become immensely popular with the staff and her intervention when she'd seen a mistake in a proposal written in Spanish, targeting a sought-after South American client, had saved them both embarrassment and thousands of dollars.

When had she learned Spanish? he wondered as he signed off on the new deal with a flourish of his pen. And what else had she learned in the years they'd been apart?

By day she was a diligent employee. Outside of business hours, she was an equally diligent student as she worked through a six-month-long pre-entry course to get up to speed for attending university again for the semester beginning in the new year. And by night—he felt that all too familiar tightening in his groin—by night she was an exceptional lover.

He looked forward to their evenings together with an enthusiasm he'd underestimated. Sex with Piper had always been good, but what they shared now surpassed anything they'd experienced before. There was a synchronicity in their movements, their desire to give one another pleasure and receive it in return. Aside from when she'd had her period some weeks ago, they'd spent every night making love. Even then he hadn't allowed her to return to her room and had instead enjoyed the closeness of simply holding her in his arms at night.

This new Piper was indeed someone else compared to the woman who'd left after demanding he give up his life's dream to follow her overseas on a tantrum-induced-whim. It was as if she was doing her level best to please and it occurred to him that above all else, Piper craved acceptance. Everything she did was with the purpose of fitting in with her peers, and of gaining a degree of respect and independence.

Last week he'd reviewed the accounts that related to the running of the house and cars and noted that there was no bill for the petrol she'd been putting in her car. On checking up with the gas station, he'd been informed that Piper was paying for her fills herself and not charging them to the account he'd had set up. When he'd approached her, she'd merely lifted her chin in that endearingly self-reliant way of hers, and said she was earning a decent wage so there was no reason why she couldn't meet her own costs. He'd wanted to argue with her, to tell her that providing for her was his responsibility now, but there had been something in her stance that made him think twice about pushing the point home.

Deep down he recognized and understood her need to stand on her own two feet—it was how he'd felt his entire life—and for some reason that commonality with her was as unsettling as it was encouraging.

He wondered anew why Rex had never encouraged Piper to achieve more with her life. Why had the man kept his daughter slotted within set confines of behavior and expectation? No wonder Piper previously had never amounted to anything more than a two-dimensional woman whose selfish demands had clouded what Wade now believed were the real issues that drove her.

She was an intelligent woman who had a quick grasp of business concepts. Not only that, but her keen mind presented solutions to issues that he would have expected from someone with a great deal of life experience. Just what *had* she done while she was away? What had made her come into her potential that he'd only ever glimpsed in the past?

Rex had done her a disservice. If the old man had perhaps been a little less chauvinistic and a whole lot more inclined to see beyond the peripheral beauty of his daughter, he could have had a formidable business partner at his side when he got sick. He could have kept Mitchell Exports a family owned business, instead of sharing that honor with the son of a stranger.

This softening in attitude to Piper was a new concept for Wade. For so many years he'd been focused on his anger toward her, on his need to even what he saw as a score to be settled between them. Now, he could at least accept that her behavior had not all been her own fault.

He shook his head slightly. Man, he must be getting soft. He'd never have believed he could feel like this about Piper again—protective, encouraging.

Wade put down his pen and picked up the contracts before rising from his desk and going to his PA.

"Could you see these are couriered to Mr. Rodriguez as quickly as possible?" he asked, leaving the contracts on the side of her desk.

"Sure thing," his PA replied. "Oh, and Piper called and left a message for you. She wasn't feeling quite a hundred per-cent so she headed home early today."

"She's not feeling well?" Wade asked. "Do you know why?"

"Not sure, could be the flu. She started here after we all had our annual flu shots." ·

Flu, or could it be something else that made her feel sick? Whatever it was he needed to find out face-to-face.

"Cancel the rest of my appointments," he instructed as he headed for the door.

"But—"

His PA's protest fell on deaf ears as the door swung closed behind him. Anything and everything else faded into insignificance. He had to know and he had to know right now.

Was Piper pregnant?

Eleven

Traffic on the way home was heavy, despite the early hour. Schools hadn't closed yet for the day, yet there seemed to be an inordinate number of cars on the road. And the rain didn't help at all. Coming down across the windshield in driving sheets, Wade's wipers were working flat out to keep the glass clear.

Everything crawled to a standstill near the turn off to his street. Up ahead, though, Wade caught a glimpse of red and blue flashing lights. Police, a fire truck and an ambulance? A sick feeling of dread took up residence in his gut. Without sparing the weather another thought, Wade pulled his car over to the side and got out, running toward the cause of the traffic jam. As he neared the intersection, the dread solidified into abject terror. There, wrapped around a power pole, was an all-too-familiar vehicle. Piper's car!

Rain streaming down his face and in his eyes, Wade elbowed past the gathering crowd. Nothing else mattered right now but knowing that she was okay.

A team of firefighters were using cutting equipment to free the driver's door of her car.

"I'm sorry, sir, but you have to stay back," a young police officer ordered, standing firmly in Wade's way and arresting his progress.

"She's my..."

My what? he thought, unable to quantify their relationship properly but desperate to explain to the policeman that he had every right to be at her side when she was brought from the vehicle.

"Sir?"

"My girlfriend. She's my girlfriend," Wade repeated, as if doing so could get it through to the officer.

"There's nothing you can do right now. Just let the guys do their job. She'll be out in a minute or two."

"Is she all right? Do you know if she's hurt at all?" he asked, looking over the uniformed shoulder of the officer and trying anxiously to make out Piper's shape through the rain and the heavily coated fire rescue team.

To his infinite relief, he saw her moving and the instant the door was removed from the car, he watched as she was helped from the vehicle and to the waiting ambulance. One of the paramedics gestured for her to lie down on the gurney he had waiting but Wade felt a swell of pride as she shook her head and walked up the steps to the ambulance under her own steam.

"Can I go to her now, please?"

"Sure."

The officer stepped aside as Wade began to barge through. Given permission or not, nothing was going to stop him from checking on Piper himself. He bounded up the stairs of the ambulance, only to be barred at the top by one of the medics.

"I'm sorry, sir, but you can't—"

"It's okay, he's with me," Piper's voice came from inside the vehicle.

The man stepped aside to let Wade into the confined area. Piper sat on a gurney, a blood pressure cuff on one arm and a wad of dressing held to her nose. She pulled the dressing aside for a moment to speak.

"Don't worry, it's worse than it looks. The air bag gave me a bloody nose, that's all."

"Don't worry? Are you sure you're okay?"

"She'll have some seat belt bruising and be pretty sore the next few days but so far she checks out okay," the paramedic who was treating Piper said. He turned back to his patient. "Don't you want to go to the hospital just to be certain?"

"Yes, she does," Wade interjected. How could she know there weren't internal injuries? And besides, what if she was pregnant? What effect would the impact of the crash have had on the baby?

"No, I don't. Seriously. I'll be fine. I'm just a bit shaken up, that's all." Piper turned to Wade. "Please, I just want to go home and have a long soak in a warm bath right now."

"Is that wise?" Wade asked of the paramedic.

"Sure, just keep an eye on her. She doesn't appear to have a concussion or anything else serious."

"I'll do that. When can I take her home?"

"Just give us a few minutes to finalize our examination and take some details."

"Okay, I'll go and get my car."

Wade exited the ambulance and was relieved to see that traffic was being directed slowly and steadily past the accident scene. A tow truck was in the process of hoisting the wreck of Piper's car onto its flatbed.

"Are you the owner?" the tow truck driver asked Wade.

"Yes, I am."

"You were lucky, then."

"It wasn't me driving. It was my girlfriend."

Again that term that just didn't sit comfortably with him.

Piper was so different from that—less in some ways, but much more in others.

Wade looked at the damage to the vehicle. The passenger side had been entirely staved in. Had anyone been sitting there, they would probably be dead right now. He fought to control the ripple of fear that suffused him. Had the car hit the pole any differently, it could be Piper that was seriously injured, or worse. The car creaked and groaned in protest as the misshapen metal was hauled onto the truck. It was only once the driver was securing it with wide woven straps that Wade realized it had sustained rear end damage too, making him wonder what on earth had caused the crash in the first place.

"Do you know what happened?" he asked the tow truck driver.

"Cops think she was clipped by another driver, someone following too close and too fast, as she slowed for the corner. They shunted her across the road in a spin then took off. At least there were witnesses. They won't get away with it."

A red haze of fury swiftly replaced the fear that had earlier swamped him. A hit-and-run driver? If only he could get his hands on the lowlife scum, he'd teach them all about hit-and-run.

"So what do you want me to do with the wreck? I can take it to your home or to a panel beater of your choice so the insurance can get an assessor out. I doubt they'll do much but write it off, though."

"Just get rid of the thing."

"Are you sure, mate? You can sell the wreck for a couple hundred if you want."

"No, I never want to see it again," Wade said, his voice seething with tension. He reached into his pocket and took out a business card. "I don't give a damn what the insurance says. Just see to it that the towing bill and any disposal fees are sent to me and I'll take care of it."

"Whatever you say."

Wade waited a few minutes to cross the road and then jogged back to his car. Easing into the flow of traffic took some time and his fingers began drumming a rapid beat on the steering wheel. Eventually he managed to pull into a driveway near the ambulance.

He had to stifle his impatience a while longer as the police took a statement from Piper in the ambulance, getting from her as much detail about the incident as possible. Then, finally, he was allowed to take her home. The rain had slowed to a steady drizzle and the cold seeped through to his bones. But none of that mattered. Right now all he wanted was to get Piper home and to see for himself that she was okay. And then maybe to wrap her up in their bed and make sure nothing bad ever happened to her again.

His hands clenched into impotent fists at his side as he thought again about the driver who'd caused the accident. What he wouldn't do to have a bit of time alone with them right now.

Suddenly he could begin to understand why Rex hadn't wanted Piper to engage fully with the realities of the world. Why he'd wanted to keep his little girl safe in a fantasy world where nothing nasty ever happened to other people and where she didn't have to face unpleasantness. After losing his wife, was it really so surprising that the man had been determined to shield his only child? It might not have been the right thing for Piper, but it would have done a great deal toward soothing Rex's parental mind.

Transferring Piper into the car was accomplished with as much speed and efficiency as he could manage. She was already starting to feel the aftereffects of the crash and had begun to shake in reaction. He held open the passenger door of his car for her and leaned down to secure the seat belt across her body.

"Wade, I'm so sorry I smashed up the car."

"You're not to blame," he said tightly.

"But it's ruined, Wade. Did you see it? I know they say it wasn't my fault, but—"

"There are no buts. Just relax, we'll be home in a couple minutes and I'll get you into that bath you wanted."

Why the hell was she so upset about a car? Didn't she realize just how lucky she was not to have been more seriously hurt? And what about the whole reason she'd left work early in the first place?

"I'll need to get a ride with you to work tomorrow."

"Work can wait. I doubt you'll be up to it, anyway."

"But I don't have any sick leave," she protested.

"It's okay, I know your boss. Leave it with me."

Wade flashed her a tense smile even as his fingers gripped the steering wheel. He tried to order his thoughts. He had to ask her, he just had to.

"Piper," Wade said, fighting to keep his voice controlled and not to let any of his fear or worry cloud what he wanted to say. "Why did you leave work early?"

"I'll make up the time, don't worry," she said listlessly.

"Again, that's neither here nor there. One of the girls said you weren't feeling well."

"I must have had something for lunch that disagreed with me. It left me feeling off color and I couldn't concentrate on anything at work. I just wanted to head for bed. Fat lot of good that did me. I may as well have stayed at work."

"Are you sure it was something you ate?" he asked.

"Of course, what else…" Her words trailed off as understanding dawned. "Oh," she said, her voice suddenly very small and her face even paler than it had been before.

"Maybe we should get you checked at the hospital after all," Wade said.

"No, really, I don't want to go to the hospital, seriously."

"The doctor, then. Why don't I get May to come to the house?"

"Wade, I'll be fine. I've had an accident and I'm a bit shaken up and bruised. That's all. And if I am pregnant, there isn't anything we can do about it right now, anyway."

There was a fatalistic edge to her voice that he really didn't like but he could see she was adamant about not seeking medical advice just yet.

"Fine," he said, his jaw so tight he thought he might shatter teeth.

How could she be so cavalier? If she was carrying his child, he wanted an assurance that both she and the baby would be okay. Whether she liked it or not, he was calling May the moment he got Piper settled.

At the house, he helped Piper in through the back door where the warm and comforting smells of Mrs. Dexter's home cooking welcomed them.

"Oh, my, the two of you are wet through, and Miss Piper, is that blood under your nose? What on earth have you been up to?"

"Piper has been in an accident. She says she's fine and doesn't need a doctor, but would you take her upstairs and get her settled in a nice warm bath? She's going to need something soothing to offset the bruises she's earned today."

Wade tried to downplay the seriousness of the incident, his words earning him a grateful glance from Piper who allowed herself to succumb to Mrs. Dexter's fussing as the older woman led her from the room. The moment the women had gone upstairs, he took his cell phone from his pocket and dialed May Ritter's number.

"Dr. Ritter, please, it's urgent," he said as the receptionist took his call.

"Who's calling, please?"

Wade gritted his teeth as he replied, "Wade Collins."

"One moment, please."

The seriously hideous tones of prerecorded music filled his ears, doing nothing for his patience or his blood pressure.

"Wade, what's the problem?"

"Piper was in a car accident today and I think she might be pregnant. If she is, will the baby be okay?"

"Is she hurt?"

"Mostly shaken. The air bag gave her a bloody nose and the paramedic said she'll have bruising from the seat belt, too."

"Okay," May said soothingly. "So nothing too serious. What makes you think she's pregnant? She hasn't yet been in to see me again, or had any tests done."

"Aside from the obvious," he said, thinking about how they'd spent nearly all their nights since that first time back together, "she left work early today because she wasn't feeling well."

"Right," May answered.

He could hear the smile in her voice. It made him grip his phone all the more tightly in his hand. Didn't anyone understand how important this was?

"May," he growled.

"Okay, Wade, I know how much you want to be a dad. Look, the upside is that if she is pregnant, there is very little likelihood that anything has happened to the baby at this very early stage. Why don't you bring her in to see me tomorrow and we'll find out for certain if there is a baby, hmm?"

"Sure, thanks."

May gave him a time in the late morning and Wade hung up from the call feeling minutely better than he had at the start of it. She said he had nothing to worry about. So why did he feel as if his entire world was under threat?

Mrs. Dexter came back into the kitchen.

"I'll put together a tray for Miss Piper, something she can eat cold when she feels like it. I don't think she'll be up to much for dinner tonight. That crash has left her quite upset."

"Was she okay when you left her?"

"She was just getting into the bath. Poor girl, she can't seem to stop shaking."

"It'll be shock setting in. She was very calm at the scene, too calm probably. Can you make that tray for two? And when it's ready, perhaps you could leave it in my sitting room. I'll go up and see to her now."

Wade ascended the stairs two at a time. For his own peace of mind he needed to see Piper was okay. As he entered his bedroom, the fragrant scent of bath crystals came from the open en suite bathroom doorway. A small sound caught his ear, a sound that made every muscle in his body tense. Piper was crying.

He was at her side in seconds.

"Are you okay? Should I call an ambulance?"

"N-no, I'm okay. I just can't stop. I keep going through it in my mind, seeing that post coming toward me and feeling the helplessness all over again."

Tremors shook her frame making ripples on the water. Wade didn't think twice. It took only a moment to shuck off his clothes and shoes and to slide into the giant old tub behind her. He pulled her against his chest and wrapped his arms around her, holding her secure, and propping her head against his shoulder. From this angle he could see the dark angry-looking bruise that was coming out on her skin. His anger against the driver who caused the accident warred with intense relief that she had not been seriously injured. The tumult of emotions was foreign to him. Usually he had no difficulty in keeping his feelings in check, in separating logic from sentiment. But there was something about Piper that scrambled all reason.

"There," he said quietly, "does that feel better?"

She nodded, the soft curls that clouded her head tickling the side of his neck as she did so. Her hair had grown in the past six weeks from the somewhat haphazard pixie cut she'd shorn it into when she'd gotten rid of her dreadlocks.

The shorter hair had suited her, emphasizing her fine bone structure and the slenderness of her elegant neck, but he preferred this slightly softer look. The lack of structure gave her a femininity that appealed directly to his core every time he looked her way.

Wade relaxed against the porcelain and let his eyes slide closed, relishing the sense of rightness that infused him as he held Piper in his arms. If only it could always be this easy to keep a loved one safe.

His eyes flew open and his hold on her tightened. Loved one? Had he done the impossible and fallen in love with Piper all over again? No, he couldn't have. What he felt right now was his own aftermath of shock. He was concerned about her. Of course he was, she might be pregnant with his baby and she had been at terrible risk today. It was his duty to look after her. To keep her safe. That's all.

She nestled a little closer, and his arms tightened automatically in response. No, he didn't love her. He couldn't.

But that didn't mean he was planning to let go any time soon, either.

Twelve

Piper relaxed against him in the delicious warm water, the sobs that shook her slowly easing, her tremors finally going away altogether. It was as if by his very presence Wade drew all that reaction and upset away and exiled it where it could no longer affect her.

Her hands rested over her belly, Wade's resting over hers. For the first moment in a very long time, Piper felt one-hundred-percent safe.

Today had been one out of the bag. She hadn't been feeling all that great when she'd risen in the morning but some toast and tea at breakfast had taken care of that. She'd hoped that lunch would improve how she'd felt again later in the morning, but instead it had left her feeling much worse.

Her mind circled the prospect that Wade had raised. Could she be pregnant already? It would be pretty soon by any standards but then again some people were lucky enough, or unlucky enough, to fall pregnant right away. Hadn't it been that way with her and Wade to begin with?

Through the whole of their relationship eight years prior, the lovemaking had been passionate and thoroughly satisfying. And yet, she'd always held something back—afraid to let herself give in to the powerful emotions he made her feel. She'd always felt she couldn't let him in all the way until she was truly certain of his love.

Then she'd made the play to win him away from her father's influence, and she'd pulled out the big guns. It had been weeks since they'd made love. Plus, things had gotten so tense between her and Rex that she'd made up her mind to leave. Wade, caught in the middle between the two Mitchells, had gotten frustrated with both of them, leading to endless arguments with Piper that had served to destroy any passion between them. Wade had extended an olive branch in an attempt to make up and during a romantic evening at the scummy flat he was living in, she'd given him her all. She'd let herself love him completely, had given up her heart and soul along with her body to him in complete abandon.

In the morning, when they'd woken, she'd assumed he would prove that he returned her love by going along with her plan to leave New Zealand behind. After all, hadn't they both just had the most amazing night of their lives? Didn't he love her enough to come with her when she left? Apparently not.

She still couldn't believe she'd been so stupid, so naive even, to have thought that she could tempt a man like Wade with what she'd had to offer him back then. Yes, she'd loved him, but what kind of life could she have given him? He was a smart, ambitious man, and she'd tried to get him to give up all his prospects for a role as her arm candy while she traveled the world. He never would have been happy with a purposeless life like that. Truth be told, she hadn't been happy with it, either. Not that she was willing to admit that—especially at first. She had tried to tell herself that she was better off without a man who would let her go after a night like the one they'd shared.

Of course, finding out she was pregnant as a result of that night together she'd seen as some kind of karmic retribution for her behavior. And then losing that baby had been harder to deal with than she'd ever anticipated. She'd never expected to want a child, or to love it. And she'd never realized what a massive hole it would leave in her life when it was gone. She'd gone back to partying afterward, trying to numb the pain, but that was her first step in really growing up.

Now she felt—hoped—that she'd left that selfish past behind her. But what did the future hold? She may already be pregnant, again. With Wade's child, again. A child conceived—again—in love on her part...but not on his. Could their story have a happier ending this time?

Wade stirred, lifting one foot to toe open the faucet and run some more hot water into the bath. She hadn't even noticed the water had cooled.

"Another ten minutes and then I think we should get out, okay?"

"Sure, the wrinkled prune look really isn't my best."

She felt him turn slightly and press a kiss to the top of her head.

"I can think of better," he murmured.

Piper leaned forward and turned off the running water. Aside from a few aches and pains, most of them centered from the pressure marks across her chest, she felt a whole lot better now. So much so, that when she leaned back against Wade, and discovered a vital part of him was also feeling pretty darn good, it was a simple matter to roll over and place her knees on either side of his legs.

"Hey, aren't you supposed to be resting?"

"I feel fine," she said, even as shifting her body made her wince a little.

"Fine, huh? Doesn't look like it to me. Piper, we don't have to—"

"I want to, Wade. I want you. I want to make love to you and make all the bad stuff go away."

Wade skimmed his hands up and down her arms lightly. "And will it go away?"

"Let's find out, shall we?"

She leaned forward and kissed him, a hot, wet kiss that sent a slow beat thrumming through her veins. Her hands slicked across his shoulders and she relished the vital strength of him. She'd never been more grateful for life than she was at this very moment. The accident had been surreal, the aftermath even more so. But this, this was something quantifiable, something valid and true.

The man beneath her had given her second chances, and with them had shown her a generosity she'd never expected, despite their very rocky start. But now, the reality of making up to him all that she'd destroyed so long ago was completely within her grasp. And it wasn't all that was within her grasp, she acknowledged as the blunt tip of him nudged against her lower belly. She lifted her hips and used one hand to position him at her entrance before slowly and carefully lowering herself until he was buried within her. Deep inside she felt the flex of his hardened length and she rocked gently against him.

Sensation built within her in steady waves as she continued to move. Wade's hands gripped her hips, his fingers taut against her skin. His eyes met and locked with hers, silently urging her on, glazing with desire as she let her hips undulate back and forth.

Water sloshed against the high sides of the bath, every now and then spilling over the side and onto the tiled floor, but she didn't care. Not when every nerve in her body was centered on the point where their bodies joined. Not when her body felt so aflame that she thought the water about them might boil off. Wade raised his head and captured one of her nipples with his mouth, his lips sealing around the tightened aureole and his teeth lightly scraping the extended tip.

A spear of heat shot directly from her breast to her core and as Wade began to suckle the rigid bud, her orgasm began to creep over her—at first a gentle swell of pleasure, but rapidly culminating in a crash of sensation that made spots swim in her vision and her body shake with its force.

She collapsed against him, even as he thrust upward, lost in the glory of his own climax. Both were oblivious to all but the passion that spent itself in tiny aftershocks that made them shudder against one another. Each clench of her body triggering another with him, each flex of his erection setting off a chain reaction that tingled all the way to her extremities.

"I didn't think it could get any better between us," she panted against his shoulder.

In response Wade wrapped his arms around her waist and held her close to him. They were each obviously as reluctant as the other to relinquish the closeness, the sheer perfection of physical pleasure they'd achieved together but, after some time, the cooling water about them became sufficient incentive to pull apart and get out of the bath.

Wade wrapped one of the big thick bath towels from the heated rail around his waist before using the other to dry Piper with gentle strokes. Under his careful ministrations she unexpectedly felt ridiculously emotional. She bit her lower lip to hold back the sob that built deep inside. Wade looked at her, worry drawing his brows together in a straight line.

"Did I hurt you?"

"No, I'm just still a bit of a mess, I think."

"It's okay," he said, reaching for one of the large fluffy bathrobes on the hook behind the bathroom door and helping her into it. "It's been quite a day, hmm?"

She nodded. Unable to speak for fear that she'd blurt out her feelings for him and ruin everything. Right now she had a deep-seated need for his undivided attention and she wasn't prepared to do anything to jeopardize that.

"Let's have something to eat. Mrs. Dexter was going to leave a tray in the sitting room for us."

He wiped an errant tear from her cheek then took her hand and led her to the sitting room. A cheerful fire danced in the fireplace behind the screen and someone, no doubt Mrs. Dexter, had drawn the drapes and switched on a pair of table lamps that cast a gentle glow about the room. Weariness seeped through her, making her feel lethargic and uncoordinated. She sank gratefully onto one of the sofas by the fireplace as Wade inspected the contents of the tray.

"Here," he said, smoothing some red paste onto a sliver of sliced French bread and passing it over to her.

Piper felt some of her lethargy dispel as the piquant flavor hit her tongue. "Mmm, that's delicious. What is it?"

"I think it's a sundried tomato hummus. Want some more?"

"Try and hold me back," she answered.

Together they ate their way through the selection of food, enjoying the cold roasted chicken drumsticks that had been coated with Dexie's special herb flavoring, licking one another's fingers clean and savoring the variety of finger foods that had been laid out for them. They eschewed the bottle of wine that sat in a frosted cooler, enjoying instead the mineral water that came from the small fridge that Wade had integrated into a wall unit along one side of the sitting room.

Finally replete, Piper curled up her legs under her and rested her head against the back of the sofa.

"Tired?" Wade asked.

"Yeah, shattered actually."

"Why don't you go to bed?"

"It's still so early," she protested even as she fought off a yawn.

"No one is going to blame you. You had a major fright

today, and you haven't been feeling well." He hesitated and drew in a breath before continuing. "I've made an appointment for you to see May tomorrow morning."

She swung her legs down and sat upright. "I told you, I'm okay. Why did you do that?"

"I need to be sure, Piper."

"Can't we just see how I'm feeling tomorrow?"

"You had to leave work because you weren't well, don't you want to find out why?"

"Whatever it was, it's passed now. I feel tired and a bit sore from the accident, but aside from that I'm okay. I really don't want to go to May tomorrow. Shouldn't that be up to me, anyway?"

Wade gave her another piercing look. "What is it that you're afraid of, Piper?"

He narrowed his eyes as he looked at her and she felt her defenses rise. She knew how much he wanted her to be pregnant, but what would happen next if she was? The prospect terrified her. She wouldn't be alone as she had been the last time she'd found out she was pregnant, but would he still want her in his bed each night once he'd achieved his objective? Or would she be tucked away, left to procreate under the clinical terms of their agreement?

She loved him. She wanted to be with him. She knew he didn't love her, but the longer she could put off him having a reason to set her aside, the better her chance of breaking through the shell he operated within. The better her chance of possibly creating a mutual affection between them that might stand the test of time. That would see them raise their child together, in a home filled with love.

"I'm not afraid. I just don't see the need, that's all," she hedged. "It's not as if I've missed a period or anything like that."

"And yet you must be feeling some changes in your body. Your breasts are slightly fuller, are they not?" He pushed aside the neckline of her robe, revealing her breasts to his glittering gaze. One finger brushed across their pink tips making them instantly taut and her insides coil tight. "And are your nipples not more sensitive than before?"

She shoved his hand away from her, even as her blood heated again in her body. Pulling her robe closed, she got up from the sofa and went to stand in front of the fire.

"That doesn't mean anything," she answered defiantly. "You're a fantastic lover, maybe it's just my reaction to you."

Wade stood and came right up to her, his hand sliding inside her robe once more, this time to rest against her lower stomach. "Or your body's natural reaction to our lovemaking—our *baby* making."

"Wade—"

"I'll pick you up at ten-thirty tomorrow, your appointment is for eleven. You will keep it, Piper. As I said before, I *need* to know."

Piper felt a stab of loss at his words. Finding out if she was pregnant or not was all that mattered to him now.

"What about work?"

"Like I said, I don't think you'll feel up to going into the office tomorrow."

"Shouldn't I be the judge of that?"

Wade sighed in frustration. "Look, you're not going to win this argument, Piper. You will see May tomorrow and that's final. Whether you go to work or not is up to you entirely, although I'd advise against it."

He turned and stalked to the bedroom, reappearing a few minutes later dressed casually in a pair of jeans and a turtlenecked sweater that made him look altogether too sexy for words. Even as angry and frustrated as she was with his high-handedness, she still wanted him on a level she'd never known before. The knowledge frightened her about as much as the prospect that she might be carrying his baby and be about to be shelved until the *happy* event.

"Go to bed, Piper. You're just about dead on your feet. I'll be downstairs catching up on some work."

He picked up the tray with their plates and leftovers and took it from the room, leaving her alone with only the sound of the fire crackling behind her as company. The instant he was gone, Piper felt every last vestige of fight leave her body. Okay, so she'd go to bed now. But it would be because she wanted to and because she was tired. Not because she'd been summarily ordered to.

Despite her weariness, sleep remained elusive until she heard Wade return upstairs several hours later. Through the open bedroom door she heard the clink of crystal as he poured himself a glass of port, then his deep sigh as he settled onto one of the chairs. It was another half hour before he quietly entered the bathroom, and a few more minutes before he then, finally, slid into the bed beside her, his naked body spooning hers, his arms coming around her in their usual nightly embrace, one hand gently cupping her left breast.

Only then did she slide into a deep slumber, her body relaxed against his warmth, her heart in his hands.

Wade waited in the reception area at the doctor's office with increasing impatience. Piper had been in May's consulting room for over half an hour now and the length of time she'd been gone was driving him crazy. How long did it take to do a pregnancy test, anyway? Maybe he should have conceded to Piper's wish not to come to the doctor today, but made her do a test at home instead.

"Mr. Collins?"

He shot to his feet as the receptionist called his name. "Yes?"

"Dr. Ritter would like you to go through now." The woman gestured down the passageway leading from the waiting area. "Second to last door on the right."

"Thanks," he said, even as his feet began to eat up the distance between torment and the answers he sought.

He tapped lightly on the door and opened it on May's command to enter. Wade's gaze flicked from one woman to the other, but he could read nothing on their faces. Piper's expression remained completely empty. Mind you, she'd been quiet this morning—her movements stiff as a result of yesterday's trauma. May, too, kept her features inscrutable but she gestured to him to take a seat next to Piper.

"I'm sure you know by now that there are no long-term issues with the minor injuries that Piper sustained in her accident yesterday," May said. "However, she will need to be very careful for the next few months."

Wade's heart leaped in his chest. "The next few months?" he repeated.

"Yes, indeed."

"So does that mean...?" He was suddenly too afraid to enunciate the words in case it might not be true.

May smiled. "Yes, you two are expecting a baby, congratulations."

Wade sat back in his chair, filled with emotion, filled with hope. Could it be that his dreams were finally coming true? And if so, why did Piper now look so stricken?

Thirteen

She was pregnant. Numbness invaded every cell in her body. When May had confirmed the result of the urine test to her, Piper had retreated behind a wall of denial. All through her physical examination she'd been in another place. A place that froze her in fear. After the confirmation, she'd asked May what was the likelihood of her miscarrying again. The answer was about as indeterminate as the wispy drifts of fog that had surrounded the house this morning.

Without knowing what had caused her to miscarry the first time, May couldn't give her any promises.

Piper slid a glance at Wade. He was ecstatic. His face glowed with the light of sheer joy. It terrified her. What if she let him down? What if she couldn't carry this baby to term?

She vaguely heard May and Wade discussing what happened next, the list of appointments she'd need to attend, when she'd have scans, etc. The words flew over her head. Wade could take care of that. Right now those matters were the least of her worries. Learning how to cope with the crippling fear

that held her frozen in her seat was going to be the biggest
thing for her right now.

On the ride home from the doctor's office, Wade exuded
a different energy. His conversation concentrated solely on
the baby they now knew she carried. Her stomach flipped
uncomfortably.

"Stop the car!" she cried.

"Stop?"

"Now!"

Wade pulled over to the curb. Before the car was fully
stationary Piper flung open her door and struggled to her
feet. Every muscle in her body ached today and moving was
difficult. She made it to a tree on the grassy verge and leaned
both arms against it, dropping her head down between her
shoulders and dragging in big gulps of the chill, damp air.

How was she going to get through this if Wade talking
about the baby was enough to made her nauseous?

She felt his hand at the nape of her neck, his fingers
stroking gently.

"You okay?"

"No," she answered with a shaky voice. She was most
definitely not okay.

"Take your time," he said considerately.

"Yeah, I'll do that."

Wade continued the gentle stroking and Piper focused on
the sensation of his skin on hers. His warmth versus the chill
that consumed her. Finally her stomach settled and the threat
of being ill diminished.

"I think we can go now," she said, straightening up from
the tree and squaring her shoulders.

"Are you sure? We don't need to hurry."

Again that consideration. If she hadn't been pregnant,
would he have been so solicitous?

"I'm fine. Can we go home now, please?"

Wade's hand drifted down her spine, resting at her lower

back as they walked to the car. He saw her settled in the passenger seat and leaned down to clip her seat belt across her. She flinched as he did so, her bruise now a painful reminder of her date with the lamp post yesterday.

"Sorry," Wade said.

"It's okay, I'm not going to break, you know."

"No, but you do need special care and attention."

He leaned one arm across the top of the doorway to the car and looked down at her.

"Why? Just because I'm pregnant?" She couldn't help it, the words sprang forth before she could hold them back.

"That and because of what you've been through. Cut me some slack, okay, Piper. Let me take care of you. Anyone can see the news has come as a bit of a shock to you. I have to admit that I'm a little overwhelmed myself. I never thought we'd get it right so quickly."

He closed the door and walked around the front of the car toward the driver's side. Piper stared out the windshield. Get it right? If that was the case, why did she feel as if everything was going so very wrong? She felt as if things were spinning out of her control. She'd expected—no, *wanted*—to have time to win Wade over, woo him back to her. Now, she was afraid his primary thought would only be for their son or daughter. She wouldn't matter as much to him as he mattered to her.

She knew exactly where she stood under the terms of their contract—for as long as she stayed under his roof at least. But how could she continue to do that, loving him the way she did, when his whole focus would be on the baby? Where would she fit in once the baby was born? Would he still want her? And what if the worst happened again? What if she miscarried? Would he believe her when she said she'd loved this child from the point of its conception, that she loved its father just as much?

* * *

The weeks seemed to race by. Wade consulted one of the baby books he'd bought and kept at work, that showed the varying stages of pregnancy and development of the fetus, fascinated by every step. Piper was fourteen weeks now and while she was still as slender as always, there was a tautness to her lower belly that hadn't been there before and her breasts had filled out, too, and continued to be highly sensitive—a fact he'd delighted in exploring when they made love.

He frowned as he considered the terminology—making love. It had been sex when it started but somewhere along the line his feelings about the act itself had changed. Who was he kidding? His feelings about Piper were changing. Especially now. He knew he was becoming more possessive and protective of her with every day that passed—even to the point that he'd soundly rejected her suggestion that now she was pregnant she move back to her old room. She and the baby were his to take care of—and he was starting to wonder if he wasn't doing a good enough job.

She'd been fragile when she'd returned from overseas but she seemed even more brittle now. As if she might shatter into a million tiny shards if the wind so much as blew the wrong way. Personally, he felt she'd taken on too much. She still worked her full days at Mitchell Exports and spent her evening hours studying or attending late classes for the pre-entry course she'd insisted on completing.

"I have to finish something in my life," she'd snapped when he'd suggested perhaps she could leave the papers since it was putting so much strain on her.

He'd been taken aback at her response, but had left her to it. She hadn't wanted her colleagues at work to know about her pregnancy, insisting it was her and Wade's business and no one else's. He'd felt the complete opposite, he wanted to shout their news from the rooftops. Even so, he'd respected her decision and remained silent on the subject, except for letting her immediate superiors know and informing them that he expected her workload to lighten somewhat. They'd been only too happy to accommodate his request, even while expressing their surprise at her condition because no one in the office, aside from his PA, had been let into the truth of their relationship.

Perhaps he'd let the cat out of the bag about the two of them prematurely, he thought. Piper obviously had her reasons for wanting to keep their relationship quiet—although they wouldn't be able to do that for much longer—and for asserting her independence. As to the latter, she had barely blinked when he'd arranged for delivery of an Audi A5 for her. Wade had elaborated on the safety features of the car including antilock electronic braking, traction control and the number of air bags. She'd merely accepted the keys and driven off as usual.

Nothing seemed to break through the mantle of eerie calm that enveloped her. The only time she showed any genuine emotion or response was when they were in bed. Even then, she was often so exhausted when she came to bed that she'd fall immediately asleep.

He'd expected some animation from her when he'd discussed redecorating the nursery, but she'd quietly agreed with every suggestion he had made and appeared quite happy to allow the interior designer he'd appointed a free hand. The decorator was supposed to be finished today. He was keen to see the final result and rued that he wouldn't be able to see it together with Piper for the first time. He'd hoped the completed room would imbue some excitement about the baby into her.

It was late when he arrived home and his stomach was growling with hunger. Despite that, Wade ignored the plate he knew Mrs. Dexter would have left in the oven for him and shot up the stairs to the next floor. When he'd walked from the garage to the house he'd seen a light on upstairs, in the nursery. He hoped it meant that Piper was in there.

The scents of new wallpaper, carpet and fresh paint filled the corridor outside the room as he approached. The door swung lightly open at his touch. A surge of satisfaction swelled inside as he saw Piper standing by the pale wooden tallboy, with her back to the door. One drawer stood open and it looked as if she was holding an item of clothing.

"They've done a great job with the room, don't you think?" he asked as he entered, his critical eye scanning the room and finding not a single thing at fault.

"Yes," Piper answered, her voice sounding thick and strained.

"Piper? What's wrong? Is it the baby?"

Wade stepped up to her, placed a gentle hand on her shoulder and turned her to face him. It stunned him to see abject misery painted on her features, her face wet with the tears that rolled off her lashes and down her cheeks.

She shook her head and moved away. He noticed the way her hands grasped the tiny one-piece suit in her hands, her knuckles white with the intensity of her grip.

"What is then?" he asked, confused. "Is it hormones?"

She sniffed a stifled laugh. "No, Wade, it's not hormones. I just…"

"You just, what?" he prompted when she didn't continue.

She lifted her face toward his, her blue eyes glittering behind the moisture there.

"I don't know how I'm going to go through with this."

"This?" he asked, a steel fist tightening around his lungs and making it almost impossible to draw breath.

What was she talking about?

"This," she said, gesturing to the room. "The baby, being a mother, all of it. I just don't think I can do it."

She couldn't do it? What the hell was she suggesting? A termination? Over his dead body. Anger rose swift and fast.

Had this been her plan all along? And to think he'd started to believe he loved her!

"You can do it and you will," he said in a voice that was barely controlled.

"There are so many things that are out of my control, I'm terrified," she sobbed. "Wade, you don't understand—"

"Understand? Oh, yes, I think I understand all right. The first sign of anything you might have to do the hard way and you run, don't you, Piper? Just like you ran before. Well, I have news for you and it goes like this. You *will* continue with this pregnancy and you *will* have this baby."

Piper looked at him with an expression akin to horror in her eyes. "But what if something happens?" she implored.

"Happens? What? Like last time? Don't think you're going to terminate my baby again, Piper. I might not have been able to prevent you from killing my son or daughter eight years ago but you can rest assured that even if I have to lock you in your room, you will most definitely bring this child to term."

Piper felt all the blood drain from her face and she swayed a little with dizziness. *He knew?*

"How did you find out?" she whispered, her throat closing on the words.

"That's totally irrelevant. The thing is that I did. You know, I really thought you were proving that you were capable of being a decent person, someone who was reliable and honest, but you just haven't changed one bit, have you? You're incapable of growing up, of taking or accepting responsibility. Well, understand this, if anything, and I mean *anything,* happens to this baby, I will hold you fully accountable and I will hunt you to the ends of the earth to make you pay."

Piper recoiled, feeling each one of his words as if it was a physical blow. She wanted to protest, but she couldn't. The words jammed in her throat. It was all she could do right now to hold on to consciousness. She dragged in a ragged breath.

"You make it sound like it was all my fault," she finally managed.

Wade shot her a look of pure venom. "Wasn't it?"

"No!" she cried. "It wasn't, how could it have been?"

"I don't believe you, Piper."

"You don't believe me?"

How could he not? She hadn't done anything to cause the miscarriage of that baby, and the loss still weighed upon her as heavily today as it had back then. Perhaps even more so. Piper's heart hammered in her chest. She couldn't believe this conversation was happening. How had he ever found out? And, even more importantly, how long ago? She forced down the fear and the shock that threatened to take over her before speaking.

"How did you find out?"

"That isn't important. What's important is that I will not let something like that ever happen again to a child of mine."

The possessive tone of his voice reverberated right through her. Here he was, claiming ownership to a child he'd never known. It catalyzed a spur of anger of her own.

"A child of yours. And what makes you so sure that it was?"

He paled before her, two deep lines bracketing his mouth as his jaw assumed a grim set.

"Are you saying it wasn't?"

"I'm not saying anything. I never did say anything. That's the point. How the hell did you know about it?"

"Rex told me. He came to work one morning an absolute wreck. He told me that you'd aborted. He never put two and two together. He never suspected it was my baby he was talking about." Wade brushed his eyes with one hand. "Do you have any idea what that did to me? I'm not a fool. While your father never would have thought to do the math, I knew. I *knew* it was my child he was talking about. The child you never told me about. How could you have done such a thing?"

How could he *believe* she would do such a thing? The question rattled through her mind. She'd loved him. She'd thought he loved her, *understood* her. They'd shared some bitter words when they'd parted but he still had to have known that deep down she would never willingly take a life.

"But I didn't do anything. I lost the baby. It was a miscarriage—I had no control over what happened. None."

"And you expect me to believe you?"

"Yes, of course I do. I'm telling you the truth."

"And you're such an advocate of honesty, aren't you? You once told me that you loved me and we both know that was a lie. Of course I don't believe you. Your father had nothing to gain by lying to me. You, however…"

He let his voice trail away and Piper knew without a shadow of a doubt that she stood no chance of swaying his belief. Deep inside, the hope that she and Wade could make something of this together shriveled and died. There was no way they could ever have a future together.

"Knowing how you feel about me, I'm amazed you could bring yourself to have sex with me."

The words tasted like ashes in her mouth. Sex? For her every intimate moment had been a silent expression of love. But clearly he'd had his own agenda all along. She'd been a complete fool to believe otherwise. A new thought bloomed in her mind.

"Is that why you loaned that money to my trust fund? So you'd have leverage over me?"

"You owed me, Piper. Big time."

"You planned this all along?" She shook her head in disbelief. "How could you? How could you harbor so much bitterness and anger toward me for so long?"

"How?" he answered. "Easy. I want what you took from me, what you denied me the right to. A few hundred thousand dollars? That's nothing. But you know that, don't you? You always treated money as nothing. To you it was merely a means to an end, not something to be earned or revered in any form. But a life? Not even you have the right to deem that as dispensable. Just think of this as a means to an end. That, at least, is something you should understand."

"It wasn't my fault," she said softly. "Please believe me, Wade. There isn't a day that goes by that I don't regret the choices I made. I've spent years trying to make that up. It's why I came home. I know I did you wrong when I left. I know I hurt my father. I wanted to make it right."

"Well, now you have the perfect opportunity, don't you?" Wade said, his words like shards of ice. "Have this baby and then move on."

Fourteen

Move on? Like she could just have this baby, a child that was flesh of her flesh, heart of her heart, and then leave? She stared at Wade in shock.

"But you said that it was my choice. To stay and be a part of our baby's upbringing or not."

"I've changed my mind," he said. "Once the baby is here I want you gone. My child deserves the right to be able to trust the people around him or her. He doesn't deserve people who will mouth platitudes when it suits them then leave the second the going gets tough."

"And you think I'd do that?"

He raised a cynical brow. "Your track record precedes you."

"I've changed, Wade. I've learned the difference between what's right and what's wrong. I've learned to value the people that matter."

"Pretty words, Piper. You were always so very good at them." He turned to leave the nursery but at the door he hesitated. "I think it would be best, under the circumstances, if you moved back into your own room tonight. I'll see to it that your things are transferred over tomorrow."

Wade lay in his bed, staring at the shadows of the molded plaster ceiling above him and missing Piper's presence by his side with a physical ache. He'd thought she'd changed, but she hadn't, and the knowledge hurt far more than he could ever have anticipated. He felt like such an idiot. He'd believed she wanted to change, to make a step forward in the right direction but she'd fooled him yet again. He thought he'd inured himself to the harm she could wreak but he'd been a lightweight in the face of everything. He couldn't afford to let her close again. If she could do this to him, what emotional hurt might she be capable of inflicting on their baby? A fierce surge of protectiveness toward his unborn child suffused him, masking the pain that dwelt deep inside. Piper was just like his father had been, paying lip service to what he wanted to hear and then letting him down yet again.

It hadn't been so bad while his mother was alive, or at least he hadn't noticed it so much with the buffer of her love there between him and his old man. But when she'd died unexpectedly, Eric Collins had been exposed for the sham he was. He'd downright refused to care for his ten-year-old son, and while Wade had bravely battled on, on his own in the house he'd been raised in, it hadn't taken long for neighbors to notice his father's absence and Social Services had been called in.

He could still hear his father's lies on the afternoon he'd been taken away, one of the rare days his father had actually been home—this time smelling of a rank combination of alcohol and stale perfume.

"I'm sorry, son," he'd said. "You know I'd keep you if I could. I'll come for you, I promise."

But Wade had recognized the look in his father's eyes,

heard the words for the platitudes they were. The look that told him his father was lying through his teeth. Wade knew that Eric Collins had no intention of ever trying to get his son back and that he couldn't wait to be free of him. It made the loss of his mother all the more painful.

Being fostered hadn't been so bad. The couple who'd cared for him were decent folk with strict rules. He'd learned that as long as he didn't rock the boat, life was pretty straightforward. But every night as he lay in the narrow bunk bed in a room with three other boys, he'd made a promise that he would always be there for any child of his. Always. No matter what.

The fact he hadn't had the chance to be there for his first baby was a scar he'd bear on his heart for all his days. But with this baby, everything would be different. And Piper Mitchell would just have to get used to the idea.

The next few days proved uncomfortable between them. At least at work Wade could lose himself in the day-to-day business that filled his time, only needing to cross paths with Piper when absolutely necessary. That wasn't to say he didn't keep a wary eye on her activity. Her movements in and out the office were carefully monitored. He didn't trust her, not one inch.

At home it was more difficult to keep his distance. He'd taken to bringing work home and eating his meals in the library. Fielding the looks of concern from Dexter and his wife became a daily chore. He hated the atmosphere that hung around the place but, he consoled himself, it wouldn't be forever. Once the baby was born and Piper had gone on to whatever it was that she wanted to do next, life would be much sweeter.

He ignored the pang of regret at the thought of Piper leaving and reminded himself that she'd done it before, she would just as easily do so again. Except this time, she wouldn't be taking his child with her.

It was two weeks after things had come to a head that

Wade faced a difficult choice. The senior manager in one of his new Pacific Island outstations had suffered a mild stroke. Most of the staff in the office had only been there a few months, and none were in a position to step in and assume a temporary management role. The one guy he could send from the Auckland office, Roy Beckett, was in Europe on other business and it was vital that Roy conclude the contract negotiations in person. It would be four days before Roy was able to travel back and pick up the reins in Samoa.

That left only one alternative, that Wade go there himself. The thought of leaving Piper behind made his stomach clench, but he didn't like the idea of her traveling with him, either. She looked so fragile these days, with a strain around her eyes giving her a haunted look that had everyone in her department constantly asking if she was okay. Here, at the house, Mrs. Dexter was like a mother hen clucking around her chick. Making sure Piper had small nutritious meals and that she did nothing more taxing than lift a cup of tea.

Surely, with so many people looking out for her, she wouldn't do anything stupid. Wade leaned back in his chair and rubbed his eyes wearily. She was sixteen weeks. The books told him that she may have felt movement by now. He couldn't imagine that even she would be able to bring herself to source a termination now.

He was in an untenable position. He had to go, but everything in him screamed not to. There was nothing else for it but to get to Samoa and back as quickly as he could. He put in a call to Roy and explained the situation. Roy assured him he could be in Samoa by Sunday. Today was Tuesday. Wade thanked him and hung up before lifting the receiver and dialing the airline. The sooner he got this sorted, the sooner he'd be home.

Piper missed Wade. Until this morning, he'd barely spoken a dozen words to her since that awful night. She'd come down to breakfast only to find him at the kitchen table, waiting for her. She didn't bother to hide her surprise. That he'd been actively avoiding her hadn't gone unnoticed. Frankly, it only served to make her even more tense as she found herself continually anticipating the moments their paths would cross. At least this face-to-face situation was something she could handle. She'd learned during her aid work that things were best faced head-on. But what was a girl to do when the person she had to face refused to believe her?

Wade stood as she came into the kitchen, scraping his chair back across the polished wooden floor. Mrs. Dexter flung a look from one to the other and grabbed a dusting cloth.

"I'll be in the morning room if you need me," she said, bustling past.

As soon as the door swung shut behind her, Wade spoke, "I have to go away for a few days."

"Away?"

That was the last thing she'd been expecting. While he'd kept his distance from her, she knew full well that he was aware of everything she did. It was suffocating, but there was nothing she could do about it.

"A situation has arisen in our office in Apia. I'll be back on Monday."

"Nothing too serious, I hope," she said neutrally.

She was well aware that the Apia office was still in a fledgling state. A serious disruption could see a major setback in operations. And it had to be serious if Wade, himself, was going.

"James, the manager there, has had a stroke. He's going to be okay but it'll be some time before he's up to speed again. Roy is coming through to relieve him on his way back from Europe, but someone needs to run things until he arrives. No one in the office already is qualified to handle it."

"And there's no one else who can go?"

"Do you think I'd be going if I had any alternative?"

She shook her head.

Wade continued, "My flight leaves this afternoon. I'll be leaving my car at the airport."

"Are you sure you want to do that? I could always take you."

"No, my return flight doesn't get in until nearly midnight on Monday."

She experienced a fleeting gratefulness that she wouldn't have to stay awake until then. Most evenings she was in bed by nine-thirty these days. Long gone were late nights, that was for sure. But she'd have done it, for him.

"Well, if you're sure," she said.

"I am. And Piper?"

She looked up, meeting his eyes for the first time in what felt like forever.

"Do not do anything you might regret while I'm gone."

"What do you mean?"

"You know exactly what I mean," he said, a thread of anger tingeing his words.

She put a protective hand to her belly, feeling the slight swelling there.

"I wouldn't do anything to hurt my baby. Not now, and not in the past. Why don't you believe me on that?"

He didn't answer immediately, then his shoulders seemed to sag beneath the fine wool of his tailored suit.

"I want to believe you, Piper, but history has a way of repeating itself and, to be frank, I don't trust you."

She reached forward, putting a hand on his forearm, absorbing the heat of him through his clothing and feeling that old familiar tingle of awareness.

"You can trust me."

"I wish I could be certain of that."

"What do I have to do to make you believe me?"

He shook his head. "I don't know. I used to think a person's word meant something, but I learned a long time ago that words are only any good when they're backed up by actions."

"You're talking about your father, aren't you? I'm not like him, Wade. I'm not."

He recoiled at her words, pulling his arm out from under her touch,

"I'm leaving straight from the office. Just do as I ask, Piper, and don't do anything stupid."

Without another word, or a backward glance, he left the kitchen. She stood there, hurt beyond belief at his words. He was a closed book, a story stubbornly unwilling to be rewritten. She went through the motions of eating breakfast, not out of any hunger but because she knew she had to provide the very best of everything for the child growing inside her. This time she had to get it right.

The house was quiet when she arrived home from work on Friday night. The Dexters were using their night off to see a live show in the city and there was a note in the kitchen with instructions for Piper to reheat her meal. She smiled at the neatly handwritten bullet-pointed note. Did Dexie not think she was even capable of reheating a meal on her own?

She shook her head, then flinched as the headache she'd been suffering from most of the day sharpened. She was reluctant to take anything for it, but if it continued to worsen she'd have to try something. A shiver ran through her. She'd felt the cold far more than usual today, and she decided to forgo dinner for now in lieu of getting on some warmer clothes.

Upstairs in her bedroom she quickly changed out of her work clothes and into a comfortable pair of stretchy sweatpants and a long sleeved T-shirt, and pulled on her father's old robe over it all. She cinched the sash around her thickening waist and rested her hand on her belly. Now at sixteen weeks, this pregnancy felt different than her last but she was afraid to hope that everything would be okay.

She needed a distraction, she decided as she stroked the fabric of the robe. Maybe now would be as good a time as any to sort out her father's personal papers. Wade didn't seem to be in a hurry for them to go through her father's room. Perhaps she could have it all done by the time he returned.

Piper lit the fire that was set in the grate in her father's suite and drew the drapes to help keep the warmth in. The Dexters had obviously been airing the room on a regular basis because not so much as a trace of his presence remained. It was more than four months since his death and yet sometimes it still felt as raw as if she'd just heard the news.

She settled by the escritoire in the corner of the room and busied herself deciding on what needed to be kept and what should be burned. It was about an hour later that she cast off the robe and pushed up the sleeves of her T-shirt. She must have put too much wood on the fire, she thought as she realized that she had begun to sweat, but hard on the heels of the sweat came another round of chills.

This was ridiculous, she thought, shrugging the robe back on again, this time leaving it open. She was making good headway on her father's papers and didn't want to stop now. She still didn't feel hungry and it wasn't too late yet. She'd just check this one drawer before going back downstairs and heating up dinner.

The drawer contained a flat file box with her name on it. Startled, Piper lifted it out. She had never known her father to express any sentimentality over her childhood certificates and awards, so what could he have in here? She lifted the lid, surprised to see a collection of her old school reports and every single childishly hand-drawn card she'd made for Father's Day or Rex's birthday. Tears filled her eyes as she looked through them. The fact he had kept every one was proof positive that, in his own way, he had cared about her, that she'd mattered to him. She felt the knowledge finally begin healing the gaping hole in her heart. Swiping away the moisture on her cheeks with the cuff of one sleeve, she set the mementos aside and pulled out the plain manila folder that lay at the bottom.

She opened the cover and was surprised to see the logo of a health insurance company. The name jogged her memory. It was the company her father had insured her under when she'd left to go overseas. But what was he doing with all these papers?

She spread them out on the desk surface in front of her. For the most part, they appeared to be a record of premiums and notifications of increases, or decreases, in available benefits. But then two words sprang out at her from a stapled set of papers.

Spontaneous abortion.

Piper's hand shook as she picked up the report and read it more thoroughly. Of course her father would have gotten the wrong end of the stick. Medical terminology had never been his forte. He probably read those two words and didn't read any farther—and then he'd done the unthinkable and told Wade.

She felt sick to her stomach. All that anger, all that sorrow, Wade had borne these past years—all for the sake of a misunderstanding? It just wasn't right. Not only that her father could think her capable of taking a life, but that Wade had believed she had done so, also. Her first instinct was to pick up a phone and call him, to tell him that she had the proof that she was telling the truth, but caution stayed her hand. This was a discussion that was far better held face-to-face.

Piper placed the papers carefully back on the desk and started to sort through the balance of information. A swell of nausea hit her hard, along with it another flush of heat that saw her body bloom with perspiration. She should have stopped to eat. She'd noticed she only suffered nausea with this pregnancy when she didn't eat little bits often. The rest of the papers would have to wait until tomorrow.

She stood and gripped the desk and groaned as a spear of pain shot through her head. The last time she'd felt this bad had been when she'd had malaria. A shock of fear hit her with seismic effect. Could she be suffering a relapse? May had mentioned this could be a serious issue, with treatment being problematic for the baby.

Piper cupped her belly with both hands. No, not again. She didn't want anything to happen to this baby. Hadn't she already borne enough loss in her life? And Wade—he wouldn't believe she hadn't done something on purpose.

She stumbled toward the door. She had to call May, but the doctor's number was in her handbag, which she'd left downstairs. As she stumbled down the first flight of stairs, all she could think of was Wade and how she needed him to know she wanted this baby to be all right, that she'd tried her hardest and that even now she wasn't going to give up. It was on the landing halfway down that she lost her fight for consciousness, the piercing pain in her head too much for her anymore.

Fifteen

"Miss Piper! Miss Piper!"

Dexie's worried voice penetrated the fog of pain and heat that held her body captive.

"Dexter, call an ambulance, quickly. And call Mr. Collins. He left his contact details in the library."

"N-no." Piper struggled to form the words her confused brain knew had to be said. "Don't tell Wade. Not yet."

"Don't fuss yourself, Miss Piper. He needs to know."

"N-not until we know what's wr-rong," she said as a violent shiver shook her body, making her teeth chatter. "D-Dr. Ritter. Her number. It's in my b-bag. Call her. T-tell her... m-malaria."

Her eyes slid shut, speech suddenly too much for her. She felt Dexie's hand repeatedly and gently stroke her forehead, the sensation soothing her as she slid back into unconsciousness.

Two more nights and he'd be home. Things had been chaos when he'd arrived but he was making headway. The most important thing was that none of the exports they'd organized out of the region had been jeopardized and everything remained on track. Now it was just a matter of waiting for Roy to show up and briefing him on what was to happen next.

Wade picked up the glass of brandy he'd ordered from the bar and looked out across the hotel pool and past it to the lagoon. It was an idyllic setting, especially considering the wintry weather he'd left behind him at home, but it wasn't a setting to be enjoyed alone. Maybe he should have brought Piper with him after all. The thought snuck into his head before he could quell it, and with it, brought a surge of longing.

Without stopping to consider what he was doing he reached into his pocket and extracted his cell phone, automatically punching in the numbers to call home. The phone rang several times before the harried voice of Dexter answered.

"Dexter? Is everything okay?" Wade asked.

"Oh, sir. Thank goodness you called. The ambulance has just been here. I was going to call you once we knew where Miss Piper was being taken."

The relief in the older man's voice was palpable, reaching across almost three thousand kilometers and delivering a punch of fear square in Wade's gut.

"What's wrong? What happened? Is she all right?"

Hard on those questions came another. Had she done something to harm the baby?

"We came home this evening to find Miss Piper collapsed on the stairs. We have no idea how long she'd been there in that state. We would have gone straight to our cottage and wouldn't have come in the house if there hadn't been so many lights on inside. Mrs. Dexter was worried. Thank goodness we checked."

"She fell?"

"No, she's ill, sir. The ambulance officers weren't sure

what it was but she kept refusing any medication in case it hurt the baby."

Wade got what details he could from Dexter before leaving his untouched drink on his table and heading back to his room. His frustration mounted as he tried to book a flight home. The soonest he could get on board a plane was at almost 2:00 a.m. He looked at his watch. There had to be another way he could get home faster.

He tried charter companies but in the end it would only have taken longer to get a plane to Apia that he could then travel on to Auckland. The hours until he could get home and make sure that everything—every*one*—he corrected himself, was okay, stretched out interminably.

Staying here at the hotel a moment longer was just going to drive him crazy. If he was out at the airport, he'd feel that he was at least a little closer to heading home. He quickly threw his things in his case and grabbed it and his laptop and headed for the door.

At the airport his frustrations increased a thousand fold as the early hour he'd gone out there meant he couldn't check in yet. But finally he was on the plane and headed in the direction he needed to be going.

His whole focus had been on getting on the next available flight home, but now he was forced by the four-hour flight to stop and wait—and think. Those thoughts immediately turning to the woman who'd never been far from his mind the whole time he'd been away.

Something just didn't gel with what Dexter had said. She'd refused any medication. Her first concern had been for the baby. This wasn't the Piper he thought he'd left behind. She'd been talking about getting rid of their child, just like she'd done before. Refusing medication wasn't the action of woman who didn't have a care toward the life growing within her. It had a lot more to do with a woman who was prepared to protect that life at all costs.

The possibility made him rethink that awful night in the nursery, turning over their conversation in his mind again and again. She'd never actually said she wanted to be rid of the baby and she'd tried to make him believe the loss of their first infant had been out of her control. Even faced with the fact that he knew about that first pregnancy, she'd been adamant—her story not wavering a millimeter.

Had he jumped to conclusions and heard only what he had believed she'd been saying, instead of what she'd meant all along? Had he been wrong about her? A fist clutched in his chest. He wanted to be wrong about her. He'd always wanted to be wrong about her. Finally he allowed himself to face the truth. He'd seen the evidence with his very own eyes. Piper had been different since she'd come home. More settled, more willing to take on responsibility. Going so far, even, to give him the child he'd insisted upon even though the prospect had clearly terrified her.

That took a new level of bravery. Sure, he'd had her between a rock and a hard place over the money and all the things that should rightfully have been hers. But she'd still had the option of walking away. Granted, *with* nothing and probably *to* nothing, but a woman who had as much pride as Piper had always had, wouldn't have thought twice about turning her back on the debt. Somehow she would have found a way to survive.

Survive. Hard on that thought came a deeper concern. If Piper was ill, it had to be pretty serious for her to collapse as she had. And it was with that thought that Wade knew that he didn't want anything to happen to her—ever. He loved her and he hoped against hope that he would have the chance to tell her face-to-face. To tell her that he was sorry for all the pain he'd put her through, and to beg her forgiveness.

It was 5:00 a.m. in Auckland when the plane touched down. Wade disembarked as swiftly as he could and processed through immigration before the interminable wait at the baggage claim. He considered just leaving his suitcase on the carousel, and sending for it later, but even as the thought formed in his mind his Louis Vuitton case appeared. He scooped it up and headed for customs, thankfully without issue, and headed straight for the taxi line outside the terminal building—one thing and one thing only on his mind. Piper.

The sun was rising as the cab pulled up outside Auckland City Hospital. Wade could only hope that the feeble rays punching through the dark clouds were a sign that everything would be okay.

May Ritter was at the nurses' station when he arrived on the floor Piper had been admitted to. She turned at the sound of his feet marching at a fast clip on the vinyl floor.

"Wade, you got here fast. What did you do, charter a plane?"

"I couldn't, or I'd have been here sooner. How is she?"

"We've stabilized Piper's fever and fetal monitoring shows everything is normal."

"Thank God. A fever? Why? What's wrong with Piper?"

May smiled and laid a hand on his arm to reassure him. "It's a particularly nasty strain of one of the current influenza viruses. It was a relief to us all that it wasn't a relapse of malaria, the symptoms presented very similarly, and Piper told me that it was her biggest fear."

"Her biggest fear, why?"

"She'd contracted malaria a while back, during her volunteer stint abroad. I believe she was working at a women's clinic in Africa at the time—it was the first of several tours she did with various agencies through many countries. It's hard work and can be soul destroying, but she stuck it out despite getting sick. Did she never tell you that?"

"No, I didn't even know she'd done volunteer work."

Wade shook his head in disbelief. Piper? Volunteering to help those far less privileged? It didn't fit with the girl who'd left him, but for some reason it seemed to suit the woman who'd returned.

"Apparently she's been all over the place. Mostly Africa and Asia. You'll have to get her to tell you about it some time."

"Yes, yes, I will," he said, admitting to himself that there was a whole other side of Piper that he needed to know and understand. "Can I see her?"

"She's resting."

"I won't disturb her, I just want to see she's okay."

"Sure, I can understand that. But don't wake her. Her fever's down and she needs the rest more now than anything. All going well, we might even be able to let her home later today."

"Don't rush her out. If this is the best place for her I don't give a damn what it costs, keep her where she'll get the best care."

"We won't let her out until she's ready, but I think she'll be fine. Usually when a flu case presents like this we'd be administering medication, but there doesn't appear to be any problems with the baby and Piper has expressed a wish that we hold off unless absolutely necessary. Bearing her wishes in mind, however, you can rest assured that if her illness presented any issues for the baby we'd be treating her."

"Thank you," Wade said, feeling relief begin to ease the tension in his shoulders and neck. "Where is she?"

May indicated the room two doors down from the nurses' station and issued a final warning not to disturb her patient.

"Don't worry," Wade said, "I want her to be well again, too."

He felt his heart hitch in his chest as he pushed open the door and entered Piper's room. The lighting had been subdued and she looked very small and alone in the hospital bed. He left his cases just inside the door and crossed to the chair next to the bed, lowering himself quietly into it. He scanned her face, noting the sweep of her lashes on cheeks stained with a faint flush of fever. She appeared to be sleeping normally and he felt himself relax by degrees, sinking back into the chair to watch the steady rise and fall of her chest.

He had no idea what time it was when he saw her move beneath the covers.

"Wade?"

Her voice made him sit upright. "Shall I call the nurse? Are you okay?"

"I didn't do it on purpose, you have to believe me," she said, her voice a weak whisper as she drifted back to sleep again.

Her words sliced through to his heart. He'd been such an ogre that her first thought on waking was to defend herself to him. It was no better than he deserved. He'd made such a total hash of all of this. He'd treated her with a complete lack of respect, thinking only of his own agenda and hoarding his bitterness over the past close to him—allowing it to color his every decision. And why? All because he still allowed his father's choices and decisions to sway his own direction.

He'd long since become his own man. Why did he let his old man's abandonment drive him even now? He was a success in business, something his father had never achieved. He had wealth and position in society, again things Eric Collins had failed at. And Wade had the chance to make something good out of something bad, instead of walking away from it and never looking back—so what was holding him in the past?

He knew what it was like to stand on his own, to fight for everything that came his way and create opportunities for those things that didn't. Had it really been so different for Piper when she'd left home? She'd been on her own, completely alone. Could he continue to blame her for decisions she made back then? Things he'd had no knowledge of, things he couldn't change now even if he'd had.

The icy grip around his heart began to soften and melt as

Wade realized that no matter what she'd done before, what mattered most to him was her well-being. Now and in the future. And he wanted to be a part of her future. He wanted to love her and protect her and stand beside her through the next stage of their lives, together.

But would she let him? Would she ever believe that he forgave her for not telling him about their first baby? Would she ever let him love her again?

Wade sat motionless in the chair at her bedside for several hours. Just watching her sleep. It was around lunchtime that May returned to check on her patient and ordered him home to get some rest. He eventually agreed, but only on the proviso that the hospital contact him the moment Piper woke. Piper's fever had returned and it was unlikely she'd be coming home today. The knowledge that she and their baby were still at risk struck fear into his heart. He wanted her to be well again so he could begin repairing the damage he'd wrought.

The cab ride home passed in a blur. He'd been on the go now for more hours than he could count. When he got home he updated the Dexters on Piper's progress and then made his way wearily upstairs. As he reached the door to his suite, he remembered that Mrs. Dexter had mentioned that last night, Piper had been in her father's old rooms.

Had she started packing up in there? he wondered. He dropped his cases inside his sitting room and walked along the landing toward Rex's room and flicked on the lights. Nothing much seemed to have changed in here, although there was a scatter of papers on the escritoire that hadn't been there before. He crossed the room and sat down, turning on the brass lamp which cast a pool of light over the papers.

He thumbed through them, quickly identifying them for what they were. He went to tidy them into a neat stack and put them back inside the file box they'd obviously been taken from when one word leaped out from the page— "abortion."

The bitter taste of regret rose in his throat. He had to learn to put this behind him, he just had to. He'd forgiven Piper already, in his heart and in his mind, but some perverse desire to know all the details saw him select the papers from the stack and sit down to read them carefully. The more he read, the more bitter the taste grew in his mouth.

Spontaneous abortion. The medical term for miscarriage, just as Piper had said.

All those wasted years of anger echoed in the room around him. Rex had misread the information from the very beginning. He'd failed to see one very vital point in the report, that the terminology said the loss of the fetus had been spontaneous. One of those tragic quirks of nature that no one could explain.

Wade leaned back in the chair and let the ramifications of what he'd just learned wash over him. No wonder she'd been so reluctant to do what he'd asked of her—asked? Hell, he'd demanded, and he'd demanded knowing that she was in no position to turn him down. He'd taken advantage of her grief over her father's death and her shock at learning of the abysmal position Rex had left her in, and he'd used both to his selfish advantage. And all of it based on a vow he'd made to himself over her perceived betrayal of the child they'd made together.

Wade made a sound of disgust at his own behavior. For so long he'd been solely focused on this one thing. On making her pay for the wrongdoing he believed she'd actively decided upon, and all along he'd been holding her responsible for something she'd had no control over. Something she'd had to endure all on her own.

The thought of her having to face what had to have been a deep personal loss, so far from home, brought a new level of admiration for her. She'd moved on from that, moved forward with her life—apparently devoting it to good deeds, if May were to be believed, and he had no reason not to believe her.

He had no reason not to have believed Piper, either, when

she'd tried to explain her anxieties to him two weeks ago. She would have been at about the same stage of her pregnancy as she'd been when she'd lost their first baby. No wonder she'd begun to doubt her ability to bring the baby to term. Such a fear would only be natural, and she'd had to face it on her own, as she'd faced so much of her entire life. In his unique way, Rex had been an absentee father almost as much as Wade's father had been.

Wade refiled the papers into their folder and placed them back in the box on the desktop. She wouldn't be alone anymore. Not ever, if he had any say in the matter—if she let him have any say, that is.

Piper sat on the edge of her hospital bed and tried to quell the nerves that twisted her stomach. Had she imagined Wade had been here yesterday? He was supposed to still be in Apia until late Monday night. She must have been dreaming. The fever that had racked her body had made everything feel as if the past couple days had happened in some crazy dream sequence.

She laid a hand against her belly, feeling the baby flutter against her hand. As long as the baby was all right, that was the most important thing. May had assured her everything was fine, even going so far as to bring a portable ultrasound to Piper's room to prove that the baby was still okay.

And now she knew the sex of the new life growing so healthily inside her. A little girl. She wondered how Wade would take the news. He had always struck her as the kind of man who'd want a son to carry on the legacy he had built with such pride. A sound at the door made her look up. As if her thoughts had conjured him, Wade stood there looking uncharacteristically unsure of himself.

"All ready to come home?" he asked.

Piper fought to hide her surprise at seeing him here. Maybe

she hadn't imagined his visit last night after all. "I...I thought you were still in Samoa."

"I came as soon as I heard you were ill. The Dexters send their love, by the way. They can't wait to get you home and spoil you."

And you? Piper asked silently. *What about you?* She dragged in a steadying breath. He'd made his feelings clear before he'd left for Samoa; she'd be crazy to expect that to have changed.

"So? Are you ready?" he asked again.

"Pretty much. I'm just waiting for the nurse to bring my discharge papers. Shouldn't be too long."

"Okay," he said, and leaned against the wall behind him, his hands shoved into the pockets of his jeans.

The silence stretched out between them. If they'd been a normal couple he'd be sitting on this bed with her, she thought, rather than maintaining casual sentry duty on the opposite side of the room.

"Wade?"

"Piper—"

"You first," she said.

"No, it's okay. What I have to say can wait. Probably best said at home, anyway."

She felt a clutch of fear grip her throat. What was it that he couldn't say right here, right now? Did he somehow hold her responsible for what had happened on Friday night? It was a particularly bad case of the flu. Surely he didn't hold her accountable for that.

"What did you want to say to me?" he urged gently, distracting her from her thoughts.

"I learned the sex of the baby this morning. Do you want to know?"

He took his hands from his pockets and pushed himself upright. "Know? Of course I want to know."

"It's a little girl."

She watched as a variety of expressions chased across his handsome features. Disbelief followed by a sheer joy that lit his eyes and made them shine like highly polished steel.

"A girl? That's amazing. Me, us, having a daughter."

"Well, it was always going to be one or the other," she said with a wistful smile.

Either way it made no difference. He didn't want her to be a part of their baby's upbringing. He'd made that patently clear.

"I don't know why but I always assumed it'd be a boy." He paced the room. "A daughter." The words held a note of complete disbelief.

"Are you okay with that?" she asked, feeling a heartfelt surge of protection for her baby. Surely he'd want a daughter just as much.

"Oh, I'm more than okay with that." He beamed. "I never thought I'd be so lucky. Thank you for telling me."

And there it was again, that stiltedness he'd exhibited when he'd come through the door. She felt a tug of sorrow that things couldn't be different between them, that they couldn't have shared this news with the mutual affection and excitement that a normal couple would have.

The nurse arrived at that moment with Piper's discharge papers and a wheelchair.

"I won't be needing that," she protested.

"Yes, she will," Wade amended firmly.

Piper flung him an irritated look. "I'm perfectly fine."

"Humor me," he asked, sending her a look she couldn't quite interpret. "Besides, you're probably not as strong as you think you are. You've been pretty ill these past couple days."

She gave in and settled herself in the chair, surprised by his consideration and, frankly, suddenly too tired to argue. He was, no doubt, quite right in his assertion that she wasn't as fit as she should be. Or maybe it was just this sensation of being on constant tenterhooks around him that made her suddenly feel so weak and incapable.

The ride home was completed in near silence, broken only by Wade asking every ten minutes if she was still comfortable. Once home, she gave herself over to the inevitable fussing from Mrs. Dexter. Finally, though, she was alone in her old room again, propped up against a sea of cushions and with a selection of magazines and a water bottle within easy reach.

Wade came into the bedroom and pushed the door closed behind him.

"Comfortable?"

"I'm fine, thanks."

If he asked her one more time if she was okay, she'd probably scream.

"Are you up for a bit of conversation?"

She stiffened. Here it came. The recriminations for not looking after herself properly, the accusation she'd put another baby at risk. Piper took a deep breath ready to defend herself.

"Bring it on," she said defensively.

"May I?" he gestured to the side of the bed and sat down at her nod.

For several very long seconds he stared at the floor and said nothing but then he turned to face her. She'd never seen him look quite this earnest or vulnerable before. It was a side of him that unsettled her, made her anxious about what it was that he had to say.

"I owe you an apology. Several apologies, actually."

Whatever she'd been expecting from him, it certainly wasn't that. Surprise rendered her dumb. He reached across the covers and took one of her hands in his, his thumb absently brushing back and forth across her inner wrist.

"I have treated you badly, Piper, and I am so dreadfully sorry. I have nothing to say in my defense aside from the fact that I've been a stubborn fool, but I ask that you consider if one day you can forgive me.

"I've always been a driven person, but one who was prepared to work hard to get where they wanted to be. You know a bit about my father and my background, how he abandoned me and surrendered me to the state rather than face up to his responsibilities. I always swore I'd never be like him, that I'd give any child of mine my abiding love and support without question. It's why I was so angry when I heard about your miscarriage."

At her startled gasp he looked up and met her eyes. "Yes, I know it was a miscarriage. I'm very sorry you had to go through that all alone, Piper. I know we can't turn back the clock but I really wish I'd known so I could have been there with you."

"How did you find out?" she finally managed to say.

"I saw the papers you were going through in Rex's rooms when I came back from the hospital yesterday."

"You *were* there," she whispered.

"Yes, and I'd have been there longer if May had let me. I wanted to tell you that I'd forgiven you for what I thought you'd done. That I could understand that, on your own as you were, you probably felt as if you'd had no other choice." His fingers wrapped around hers more firmly, giving her hand a squeeze. "But I was wrong about that as I was wrong about so many things. If I had the chance again, please believe that I'd do it all very differently."

"As you said, we can't turn back time," she said sadly.

"No, we can't. But we can go forward, and I'd really like to go forward with you, Piper. If you'll let me. I'll understand if you don't want to, if you don't want me, God alone knows I deserve worse, but can I ask you to at least consider staying here with me and raising our daughter together, as a proper family?"

"As a proper family?" What exactly did he mean? Did she dare begin to hope?

"I love you, Piper. More than I ever did before and more

than I ever believed I could possibly feel for another human being. I beg of you, please give me another chance. Let me make it right with you this time around. Let me be the man to love you and protect you and stand by you every day for the rest of our lives."

"Wade—" Emotion swamped her, making her eyes tear up and her voice tremble. "I don't deserve this."

"You deserve more, trust me."

"When I was younger, I always thought I loved you as much as one person was capable of loving another, but I know now that those feelings were nothing compared to how I feel about you now. I was too young and immature to understand what I was asking of you when I demanded you come away with me. All I wanted was the reassurance that I came first with you. All my life I'd been second string to my father's work. Nothing I ever did was good enough to get his attention for more than five minutes. I know he loved me in his own way, but it was never enough for me. It made me push so hard for what I wanted that, in the end, I pushed it all away."

She reached out one hand to cup his face. "I didn't deserve your love back then, Wade, but I would like to have another chance to prove to you that I'm worthy of it, of you, now."

"You're more than worthy," he protested before turning his head to place a kiss in the palm of her hand. "I let you down. I didn't understand how much you needed me then. I had my life compartmentalized, my plan ahead of me. You totally upset that apple cart and I didn't know how to do what I wanted to do and keep you at the same time."

"We were both too young to understand it then. I think what I always craved, more than anything, was the reassurance that I was good enough. But I never realized until a few years ago that that acceptance had to come from within me. I've learned that now. I understand that my behavior toward you and Dad was dreadful, but if you can forgive me that, then yes, I would like to be a family with you and our daughter.

"I love you, Wade, more than I ever did before. I want to prove to you that I'm grown up now and worthy of your love, that I'm someone you can rely on in any circumstances, and that I can be a good mother to our children."

Wade leaned forward to brush away the tears she didn't even realize she was crying.

"I know I can rely upon you, Piper. We've both made some pretty terrible mistakes, but at least we've had the courage to learn from them. Will you marry me? Will you be my wife and help me steer a true course for the rest of my life? And then maybe we can keep growing up together?"

"Yes, I will. I'd be honored to be your wife."

"Then there's one place you really need to be," Wade said as he stood and pulled her bed covers aside.

"Where's that?" Piper said, laughing softly.

"With me," he said simply, scooping her up into his arms and taking her to his suite.

And she knew as he placed her gently in their bed and then gathered her in his arms to hold her close that she'd always be number one in his life. Always.

* * * * *

MILLS & BOON®
By Request

RELIVE THE ROMANCE WITH THE BEST OF THE BEST

A sneak peek at next month's titles...

In stores from 11th January 2018:

- **A Diamond in the Rough** – Catherine Mann

- **Call Me Cupid** – Fiona Harper, Nina Harrington *and* Heidi Rice

In stores from 25th January 2018:

- **One Passionate Night** – Susan Meier, Jessica Gilmore *and* Caroline Anderson

- **Save the Date!** – Michelle Douglas, Lucy Gordon *and* Kate Hardy

---

LET'S TALK
Romance

For exclusive extracts, competitions
and special offers, find us online:

f facebook.com/millsandboon

⊙ @millsandboonuk

🐦 @millsandboon

Or get in touch on 0844 844 1351*

For all the latest titles coming soon, visit
millsandboon.co.uk/nextmonth

Want even more
ROMANCE?

Join our bookclub today!

'Mills & Boon books, the perfect way to escape for an hour or so.'

Miss W. Dyer

'Excellent service, promptly delivered and very good subscription choices.'

Miss A. Pearson

'You get fantastic special offer and the chance to get books before they hit the shops'

Mrs V Hall

Visit millsandbook.co.uk/Bookclub
and save on brand new books.

MILLS & BOON